PRAISE FOR *IN DARKNESS VISIBLE*

'So much more than an intriguing thriller . . . Tony Jones has written a thought-provoking political novel spanning decades.'

Good Reading

'Engrossingly interesting . . . the historical material is worthy of elaboration and remembrance.'

The Weekend Australian

'Jones is a natural fiction writer. He combines the incisiveness of Helen Garner with the pacy absurdity of Michael Crichton.'

The Australian Financial Review

'An assured and compelling read.'

The Sydney Morning Herald and The Age

'*In Darkness Visible* takes the story started in *The Twentieth Man* in an interesting and topical direction. Drawing on tragically real events and characters to craft a rich narrative, once the pieces are in place this becomes a fascinating and fast-paced narrative.'

PS News

'Undeniably gripping . . . a compelling, racy political thriller. It's satisfying to read a story of this nature with an Aussie twist.'

On the Town

'Brilliant, immensely readable and for lovers of political thrillers, the perfectly constructed read. Better than ideal for the long hot days of summer, if you have not read it already.'

e Wolf Review

T0347754

PRAISE FOR *THE TWENTIETH MAN*

'Jones' debut novel uses his experience as a journalist to reprise a series of events in the early 1970s ... the action of the novel is deftly strung together [and] the research is palpable on the page.'

The Australian

'*The Twentieth Man* is a political thriller in the Robert Harris mould ... Jones cleverly weaves fact and fiction—and has great fun painting "real" characters like the wilful Lionel Murphy.'

Jennifer Byrne, *The Australian Women's Weekly*

'An engaging political thriller ... Anna [Rosen's] key role serves to remind us of the importance of investigative journalism in a democracy.'

Spectrum, The Sydney Morning Herald

'Mixing bombs in Melbourne, Balkan politics and a slice of seventies sexism.'

The Guardian

'Alongside the hefty doses of political and bureaucratic intrigue, there [are] romantic complications, family tensions and a nearly pitch perfect feel of time and place ... Extremely readable, fascinating and very cleverly done, *The Twentieth Man* is unfortunately a bit of a rarity in Australian fiction—an historical political thriller covering our recent past.'

AustCrimeFiction.org

'*The Twentieth Man* is an incredibly assured debut novel and Jones has delivered a pacey and original historical thriller. While historical detectives seem to be everywhere, historical political thrillers are not a genre we have seen much of in Australia. And this one shines a light on a fascinating period of Australian history, contemporaneous with Watergate, in an engaging and interesting way.'

PS News

IN DARKNESS VISIBLE

TONY JONES

ALLEN&UNWIN
SYDNEY · MELBOURNE · AUCKLAND · LONDON

This edition published in 2021
First published in 2019

Allen & Unwin
83 Alexander Street
Crows Nest NSW 2065
Australia
Phone: (61 2) 8425 0100
Email: info@allenandunwin.com
Web: www.allenandunwin.com

 A catalogue record for this book is available from the National Library of Australia

ISBN 978 1 76106 502 6

Set in Minion Pro by Midland Typesetters, Australia
Printed in Australia by McPherson's Printing Group

10 9 8 7 6 5 4 3 2 1

For my three sons

'Now conscience wakes despair that slumbered; wakes the bitter memory of what he was, what is and what must be . . .'

John Milton, *Paradise Lost*

THE PRISONER

1

ROVINJ, CROATIA

AUGUST 2005

TRAILED BY A LONG shadow—his spindly, striving familiar—
Marin Katich walked across the gleaming limestone towards the
boat harbour. A woman sitting at an outdoor café glanced up as
he passed, shading her eyes against the balled sun, so low now that
the yellow umbrella above her had become redundant.

Marin was moving fast and she saw he was carrying some kind
of long pole. He didn't stop when he reached the water's edge
but leapt straight across a wide gap onto the bow of a moored
speedboat. He was a big man, yet he kept his balance easily
as the boat dipped beneath him. He took three quick steps
around the narrow gunwale, jumped into the cockpit and swung
the pole out over the stern. She noticed there was a hook on the
end of it with which he grappled the bowline of the nearest boat,
dragging it close enough to step aboard. He scampered across
the second boat from bow to stern, and hooked up the next
nearest one.

The woman grabbed her mobile and keyed in a number,
watching as he repeated the odd sequence, bounding from boat
to boat in an unconscious display of agility.

'He is coming,' she whispered, then swapped the phone for a Campari spritz. She drank a little, dabbed her plum-coloured lips with a napkin, popped a piece of nicotine gum into her mouth and chewed on it thoughtfully.

Marin's destination was a wooden-hulled vessel at the back of the tethered fleet. He climbed across the varnished mahogany deck and unclipped the boat's vinyl cover, raising one edge to let the pooled rainwater run off. He folded the cover, stowed it away and stripped off his T-shirt, folding and stowing that too before crawling onto the bow to mop the damp deck.

The woman watched the boatman's ritual from a distance. His fastidiousness would otherwise have bored her, but she was transfixed by the disfiguring striations that furrowed his belly and chest. She took a series of shots with a telephoto lens, focusing on the telltale wounds. Then, to remain in character as an inquisitive tourist, she turned the camera up to the church of St Euphemia, whose spire rose high above the medieval houses that packed the steep hillside above the harbour. Through the scope she saw the statue of the martyred Euphemia atop the spire—or rather it was the idealised image of her, made whole again in the kingdom of heaven after she was torn apart in the arena by a bear. Now St Euphemia revolved gently on a spindle, the highest point in the town, a holy weathervane for fishermen and sailors to judge the wind.

•

Marin never once glanced up at the luckless saint. He finished his preparations, drew his T-shirt back over his broad, ravaged torso and straightened his sunglasses. The engines roared reassuringly at the touch of the starter and he gunned the boat fast into a long arc to pick up his passengers at the end of the breakwater known as Veliki Mol.

As he tied up at the jetty, Marin picked out the two Englishmen waiting for him. They were tanned and fit and wore matching shorts and sunglasses. His immediate thought was that they were homosexuals, but that didn't bother him. He had fought alongside such men and they had proven to be as tough as any under his command.

'Mr Maric?' the taller one asked.

'Tomo,' said Marin, reaching out to shake his hand.

'I'm Greg, this is Derek.'

'Climb aboard.'

The men dropped nimbly into the cockpit behind him. Marin turned to them as they settled into their seats.

'If you want a swim now, to cool down, we can go first to the town beach. It's very close, just beyond the breakwater.'

Derek nodded. 'Let's do—'

Greg interrupted. 'Will we still have time to get to the islands?'

'No worries,' said Marin. 'They're ten minutes away. We'll go around Katarina.' He gestured to the cypress-covered island just offshore that was framed by the outer points of the harbour. A small wooden ferry was plying its way towards it. 'Then we go south a ways to Zlatni. There are many islands in the national park. Good places for swimming and snorkelling and to watch the sunset.'

'Your English is very good, Tomo,' said Greg. 'Is that an Australian accent?'

Marin paused, scrutinising the man from behind his dark glasses. Then he turned to start the engine.

'You want to swim now or wait?'

'Let's have a look at this town beach, shall we?' said Derek.

•

Marin tied on to a buoy, fished out masks and snorkels for his passengers, and watched them dive in and stroke powerfully towards the town beach. In truth, it was not so much a beach as a natural inlet set against the backdrop of a great limestone wall, part of the fortifications built centuries ago by the Venetians, who colonised the port and called it Rovigno. Their engineers were men who understood how to make an organic connection between sea and land.

High on the upper reaches of the structure, dozens of white tablecloths had been hung out to dry in the sun. Tall, indented stone archways punctuated the length of the wall just above the water, creating perches for somnolent sunbathers. A topless woman with bleached white hair and leathery skin slid from hers down into the water, barely creating a ripple as she pushed slowly through the shallows.

The human rookery created bright swatches of colour on the rocky outcrops at either end of the cove. The water was turquoise in patches and darker over the submerged rocks. A small child ringed with a plastic float climbed down the stainless-steel ladder embedded in the rock. From a large, round boulder, silhouetted teenagers threw themselves screaming into the depths, ignoring the angry cries from two old women breaststroking side by side, their heads held high to preserve Tito-era perms.

Presently Derek, limber as a seal, hauled himself back into the boat, and pulled off his goggles.

'Brilliant,' he said, wiping water from his face and throwing himself onto the vinyl seat to laze in the sun. 'Clear as glass and hundreds of fish down there.'

Greg came over the stern rail and stood, spare and toned, dripping onto the deck as he towelled his hair dry. He edged his way into the front cockpit, standing a little too close to Marin as he dried the rest of him.

'So where are you from, Tomo?' he asked.

'I live here.'

'Lucky man,' said Derek, opening his eyes. 'Were you born in Rovinj?'

Marin shook his head. 'I just washed up here one day.'

'So where were you born, then?' the taller one persisted.

'What's this, Greg,' said Marin. 'Twenty questions?'

'Just making conversation. Me, for instance, I was born in East Anglia.'

Marin gave him a blank look.

'Have you heard of Essex?' Greg asked.

'Sure.'

'And I'm from Sussex,' Derek chipped in.

Marin looked at each of them before responding.

'So you do have sex in common.'

'Funny man,' said Greg.

Marin hauled up the buoy and untethered the boat. He started the engine.

'Shall we go?' he said, but he wasn't really asking. He'd had enough of these inquisitive bastards. He opened the throttle, the bow kicked high and the big engine churned up a neat white wedge in its wake. Greg braced himself next to Marin and raised his voice.

'I'll tell you what we have in common, Tomo. We both served with the paras in Belfast. We have that in common.'

Beyond Katarina Island now, Marin had the boat slapping the light swell at top speed.

'I'm not Irish,' he replied, keeping his eyes to the front. 'That's not my problem.'

Greg leant in closer. 'But there's a problem?' he said.

Marin was puzzled by the man's belligerence, but decided to play a dead bat. 'It's not my fight,' he said.

'You're not Catholic?'

'I was,' said Marin. 'A long time ago.'

'So what is your fight, Tomo?'

'Just keeping my head above water. That's enough.'

'Come on!' said Greg, clearly annoyed. 'No one escaped the shit here. Tough guy like you, you must've picked up a gun, right?'

'What's with all the questions?'

'Just pegged you for a soldier, that's all. Derek and me, we've seen plenty of shit. But what happened here—that's something else. I'm just curious about it.'

'You've come to the wrong place,' said Marin. 'There was no fighting in Rovinj.'

'I've heard it's full of veterans.'

'That was years ago.'

'They sent the wounded here to recuperate, didn't they?'

'What are you getting at?'

'Were you one of them?'

Marin turned sharply to his inquisitor and let the boat slew off course.

'That's enough fucking questions.'

'Hey!' Derek yelled from the back. 'Up ahead! Watch out for those rocks!'

Marin ignored him, his eyes fixed on Greg, who now saw the reef coming at them fast.

'Fuck!' Greg yelled, reaching for the wheel. Marin caught his hand and squeezed it hard until he saw him wince. With his other hand, Marin flipped the wheel and came about at a steep angle, missing the reef by a whisker.

'Jesus Christ!' Greg exclaimed when Marin finally let his hand go.

'You could've killed us!' Derek had leapt to his feet.

Greg was spluttering with anger. Marin saw that he was the one most likely to retaliate, but dealing with two of them would be difficult. He turned and pushed Derek hard in the chest so that he fell back into the chair in the rear cockpit.

'Stay there!' he ordered him, yawing the boat again.

Greg was now caught off balance, forced to grip the taffrail to avoid going overboard. There was fury in his face. He seemed ready to throw himself at Marin.

'Sit down!' Marin shouted. 'Or I swear I'll put you over the side.'

'You maniac,' Greg seethed. 'I've killed men for less.'

Marin laughed. 'You don't look too dangerous in your speedos, mate . . . Sit down, I said!'

To Marin's surprise, Greg did as he was told. 'That was fucking crazy,' he muttered.

'Maybe I am crazy. Don't push your luck.'

'I was just talking soldier to soldier.'

'You sounded more like a cop to me,' said Marin.

He put the boat into another fast turn until they were pointed back towards Rovinj.

'The sunset cruise is over.'

•

The woman with the plum-coloured lips knocked three times on the hotel room door, then once more. It opened a crack.

'Jasna,' said a British voice.

'I suppose I can come in,' Jasna barked, pushing through the doorway. She shoved aside military gear piled around the sofa and picked up a sleek black submachine gun from the cushion.

'Hey, careful with that,' said Greg.

Jasna gave the Englishman an imperious look and rolled her eyes. It was her view that Greg and his partner, the ludicrously named Derek, had spooked the quarry. She flipped open the stock of the weapon, braced herself and sharply pulled the cocking lever back several times to make sure it was empty.

'Now I *know* is safe,' said Jasna, tossing the weapon to the other side of the couch. She sat then in the cleared space and sighed loudly as she rummaged through her voluminous handbag, piling item after item on the coffee table: the camera and its telephoto lens; a manila folder; a packet of nicotine gum; a plastic bag full of cigarettes; a Zippo lighter; and a small jar of Nescafé granules.

The other members of the team, all men and dressed like summer tourists, watched this performance without surprise. Like her, half of them were Croatian, on loan for the operation and with orders from Zagreb to cooperate with these tight-arsed Brits. Such were the compromises their political masters were forced to make to prove themselves worthy of European citizenship.

Captain Duncan held up a pot and waggled it.

'Coffee, Jasna?'

The officer was a tall, upright blond man with a neat moustache. He seemed to have stepped out of one of those BBC Jane Austen serials they liked to show on Croatian TV, poorly dubbed into her own language. She found it strange listening to the original.

'No,' she said, picking up the Nescafé jar. 'Bring me just hot water in a cup. Croatian coffee is strong and I drink many cups, so I prefer this.'

Duncan passed her a steaming mug.

'Must be like a holiday for you,' he said. 'Coming to Rovinj.'

She ignored him for a moment, heaping in coffee granules. 'Actually, I don't like it here at all,' she said when she had finally gotten the drink to her taste. 'I don't like that they speak to me in Italian. I don't want to hear them say "Hello" in Italian even before I speak. And all the signs are in Italian so I don't understand it.'

'It's true,' said one of the Croat soldiers, nodding fiercely. 'Everything is in Italian here. They're taking over.'

'But surely you do understand,' said Captain Duncan reasonably. 'Everything's written in Croatian, too.'

'No, *you* don't understand,' said Jasna. She plucked the gum from her mouth and wrapped it in an old supermarket receipt. 'It wasn't like this before the war.'

The Englishman had read Fitzroy Maclean. He thought he had a pretty good grasp of the history.

'Come on, Jasna,' he said. 'This used to be part of Italy. Italians and Croatians have always lived here side by side.'

'Listen, honey.' Jasna wagged a finger at him. 'It was never *part of Italy*—this is Croatia, always Croatia. Then Yugoslavia, now Croatia again.' She laughed and slapped her knee. 'If they don't speak Croatian, fuck them.'

'Fuck them!' echoed the soldier. He was a thuggish-looking Special Forces man who had cut his teeth a decade earlier expelling Serbs from the Krajina.

'Okay, forget about it. It's not important,' said Duncan irritably. 'Let's get down to business. What have you got for us, Jasna?'

She passed him the manila folder. 'Look at these photos.'

Duncan pulled a seat over to the coffee table and spread a series of enlarged images across it. The other team members gathered to look over his shoulder.

'Greg, Dez,' he said. 'You fellows see these wounds?'

Derek let out a sharp whistle. 'Nasty,' he said.

'No,' said Greg. 'He never took off his T-shirt.'

'You scared him off, honey,' Jasna chided. 'Should have been softly-softly.'

Greg's face darkened. 'The man's a fucking nutter.'

'You did come it a bit strong with him,' said Derek.

'I'll tell you one thing,' Greg responded. 'There'll be no softly-softly when we pick him up.'

'*If* we pick him up, sergeant, *if*,' said Duncan. 'But these pictures do fit the intel—a pattern of wounds right down his left side, below the heart. Must have taken out a lung, at the very least. It's a miracle he survived. Well done, Jasna.'

'These I have emailed to Zagreb,' she said, and surprised them all by lighting a cigarette. 'I need this one. Fucking gum doesn't work. We will have an answer soon.'

•

In the early evening, Marin hiked up the steep cobbled streets of the old town to Giannino's where the old man was waiting at their usual table under the awning, a chessboard set up. It was Rossi's turn to play white and Marin saw that he had already pushed up his queen's pawn. He knew what was coming. As the unofficial historian of Rovigno, Rossi naturally favoured the Italian opening.

'Sit, sit.' Rossi spoke in English. 'Is your move.'

Since the old man refused to converse in Croatian and Marin's Italian was rudimentary at best, they had long ago agreed to stay on neutral ground. Marin poured himself a glass of malvasia from the carafe at Rossi's elbow and pushed up his own queen's pawn to meet its opponent. The old man immediately threw forwards his queen's knight to threaten it, as Marin knew he would, so he paused to take a drink.

'You've ordered?' he asked.

'*Calamari alla brace* to begin.'

Marin smiled with relief. 'I'm starving,' he said. 'It's been a shit of a day, first the rain and then some mad fucking tourists who refused to cough up.'

The old man raised an eyebrow. 'Relax, Tomo, is my treat tonight. Perhaps you need to work on customer relations?'

Marin moved his king's knight to protect the endangered pawn. 'It wasn't my fault,' he insisted.

'Not this time, eh?'

'No, not at all. They were a pair of English *finocchi*, though I say that without prejudice . . .'

'You call a man faggot without prejudice?'

'I don't care who they fuck,' said Marin. 'I told you they were Englishmen. That's enough to justify any prejudice.'

'*Si*, you have a point.'

'It was how they behaved, pestering me with questions. They just wouldn't stop. *Where were you born? Why are you here? Did you fight in the war?* On and on.'

Rossi pushed up his open bishop. 'Just curious, perhaps.'

'No, it was more than that.'

The old man drank some wine, pondering this. After a while, he asked, 'Who would send a pair of English homosexuals to torment you, Tomo?'

'I don't know,' said Marin. 'But it felt like the old days.'

Rossi regarded him with something like pity. '*Capito*,' he said with a sigh. 'The old days leave deep scars.'

Marin made his next move, keeping his finger on the piece. 'They remind you that no one can be trusted.' After he lifted his finger, he looked into Rossi's perpetually worried eyes and smiled. 'Present company excluded, of course.'

A waiter came with plates of charred calamari, served in the local style with potatoes and garlic spinach steeped in green oil and, as the two men fought out an increasingly complex battle on the chessboard, the meal unfolded with perfect timing. The carafe was refilled again and again as fresh courses arrived. The aromatic wine, the food, all of it fresh from the morning market, along with the old man's gentle companionship, began to ease Marin's tension, a slow unwinding welcome to both of them. Yet one phrase lingered in each of their thoughts:

Like the old days.

As Rossi stared down at the board, Marin studied the old man's face. It was marked by the secret history for which he was the only keeper. There were baggy pouches under the hooded eyes and deep lines flowed up his brow as if a succession of waves were gradually eroding his hairline.

Then Rossi's untidy eyebrows shot up. He had realised too late that Marin had outmanoeuvred him; there was sadness in his eyes as he glanced back at his younger opponent. Rossi carefully laid down his king in surrender, reached for the grappa and raised his glass.

'A worthy contest,' he said. '*Saluti.*'

'You're too generous. We should have played it out.'

'It is better, more *elegante*, to die with dignity.'

'This has nothing to do with death,' said Marin.

Rossi looked at him wistfully, as if at a foolish child.

'You're wrong about that, Tomo. At my age every defeat, it is *una piccolo morte*. The staircase that has become too steep, the summer you stop swimming in the ocean, the faltering flow of your own piss, the chess game you can't win—'

'Come on, Alberto . . .'

'—the book they refuse to publish.'

'What?'

'The Italians rejected my manuscript. The letter came today.'

'Oh, fuck. You kept this to yourself? They seemed so sure, they were—'

'—encouraging, *si*,' said Rossi.

'It was perfect for them.'

'So you would think. A forgotten Italian tribe *viene decimata*— decimated.'

'More than that, I think,' said Marin.

'*Si, si.* Tito's true legacy is *genocidio, GEN-O-CID-IO!*' Rossi slammed the table and began a tirade long familiar to Marin. 'This town is full of ghosts! It is my duty, my one duty in life, to speak for them. Who else will do it? Perhaps these fools really believe in the myth of Tito. Didn't I give them enough evidence of his tyranny? Tito's partisans came here with blood in their eyes. They stole Rovigno, they stole all of Istria for Tito's dream of Yugoslavia. A dream for him; for us, total nightmare—'

'Alberto,' said Marin gently.

'—they condemn thousands of Italians as collaborators, thousands! My brother, his best friend, two of my uncles were among them. They throw them into deep chasms in the hills, dead or alive; it didn't matter. None of them do we ever see again. Forever more they are *Il enfoibe*—The Buried.'

'They were murderers,' said Marin, no longer trying to stem his friend's flow of words.

'*Si*, murderers! Assassins! Monsters! But these are just words.' Rossi poured another grappa and downed it immediately. 'Without consequences, without history, without even the memory of their acts, none of these words have meaning. I say this to you before, Tomo—the ethnic cleansing of the recent wars, it all begins here. They broke the tissue of our world.'

Soon after they had first met each other and recognised a common understanding, the old man had invited Marin to the Historical Centre he ran in the old town. Rossi had unrolled a map to show him how Tito's partisan army had occupied the Istrian peninsula after the war. Hundreds of thousands of Italians had been terrorised into leaving their homes to flee north and Rossi alone had recorded it. In an old safe he kept a folder full of fading typewritten pages, the evidence he had gathered which included the testimonies of survivors and witnesses, but he had refused to show them to Marin.

'Some of these people are still alive,' he had explained. 'You must understand that there are many taboos of World War the Second.

People here know what really happened and they worry it could happen again. Those now in power in Zagreb are old communists, but they're also rabid nationalists. Before he died, Tudjman accused us as irredentists. The president! He called us the spies of Italy. Then comes Mesic and he is just as bad. He blocks any investigation of the partisans' war crimes. They wish to control history.'

Rossi had waited until all the witnesses had died before finally sending his manuscript to the publisher, but now came the rejection. Marin knew what an unbearable blow it was for the old man. He watched Rossi down another shot of grappa and promptly refill his glass.

'Forget about them,' said Marin. 'You must send it to others.'

'Only God knows what would be enough *per quei bastardi*. I have to accept they've said no to me—no to my work, no to my people.'

•

It was late when Marin made his way back down the steep, deserted streets. He had early morning tours booked and had left Rossi working his way steadily through the bottle of grappa. Lamplight yellowed the cobbled limestone paths. They were so shiny-smooth that they appeared wet, although it hadn't rained at all that evening.

He kept his head down, unaware of the shadow he cast on the ancient walls. As he passed, his hulking familiar stained shuttered windows and doors with darkness.

Marin reached the bottom of the hill where the narrow lane ended at a wide square from which five paths radiated, each climbing into different quarters of the old town. A dual sign named the square in Croatian—*Trg Na Mostu*—and beneath that was its Italian name—*Piazza Del Ponte*. Evidence of the town's bipolar nature was there on every signpost.

Even at this late hour, people were crowded into a few bars and cafés. A small boy on the loose from an outdoor table found himself staring up at the man who had just lurched into the piazza. Marin stopped, looked down at the little fellow and felt a twinge of sadness, of pain for the child in his dreams, the son he would never have. The boy stared back at Marin wide-eyed until his mother called and he ran back to lean against her legs and peer out at the strange giant. Marin left the square on the wide street that took him to the harbour. Hundreds of small boats sat there jostling against each other in the light breeze. He looked up at the dark spire of the church, silhouetted against the star-filled sky, and he recalled that this was where Rossi's manuscript had begun.

•

It was the summer of 1944 and the twelve-year-old Rossi was horsing around with his mates on the quay. The boys heard a roaring noise and looked up to see two fighter planes coming in fast and low over the cathedral. The planes dived either side of St Euphemia, levelling out just above the masts of the fishing fleet. They angled towards a small motor launch that had just entered the harbour. Rossi saw flames erupt from the guns in the plane's wings, then heard the deafening racket as both aircraft strafed the launch, riddling it with deadly fire. The tri-colour roundels on the underside of the wings told him these were British fighters.

When the shattered vessel reached the dockside there was pandemonium. A bloodied body was hauled up from the bottom of the boat and the boy recognised it as the Nazi commander of Rovigno, a lofty and aristocratic presence in the town with the power of an ancient satrap. The guileless German had been targeted returning from lunch at the home of an Austrian baroness, widowed now and living on the island of Sant'Andrea. As it transpired, neither party would survive the consequences of that fateful meal. The German soon died of his wounds, but what happened to the baroness and her daughter would help inspire Rossi's hatred of Tito's Yugoslavia.

Having survived the war in the relative splendour of their island villa, the mother and daughter were seized in its immediate aftermath by the local partisans. The two women were accused of collaboration with the Nazis and, without trial or charge, summarily bludgeoned to death. Their battered bodies were tossed into the sea like garbage. It was a single act of terror set against a searing global conflict, but for Alberto Rossi this unrecorded act of savagery was a portent of worse to come.

•

Marin walked the length of the darkened quay. Just offshore, the outline of Sveta Katarina was clear in the starlight. Many years ago, while he was recovering from his wounds, Marin used to swim out to the island on hot nights. He did so many times until one morning he watched a fisherman haul an eight-foot shark onto the dock. It was a beautiful thing, blue as the Adriatic, but Marin knew that beauty and savagery could exist in the one place. The history of Rovinj was proof of that, although for him the old town had been his sanctuary.

The limestone flagging around the harbour's edge, spectral white under the stars, had been worn smooth. It was not hard for Marin to imagine that the ancient buildings and their narrow connecting pathways really were full of ghosts, as Rossi claimed. He imagined they were like the ones who would always follow him through his life.

For years now he had lived in an apartment he rented from Rossi. It was on the waterfront, above the Sportz Bar—three storeys up, overlooking the harbour. Marin threw open the shutters. He had rationed himself to one cigarette a day and he smoked it now, watching his old wooden boat bobbing at the back of the fleet.

He cared little for material possessions, but this superannuated Venetian water taxi was an exception. He had found it for sale in a port in Giudecca. After haggling with the owner, he finally settled on a price and used much of the inheritance from his father to pay for it. He fuelled it up and put his trust in the misfiring engine to power him back across the Adriatic to Rovinj.

No one in the town knew him as Marin Katich. He had been Tomislav Maric for more than a decade. Those who got close to him, or thought they did, called him Tomo—but there were very few in that camp. From time to time a woman had entered his life, but they had never stayed for long. There were many rumours about this man Maric, who had arrived during the war in need of much more repair than the old boat from which he now earned his livelihood. But people had learned not to ask too many questions. His scars, they understood, were too fresh; his temper too easily aroused. Mostly they left him in peace, and he clearly preferred it that way.

It was only the ghosts who refused to leave him alone. And though in recent times they had been quiet, he sensed that something was stirring.

The boat, concentrate on the boat!

He would have to have a look at the engine. Today he thought he had heard something—a ticking, an arrhythmia, an off beat in the music of the twelve cylinders, something barely noticeable but out of kilter. He went to sleep rehearsing the mechanical steps he would take to return the engine to smooth running.

•

In the middle of the night, Marin was woken by a noise. He switched on a light and sat up, instantly alert. Dark figures rushed into the room, crowding in, five or six, dressed in black, wearing balaclavas, carrying stubby submachine guns. Military. Hard, black eyes in the slits, a babble of Croatian voices.

Someone cried: '*Uzmi mu ruke!*' Take his arms!

Marin hit the nearest of them hard, a short-armed jab. The man's legs crumpled. Weapons were pointed at him. He knew they'd have shot him already if they intended to. A man grabbed at Marin's arms from behind.

A masked figure appeared in front of him and he yelled at it: '*Jebi se!*'

Marin headbutted the masked face, felt the crack of cartilage.

'Ahhh! You fucking cunt! You'll pay for that!'

The curses were in English. Marin recognised the voice. He managed to tear off the man's balaclava, uncovering a grimacing bloody face full of anger, a face he had already seen that day.

Marin only had time to cry out: '*You!*'

Two more powerful men pinned his arms from behind. One of them yelled in his ear, 'On your fucking knees, Maric!'

English again. He knew that voice too—Derek. Greg and Derek. He barely had time to process the thought before Greg began thumping his face. Left fist, right fist, punch after punch.

'I told you,' said Greg, hitting him again, 'I've killed men for less.'

Marin felt his legs go from under him.

'Stand down, Sergeant!' A third English voice. The beating continued. 'Stand down, I said! That's an order.'

Marin clung on to consciousness. His body was a dead weight in the arms of his captors, but still he registered a woman's face floating before him—a pair of smiling plum-coloured lips.

'Hi, honey,' she said, producing a hypodermic. 'I'm Jasna. And you're under arrest.'

'I'm Croatian,' he blurted out as she plunged the needle into his arm.

'Believe me. We don't want you. You're on your own.'

Marin felt his brain shutting down as Jasna leant in close.

'Tell me one thing, honey. Your funny Italian boat. Why you called it *Anna*?'

Marin didn't answer. His eyelids drooped, then closed. A hood was pulled over his swollen face. He was shackled hand and foot, hauled from the floor, and carried from his apartment trussed up like an animal.

2

SYDNEY, AUSTRALIA

12 DECEMBER 2005

ANNA ROSEN, BURDENED by heavy bags of groceries, climbed the four flights of stairs to the apartment her father had left her. To be precise, she had inherited one third of the property, but she had bought out her brothers' shares and thus ended up with a sizable mortgage.

Anna had found every aspect of the transaction grimly amusing. Thanks to her communist parents, she had grown up strictly opposed to inherited wealth; but the further necessity of dealing with moneylenders had made it even worse. She felt her skin crawl when she was forced to submit to a bank manager's capricious will. The punctilious prick had questioned why she'd never borrowed money in her life. He seemed to believe that she was in the grip of some strange deviance beyond his comprehension.

Anna had persisted because her brothers had convinced her they could use the money to reduce their own mortgages, but she had also begun to think, after a lifetime of renting, about what she could leave to her own daughter. The dwindling royalty cheques from her books would not amount to much. Nor would her meagre super-annuation accounts and she really must get around to the boring job of corralling them into a single compound-interest-bearing entity one day. Such a task made her nauseous.

Not that Rachel would ever need what little Anna had to offer. When it came to money, her daughter was an apple fallen far from the tree, then picked up by a passer-by and tossed over a high fence. As if in mockery of her mother, Rachel was steadily making her own fortune working for a private-investment fund in some capacity that Anna still struggled to comprehend. Rachel had already bought her own city apartment and a European sports car to occupy its precious garage.

Anna reached the landing, lowered her bags and opened the apartment door. She preferred the American term *apartment*—as in a suite of rooms—with its subtle implication of elegance. Her father, Frank, had called the place a unit, reducing it to a component, a module or a segment of something larger. This gave it a kind of socialist connotation that perhaps helped salve his conscience at having bought it in the first place. Her mother had suffered no such pangs of guilt. Eva had grown up in a spacious, high-ceilinged apartment in Vienna, filled with Ottoman carpets and fine furniture and valuable paintings, all of which had been stolen, in due course, by the Nazis.

Anna picked up the groceries and entered her home. Her home! She bumped the door closed with her bottom and felt the same sense of elation she always did. She was grateful that Eva had finally gotten her wish; pleased that Frank had not denied it to her after four decades living in public housing. After all, during the many years he had devoted to The Party, as an apparatchik and an evangelist, Eva had stood by his side, unwaveringly loyal through the worst of times.

The apartment was European in style. It was the closest thing to her childhood home Eva had been able to find in Sydney. When Anna finally took ownership of the place, she, as her mother had done, set about making it hers. On the parquetry floors with their patina of old polish she had laid her Afghan rugs, rugs whose price she had negotiated while drinking mint tea during a lull in the fighting in Kabul. She had filled the rest of the apartment with paintings, objects and photographs gathered during a lifetime of travelling.

Anna carried the grocery bags down the intricately patterned runner in the hallway and past the two bedrooms, past the bathroom and the study, which Frank had lined with old cedar bookshelves. She entered the living room with its high pressed-metal ceilings. Here tall windows looked down over Woolloomooloo. The long finger wharf and the green peninsula of the Botanical Gardens reached out into the harbour. Beyond and above the gardens was a section of city skyline, a slice of the Opera House and the arch of the Harbour Bridge.

Anna put her bags down. She never once saw the familiar shape of the bridge without it triggering memories of two men. One was more a demon than a man and, though long dead, he would forever inhabit the structure as a dark presence. The other had been lost to her for decades, yet he still existed in her life as a tangible, living presence.

After methodically unpacking the groceries, Anna reached up to a shelf of spices and took down the jar of tarragon. She put two fingers inside, feeling for what was hidden there. She found it easily enough and placed on the counter a green lump with tiny fibrous branches and pale seeds nestling among its resinous foliage.

It was all that remained of the bag of hydroponic dope she'd bought more than a year ago, dried and compacted like the Buddha sticks of her youth. Soon she would face the same old dilemma of how to replenish supplies. Her once-reliable dealers had evaporated, died or simply gone straight in middle age. The fellow she'd been most comfortable with, like the one mechanic you trust with your car, was now a website designer who wanted his friends to forget how he used to make his living.

Artists tended to retain their connections to the black market and there was a painter Anna knew pretty well who liked a smoke, but she was too embarrassed to ask him. She pulled out her papers from a kitchen drawer and rolled a thin joint using the dried tarragon as a tobacco substitute. She lit it up and drew on the fragrant smoke.

Anna liked cooking when she was stoned. It gave her focus. She thought about that and then, realising that the very idea sounded silly, she laughed at herself.

'Focus,' she said aloud. 'Some music.'

She wanted up, not down, and she found waiting on top of the CD player an album by Amadou & Mariam.

Not too hot, not too cold—just right.

The gentle ringing tones of '*M'Bifé*' filled the room and she danced to it a bit until she saw herself in the mirror across the room—or, rather, what seemed to be an incarnation of her former self, swaying rhythmically, sexily. She moved closer until she saw a truer reflection. As always, the first thing she noticed was the tear-shaped scar below her left eye, damage wrought by men, but it could have been much worse. When she changed focus and saw the whole picture, she wasn't unhappy with it; she didn't mind the face that the years had given her. Anna toked on the joint, blew smoke at the mirror and watched her clouded reflection smile at the gesture.

In the kitchen she lined up the ingredients for Rachel's meal, a simple ritual she had done time and again. It was an act of devotion, after all, the preparation of a meal for a loved one on her birthday. For a present she had chosen a painting which had lived for years on her bedroom wall. Rachel had always loved it and it was now wrapped and leaning against the living room couch. Like the meal, it was a peace offering. She felt guilty that she'd seen so little of her daughter in recent months. Both of them had been busy, but the lapse seemed to cover most of the time that Rachel had been together with Leah. How many months was it? Anna tried to harness her drifting thoughts. Three or four perhaps, and in that time Anna had met the young woman only once at a café, and after what seemed like ten minutes Leah had made a lame excuse and run off, leaving Rachel to interpret what had happened.

'She finds you intimidating, Mum.'

'I can see that. I just don't get it.'

'You're scary, that's why.'

'Oh, come on.'

'She's seen you on telly tearing shreds off people. Imagine holding a contrary opinion. Even I used to find you intimidating.'

'Well, you got over it.'

'Really,' Rachel had said, raising her eyebrows. 'You think so?'

•

The squid and the blue swimmers were packed in ice, which Anna tipped into the sink. She cleaned the crabs first, flipping them onto their backs and, finding with her fingernail the triangular key to unlock the carapace, she prised them apart to peel off the grey lungs and wash out the mustard. Then with each squid she forced her fingers in behind the head, with its cloudy, dead eyes, easing out the gut, the ink sac and then the quill, setting aside her disgust at the partly digested fish in some of them and the white viscous substance that always gave her the unpleasant sensation of rinsing out used condoms.

Anna's fingers were deep in squid entrails when the landline phone rang.

'Oh fuck,' she cried and dropped the slimy dead thing into the sink. She thrust her hands up like a surgeon waiting to have her brow mopped and the call diverted to the answering machine.

This is Anna Rosen. I'm not here, please leave a message . . .

Anna rinsed and dried her hands as a voice boomed through the machine's small speaker:

'Anna, it's Leon. Are you screening? Pick up! I need an answer on Aceh. Don't fucking screen me, Anna! I've got a queue of writers begging me to put them on that plane . . .'

The voice was still squawking when she grabbed the receiver. 'Leon?'

'Ha,' he said. 'I knew you were there.'

'Uri Geller now, are you?'

'I wish. You got to love a magical Jew.'

'It's not magic.'

'Don't tell me what's magic. You ever tried bending a spoon? What are you up to?'

'Rinsing out condoms.'

'What?'

'Cleaning squid and trying not to puke . . . A birthday dinner for Rachel. Give me some time, will you? I'm still trying to decide if I want to go back to Aceh.'

'Who else should I send?' Leon responded peevishly. 'You were there.'

Anna's brow creased and she rubbed her eyes with her free hand. 'That fucking place is full of bad memories,' she said. 'And, anyway, I hate anniversaries.'

'Don't tell Rachel that when she's blowing out the candles.'

'I still have tsunami nightmares, you know. Thing is, I'm not going to give you an answer now. I'm nervous as a cat about tonight. Rachel's bringing her new girlfriend. I've only met her once and we didn't exactly hit it off.'

'Such a lovely girl, Rachel. I was sure she'd grow out of this thing for women.'

'Leon!'

'It happens you know . . .'

'That's wrong on so many levels. I'm hanging up now.

'Call me tomorrow!'

•

Anna cursed herself for answering the call.

Aceh.

She was still high and this hydro weed could take you down as quickly as up. Unwanted images played in her head—black water, bodies large and tiny, countless; bodies, tens of thousands, hundreds of thousands of bodies entombed in mud, and she smelled again the stench of their dissolution and heard again the wailing grief of the living.

Just under a year ago, on Boxing Day, she had rushed to Aceh when news of the tsunami broke. Her piece for the magazine had ended with the mothers who crowded the bridge every night where they heard their lost children crying out to them from the river. It wasn't only mothers. Husbands heard the cries of their wives, wives heard their husbands, children their parents. Now Leon was pushing her to go back, and though she had agreed she dreaded it.

When she went back to the dead animals in the sink she remembered helping a man pull the bodies of his wife and daughter from a mud-filled house and hot tears gathered in her eyes. She grabbed up a paper towel and blotted them away.

'Bloody hell,' she muttered, throwing the damp thing aside.

•

By late afternoon her preparations were done. Anna made herself a gin and tonic and surveyed her work. A curry base awaited the crabs. The squid had been stuffed with their own chopped tentacles and a mixture of pork and spices, and then sewn up with thread, ready for the wok. There was a large bowl of *nuoc cham* with sliced chillies floating lethally on the surface, and bowls of rice noodles, lettuce leaves, mint and basil, with bok choi and *gai lan* waiting in steamers. The cake she had bought from her favourite bakery on Macleay Street was safely on a shelf.

Her own mother would have been bemused by the exotic choices, but Eva had always gone to great trouble for special meals, and Anna knew how much she would have loved to have been there tonight with her daughter and grand-daughter.

She glanced automatically at the photo of Eva and herself on the wall. It had been taken two decades ago when they visited what was left of Ravensbrück concentration camp. Eva was in a wheelchair. She had less than six months to live when she finally decided to go back and confront the past, and only then was she able to tell her daughter what had happened to her in the camp. Anna turned away from the picture and the train of thought that had taken her in swift steps from the Holocaust, back to Aceh and to the fallacy of a merciful God.

Anna was heading for the shower when the Blackberry chirped. She had to change that irritating fucking tone. She considered just ignoring it, but then thought that it might be a text from Rachel, caught up at work or something worse. She was relieved but surprised to see the sender: *Pierre / The Hague*.

Pierre Villiers, that was. A year ago, her old friend had got himself a job at the War Crimes Tribunal. She had heard from him only once since then and that had been early on as he was settling in to his new life, so she was surprised at the abrupt tone of his text.

I've emailed you some pics. Have a look as soon as you can and call me.

Anna had never figured out how to open attachments on the Blackberry so she went to the study, woke up the computer and activated the modem. The familiar beeping dial-up tones gave way to the eerie electronic whale song, and it squealed away before transitioning into an orgasm of white noise as the connection was made. She had resisted the advice of tech-savvy friends to upgrade to ADS-something or other which, they assured her, could achieve download speeds of five hundred and twelve kilobits per second. Anna didn't know or care what a kilobit was. She reasoned she could get whatever she needed from the internet with her old dial-up modem but, she had to admit, it was a real bugger opening attachments.

She found Pierre's email at the top of her inbox with a second intriguing message:

Have a look the attached photos. Do you recognise this man? Call me!

Anna found four files at the bottom of the email and opened them all, leaving them to download while she went to the bathroom. She washed her hair and languished under the shower, letting it stream at high pressure over her shoulders and down her back. The tail of the marijuana high added a sensuous note that made her reluctant to leave the warm water.

Anna was in a bathrobe, drying her hair, when the doorbell rang. She ran to peer through the spyhole. It was Rachel, alone. She unlatched the door and pulled it open.

'Hi, Mum,' said Rachel, in a small, embarrassed voice.

'Hello, darling.'

Anna threw her arms around her, dampening her daughter's pale silk blouse.

'Oops, I'm still wet. I wasn't expecting you so soon.'

'Sorry, I thought I should come early.'

'Don't be silly. I'm just happy to see you. It's been too long.' Anna stroked her daughter's cheek and pushed strands of wayward hair back behind Rachel's ears. 'You look tired.'

'I am. It's not easy taking care of other people's money.'

Anna hesitated, then caught her tongue. 'Come in,' she said. 'Come in.'

She drew Rachel inside, an arm around her waist. Halfway down the hallway, her daughter stiffened and stopped.

'Mum! Have you been smoking dope?'

'What?'

Rachel pulled herself free and stared into Anna's eyes. 'You're stoned.'

'Well, mildly buzzed.'

'What are you, sixteen? *Buzzed*?'

'It was hours ago.'

Anna watched with alarm as her daughter raced about the living room, hauling up the tall windows. Once all of them had been thrown open, Rachel turned to her mother and Anna was taken aback by her apparent distress.

'Christ, Anna, what were you thinking?'

'Come on, darling. It's not like you to be such a puritan. It's mostly tarragon you can smell, anyway.'

'It stinks like a hippy campervan. Leah would have a fit.'

'This is *my* apartment Rachel, I'm not sixteen and the world's not going to end because I smoked a joint.'

Rachel nodded and took a breath, deliberately composing herself. 'I'm sorry, Mum. It's my fault. I should have told you before now.'

'About what?'

'It's Leah. She's . . . Orthodox.'

'Are you serious?'

Rachel gave her mother a pleading look. 'Please understand, Mum. It's bad enough what we're going through with Leah's family. I didn't want you on my back, too. On top of everything I've been working around the clock. That's why I came early. Let me make us a drink.'

'You mean Orthodox, Orthodox?'

'Yeah, well, Modern Orthodox.'

'What does her family think of you?'

'It's complicated.'

'I'll bet it is,' said Anna, constructing in her mind the whole world that Rachel had kept from her and feeling ashamed that her daughter had been too wary to share any of this with her.

'You want to sit down?' asked Rachel.

'Oh fuck,' cried Anna, slapping her head theatrically. 'I've just made the most non-Kosher meal imaginable: crabs and squid—no fins, no scales—and the squid's stuffed with pork. It's like I set out to offend her.'

Anna laughed with a slightly hysterical edge, but then Rachel joined in and it ended in a tight hug.

'It's my fault, Mum,' said Rachel. 'I'm sorry, I really am. Look, I bought fish on the way. Can we start again?'

Anna saw that Rachel's eyes were brimming with tears and imagined the fraught nature of the love she had given herself over to.

'We can do that,' she whispered. 'Don't worry. It'll all be fine.'

'I wonder sometimes if it ever will be.'

'Look,' said Anna. 'I'll go put some clothes on. You cut up the fish and we'll make a kosher curry.'

•

The two women spent an hour or more, their good humour largely restored, working together in the kitchen to transform Anna's menu—as she put it—from the profane to the sacred. Only when it was done did she remember Pierre's email. She left Rachel setting the table and went into the study to wake up her computer again.

The photos Pierre had sent her had downloaded, but they had opened sideways. Anna twisted her head to look at the first image. It was the figure of a hooded man wearing a set of orange overalls. He was handcuffed and shackled at his ankles. Two men in military uniforms were on either side of him, grasping his arms as they led him down the stairs of a Jetstream aircraft parked on a darkened tarmac. Her immediate thought was Guantanamo Bay, but, looking closer, she saw, distorted by the angle, what appeared to be UN markings on the side of the plane.

She scrolled down to the next picture, a wider version of the first one. The hooded man and his guards were heading for a black-windowed van parked on the tarmac near the jet, and she saw part of a sign that indicated this was Schiphol, the main airport of Amsterdam. Pierre had offered no explanation, but Anna deduced that this was an accused man on his way to the war crimes prison in The Hague.

The next photo seemed to confirm that assumption. It was a typical police mugshot. The man in the orange jumpsuit was unhooded now and his face showed the obvious signs of a severe beating. He was middle-aged and powerfully built. His nose and both his eyes were badly swollen and discoloured by bruising, as were his cheekbones; there were bloody butterfly bandages holding together cuts that seemed to require stitching. Below the image was a name:

MARIC, Tomislav

D.O.B. 13.11.51

Rijeka, Croatia

Anna stared hard at the photo. Pierre had asked her if she recognised this man and all her nerve endings now seemed to be tingling. Was there something there? She scrolled down to the final image, hoping for clarity. It showed a man from the waist up wearing a hospital gown. It was the kind of photo taken by medical staff for their records and she imagined doctors and nurses appalled by the damage done to this patient, whatever he might be guilty of. The man's face was still discoloured by the bruising, but the swelling around the eyes had subsided. Anna drew a sharp breath.

There was a tremor in her hand as she used the mouse to enlarge the image, focusing on the man's eyes.

They were a distinctive green. She sat up, blinking with shock. What she was seeing was simply not possible. Her heart was pounding so hard she reached for her chest as if to hold it in. He could not be alive. She did the mental calculations—Bosnia, June 1992, more than thirteen years ago—that's when she had seen, with her own eyes, his car shot so full of holes it was like a giant colander. Black flies swarmed over seats pitted and perforated and sweetened with gouts of congealed blood. She remembered how the flies had risen from the gore, dotting the air around the car, and how she had swatted them away from her face in disgust.

And what of the mourning men? Their grief could not have been feigned. No, he had died in that car. No one could have survived such an ambush. In her imagination, he had died like Sonny Corleone, shot to pieces by machine guns as he tried to tear himself from behind the wheel of his Cadillac. Yet she could not ignore the evidence on the screen in front of her. She was absolutely sure that these were the eyes of Marin Katich. There could be no doubt. They were the same green eyes possessed by their daughter.

At that moment the doorbell rang, and she heard Rachel rush past her, down the corridor to welcome Leah.

3

SCHEVENINGEN, THE HAGUE

12–13 DECEMBER 2005

MARIN KATICH was in a locked box. Four storeys up on the western face of the building, part of the E1 wing where all the windows have steel bars and frosted glass. Here the accused were hidden away from the world according to strict codes set by The Registry.

In the late afternoon, Marin could hear the cries of gulls circling over Scheveningen beach. Sometimes they dropped down to perch between the bars and their shuffling forms were shadows behind the glass, quivering in the freezing winds. The North Sea was so close that in the exercise yard he could taste salt in the air. In his closed cell there was only the faint stench that circulated through the air vents: rotting vegetables and something worse. He believed that stench came from the inmates, that it seeped from their pores, and from his own.

Watery light leaked in through the translucent glass, but the winter sun did nothing to warm his blood. At this time of the year the weak glow of the afternoon sun dwindled fast, but he was reluctant to turn on the electric lights, whose tungsten brightness produced in him a wave of despair.

Dr Vladka told him his despair had physical causes. It was all to do with the hypothalamus, she explained—that mysterious gland located above the optic chiasm. The theory was that he had learned to crave bright sunlight when he was a boy growing up in Australia so it was no accident that he found the prolonged northern gloom debilitating. It disrupted his circadian rhythms.

He found it strange that a well-credentialled psychiatrist like Dr Vladka was fascinated by New Age methodologies. As a lifelong sceptic, he had berated her when she made the mistake of suggesting he join the prison's meditation group.

'What kind of doctor are you?' he cried. 'You seriously think I could reach a higher state of consciousness in a room full of murderers? That's an obscenity!'

Dr Vladka took his outburst calmly. She liked to provoke him and he didn't resent her for it. She played the lion tamer with chair and whip while he was the unpredictable, clever predator.

'It might work for you,' she said. 'Something apart from masturbation to help you relax.'

'But then at least'—he shrugged as he said it—'you're always in my thoughts.'

She wrote something in her notepad and he let the silence settle before asking: 'Your notes on my sanity? Is that meant to be intimidating?'

'What's intimidating for you, Tomo,' Dr Vladka said calmly, 'is saying anything about yourself, except bad jokes.'

He looked at her for a moment before responding honestly.

'I've got too many secrets.'

•

Dr Vladka—he knew no other name for her—had broad shoulders, heavy limbs and a face with large features. He was not attracted to her, but he liked her soulful eyes, her seductive voice and her sardonic sense of humour.

At first, it had struck him as odd that they would fly in a psychiatrist all the way from Belgrade and, in a rare moment of candour, he had told her how ironic it was that they had placed him in the care of a Serb, given his history, which must surely be set out in his file.

She said there was no irony involved. It was just that the psychiatrists of Belgrade had become renowned for dealing with men like him. During the war and in its aftermath, the city's psychiatric wards had been overrun by an epidemic of men driven insane by the atrocities they had committed. Their treatment had become a rare Serbian growth industry.

Apart from remaining taciturn, Marin had no alternative but to play games. He could not be truthful with her while he was living a lie. Since his arrest, he had maintained the fiction that his name was Tomislav Maric and, since no one had proven otherwise, he was locked in his false identity as securely as he was locked in the prison.

Nonetheless, he needed to keep Dr Vladka on side, or at least sympathetic to him, since she was the source of his sedating pills. However, when she probed into his past, seeking details about his family or his upbringing, he remained tight-lipped. He had certainly not told her about his ghosts, even when they appeared behind her ample shoulders, demanding attention, distracting him as she spoke.

'Tomo?' she said. 'Are you listening to me?'

He stared at her blankly until it came back to him that this was the name by which she knew him.

'Sure, I'm listening.'

'I was asking about your father.'

•

Although Marin had refused to answer any such questions, they were not without effect. Back alone in his cell, thoughts of his father were never far away. Only this morning, in the timeless darkness before dawn, he had had one of his many dreams about Ivo. In the last beats of the dream, the old man had been singing the *ojkanje* with a terrible passion. It was one of the wolf songs his father had tried to teach them when he and Petar were boys. As Ivo howled its strange cadences, the old man's face transformed into a yellow-eyed beast, and Marin woke, drenched in sweat and shaking. For a moment, as the last note of the song echoed in the hard space of his cell, Marin had no idea where he was. He fumbled for the pills and swallowed two of them to ward off the panic. He lay trembling, as if waiting out an earth tremor.

This was by no means the first visitation. Long ago his father had joined the others who trailed in Marin's wake—those who spoke to him in the dead of night, who continued to haunt him. They were always there: the ones he had killed from a distance, the ones he had killed up close, and the ones whose killing he had caused. His brother Petar had been silent for many years, perhaps because he had no reason to blame Marin for his own death. He hoped Petar was not trapped in this purgatory, endlessly punished by the presence of the father he hated.

Marin remembered that, in the dream, before Ivo had started singing, he had spoken to him almost tenderly.

Remember what I told you . . .

He had noticed Ivo's fist was closed around something. Then it opened and there was a black cicada, throbbing in his father's palm like a living engine with alien eyes, red and implacable.

You are like him, Marin. Remember this. This life in Australia is not real. You are deep underground. One day it will be time to come out.

Remembering his father's words, Marin now sat up on the hard bunk and stepped over to the desk to write them down. There was much he had forgotten. When he was done, he flicked back through the journal to the notes he had written about the last time he saw Ivo alive.

•

His father had been restrained in a reclining chair and propped up with pillows. The curtains were drawn on one side to dissuade him from yelling abuse at the frail old soul in the next cot. Ivo's wrists were strapped to the chair's padded vinyl arms. Before the nurse led him to the room, she had warned Marin to prepare himself. The binding, she explained, was to stop the old man tearing out the plastic tube that drained his bladder through an incision in his lower belly. Ivo had managed to do this more than once, spraying piss all over himself and the nearest nurses.

Marin watched from the doorway, reluctant to go in as his father writhed about, trying to free his wrists. Ivo's fingers clawed at the arms of the chair and his body contorted in fruitless efforts to bite at the straps. All the while he ground his hips, stiffened his legs and arched his back. Marin was reminded of the slow-motion, repetitive movements of a reanimated corpse, and he imagined that this was how Ivo's precious God had chosen to punish him, confining him like this in an earthly purgatory.

By losing his mind, Ivo had once again escaped justice—or, at least, the trial prepared for him. More than forty years after the war ended, they had indicted him for war crimes and, irony of ironies, they'd done so based on evidence gathered by Anna Rosen. Ivo's one-woman Jewish conspiracy had finally caught up with him.

Marin had taken a huge risk in flying back to Australia and, when he finally went in to sit beside his father, it seemed there was a glimmer of recognition.

'I know you,' said Ivo before his eyes rolled up. After a moment, they returned to refocus on his son. There was cunning in the old man's face. 'I know you,' he whispered. 'I know you.'

Marin bent in close and pushed greasy strands of white hair from his father's eyes.

'Of course you do,' he said.

The old man flinched at the physical contact and struggled to formulate a question in Croatian.

'Did . . . did *they* send you?'

'Who?'

'Belgrade . . . Or maybe the Jews . . . Huh? The Jews! I can see it in your face. They have the longest memories.' Ivo laughed until the exertion produced a hacking cough.

'What are you talking about?'

'Fool! I know who you are . . .'

'For fuck's sake, Papa. I'm your son, Marin.'

'Liar!' Ivo shouted. His eyes were ghastly, protruding as if swollen by the sudden anger. 'You . . . you . . . You I know. You're the slaughterman!'

Marin reeled back.

'No! That's crazy. It's me, Marin. I heard how sick you were. I came to see you. I came to say goodbye.'

'Come, then,' Ivo rasped. 'Come closer.'

'What is it?'

'I'm waiting.' Ivo tried again to free his arms. 'See? Tied up like a pig.' He rolled his head back, exposing the corded arteries and veins in his unshaven, emaciated neck. 'Go ahead.'

'Don't be crazy, Pop!'

'What are you waiting for? Coward! Waverer! Incompetent! Leftist scum! Don't think twice. It's easy, it is, it's so easy . . . A knife through butter, then it's warm on your skin, warm on your chest . . . I know how that feels, I know.'

Ivo's tongue flickered across his lips and he smiled at some sickening memory.

Marin's stomach roiled as his father continued in a hoarse whisper: 'Take my confession, Father. I've done mortal sins. No

penance can answer for them. The only recompense is blood . . .
Only blood can answer for blood. Now get on with it! *Do it!*'

Ivo's laugh was mirthless. It was like the barking of a seal. Then,
as suddenly as it had come, the light in his father's eyes faded and
he returned to the slow writhing attempts to free himself.

•

Marin sat at the desk, the memory curdling inside him, as he
thought of the wartime photographs depicting the crimes of the
Ustasha—black-and-white images Ivo had always laughed off as
communist propaganda. A monstrous library of such photos had
been compiled by American prosecutors at Nuremberg, and many
of them had been reprinted in Anna Rosen's book about his father:
an Ustashi soldier posing in a group with the severed head of a
Serbian Orthodox priest; a man forced to his knees by a crowd of
grimly posing Ustashi as they prepared to hack off his head with
a logging saw; prisoners at Jasenovac camp whose skulls had been
smashed open by steel mallets; others slaughtered like sheep by
men wearing custom-made curved blades buckled to their wrists
with leather straps. And the image that had leapt into his head as he
listened to Ivo's demented ravings in the hospital: two young, bare-
chested men, arms linked in the manner of drunks holding each
other up, both howling with laughter, their faces drenched in blood.

A scraping sound at the door brought Marin back to the present.
He saw the spyhole go light, then dark, then light again. It was
7.30 am. A key penetrated the lock, the steel door swung towards
him, and the guard Zwolsman thrust first his head, then much of his
large body, through the door. Zwolsman had the face of a Bruegel
peasant who'd been rudely stuffed into a prison guard's uniform.
His was the first face Marin saw each day.

'Mr M, not a nice day to be out today. I must book first if you
wish to use the gym this morning?'

'No, thank you, Zwolsman. I want to walk outside. I need to see the sky.'

'Today you will only see clouds and raindrops, perhaps.'

'I don't care if it rains.'

'Dress warm. It is very cold,' said the guard. 'I will come and get you at zero nine hundred.'

Zwolsman backed out of the cell, leaving the door open. Marin pulled on winter clothes, grabbed his jacket, gathered up a pile of dirty garments and a sachet of washing liquid, and stepped into the corridor. He headed for the laundry in the communal bathroom.

Behind a closed shower stall someone was singing loudly. Marin stopped, clutching his bundle of clothes, unable to move. The song was Milosevic-era turbo folk, vulgar and taunting—'porno-nationalism' they called such music.

Marin's pill-induced calm evaporated like morning fog. He knew the song well. It was a favourite of the Chetniks in Vukovar: *I punu saku olova, i nesto protiv bolova* . . . Leave me a handful of bullets and something for the pain.

When drunken Serbs, their own frontlines only metres away in the ruined city, used to belt this out as a provocation, Marin would order his snipers to wait for one of the intoxicated imbeciles to expose himself. No need for a handful of lead, just one round—that had been the best coda to their shouted chorus.

He knew the singer in the shower. The voice was unmistakable—it was one of Milosevic's cronies, a dumb, murderous thug. Marin saw himself tearing open the cubicle door, smashing an elbow into the fool's fat face, forcing him onto the tiles beneath the hot downpour and shoving a cake of soap down his throat.

But he remained standing where he was and the singer kept on singing.

Eventually Marin walked stiffly to the Miele washing machine up against the wall. He knew that this was exactly why they had rules against talking politics, or even discussing your case with other inmates. They were afraid the murderers would start murdering each other.

He shoved his clothes into the front loader and slammed it shut. He ripped the sachet open with his teeth and the bitter tang in his mouth made him wonder if that's what a bar of soap down the throat would taste like. He poured the blue liquid into the machine, set the dial to *Miniwas 40 graden*, pressed the start button and heard the water come shushing in. The man in the shower was still singing.

Marin went to a basin and splashed cold water on his face. A death mask stared back at him in the mirror. He noticed a tremor in his right hand. He left the washing churning and walked out, down the corridor to the common room. This long neon-lit space was where inmates in E1 spent most of their spare time. Just inside the doorway a table football game sat idle. Marin hated seeing grown men hunched over this apparatus, twirling the knobs like idiots, as the ranks of tiny players performed backflips. A pool table would have been better, but a game that furnishes you with a lethal weapon would never be approved.

Chess and backgammon boards were stacked in an open cupboard and he thought again of his improbable chess opponent, Slobodan Milosevic. Marin had been playing regular games with the prison's alpha male until he was carted off to the hospital wing for more tests on his ailing heart.

Two microwave ovens, one on top of the other, sat on a table against the wall. Beside them were two large refrigerators—two of everything to reduce the potential for conflict. At the far end of the room, side-lit by a barred window, was an open kitchen with a gas stove and a white Formica table with eight chairs around it. There were two men seated at the table, huddled together, drinking from matching mugs. They looked at Marin but said nothing.

He walked into the kitchen, smelled burnt coffee and turned to the nearest man.

'You'll never learn will you, Mejakic?'

'Good morning to you too, Maric. What are you whining about?'

Marin stared into the dead eyes of Zeljko Mejakic, set deep in a long, mournful face. During the war, the Bosnian Serb had been the commandant of the Omarska concentration camp. Marin picked up the coffee pot and emptied the dregs into the sink.

'It stinks in here,' he said. 'You always burn the coffee.'

Mejakic's companion responded: 'If you're such an expert, you should get up earlier and make coffee for us all.'

Marin regarded the pair of them. They might have been brothers. Ljubomir Borovcanin was another long-faced Serb, with heavily bagged grey skin under his black eyes. In his pomp, he had boasted the title *Republika Srpska Police General Ljubomir Borovcanin*. He was under indictment on charges of genocide for the deportation of thirty thousand Bosnian Muslim women and children from the Srebrenica enclave, and for the slaughter of seven thousand of their husbands and sons during one murderous week in July 1995.

Since his incarceration six months ago, Borovcanin had grown a Van Dyke beard. Marin wondered whether it was there to hide the incongruous dimple in his chin, or simply because he imagined that with it he would cut a more impressive figure in the televised courtroom. Whatever the motive, the fastidious beard encouraged in him a nervous habit. He repeatedly ran his thumb and forefinger across his trimmed moustache and down to tug at the thatch of hair on his chin.

'You'll pull that silly beard right off if you keep doing that,' said Marin.

Borovcanin dropped his hand abruptly and Marin turned away to complete his task of cleaning and refilling the coffee pot.

'That was very rude of you, Maric,' said Mejakic, his face reddened with indignation. Marin glanced back and smiled, sizing up each man, then he returned to packing the ground coffee into the machine and tamping it down.

'I'd be happy to make coffee for you, *Generals*,' he said when his task was done. 'But would you really want to drink it without a food taster?'

The two men stared back at him.

'Are you drunk?' asked Mejakic, and Borovcanin chimed in: 'Is that a threat?'

'I'm just making coffee,' Marin said as he plonked the steel pot loudly on the stove and lit the gas. 'I'll try not to burn it.'

'What's up your arse?' Mejakic demanded. 'It's not like you to start fights.'

'You should apologise,' said Borovcanin.

Marin ignored them, filled a bowl with muesli and poured milk over it. He sat down opposite the two and began to eat.

'I mean it,' said Borovcanin.

Marin stared at the man and slowly munched a mouthful of muesli. A line of milk ran from the side of his mouth to drip on the table.

'Are you feeling all right, Maric?' asked Mejakic.

When Marin didn't answer, Borovcanin abruptly pushed his chair back and stood up. The Serb grabbed his coffee mug off the table and walked to the sink; with rapid movements, he rinsed it out and put it in the dishwasher.

'I'll see you later, Zeljko,' he told his companion as he left the room.

'Sure, Ljubo. You booked the court, yes?'

'I did.'

Mejakic turned back to Marin.

'You've upset him.'

'Why? Does he really think I'd put rat poison in his coffee?'

The coffee pot was bubbling now. Marin wiped his face with the back of his hand and went to pour a cup.

'You want one?' he asked Mejakic, holding up the pot.

'No, thank you.'

'I didn't think so,' said Marin, blowing gently into his coffee before taking a sip.

'I'm serious,' said Mejakic. 'You are not normal. You have me worried.'

'Worried?' Marin looked him in the eyes. 'About what?'

'You know what I mean. You'll scare people if you behave like this.'

'And do I scare you too, Zeljko? Really? I imagine you must understand fear very well, how to nurture it so it grows and grows. How brave you must have felt terrifying those women and children out of their wits.'

'Maric!' Mejakic cried. 'I will have to report you for this.'

Marin leant in close. 'I wouldn't do that if I were you,' he said quietly, almost in a whisper, holding the man's gaze until Mejakic dropped his eyes.

Mejakic stood, grabbed his empty coffee cup and turned to walk out. As he reached the door, he turned back and said loudly: 'Filthy fucking Ustashi!'

Marin froze. He knew that if he looked up and saw the man's hideous, mocking face he would have to kill him. It was as simple as that.

But when he left the common room the corridor was empty. He looked down at the steaming cup he was carrying. The black surface was vibrating.

Ustashi. That word had been with him for as far back as he could remember. Then he caught a whiff of something in the air: old tobacco, *rakija* and decay. Ivo was close by.

4

SYDNEY, AUSTRALIA

12 DECEMBER 2005

ANNA WAS STILL SITTING in her study, staring dumbfounded at the photos, when she heard Rachel's cries of delight as she greeted Leah and pulled her into the apartment. Rachel called out to her mother and she answered with an apology, saying she would be out in a moment. Instead she found a packet of stale cigarettes, threw open the window and lit up a smoke to settle herself for the ordeal to come.

When she finally felt able to join her guests, Anna composed herself and came out to find Rachel and Leah drinking tea in the living room.

'Leah,' said Anna. 'I'm so sorry, I got caught up with an urgent work thing.'

'Don't worry,' said Leah as she stood up. 'It's nice to meet you properly.'

'Welcome.' Anna put her hands on Leah's bare shoulders and felt the young woman flinch almost imperceptibly as she kissed her lightly on each cheek. She stepped back and gave her a brief appraising look. 'You look lovely.'

Leah whispered: 'Thank you.'

Leah was wearing a floral cotton dress whose bright colours emphasised her almost ethereal paleness. Her face, neck and limbs were strangers to the sun and she crossed her arms, as if shy of the exposure. Anna sensed that the young woman was uncomfortable in her own skin, unaware of her beauty. She wondered if Rachel had bought her this dress and perhaps, too, the tiny gold Star of David that hung on a fine chain above her breasts.

'Can I get you a proper drink?' Anna asked her.

'We're fine with tea, Mum,' said Rachel.

'You sure?' said Anna. Rachel sent her a warning look but she went on mischievously. 'We can't open your present without a small glass of champagne.'

'That would be lovely,' said Leah and Rachel nodded sheepishly.

•

Anna pulled the cork with a single twist, which produced a small, controlled explosion. It was one of her few practical skills and she was pleased with herself as she poured the champagne and raised her glass to Rachel.

'Happy birthday, darling.'

They each clinked glasses and Anna waited discreetly for Leah to take a sip before reaching behind the sofa for the wrapped present, which she placed on Rachel's lap.

'I hope you like it,' she said.

Rachel unwrapped it quickly and blushed when she saw what it was.

'Oh, Mum,' she said. 'You can't give me this. You love this painting.'

'You love it too, don't you?'

'Yes, I always have.'

'It's yours now.'

There were fresh tears in Rachel's eyes as she pulled off the last of the wrapping and set the black and ochre abstract in front of them.

'It's beautiful,' said Rachel. 'So serene. I don't know what to say.'

'Serenity is enough,' said Anna, but despite her efforts to appear lighthearted her own thoughts were far from serene.

Leah put down her glass and examined the painting closely.

'Is it a Rover Thomas?'

'It is,' said Anna. 'I bought it in the eighties.'

'Before . . ?'

'Before he became Rover Thomas, "old master".' Anna used both hands to make exclamation marks. 'Back then he was a retired stockman who did paintings to make a bit of extra money. I just liked it. Who knew?'

'That was a great investment,' said Leah. 'I can't imagine how much it's appreciated since then.'

'I forgot you were an art dealer,' Anna responded harshly. 'But I didn't buy it as an *investment*. It wasn't about money.'

'Sorry, no,' Leah stammered. 'I didn't mean . . .'

Anna realised that Leah had been hit unfairly by a wave of the tension she had been holding in.

'Of course, I'm sorry,' she said. 'Right, I'm going to get the dinner ready.'

'Can we help?' said Rachel.

'No, we'd just get in each other's way,' said Anna and she barked out a brittle laugh. 'You can talk among yourselves about the cranky old woman in the kitchen.'

By the time the meal was ready, Anna had downed a strong G&T and started on a bottle of chardonnay. Her mind was elsewhere as she laid steaming bowls of curry, raita and rice on the table. She lit a pair of tall candles and opened Rachel's wine. The lovers were still chatting quietly in the living room. Let them decide to drink or not to drink, she thought, setting the bottle down.

'Come in, you two,' she called. 'Supper's ready.'

'Rachel's been showing me your photos,' said Leah as she sat down. 'You've been to so many places.'

'I'm afraid it's proof of what an itinerant mother I was,' said Anna, spooning rice into Leah's bowl. 'I hope you like curries. The fish one's not too spicy. I sometimes wonder if Rachel will ever forgive me.'

'Don't be silly,' said Rachel, taking over the job of serving Leah and herself. 'You wouldn't be you if you hadn't done all those things.'

'I know I could have been a better mother,' said Anna, looking into Rachel's eyes, inevitably comparing them to the emailed photos and worrying about the enormous lie that hung over their lives. She topped up her wineglass, raised it and said, 'Happy birthday, darling! For better or worse, you got me.'

'Happy birthday,' said Leah, kissing Rachel's cheek.

'Thank you,' said Rachel. 'It's always been *for better*, Mum.'

Anna gave her daughter a bleak smile.

'I hope that doesn't change,' she said.

•

Anna barely touched her food, dutifully chewing small mouthfuls as she watched the young women prattling on about the various dishes as Rachel described the spices, the countries of origin, and her mother's painstaking efforts in making the curry sauces. She found it difficult to lift the invisible barrier between her and them, and instead kept refilling her own wineglass, getting another bottle from the fridge when she had emptied the first. Leah's attempts at polite inquiry were met with blunt responses and awkward silences.

'Rachel told me you're going back to Aceh,' she said at one point.

'That might not happen now,' Anna replied, taking up her glass. Rachel looked at her, puzzled.

'You were all ready to go.'

'I may have to go to Europe instead,' said Anna. 'We'll talk about it later.'

To Rachel's evident annoyance, Anna kept drinking and even lit up a cigarette at the table after the curries were cleared away. Anna was well aware that she must seem like the cliché of a disaffected future mother-in-law, but she simply could not find a way of altering her mood. Then, with terrible inevitability, Leah strayed recklessly into the quicksand of the Middle East.

'That photo in the hallway of you in front of a bombed building with all those men in the white protective suits,' she said to Anna. 'Is that Tel Aviv?'

'Yes,' said Anna. 'After a Scud missile attack. Those are chemical weapons suits. The big fear was that Saddam would arm a missile with sarin gas.'

'And the Palestinians were sitting on their roofs cheering as the missiles flew over,' said Leah, shaking her head. 'That tells you everything we need to know about living with them as neighbours.'

Rachel sent Anna a psychic warning: *Don't go there!* But it was too late. Anna was already crushing the cigarette packet in her fist under the table.

'It's hard to have happy neighbours,' said Anna, 'when you've driven them off their land and out of their houses and towns and villages, and forbade any right to return to the ones who ran for their lives.'

Rachel gripped Leah's arm and her silent mediation failed again.

'Sharon tried to compromise with these people.' Leah spoke with righteous anger, emphasising *people* as if to throw doubt on whether the word truly applied to Palestinians. 'He used our own army to tear settlers from their houses in Gaza. He freed hundreds of terrorists from jail. He said it was for "peace". And how did they respond, his peace partners? They sent suicide bombers! First the marketplace in Hadera. Did you see that bloodbath? I used to shop there. Then, a few days ago, the mall in Netanya.'

So, thought Anna, this is the real Leah. The shy, fragile beauty has a hard core of belief.

'I always thought Ariel Sharon was nothing but a warmonger,' she said. 'Even a war criminal, after Lebanon. It's ironic that he was the one to move against the illegal settlements. But even Sharon has come to realise that it's the extremists on *both* sides who pose the biggest threat to Israel's future.'

Leah's eyes widened in disbelief. 'You think settlers and terrorists are the same? That's the argument of self-hating Jews. Have you forgotten your own history?'

'That's enough!' cried Rachel.

But neither antagonist was ready to step back from confrontation.

'What a meaningless cliché,' said Anna. '*Self-hating Jews*, who came up with that? I'll tell you what I am. I'm a Jew who knows the consequences of hatred. I've seen what happens to communities full of religious animosity when someone is reckless enough to light the fuse. You don't have to go back as far as the Holocaust for examples.'

'You don't understand, Anna,' said Leah, raising her voice. 'The Holocaust is the only example we need. It's why we can never compromise on the safety of our people.'

Anna put both hands on the table and stared wide-eyed at Leah. 'Do you think our family doesn't understand the Holocaust?'

'Stop this both of you!' Rachel beseeched her mother, then turned to her lover, tears in her eyes. 'This is meant to be my birthday celebration.'

'Excuse me,' said Leah, standing up. 'I have to go to the bathroom.'

•

'What's going on, Anna?' Rachel demanded in an angry whisper as soon as Leah left the room. 'You've been hostile since she arrived.'

Anna looked into Rachel's unmistakeable green eyes and suppressed the urge to shout: *Your father is alive!*

'It's nothing to do with Leah, darling,' she said. 'I know I handled that badly. I'm not myself tonight. I just got some bad news before she arrived.'

'What bad news?'

'I got a pretty confronting email from Pierre.'

'Uncle Pierre? Is everything all right?'

'I'm going to have go to The Hague to see him as soon as possible.'

'Oh, Mum. Poor Pierre . . . Is he sick?'

'No, he's fine. It's something . . . from a long time ago.'

'But what is it?'

'I can't say anything yet. I'm going to fly out tomorrow. Look, I know I've been shitty. I'm really sorry. I'll apologise to Leah, I will.'

Anna hated lying to her daughter. But she told herself it was necessary. She did make an apparently sincere apology to Leah before she brought in the cake. They lit the candles and dutifully sang the birthday song, but there was no joy in it and Rachel took Leah home soon afterwards. Anna hugged them both at the door, knowing that she had failed Rachel. She promised herself she would try again as soon as possible, but the truth was that she could not get them out of the apartment quickly enough.

The moment they had gone, she rang Pierre and lied to him as well. She told him she couldn't be sure if the man in the photographs was Marin Katich. There was, she agreed, a genuine resemblance but, as Pierre would know better than anyone, Marin had been killed in Bosnia thirteen years ago.

'We never saw his body, Anna,' said Pierre. 'And this man Maric could be his twin, don't you think?'

This man, Ma-wich. That's how Pierre said it, for he had never overcome his mild rhotacism. It was now integral to his persona—a slight glitch, thought Anna, like a crooked tooth that only made him more endearing.

'I'm not saying it doesn't look like him,' she said. 'And this man is so beaten up that it's hard to tell. But there's enough there for me to get on a plane. I'm coming to see you. I'll leave tomorrow if I can get a flight. Have you got time to see me?'

'Yes, I'm in town for a while. I don't have anything planned. And of course I'd love to see you. But it is him. I'm damned sure of it, and there'll be hell to pay when his identity is revealed. The press in Australia will go crazy.'

'Pierre, please,' Anne implored him. 'Promise you won't tell anyone what you suspect, at least not until I get there.'

'I know you want the story to yourself.'

'That's not the only reason . . .'

'Christ, don't tell me you still hold a candle for this fellow?'

'We really don't know it's him.'

'You didn't answer my question.'

'It's completely hypothetical.'

'Right, so you say.' Pierre didn't try to mask his scepticism. 'Look, I'll keep shtum for now, but only because you're asking me to. Meantime I want to send you something to read on the plane.'

'What is it?'

'The war crimes indictment against this fellow. Maric or Katich, or whoever he is. There's just one thing . . .'

'Go on.'

'You can't let anyone else see it. It's a sealed indictment. I'd be sacked for leaking it to you.'

'You have my word, Pierre,' she said, 'and honestly, as far as I'm concerned, the fewer people who know about this the better.'

'A warning, though. It'll turn your stomach. This is an evil bastard and, if it turns out to be Marin Katich, you won't be able to mount any defence for him. Do you understand?'

'Of course. Can you also send me the mail address for inmates in the war crimes prison?'

'I'll do that, but Anna . . .'

'But what?'

'I just want to say that I was right about him all along.'

•

Anna retreated to her study to rummage through the boxes she kept locked in her filing cabinet. She hid them away because they held her biggest secret, or rather clues to the secret she had always kept from her daughter. The boxes contained her ASIO file—at least those parts of it that the spies had been forced to release under the Archives Act.

Anna knew for a fact there were big holes in the file. There was nothing in it at all, for example, about her knowledge of the attempted assassination of the visiting prime minister of Yugoslavia, Dzemal Bijedic, in March 1973. The Official Secrets Act had been invoked to stop her publishing what she knew about it; her editors had been intimidated and she'd had to shelve one of the most extraordinary stories of her career, a story bound up in her own life. The facts had been buried so deep they would never see the light of day.

After more than thirty years, all this might have remained buried deep in Anna's memory but for one thing: the man tasked with assassinating Bijedic had been her ex-lover Marin Katich, who had walked out on her three years before these events. Just disappeared without a word. At the height of a nationwide manhunt for him, Marin had come secretly to her hotel room in Canberra in the middle of the night. He was about to commit an audacious public act that would put him beyond reach forever, but he had risked exposure to finally explain to her the mystery of his long disappearance.

When Marin's confession was ultimately interrupted by the ASIO spy Moriarty, he fled her hotel room, barely evading capture by armed police. He had then disappeared from Anna's life for a second time, without knowing that a child had been conceived that night.

Anna looked at the photo of baby Rachel on the desk in front of her. It had been taken on the day Rachel was born, when Anna was attempting to breastfeed the tiny swaddled being for the first time. At the memory, her eyes glistened with tears.

Her father had taken the photo. She remembered that Frank was completely unabashed; he would have regarded embarrassment as a bourgeois conceit. He never asked her who the father was; she told him only that the man had come and gone from her life, and she saw no reason at all to acknowledge him. Anna insisted to her parents that there was no reason why she would need a man to help her bring up Rachel, but she would be forever grateful for their help.

In the last year of her mother's life, Anna decided to reveal the truth to Eva and it proved to be a terrible mistake. It happened in the lead-up to Rachel's eighteenth birthday. Anna had become more and more anxious about whether she owed it to Rachel to tell her who her father was. She felt that her duplicity threatened to cause a rift, and that the longer she held back, the harder it would become. Rachel's coming of age was an obvious opportunity.

Eventually, Anna chose to set aside her fears about her own mother's failing health and seek her counsel. She could not avoid explaining that Marin Katich was the son of a man who had played a brutal role in the holocaust in Bosnia. After hearing the story, Eva closed her eyes and was silent for a long time before she responded.

'Rachel must never know this,' she said. 'That pain you must bear yourself, Anna. It would destroy her idea of herself. I suppose I should be grateful that you trust me enough to tell me this, but I'm old and unwell and, to be honest, it saddens me that I must now carry this burden with you. I can only manage it if you promise you'll never tell her.'

Anna had kept that promise, but as the years passed she regretted it more and more. Now the revelation in Pierre's email, that Marin Katich had come back from the dead, threatened her relationship with Rachel again.

•

Anna's ASIO file, much of it spread out now on her desk, was only part of an extensive surveillance operation that had expanded from her communist parents to include their children and close acquaintances. And despite the obvious holes in her secret file, there was much more in it than she could have imagined, especially when the spies became obsessed with her role in the anti-war movement and her activism as a leftist university agitator. There were interviews with informants, agency assessments, surveillance reports, transcripts of phone taps and, of course, photographs taken by the patient grey men who always seemed to be waiting for her to come in and out of meetings, or following her during marches against the war, or even attending events that had little or nothing to do with politics. Overall, they had done a marvellous job of documenting her university life.

Many now-forgotten details were in these documents and they revived memories of people she used to know but who had faded into the shadows of the past. There were banal transcripts of tapped phone conversations with early boyfriends, young men from within the movement who had come and gone quickly from her life. There was feverish speculation about her relationship with her Trotskyite flatmate, Pierre Villiers, as if they might be establishing the Glebe branch of the Weather Underground. Some of those who got special mention were old comrades. And some of them, it was clear, had been ASIO informants.

Then there was Marin Katich.

ASIO had taken an intense interest in her relationship with Marin from when she first started to see him in 1970. She knew this from the stuttering spy, Don Moriarty, who walked alone in the wilderness of mirrors, and had insinuated himself into her life a few years later. He had a mysterious connection to the Katich family that she had never got to the bottom of.

Moriarty once told her that whimsical, if not entirely literate, analysts within the Organisation had characterised her relationship with Marin as something Shakespearean: 'Your f-father, his father—our enemy and our f-friend. All of a sudden there's a Romeo and J-Juliet plotline going on with their children. That certainly p-piqued their interest, I can tell you.'

That interest had been largely erased from her ASIO file—on national security grounds, she could only presume. There were no transcripts of phone conversations with him, although there must have been many. There were no informant notes on the relationship and no analysis. There was nothing to indicate that the spies had gone to Marin's father, Ivo, to tell him of his son's romantic attachment to the Jewish daughter of a leading communist, although she was certain they had done precisely that.

No one reading her cleansed file would have known anything about her relationship with Marin Katich were it not for one strange anomaly where the Organisation's censors seemed to have slipped up. They had left in the file four crucial photographs. The images were part of a sequence of photos taken in late 1970 by one of those anonymous grey men hidden away in a high window or on a rooftop with a telephoto lens.

Two people in motion were the photographer's subject. In the first image, Anna is running towards a man, whose back is to the camera; she is calling out to him. In the second, he has stopped and turned—a close-up. It is Marin Katich. In the third, Anna has moved in close and is pulling him towards her. In the last image, her head is buried in his chest; he is looking into the distance over her shoulder, and on his face—this she chooses to believe—there is an expression of unbearable anguish.

Looking at this image again, Anna now marvelled at its very existence. That little grey man, high in his eyrie, must have felt like a god looking down on the lives of mortals. Marin had just told her, there on the street, without explanation, that it was over; he could no longer see her. And then he had disappeared from her life for the first time.

Anna took the photograph, flipped it over, and on the back of it wrote the briefest of messages:

I'm coming to see you,
Anna

5

SCHEVENINGEN, THE HAGUE

13 DECEMBER 2005

PROMPTLY AT NINE o'clock, Zwolsman collected Marin from his cell to join the group from E1 waiting to be escorted to the yard or to the recreational facilities. His floormates were loitering in the wide corridor adjacent to the locked stairwell and he regarded them sourly. They were mostly Serbs or their allies. These were self-absorbed, middle-aged men who had held command positions of one form or another. They were regional powerbrokers, party bosses, army and police generals—men for whom imprisonment had barely dented their impenetrable egos. His breakfast companions, Borovcanin and Mejakic, were there in matching tracksuits chatting to the Gypsy, Nicolae Hasimovic. They took turns to cast withering stares in his direction.

There were two other men in the group who bore him particular malice: one a Serb, the other an Albanian. Their names were Miroslav Andric and Albion Ademi. Both were lower down the food chain on the E1 wing, being neither politicians nor commanders. They also considered themselves to be the Praetorian guard of the prison's top dog—the man they still referred to as Mr President. It was their self-appointed role as protectors that incited their resentment of Marin.

It had been the Serb Miroslav Andric singing in the shower that morning. The man was a crudely constructed giant, with a low brow and a curiously flattened face. He was on trial for his role in the Ovcara Farm massacre. The mere sight of him caused Marin's fists to bunch.

Albion Ademi, the Albanian, was a beast of a different order. He was a Belgrade-trained secret policeman who had worked assiduously against his own people in Kosovo. When Milosevic ordered that region to be ethnically cleansed of terrorists, by which he meant Muslims, Ademi sided with his Serbian masters. The Kosovars would have hung him as a traitor after the war, but NATO troops got to him first and sent him to The Hague, indicted for the torture and murder of Albanian Kosovar civilians. Ademi reminded Marin of someone he'd known as a young man, a vicious little assassin called Horvat. They had the same furtive, treacherous qualities. You would never want to turn your back on either of them.

A grey-bearded Bosnian nodded to Marin. General Adem Halilovic was standing apart from the others, brooding alone as he often did, a silent sentinel hunched into his long dark coat. Marin walked over to him.

'I see you have angered our Serbian friends,' Halilovic said quietly. 'One senses a fresh disturbance.'

'It was just a little dispute over burnt coffee.'

'They have it in for you, Tomo. I would be very careful if I were you.'

'Don't worry about me.'

Halilovic raised a quizzical eyebrow and by rearranging the features in his crumpled face, he produced a gesture both comical and sad. 'It's nothing to do with coffee,' he said. 'They are burning with indignation that you have privileged access to The Boss; that he favours you, a Croat. Even I am surprised by this, but they . . . they are incensed.'

'I've played a few chess games with the old devil. What's the problem?'

'I have warned you. That's my duty before God.'

'Thank you.'

'He's back, you know, the old devil.' Halilovic nodded to the end of the corridor. 'They let him out of hospital.'

Marin followed the Bosnian's gaze and saw there was a guard waiting at the doorway of Milosevic's main cell. The former dictator occupied two of them. One cell he lived in, while the neighbouring one had been set up as an office in which he prepared his own defence in the biggest war crimes trial since Nuremberg. The guard stepped back and Slobodan Milosevic himself came bustling out, like an actor who had delayed his entrance to build up anticipation in the crowd.

Milosevic was bundled up, like Halilovic, in a long coat, but the former president's was far more theatrical, with a luxuriant mink collar that framed his bloodless face, like a severed head on display. Some of the Serbs called out greetings to him. *Dobro jutro, dobro jutro, Slobbo.*

The old politician gave a wan smile and a restrained regal wave, nodding here and there and raising his hand to quieten the more enthusiastic. Marin was surprised as usual that this sickly creature could still project an aura of command. There was no denying that he was the prison's apex predator and that his was the most impenetrable ego of them all. Even the flickering light of his power remained irresistible to some.

Zjelko Mejakic fluttered over.

'*Dobro jutro, Gospodin President.*'

Mr President! Marin winced at the sycophancy.

Milosevic replied politely: '*Hvala lepo, Zjelko.*'

Then he did something odd—he silenced Mejakic with an abrupt gesture. The disgruntled general was left frozen mid-sentence as his former commander-in-chief gazed around to see who else was there. He spotted Marin and graced him with a perfunctory nod. Milosevic had been away in the hospital wing undergoing medical tests for nearly a week, putting his never-ending trial on hold as effectively as he had just halted General Mejakic. Marin had read that the sceptical prosecutors believed their star defendant was feigning illness to frustrate them, but looking at him now he wasn't inclined to agree.

In the yellowish light of the hallway, the Serb's face seemed as bruised and puffy as old dough. Milosevic's thinning mane of white hair had been swept back in a widow's peak from his exceptionally high forehead, as bulbous as the large end of a light globe. The face beneath it had a sickly pallor, coloured only by purplish blood vessels on his cheeks and the red rims of his eyes.

When Zwolsman reappeared with a huge bunch of keys, the group started shuffling forward and Marin found himself alongside Milosevic.

'These little holidays aren't doing you much good.' Marin spoke to him in English. 'You're starting to look like Grandpa Munster.'

Milosevic's brow creased. 'What?'

'You won't have heard of him. An old TV vampire.'

Milosevic rallied quickly. His head tilted to the familiar pugnacious angle it so often assumed in the witness box; arrogance returned to the set of his jaw.

'You look like shit yourself, Tomo,' he said softly. 'You've lost weight. Your stomach is like a five-dinar bill.'

'I'm in training,' said Marin. 'For when you set your thugs onto me.'

'Don't be a donkey,' Milosevic barked, a flush of colour returning to his face as the harsh banter brought him back to life. 'My son, Marko, he's touchy like you. Nervous boys like that always lose weight when things go wrong. I tell Marko that to be skinny is a violence against nature. Even a chicken has a little meat behind its ear.'

'This must be hard for him, then.'

'It is, for all my family,' said Milosevic. A tear glistened in the corner of his eye and he blinked it away. 'It's hard for sons trying to be like father.'

Milosevic turned his bloodshot eyes away and they waited in silence while Zwolsman searched for the right key. Marin thought again of Ivo. He noticed that Mejakic was scowling at him. Then Zwolsman finally got the steel door open and they started shuffling forward.

At the top of the stairs, Milosevic held back.

'What's this about you threatening Zjelko and Ljubo?' he asked. 'A little bird told me what happens this morning.'

Another guard urged them to keep moving and they started slowly down the stairs.

'That little bird is shitting on your head,' said Marin.

Milosevic stared hard at him. 'Did you threaten to poison them?'

Marin laughed. 'Well, I did ask the brave general if he would dare drink a coffee I gave him without a food taster.'

'You were twisting his ear?'

'I was.'

'Listen, this is no joke. If they go crying to McFadden, he will push you to another floor. And you're the only decent chess player on E1.'

The group reached the bottom of the stairs and the guards took them to their different activities—some to the gym, some to indoor tennis, others to the open courtyard. Marin, heading outdoors, was still alongside Milosevic.

As they entered the courtyard, The Boss turned to him again.

'I'll smooth it over this time,' he said. 'If you let anything like that happen again, I'll leave you to their—what is phrase?—tender mercy. So . . . tomorrow at three? Is your turn to play black.'

'I'll check my diary.'

Milosevic gave him a blank look and turned away, sinking deeper into the big coat as he walked briskly to the part of the courtyard where the Serbs from the other floors had gathered. Stamping his feet in the chill, Marin watched as the former president's courtiers zeroed in like pilot fish, gripping onto the old shark, who kept moving, as sharks do, to stay alive. They bunched together around him, smoking cigarettes, swapping aggressive banter and trading insults with the football players in the yard:

'Ho, Petrovic! Missed again. You son of a whore!'

'Ah, fuck off! Crawl back in your mother's cunt!'

Marin made a solitary circuit of the courtyard, crunching frost on the untrammelled areas on the perimeter. Zwolsman was right: there was no gap in the clouds hanging over the prison in a low ceiling. Steam huffed from his mouth and the cold air was numbing. But it was a relief to taste the North Sea on it.

The football came bouncing towards him and he stepped over it, ignoring calls from the closest player. The man was about to unleash a stream of abuse, but Marin stared him down. The fellow held his tongue and scrambled to fetch the ball. There were sudden peals of hilarity from the Milosevic gang on the other side of the yard. For a moment, Marin imagined they were laughing at him but, no, they were engrossed in their own banter. Milosevic was holding court and his subordinates hung on his every word.

Watching the Milosevic gang, Marin was reminded of scenes from *The Sopranos*. Today's gathering was like the Mafia bosses and their 'made' men hanging out on the street outside Satriale's Pork Shop to avoid being overheard by FBI bugs. Even outside, they habitually spoke in coded language. Milosevic and his cronies did the same. In intercepted phone calls put into evidence at his televised trial, the then president of Yugoslavia referred to weapons as 'bags of flour', to bodies as 'loaves of bread' and so on. Marin wondered if life was imitating art, or vice versa.

Milosevic seemed to have no problem with the art/life dilemma: the old vampire kept box sets of *The Sopranos* in his cell. These DVDs were avidly passed around among Milosevic's favourites on E1, and since they had begun playing their chess games, Marin had been permitted to borrow them too. Watching them in his cell, he began to speculate about which character Milosevic most resembled. It wasn't Tony Soprano. That piggish thug, with the hair-trigger temper, deep insecurities and panic attacks was not far enough up the mob's chain of command. Besides, Milosevic would never allow his own shirtsleeves to be stained with blood.

The Serb gave killers their orders and then joined his family for a weekend at Tito's hunting lodge. For such men, the consequential spilling of blood was an intellectual abstraction; they automatically denied any responsibility or even that deaths had taken place. Marin had watched what happened when Milosevic was confronted by prosecutors in the televised courtroom with photographs of a massacre, how he had cried out: 'Where's the blood? These are fakes.'

Marin concluded that Milosevic's true *Sopranos* doppelganger was Johnny Sacramento, aka Johnny Sac. Sacramento was a venal mob boss who had climbed over piles of bodies to get to the top of the Lupertazzi crime family. Just like Milosevic, Johnny Sac was behind bars, indicted for the many murders he had ordered, and, as with Milosevic, wiretaps, stoolies and supergrasses from within his own inner circle had also threatened to keep him imprisoned. They were similar in other ways: their pinched expressions; their griping faces; their self-obsessed whining; their mawkish sentimentality about their ghastly wives and their spoilt-brat children; and the fact that both spent much of their time moping in the prison hospital, wallowing in self-pity.

As he watched Milosevic in the prison yard, Marin reflected that the nature of gangsterism was universal. As a means of social organisation, it was remarkably adaptable: it had the capacity to transform itself from a parasitic criminal enterprise into the governing principle of a nation. All you needed were the right conditions and men ruthless enough to exploit them. Therein lay the secret of Slobodan Milosevic's power, just as with Tito, Stalin, Mao, Hitler and Mussolini. They were all gangsters of greater or lesser orders of magnitude, each tyrant reliant on the brutal rules of criminal power for his irresistible rise.

Then Marin noticed, or thought he did, a ravaged old man in a dressing gown standing behind Milosevic. When the old fellow dipped behind someone's shoulders, Marin searched among the faces; but the spectre was gone.

He did another circuit of the yard to shake off his father's ghostly presence. When darker clouds unleashed an icy drizzle, he hunched his shoulders and quickened his pace. Ahead of him he noticed a diminutive figure walking slowly, shivering and cursing. Marin ignored the little man as he passed him. It was the wretched Gypsy, Hasimovic, whose rec room antics with his piano accordion frequently drove Marin back to his cell. Hasimovic had an endless repertoire of Macedonian folk tunes which he liked to play, grinning all the while like a village idiot at a wedding. Marin hated piano accordions as a matter of course but he found the man's insincere smirk, with its flashes of gold, especially offensive. The Gypsy was here for organising the mass rapes of Bosnian women.

When Marin reached the far end of the yard he saw a hooded figure walking briskly towards him, head down. Only when they were close did the head bob up. It was Milosevic's crony, Ademi. The Albanian stopped, blocking Marin's path. There was unrequited grievance in the upturned face.

'His master's voice,' said Marin. 'What the fuck do you want?'

'You trying to be funny?' Ademi lisped in English.

'You wouldn't know one way or the other.'

'Shut up and listen, Maric, if you value your health. I'm here to tell you a warning.' Marin heard the interrogator's arrogance, the torturer's confidence.

'Spit it out, then.'

'Stay away from President Milosevic,' Ademi snarled. 'Or you'll regret it.'

'Did he send you?'

'I'm not here to answer your questions.'

'Maybe you're just another mongrel running off his leash,' said Marin, unable to avoid sneering down at the man. 'I asked if your master sent you!'

There was a sudden presence behind him and Marin felt something snake under his jacket. Before he could react, the tip of a blade was pricking into his lower back. The vile scent of cheap cologne cut through the sleet. The Gypsy. He stiffened as Hasimovic leant into him. The Gypsy rested his head on Marin's shoulder; the man's arm was around his waist, like lovers in a park.

'Be still, Mr Croat,' he whispered, prodding Marin with the knife. 'One move and you could have a sudden kidney failure. Very bad. Very painful.'

Marin, face composed, stared at Ademi.

'See what I have to do to get your attention?' said the Albanian.

Marin said nothing. Flanked by the evil twins, he forced himself to remain still. He quashed his impulse for violence, controlled his breathing.

'I'm listening,' he said.

'You have no friends here, Maric,' said the Albanian. 'And no way to avoid your enemies. I could have you carved up now or any time. Show him, Nicu.'

The knife bit into Marin's back. Ademi pushed his face towards Marin's, so close he could smell the Albanian's rancid breath. He felt a line of blood run down the small of his back all the way to his buttocks.

'I hope the message is clear,' Ademi hissed. 'Stay away from the president. Your life depends on it.'

The two men detached themselves from him and walked off together. Marin didn't move. The freezing rain stung his face.

6

THE HAGUE

14 DECEMBER 2005

ANNA ROSEN EMERGED on the escalator from the underground railway platforms into the vast hall of Den Haag Centraal. Prepared for the cold, she was wearing black gloves and her narrow-waisted black coat with the high astrakhan collar. Over her shoulder was the black leather bag that contained her laptop, a hard-cover notebook, Blackberry, passport, wallet and a comprehensive guide to The Hague. In her wake, she wheeled her newest possession, a Briggs & Riley suitcase in matching black. She moved fast, an elegant ink smudge under the halogen lights.

She looked up at the large wall clock. 3.50 pm. The *sneltrein* from Amsterdam had delivered her to the capital in just over thirty minutes, but she was so tired after the interminable journey that she repeated a mantra to herself: *Lose that bag and you're a dead woman.*

At a station kiosk, she bought a tram *strippencaart*, a city map and a short espresso in a paper cup. Balancing the coffee, she carefully made her way out to the tram stop. Soon the Number 1 to Noorderstrand rolled smoothly towards her, sparks crackling on the overhead wires in the dim light. She hauled her chattels aboard, punched the journey into the *strippencaart* and sat down, keeping one hand on the luggage.

Lose that bag and you're a dead woman.

Anna felt a small surge of alertness as she sipped the espresso, a faint echo of what could have been achieved by, say, a line of powdered Benzedrine. The thought prompted a metallic taste in the back of her throat. Her mind wandered. She caught herself floating in a daydream and quickly grasped the handle of the suitcase.

Lose that bag . . .

The tram hummed across a bridge, past statues of dead kings and their palaces, past lakes and parliament buildings and court-houses and down wide streets lined with skeletal elm trees. Snug inside the warm capsule, Anna liked the look of this civilised, orderly city.

She gazed with envy at the endless stream of elegant old mansions set back from the traffic. Floating alongside the tram, cyclists kept up an easy pace through the city's prosperous old neighbourhoods. She followed the procession of place names on the route map as a woman's recorded voice announced each stop on approach, warning people to alight safely.

Kneuterdijk, Adriaan Goekooplaan, Frankenslag, Duinstraat, Keizerstraat . . .

This last leg of her journey, from the city centre to Scheveningen, should take about twenty minutes. According to her guidebook, the ancient fishing village had been transformed into a popular nineteenth-century seaside resort before being gradually absorbed into the capital's sprawling development. There on the map was Scheveningen with its boat harbours and long beach, and on its eastern edge, clearly marked out, across the road from sand dunes and horseriding trails, was the prison. Anna had imagined the place isolated like a leper colony in a remote coastal wilderness, but there it was—nestled in the suburbs.

She thought of him alone in his cell, the resurrected Mr Katich. Or, rather, Mr Maric. How long had he had that name? What had he become? Was he coarsened with age, hardened by bitterness and violence? Would she find him repulsive, or would there be some trace left of the boy she had known?

No, she was drifting again. Marin Katich had not been a boy back when she knew him. That would imply a lightness of spirit, an unformed soul, and he was never that. His self-possession was one of the things that had drawn her to him. Her previous lovers had been spoilt children by comparison, known quantities, whereas he had come to her out of the shadows.

Anna's eyes flicked open. She castigated herself; surely she must be delirious to entertain such thoughts. She reconsidered the wisdom of sending that thirty-five-year-old photograph to him, worried that he might take it as some kind of romantic gesture. She shook her head. No, he couldn't possibly think that. Her own memories of him were of loss, betrayal, disbelief and anger. This man had not defined, and would not define, her life. Except in the one, crucial thing that bound them together, whether she liked it or not—their daughter, Rachel. She was Anna's overriding reason for coming here.

On the long journey, mostly cramped and sleepless in pressurised cabins, Anna had continued to agonise over what to tell Rachel. The sudden death of Marin Katich in Bosnia in 1992 had made it easier to keep the promise she made to her mother to never reveal the truth. But his incomprehensible resurrection changed everything.

Anna had considered going straight to Rachel, but she knew the edifice of lies she had built was insurmountable. Examining her own motives, she realised that keeping her promise to Eva had never been entirely selfless—it had just taken the decision out of her hands. It had let her off the hook. Now she was forced to reconsider all the arguments she had made to herself and she found she was focused on one question: What possible good could come from burdening Rachel with the knowledge that her father was a murderer?

•

On the plane, Anna had read the sealed war crimes indictment that Pierre had sent her. As if designed to quash any doubts she might have, the formal juridicial nature of the document seemed to add weight to the allegations:

THE INTERNATIONAL CRIMINAL TRIBUNAL FOR
THE FORMER YUGOSLAVIA

CASE NO: IT-98-34-PT

THE PROSECUTOR v. Tomislav Maric.

AMENDED INDICTMENT
The Prosecutor of the International Criminal Tribunal for the former Yugoslavia, pursuant to her authority under Article 18 of the Statute of the International Criminal Tribunal for the former Yugoslavia (hereinafter the Statute of the Tribunal), charges:

Tomislav Maric a/k/a Illija Lovric a/k/a Cvrčak (Cicada)

with *CRIMES AGAINST HUMANITY, GRAVE BREACHES OF THE GENEVA CONVENTIONS and VIOLATIONS OF THE LAWS OR CUSTOMS OF WAR.*

Anna was intrigued when she saw the alias Illija Lovric. She recalled that a man by the same name had been one of the twenty Australian-trained insurgents who infiltrated Bosnia in 1972 to try to foment a rebellion against Tito's communist regime. Young Marin Katich had been the last recruited, the twentieth man, and the only survivor of that doomed mission planned by his father. She wondered now if he had assumed Lovric's identity after the man was killed; she certainly knew well enough the *nom de guerre* Cvrčak. Indeed, she had gone to Bosnia in 1992 to track down General Cvrčak, on the strong suspicion that his true identity was Marin Katich.

There were eight counts in the indictment, but the detail contained in the first one was especially chilling:

Between about June 1992 and at least August 1992, Tomislav Maric AKA Illija Lovric AKA General Cvrčak helped plan, instigate, order or aided and abetted the planning, preparation or execution of a crime against humanity, through the widespread or systematic persecutions of Bosnian Serb civilians on political, racial, ethnic or religious grounds, throughout the territory claimed to belong to the HZ H-B and HR H-B by the following means, including, as applicable, the acts and conduct described in Counts 2 through 22 below:

(a) *unlawfully confining, detaining, forcibly transferring and deporting Bosnian Serb civilians;*

(b) *subjecting Bosnian Serbs to torture and inhumane acts, inhuman and cruel treatment, murdering and wilfully killing them, wilfully raping them, wilfully causing them great suffering;*

(c) *destroying and wantonly devastating Bosnian Serb dwellings and buildings; and*

(d) *plundering public and private property of Bosnian Serbs.*

By these acts and omissions, Tomislav Maric committed:

COUNT 1: persecutions on political, racial and religious grounds,
a CRIME AGAINST HUMANITY, as recognised by Articles
5(h), 7(1) and 7(3) of the Statute of the Tribunal.

Reading this for the first time on the plane, Anna had puzzled over the vague dates for these terrible offences: *Between about June 1992 and at least August 1992.* That would mean at least some of this had been happening when she was in Bosnia with Pierre. She searched back through her notes from that time and found that they had discovered that General Cvrčak had been killed on 15 June, shot dead in an ambush. Of course now she believed that he hadn't been killed at all, but she still couldn't understand why he and his men had constructed such an elaborate charade, a deception designed to fool two journalists who, in the prevailing wartime conditions, could simply have been refused permission to enter the area. The more she thought about it, the more implausible it seemed, but there was no doubt at all that Marin Katich was still alive at the time of these crimes. With a sense of dread, Anna read on through the rest of the eight counts in the indictment; all were charges stemming from the first overarching count:

COUNT 2: torture, a CRIME AGAINST HUMANITY, under
Articles 5(f), 7(1) and 7(3) of the Statute of the Tribunal.

COUNT 3: torture, a GRAVE BREACH OF THE GENEVA
CONVENTIONS OF 1949, under Statute Article 2(b), and
7(1) and 7(3) of the Statute of the Tribunal.

COUNT 4: cruel treatment, a VIOLATION OF THE LAWS OR
CUSTOMS OF WAR, under Statute Article 3 as recognised
by Article 3(1)(a) of the Geneva Conventions, and Articles
7(1) and 7(3) of the Statute of the Tribunal.

COUNT 5: *wilfully causing great suffering or serious injury to body or health, a GRAVE BREACH OF THE GENEVA CONVENTIONS OF 1949, under Articles 2(c), 7(1) and 7(3) of the Statute of the Tribunal.*

COUNTS 6 to 8

OUTRAGES ON PERSONAL DIGNITY INCLUDING RAPE AND UNLAWFUL CONFINEMENT.

Pierre had been right. The contents of the document left her sickened to her core. There was a small but diminishing part of her that clung to the hope that none of it was true, but she knew too much about the sins of his father, Ivo. If Marin really had come from the shadows, then deep in his darkest recesses lurked that man's presence, a man beyond redemption, a man who had sought to shape his son in his own image.

She remembered her confrontation with Ivo Katich on the Harbour Bridge, when he had revealed himself as the monster he truly was. Anna knew better than anyone that Ivo Katich was guilty of the war crimes he had been charged with. She had made it her business to uncover the evidence that had been cleansed from his record before he came to Australia.

In 1941, as a young officer in the Croatian Ustasha, Ivo Katich had collaborated with the Gestapo as they rounded up the Jews of Sarajevo and sent them to their deaths; tens of thousands of them had been exterminated. For that murderous effort, the elder Katich had been rewarded by the high command of the Ustasha in Zagreb. He was appointed as a judge on Bosnia's Mobile Court Martial—not that it offered any form of justice. The court was nothing more than a sanctioned death squad moving from town to town, murdering political opponents. As a further reward for his loyalty, Ivo Katich would later be promoted to the elite personal guard of the Croatian Führer, the Poglavnik Ante Pavelic, a man whose authority to command the puppet state flowed directly from Adolf Hitler.

When the Nazis' power disintegrated in 1944, the Pavelic regime collapsed along with it. By then, Ivo Katich was so steeped in blood that it should have drowned him, but he was able to escape from the wreckage of Croatia by claiming to be a refugee from Tito's communists. After the war, while resident in an Austrian Displaced Persons camp, Katich had been indicted for his many crimes, but was rescued by Western intelligence agents who recruited him and other Nazis with the potential to become valuable assets in the Cold War. The Western spies made many deals with many devils. In the case of Ivo Katich, his recruiters cleansed the war crimes from his record. They allowed him to escape justice and, in due course, allowed him to migrate to Australia.

And now Anna could barely comprehend the irony that, a generation later, his son Marin would be the one to face a war crimes trial. Anna had been a rationalist all her life, but it was hard to shake the feeling that fate was playing a role in Marin Katich's life, and perhaps her own. Before she left Sydney, she had pulled from her bookshelves Jean Anouilh's retelling of the Antigone myth. During the endless night on the plane, she had thumbed through the play until she found the passage she had been trying to remember: *'The spring is wound up tight. It will uncoil of itself. That is what is so convenient in tragedy. The least little turn of the wrist will do the job. Anything will set it going . . .'*

•

Above the hum of the tram, a Tibetan temple gong rang from Anna's shoulder bag. An ancient Dutchman sitting opposite gave her a hard stare as she fished out her Blackberry. She found a text from *PierreMob*: *Welkom bij Den Haag. I'm in the neighbourhood. Meet you at the Kurhaus Bar in 45? P x*

Relief crowded out both embarrassment and fatigue, and she texted back: *Yes. Wonderful. See you there soon, Anna.*

The machine was in perfect order, she thought, the spring uncoiling of itself. No need to lift a finger. Then came again the harsh recorded voice, cutting through the over-heated air in the stuffy cabin.

Scheveningseslag halte.

Anna peered out the windows, expecting a view of the North Sea. The map showed she should be on a wide boulevard running along the coast, but the sea was hidden behind a barricade of cheap hotels and holiday apartments. The next stop, Kurhaus, was hers and she struggled from the tram, dragging her luggage into a cold drizzle. She put her head down and raced for shelter, stopping halfway to look up at the massive edifice of the Kurhaus Hotel, looming over her like a baroque cathedral. Fine rain wet her face and she wiped it out of her eyes.

The building glowed surreally in the dusk, its central dome and cupolas already lit by floodlights. She recognised it from old photographs, but the palatial nineteenth-century hotel had now been hemmed in by shoddy modern construction and encroached upon by ugliness—a grand dame jostled by street thugs.

In the sheltered forecourt was a brightly lit ice rink, a stubborn remnant of the old world, and she paused to watch skaters wheeling around the frozen space, graceful gliding couples and teenage racers bent at the waist, beginners left skittering in their wake, clutching at the outer railing. She recalled her mother's stories of skating on frozen ponds as a girl and of a fairytale world of snow-drifts and horse-drawn sleighs and winter markets. Eva had always refused to let the rise of the Nazis and the horrors she survived in Ravensbrück redefine her childhood memories. She had never forgotten how her world was before it ended.

Anna had none of those nice memories, and her own thoughts always leapt, as they did now, to the dark winters when bodies were stacked like firewood in the bloody snow while Jews were forced to dig their own burial pits in the frozen earth.

7

SCHEVENINGEN PRISON, THE HAGUE

14 DECEMBER 2005, AFTERNOON

SLOBODAN MILOSEVIC was peering intently at a bundle of papers when Marin came to his cell door. Surrounding the former president were piles of court documents in ring-bound folders, amounting to thousands or even tens of thousands of pages. So much paperwork, so many transcripts and witness statements that the Irish prison commandant McFadden had been forced to grant Milosevic access to this extra cell for use as an office.

Marin coughed, more a clearing of the throat, and Milosevic looked over the top of his reading glasses. It was an actor's gesture and, when he saw who had interrupted him, he removed the spectacles with a quick movement, grasping the frame between his thumb and forefinger and holding them defensively.

'Maric,' he said. '*Dosao si da me ubijes?*' Have you come to kill me?

Despite the attempted mirth, the older man's voice was strained, weaker than the previous morning. Marin entered the cell and took the only other seat.

'Shall we speak English?' he asked.

Milosevic put down his spectacles and took a sip from the cut-crystal whisky glass beside him.

'That is whole point,' he said.

'That's *the* whole point.'

'Maric, I asked big question. But now is not spontaneous.'

'I can let you make grammatical errors and keep it spontaneous, but that would defeat the purpose.'

'*Defeat the purpose*? You would have me speak like Shakespeare?'

'*Reason not the need*, Slobodan.'

'What?'

'*Reason not the need. Our basest beggars are in the poorest things superfluous* . . . King Lear.'

'You think I am mad old king?'

'The story goes like this. Lear gave up all his power and now his own daughters are questioning what he needs to live. What comforts? How many bodyguards? They're greedy, these daughters. He's angry and he tells them: *Reason not the need*. So here you are, an old man who's lost his power. Alone. Unprotected. And you ask: *Have I come to kill you?* If he were still alive, Shakespeare might make a play about you.'

'And what character would you be, Maric?'

'The fool, of course.'

Milosevic nodded, a glimmer of infernal light returning to his bloodshot eyes.

'Make me laugh, then.'

'The real job of the fool is to make you think. So, you asked: *Have I come to kill you?* My *spontaneous* answer is: *Why would I take the trouble to alert you first?*'

'You might,' said Milosevic. 'If you want look in my face when you did it.'

'No, *Gospodin President*, I'd just whack you over the head and get it over with.'

The smile lingered on Milosevic's lips, but there was no humour left in his eyes. He jabbed his forefinger on the court documents.

'If you're going to do it, make it quick. This endless fucking trial is just killing me slowly.'

Marin shifted in the chair, feeling pressure on the bandaged knife wound on his back. When he had treated it in the bathroom, twisting to see in the mirror the damage the Gypsy had done, he saw that the wound was a U shape. He remembered Mejakic hissing at him—*Ustashi*. He looked at Milosevic over the table, feeling contempt for the man's self-pity and wondering if, despite his promise to 'smooth' things over, he had gone ahead and authorised the attack.

He asked himself, not for the first time, why he was sitting across from this man. The simple answer was that McFadden had sought him out and asked him to help Milosevic with his English. Marin had resisted at first, for it seemed an absurd proposition, but the commandant was persuasive. McFadden seemed to have the crazy idea of recreating the old Yugoslavia within the little world that he controlled, of stitching the multi-ethnic community back together, forcing enemies to live cheek by jowl in their confinement and compelling them to find ways to get along. The Irishman encouraged them to eat together, to cook meals for each other, to share communal spaces and activities. Marin deduced that this was an experiment in human nature, motivated perhaps by the fratricidal conflict in McFadden's own homeland.

Of course Marin had not been compelled to go along with this. He could have refused to play the game and kept a scowling distance from Milosevic. But he could not deny his own curiosity. Perverse curiosity, perhaps, but a chance to glimpse the power behind the curtain. He found that he wanted to look into the eyes of the man who, like some vengeful potentate from a bygone age, had ordered the sacking of Vukovar and the razing of the city to terrify and subdue his enemy.

Marin understood why The Boss's prison cronies distrusted his motives. On several occasions, while playing chess with Milosevic, the impulse to reach out and strangle the monster had welled up in him, like bile rising suddenly in his throat. Each time Marin had suppressed the urge, and it occurred to him that, having grown up with a monster, perhaps Ivo's madness had immunised him like a pathogen that didn't destroy but left you resistant.

'All this talk about me killing you,' he said now, probing the Serb. 'Sounds like you've been listening to that poisonous little shit Ademi. He's warned me to stay away from you.'

'I did not tell him to do that,' said Milosevic, thrusting out his chin. 'You know, this Albanian is born conspirator.'

'*A* born conspirator.'

'Fucking hell! A . . . A . . . A . . . He has many theories. He says some big shot would pay you a lot of money to kill me. Culprit number one: Your fucking president.'

'He's not *my* president.'

'Your people elected Mesic, didn't they? Who would vote for such an ordinary swine? Three years ago, he comes here to testify against me. Milosevic alone wanted war, he says. Milosevic was in control of everything. Every big decision, every small decision. There's a massacre in Prijedor, must be Milosevic. Someone's throat is slit in Kosovo, it's fault of Milosevic. Mesic tried to bury me in courtroom then, but now he's panic. Maybe Milosevic will win his trial. Better send an assassin.'

'Ademi's telling you this?'

'Not only him, Mira too. She says my enemies will try to kill me in here.'

Mira! Marin was instantly alert. This was a danger of a different order. Mira Markovic was the lifelong companion of Slobodan Milosevic: his childhood sweetheart, then his wife and political partner. She had been a sociology professor in Belgrade, a virulent left-wing theorist, and a key figure in Tito's communist aristocracy, more than enough reasons for Marin to hate her. He knew that in Belgrade she had powerful enemies. They called her the Red Witch. Many close to the centre of power believed she was the real engine of her husband's ambition, his Lady Macbeth. By the force of her will, she had taken this dull bureaucrat, this lawyer and economist, a mid-level party apparatchik, all the way to the presidency. She had wheedled and cajoled him into taking up the killing knife. She stiffened his spine, screwed his courage to the sticking place.

Now she had her own troubles. The new Serbian government wanted to put her on trial for corruption and abuse of power. To avoid that prospect, the Red Witch had fled to Moscow two years ago and she had been stuck there ever since in self-imposed exile. Mira knew full well that behind the corruption charges against her were hidden indictments for murder. Belgrade's new generation of political leaders and prosecutors wanted to put her on trial for ordering the assassinations of her husband's enemies.

During these years in exile, Mira had not been able to travel to The Hague to see her husband for fear of being arrested and deported back to Serbia. Milosevic was bereft at the long separation and spoke to her regularly by phone. Marin could not imagine the lovelorn Slobodan wasting time telling her all about his Croatian chess opponent, but he knew that one word from the Red Witch and he could end up as another of her victims.

'How is she going?' asked Marin.

'Don't talk to me of Mira.'

'Has something happened?'

'We spoke today. Nothing but tears. She still cannot leave Moscow.'

'Two years since you saw her? That's a long time.'

'Yes,' said the older man before lapsing into silence.

Under the fluorescents, Milosevic looked like a dying animal. There was a framed photo of Mira on his desk, a decades-old image of a plump, smooth-faced young woman with a coquettish smile. Her ink-black hair was cut in a straight fringe and there was a purple flower tucked behind her left ear. Marin knew very well that, like her husband, the present-day Mira was a worn and ravaged creature. She had ended up with a face that reflected her character, but Marin imagined that her Slobodan still saw her as the girl in the photograph.

'You know what I tell to the Albanian?' Milosevic said eventually. 'I tell him: Don't worry about Maric. The real assassins are in courtroom. This prosecutor, Mr Geoffrey-not-so-fucking-Nice, he is the worst of them, but the judges, too, they try to kill me. Mr Fucking Robinson, you know him? The black man . . . Robinson is from Jamaica! Can you believe? Is that really where to find the best judges? Does it not seem a little grotesque? Sugar cane, rum and reggae, God save me, that's all that comes from that pathetic little colony. They send to judge me a man descend from plantation slaves . . .'

'Descend*ed* . . . descend*ed* from . . .'

'Descend*ed from* slaves owned by a past generation of Englishmen, perhaps the ancestors of Geoffrey Fucking Nice. Justice can be poetic, no? Black and white. Now Mr Nice and Mr Robinson both work for UN, their salaries are paid by new masters in Washington. These lawyers and judges, they are nothing but America's assassins sent kill me day by day, question by question, a Chinese water torture to death.'

'For fuck's sake,' said Marin, annoyed by the constant whining. 'Why don't you just admit you gave the orders in Bosnia and Kosovo? It's obvious Yugoslavia had a chain of command and you were at the top of it. They don't call you Gospodin President for nothing.'

Milosevic's mouth twisted into an ugly smile.

'According to Mr Fucking Nice, I was head of every Serb citizen. I suppose if someone ran over a pedestrian in Pristina that was my fault too?'

'*The* head of every Serb citizen. *The*. You always forget the definite article. Anyway, I came here to play chess. That's all.'

'That's not all, Maric! You take sides with those who persecute me and expect me to remain silent? These same Americans, and English too, they talk of a New World Order. Tell me: How do you make a New Order by bombing innocent Serbian people, by sending missiles onto trains and refugee convoys and into TV stations? Who are murderers here? Tell me why are *they* not on trial? They find not one piece of paper with my name on it. No orders to kill, nothing. Now their false tribunal finds me responsible for everything they have done themselves. All Serbs know that President Milosevic and the will of the Serbian people are inseparable. They are one and the same. Milosevic *is* the expression of their will.'

'Here's some advice for nothing,' said Marin. 'You should stick to the first person. Every crackpot dictator in history refers to himself in the third person. That's when people stop listening. And as for your *triumph of the will* . . . Wasn't it Leni Riefenstahl who came up with that?'

'Oh, I see, now you compare me to Hitler? You? A fucking Croat! Are you so ignorant of your own history? It was Ustasha who embraced Hitler. Your fucking Poglavnik did that. Fascist pig Ante Pavelic . . . *the* fascist pig . . . Pavelic crawled to Berlin like a craven dog to get his Fuhrer's blessing. He genuflects to Hitler, his Ustashi kill for Hitler, for Hitler they murder all the Jews, and to please themselves they make a great slaughter of Serbs. And all the time the partisans—*my* people—fight *against* Hitler. Fifty German divisions cannot defeat them. That is the will of Serbian people!'

'Why do you want to play chess with me,' asked Marin, 'when you think of me as your worst enemy?'

Milosevic ran two hands through his hair and took another slug of whisky before answering.

'I could ask you same thing,' he said. 'To tell you truth, I have to find some way not to think of trial all the time. I have to relax my mind. My blood pressure is boiling. I do not trust these Dutch doctors, but even these ones tell me I need more time to rest and recover. But my countrymen in here do not play, not like you, and when I do spend time with them they speak only of my trial. And when I listen to their anger my blood boils even more. You, Maric, you are different. You don't talk about trial. Perhaps you just don't care? Yes, you are my enemy. Yes, you are insolent and sometimes you are intolerable. All true, but, strange to say, you mostly do not make my blood boil.'

•

Marin was enthralled by one aspect of this most unusual prison: the live video link to Courtroom One, which all prisoners could access in their cells. It reminded him of watching the action on the centre court at Wimbledon, but instead of tennis matches you got telecasts of the trials of top-seeded war criminals. Before he even met Milosevic, Marin had seen a good deal of his courtroom antics. He watched, knowing that he too was destined to play at some point, albeit on an outer court. Of course, he might have to wait two years or more, that being the average time it took to put a defendant on trial.

Slobodan Milosevic was the number-one seed and the tribunal's biggest drawcard so his trial had begun within months of his incarceration. But after this rapid start, it had dragged on for years and now seemed to be grinding into the final games of the fifth set without a clear winner. Not long ago, Marin had watched in his cell a cable TV documentary marking the third anniversary of the Milosevic trial. It was his first chance to see the opening games of the contest.

On day one the large courtroom had been crowded with judges, lawyers and court officials. A theatrical blue curtain hung behind the bench, framing the three justices in their black gowns, red silk vests and pleated white bands. Marin thought they looked like overdressed men waiting for a meal with big white napkins tucked into their collars.

A grey-faced official had come on stage to play the chorus.

'Good morning, your honours,' he intoned. 'Case number I-T 0-2-54, the prosecutor versus Slobodan Milosevic . . .'

Then on he went, and on and on.

Milosevic sat opposite the bench, flanked by two policemen, one black, one white, each turned in towards the accused like a set of racially balanced bookends. This younger Milosevic was much healthier-looking than the raddled creature Marin knew. He was soberly attired in a black suit, white shirt and striped tie. His fierce brown eyes were fixed on the judges. The effort to bend the judges to his will seemed to deepen the furrows in his high forehead and exaggerate the twin grooves that ran from his nose to the sides of his disaffected, downturned mouth. Then his right eyebrow lifted, his chin jutted forwards and his body shifted around in the revolving chair as he prepared to say his first words to the court.

'I consider this tribunal false tribunal,' he announced with a sneer. 'So I have no need to appoint counsel to an illegal organ.'

In the centre of the bench, the presiding judge, Richard May, a diffident Englishman, peered at the accused over his heavy reading glasses, his inborn dignity already unsettled by the head-phones clamped over his ears.

'Do you want to have the indictment read out on your behalf?' he inquired mildly.

'That's your problem,' Milosevic snarled.

May's gentility gave no hint of the ordeal to come, but Marin knew that the judge would be the trial's first casualty. Forced by ill-health to step down after two years, he would die soon afterwards.

Then it was the turn of the prosecutor. Geoffrey Nice QC had been seconded to the tribunal from London's Temple Garden Chambers, which had famously supplied Britain's main prosecutor to the Nuremberg trials. With this weight of expectation on his shoulders, Mr Nice would lead the prosecution in the biggest war crimes trial since the end of the Second World War, and the first of a former head of state. In deference to the location of the international court, Nice went wigless and wore the simple garb of Dutch lawyers—a plain black robe with a pleated white band.

Geoffrey Nice had a finely drawn aesthetic face, shrewd eyes and closely trimmed, blue-black hair. That hair was surely dyed, Marin had thought, which suggested, as did the two gold rings on the little finger of his left hand, an unpromising level of self-regard. The prosecutor's microphone, like the long stem of a brutalist flower, reached to just below his chin.

'This trial,' Nice began, speaking slowly and clearly for the interpreters, 'is about the rise of this accused to power, power that was exercised without accountability, responsibility or morality.' He paused here to remove his glasses, then slowly put them back on. 'At the outset, he thought he could have it all—perhaps a new Yugoslavia, himself a second Tito.'

At this, Milosevic tilted his head ironically, but Nice was speaking beyond him to a global audience, aware that hundreds of journalists were watching on a big screen in the nearby media centre.

'Ethnic cleansing happened over and over again,' the prosecutor continued. 'Did he know what was happening? Of course he did. Was there a piece of paper that said, "Go and commit these crimes"? Of course not. People aren't like that.'

The stage had been set as if for a grand opera. Nice would supply the soaring rhetoric, the evidence, the motive, the psychology behind it all, the scale of Milosevic's ambitions and his hubris. Yet at the centre of this ennobling theatre of justice, the accused was sublimely disinterested in playing the role allotted to him. In the years that followed, Milosevic would drag out the proceedings until the global audience and the holdouts in the media centre succumbed to boredom and simply left. Representing himself, the former president lectured and hectored the judges. He refused to accept a single piece of evidence and insisted on cross-examining every last witness in minute detail.

Marin understood that the prosecution had played into the hands of the old devil from the very beginning. The crucial mistake came when Geoffrey Nice announced his intention to introduce more than a thousand witnesses.

'Over a thousand witnesses?' Justice May protested. 'No trial can take place under those circumstances.'

May's even temper failed him for the first time that day and Marin wondered if the judge had glimpsed, at that moment, his own mortality. The trial that killed him really was like no other in history, encompassing sixty-six charges and more than a thousand events. The prosecutors would generate a million pages of material, requiring Milosevic to read more than a thousand pages a day, an impossible task, on top of the thousands of hours of video evidence he was expected to review. As the former president's health worsened, the trial would be interrupted by frequent stoppages as he complained to the judges that the burden on him was intolerable.

'A superhuman could not do it,' Milosevic told the court. 'They bombard me with documents, not evidence, quantity over quality, I am the victim of being bombed by documents. This is a form of torture and a form of cynicism.'

Marin felt no sympathy for Milosevic, but he did understand that the trial of the century was collapsing under its own weight. Nevertheless, amid the interminable white noise of testimony, one witness cut through to Marin. He was a fellow who had known Milosevic personally when he was president. He told the court that his impression was of a man who felt that, when he said something, the very saying of it made it *true*. If he uttered it, it simply must be true.

•

'Shall we play chess, then?' Marin now asked.

'Yes, but not here surrounded by all this shit. We will go next door. I have more whisky there,' said Milosevic, holding up his empty glass.

The Serb played white and pressed his advantage hard, forcing Marin to build a defensive fortress around his besieged king. Not for the first time during one of their contests, Marin thought of Vukovar and found himself employing his pawns like the small groups of men who used to risk their lives to go out and attack Serbian tanks.

When Zwolsman came to lock down the cells, the game was in the balance. A slip-up by either player would be fatal. They carefully moved the board to the top of a cupboard to keep it safe until they could resume the battle. The guard escorted Marin back to his own cell and shepherded him inside like a farmer herding a prize cow into the barn ahead of a cold night: 'In you go, Mr M. Take care. Sleep well.'

Marin did not look at him.

'Oh, I almost forgot,' said Zwolsman. 'A letter came for you.'

Marin looked up now, staring at the man's stupid face. 'What did you say?'

'You got a letter, by courier. I put it on your desk.'

Zwolsman smiled inanely and clanged the door shut.

Marin suddenly felt claustrophobic. *A letter!* He found it on the desk—an envelope addressed to Tomislav Maric c/- the prison.

He tore it open and a photograph slipped out, falling face-up on the desk. He looked at it for a moment, then picked it up with trembling fingers.

It was an artefact that should not exist. He saw his younger self and felt a profound shock. The young woman was in his arms and Marin seemed to hear her pleas, faint echoes from the distant past. In the photograph his own face was unreadable. It was like seeing an actor playing a crucial scene in his life. After a while he thought to turn the photograph over, and on the reverse side he found the message:

I'm coming to see you,

Anna

Marin clutched the photograph so hard it began to bend. He dropped it and stood up. He stepped to the window and turned his back to it, standing in the narrow gap between the bunk and the desk. He took four long paces to the cell door, his rubber soles squelching on the vinyl floor. He put both palms on the door. Cold steel. He turned and paced back. The same noise, the same rhythm. He touched the window. It was damp with tiny beads of condensation; he pushed off from it like a lap swimmer and repeated the sequence again and again.

Pressure rose in his veins so they seemed to pulsate, pressing against his skin. The cicada cry of tinnitus was in his ears as he sat heavily on the bunk, squashing the thin mattress.

He clicked on the TV.

Bewitched. That infuriating fuckwit Darren, the pop-eyed, unreasonable prick, was babbling away as usual. What man wouldn't be happy that his wife could grant his every wish? *Click.* CNN. More infuriating fuckwits. *Click.* Crap. *Click.* More crap. He turned it off.

Marin Katich was filled with helpless anxiety. He wanted to pull the television from its swivelling metal arm and smash it to pieces. He wanted to tear the bunk apart; to drag out the sink; to rip the plumbing from the wall; to break the spines of his books and scatter the pages; to tear up his indictment and the investigators' reports and the witness statements, and throw them about like confetti.

But he did none of this. Instead, he lowered himself back onto the narrow bunk and closed his eyes. It took some time for him to calm down.

Eventually, he was able to sit up. He stared at the desk. It was plain and orderly. The photograph was still there. He picked it up again and examined it closely. It had obviously been taken from a distance, looking down from a building, and the photographer had been good at his job. He could see that from the detail in the image and its clarity. The young woman cleaves to his body and he feels again the pressure of her against his chest.

Then tears came to flood Marin's eyes and he began to sob like a child. It was an immense relief to feel something, to remember what it was like to be human.

8

SCHEVENINGEN, THE HAGUE
14 DECEMBER 2005

ANNA WAS EXHAUSTED by the time she reached the Kurhaus reception desk and gratefully handed her belongings to the porter who stood next to a large Christmas tree like a helpful elf. Booking a room here had stretched her thin budget and she winced as she handed over her credit card. All she wanted to do was climb into a warm bed with fresh linen, but Pierre would be here soon, so after she had the luggage sent to her room she headed up the wide marble staircase to the bar. A song, popular when she was a teenager, grew louder and louder as she ascended. At the top of the stairs, she looked up into the vast space beneath the hotel's dome. A raucous, booming voice filled the space and, looking for the source of it, she saw a diminutive black man in sunglasses bent over a grand piano. The man's head rolled about with the unself-conscious awkwardness of the blind. He sang about feeling kind of seasick and of a room humming harder and a ceiling flying away, words that seemed wildly out of place here in this nineteenth-century ballroom. Far from crying out for more, the crowd of elderly women, scattered about the place taking high tea, merely wobbled their coiffured heads like novelty nodding dogs.

Behind a circular bar near the small stage, a man in a mono-grammed waistcoat with the moustache of a 1970s cricketer sang along as he cleaned glasses and lined them up neatly on the counter. The bar occupied an alcove framed by high walls with trompe l'oeil drapery that suggested old stage curtains.

As the blind man sang of vestal virgins leaving for the coast, Anna slid onto a bar stool. High up in the frescoed dome she made out, on its largest panel, a corpulent Neptune afloat in a giant conch shell. Surrounded by dripping mermaids and minions, the dissolute fellow clutched a trident in one hand and draped the other over the shoulders of a naked nymph. Anna found something oddly appeal-ing about his concupiscence. Then again, like all immortals, he was careless of the creatures around him: he paid no heed at all to the panicky horse hauling him through the sea with its foaming head and nostrils barely above the waves.

'Can I get you something?' the barman's mildly accented English interrupted her reverie.

'Some binoculars?' Anna squinted at the immense chandelier that hung from the centre of the dome like a great crystal stalactite but did little to illuminate the frescoes.

'You can see it better in the daylight,' said the barman.

'I'll have a martini.'

'To ease the pain?'

'To pass the time.'

'Gin or vodka?'

'Do you have to ask? You've got London Number 3—I'll have that.'

'Olive or twist?'

She raised her eyebrows.

'Olive,' the barman said, and began the ritual. 'Have you come far?' he asked without looking up.

Anna paused, then relented: 'Australia.'

'Ho! You'll need this, then.'

The puckish piano man was building to a big finish. There were wild thatches of remnant hair on his shiny head and Anna noticed that the trousers of his outmoded suit were too short. These little signs of decrepitude made her sad. So did thoughts of the ghostly woman whose face had just turned a whiter shade of pale. The singer repeated that line over and over, his voice rising in volume until the lower chandeliers quivered on their flimsy chains.

The barman wiped the marble top and placed a chilled glass in front of Anna before pouring.

'What brings you so far?' he asked.

'I've come to see a man I once knew,' said Anna, and abruptly decided she had revealed too much. She took the martini and a bowl of nuts and moved to an empty table. Before long she heard a familiar voice, and looked up to see a dishevelled figure shambling across the room. Pierre Villiers skirted tables, moving gracefully for a big man. Anna stood to greet him and he hugged her hard, then held her at arm's length, clutching her shoulders.

'Hello, Pierre,' she said, modest under the scrutiny of his clever eyes. They were swimming, as ever, in and out of focus behind the Coke-bottle lenses that made him look a lot like the Trotskyite revolutionary he once claimed to be.

'Still a beautiful creature.' Pierre gave his verdict at last, pronouncing the last word 'cweature'. Anna smiled, recalling his famous radio sign-off: *Pierre Villiers weporting fwom Zagweb.*

'That's very kind of you,' she said. 'Especially after another decade of the great unravelling.'

'Oh, come on,' Pierre chided her. 'Time's stood still for you. There's no gruesome portrait in *my* attic, but at least I've lost a few pounds with all the cycling.'

'Sit down, sit down,' she urged. 'Let me get you a drink. I couldn't wait.'

'Right.' He pointed at the martini. 'I'll have one of those and some more nuts.'

From the bar, Anna watched her friend hoover up the little bowl of peanuts. Pierre was certainly trimmer, but his generally unkempt appearance hadn't changed much. It had been a long time between haircuts and there were unshaven patches on his cheeks. He had never managed basic maintenance very well, nor cared about it. Clearly no one was taking care of him and she wondered about that. The barman tipped his head towards Pierre, as if to say, 'Is this really the man?' Anna shrugged, scooped up another bowl of nuts and left him wondering.

'He thinks you're my squeeze,' she said as she passed over the bowl.

'An easy mistake,' said Pierre, straightening his spectacles in a mild effort to measure up.

'Still got the same goggles.'

'Propinquity. I got so used to them that I don't look like myself when I take them off.'

'Propinquity, propinquity,' Anna laughed. 'Zelda Gilroy, right?'

'That's right, good memory.' Pierre grinned back. '*The Many Loves of Dobie Gillis*. Poor Zelda could never get him to take an interest.'

Anna crumpled her nose.

'Dobie was a dickhead. Zelda could have done better.'

'But it was Dobie she wanted,' said Pierre. 'And she hung in there waiting for it to kick in—propinquity, I mean. It's from the Latin *propinquitas*, by the way, a genuine sociological theory about how proximity eventually leads to attraction.'

'Right,' said Anna, remembering that Pierre never missed an opportunity to display his erudition.

'But somehow,' he sighed, 'it never worked for you and me.'

Anna smiled at the old trope and raised her glass.

'That's why we're still friends.'

'I'd have coped if things had worked out differently.'

'Really? What about Chiara?'

'Chiara! We have been out of touch, haven't we? She left me years ago . . . And so you've obviously missed out on Emina altogether.'

'Emina?'

'I met her in Sarajevo. She's a philosopher.'

'I guess you do look a bit like the young Sartre.'

'I'm not sure that's a compliment,' said Pierre. 'Anyway, she had an existential crisis and ran off with a Bosnian house painter.'

'Ten years reduced to a haiku.'

'Well, I did leave out all the important stuff. How we met. Who the house painter was. All big issues, not that it matters now . . . So, tell me, are you with anyone?'

'No,' Anna said as the waiter interrupted them, putting the cocktail down on a placemat. Pierre sipped it, then had a longer drink. Anna took the opportunity to change the subject.

'Have you said anything about Marin Katich?'

'I told you I wouldn't do anything until you got here,' he said, unable to hide his irritation. Then he stopped, realising what she'd just said: 'So it *is* him. You were bullshitting when you said you weren't sure.'

'I was. Sorry about that. I had to be sure you wouldn't tell them.'

'Why the hell are you wasting energy on this fellow? Did you read the indictment?'

'Yes,' she said. 'Why is it sealed?'

'I couldn't find out. Something to do with the danger to witnesses. The prosecutor keeps this stuff close to her chest. But what did you think about it?'

'It's unspeakably horrible.'

'It's hardly a surprise, is it? He was raised to be a fascist. Anna, you've got to let me tell the investigators who he really is. I don't even know why I sent those pictures to you.'

'You needed confirmation.'

'I could have worked it out myself. I was just trying to make a point, I think. I shouldn't have involved you. I shouldn't have made it personal.'

'But you did, Pierre, and it is personal, in ways you can't imagine.'

'What are you talking about?'

Anna paused, watching her old friend. She had always treated his amorous approaches as comical, but she realised now that he had nurtured deeper feelings. She saw him compose his face as if preparing for a blow. Before this moment, she had been debating whether to tell him everything. She knew now that she had no choice.

'Marin Katich is Rachel's father.'

Pierre blanched. Speechless for a moment, he gulped down the rest of his drink.

'I need your help, Pierre,' she said. 'I have to get in to see him before anyone finds out who he is.'

'I'm going to need another one of these.'

'Me too. I've got a story to tell you that won't make a lot of sense if we're sober.'

THE LOVERS

9

SYDNEY, AUSTRALIA

6 FEBRUARY 1970

ANNA ROSEN STARED UP AT THE BRIDGE, into the high mass of steel girders tinged green under the floodlights. The tall figure next to her was silent, waiting for her to take it all in. Suspension cables as thick as tree trunks reached down from the arch to the roadway. The rest of it was an incomprehensible cross-hatching of steel spans. She felt the weight of the great structure, the pull of gravity and the tension in the cabling.

Even now, at 2 am, a constant flow of vehicles droned past and vibrations rang through the metal structure beneath her feet. These sensations were amplified by the drug, which gave her an icy clarity.

Anna jumped when Marin Katich touched her bare shoulder.

'You ready?' he asked.

'Not until you explain to me how,' she said.

'Come here, then.'

Marin led her further along the empty pedestrian pathway until they were standing adjacent to the base of the nearest arch.

'This is where we'll go across.'

He pointed to the top of the high corrugated iron fence that ran the length of the bridge in order to separate walkers and cyclists from the two sets of train tracks going to and from the city.

'I'll climb up. Hoist you over and down. Stay low and wait until I join you. Then we go quickly across the tracks together.'

'Aren't they electrified?'

'That's just in American movies. Power's in the overhead wires.'

Marin was standing behind her, so close that she felt the heat of his body. He put a hand on her shoulder and pointed to the base of the arch.

'See that steel ladder? That's where we're headed. We go up the ladder, then on—right up the north face.'

Anna went up on her toes to see over the fencing. She saw a twenty-five-foot ladder that ended at a closed metal trapdoor. Above the trapdoor, she made out a narrow staircase ascending into the superstructure. This, she presumed, was 'the north face'. She found this Everest terminology irritating.

'Yes, sir,' she said.

Marin raised an eyebrow. 'You know I didn't mean it like that.'

Anna didn't respond. She was looking at the top of the ladder and she could now see an obvious flaw in his plan. Long metal spikes protruded from the frame of the trapdoor, precisely to stop intruders climbing around it so as to reach the staircase.

'Have you got a way of opening that trapdoor?'

'Not exactly,' said Marin, clambering up onto the high fence. Straddling it, he reached down to her, but Anna hesitated.

'You'll have to trust me,' he said, and she took his hand reluctantly, allowing herself to be hauled over the fence before jumping down onto the gravel beside the train tracks. A moment later, Marin dropped down into a crouch beside her.

'C'mon, quick.' He grabbed her hand again and they flitted across the tracks. 'Follow me,' he called and sprang up the ladder with the assurance of a monkey.

Anna stayed rooted to the ground.

Halfway up, Marin leant back and called out: 'Quick, before someone sees us.'

'This is insane,' she muttered. Then she drew a deep breath and began climbing hand over hand, with great deliberation. She looked up as she reached Marin's feet and saw him stretching out to the metal spikes around the trapdoor.

'This is the only hard part, but I'll be there to pull you up. You take the spike like this . . .'

Marin wrapped both hands around one of them, took his feet off the ladder and swung out over the train tracks. He dangled there for a moment, face to face with Anna, who had edged up the last rungs of the ladder. He was grinning.

'Then you swing your legs up and over,' he said, executing the manoeuvre like an acrobat, pulling his legs above his body and throwing them over one of the spikes before, in a single fluid movement, dragging himself up to sit astride the obstacle.

Frozen at the top of the ladder, Anna looked up at him.

'You've got to be joking!' It was an absurd risk to be taking. 'This is a stupid boys' game.'

'Come on! I won't let you fall. You won't forgive yourself if you have to climb back down.'

Anna eyes flashed with anger.

'Oh, fuck off.'

'Go on,' he said with a laugh. 'I dare you.'

'Stop laughing, you bastard!' Anna yelled before she lunged out and grabbed a metal spike with both hands. Gravity pulled her body into space. As she hung there, both of them heard the sound of a train. It was quickly getting louder.

'Hold on tight!' called Marin and he grabbed her wrists. 'Don't look down!'

But she did and panicked at the sight of her feet dangling over the electrified wires.

'I've got you! I've got you! *I've . . . got . . . you!*'

Marin repeated the words as the noise of the approaching train became a clattering roar and its headlights flooded the track with light. Anna saw sparks jumping on the wires. She pictured herself electrocuted, crushed and dismembered on the tracks. She felt his grip tighten.

'Hold on!' he yelled.

Hurtling beneath her, the train seemed to tear the atoms out of the air. Her feet scrabbled against nothing as the carriages rattled past in a long blur. Then, as quickly as it had appeared, it was gone— rocketing on to Milsons Point station.

Marin strained and pulled her up and over until they tumbled back into the enclosed staircase, collapsing together in a heap. Anna was on top of him and he held her tightly. She pulled herself free.

'Fuck, fuck, fuck, fuck—'

'Are you—'

'Fuck, faaarck!'

'—okay?'

'No, I'm not okay!' she shouted into his face. 'You nearly got me killed!'

'You didn't have to do it.'

'You dared me. I hate that.'

'Sorry, but it worked.'

Marin pulled something from his pocket. A steel flask. He unscrewed the cap and passed it over. Anna took a long pull and felt the harsh liquor burn its way to her core.

'Ahhh.' She wiped her hand across her mouth. 'What is that?'

'*Rakija.*'

'What?'

'Plum brandy. My dad makes it.'

She took another long swig, holding onto the flask when he tried to take it back.

'Steady, it's pretty strong.'

'Bloody train.'

'That never happened before.'

'"Trust me," you said.'

'Sorry.'

She felt the calming effect of the liquor and handed him the flask.

'Thanks for not letting me fall.'

Marin jumped to his feet and pulled her up.

'C'mon then, let's go. It's quite a way to the top.'

After they climbed the first staircase, Anna found they were inside the superstructure on a steep zigzag route to the top of the arch. She could see the long line of suspension cables extending off into the distance. Now, above the floodlights, Marin cast a Nosferatu shadow ahead of them, and her own spindly darkness was soon entwined with it as she hauled herself up after him. Eventually he paused on a landing, and she was grateful to take a moment to her get her breath.

'This is a maintenance route,' he explained.

'Phew, steep.' She was breathing heavily, in no hurry to move on. 'How on earth did you find out about it?'

'I've been coming up since I was a boy. My dad works here.'

'You're kidding.'

'He's in charge of the maintenance crew.'

'Okay. What's his name?'

'It's Ivo, but on the bridge they call him Steve.'

'Does he know you come up here?'

'Christ no!' said Marin, his face moving into shadow. 'He'd wring my neck.'

'Let's get going then before he catches us.'

'There's no one here at night. He's not the bogey man.'

Marin led her up a series of steep staircases. Through gaps in the metalwork, she glimpsed odd corners of the harbour and random lit windows in otherwise dark buildings. She began to imagine the bridge as a living organism. The maintenance stairs and passageways were the venous system, and way down below her were the arteries—traffic lanes, along which tiny vehicles moved, metal cocoons pushing twin cones of light ahead of them.

'Nearly at the top,' Marin said at last, pointing up to another steep ascent. Beyond his silhouette, Anna glimpsed the sky. She pushed on as fast as she could manage until she emerged breathless from the hatch into a night swarming with stars.

In spite of herself, she gasped, as rapt as a child who had climbed to the top of the world. 'It's beautiful.'

They had come out at the low end of the arch, close to the two hulking granite pylons flanking the northern end of the bridge. Down below, on the eastern harbour, the first signs of a breeze ruffled the black surface. The winking fore and aft lights of slow-moving watercraft crisscrossed it. On the western side was an array of massive petrochemical tanks and also docks, where the prehistoric outlines of cranes overhung the sleeping ships waiting for their cargo.

Marin came up behind Anna and wrapped her in his arms, breathing lightly into the nape of her neck. Surprised by his tenderness, she leant into his body. After a moment, he pulled away, and Anna found herself oddly moved by his unfamiliar touch but also puzzled by it.

'Come on then,' he murmured. 'We're only halfway there.'

The physical attraction was no surprise. She knew they had both felt it the moment they met. Such things happened—not often, but sometimes. Anna looked at him and wondered if she could possibly fall for such a man. They weren't just strangers; they were ideological enemies, here together tonight, in this strangest of places, because of an unspoken truce that she could have barely imagined possible after the furious days she had just lived through.

10

EARLIER THAT WEEK, Anna had picked up *The Oz* and read that the prime minister was planning a cabinet meeting at the Commonwealth Parliamentary Offices in Martin Place. Ever since the protests against the Vietnam War began, the PM's people had rarely given out his schedule in advance. They had fucked up this time and created an unexpected opportunity to confront him directly. And not just him—the ministers responsible for the conscription laws and the conduct of the war would be there with him. Anna rang around the leaders of Students for a Democratic Society to convene an urgent meeting of its Action Committee.

There was a brief and intense debate at the meeting as the SDS had recently agreed to concentrate its resources on organising the first national Moratorium March. But that was months away, Anna had argued, and this was an opportunity to confront the top dogs now. The committee finally agreed with her that it was time to mobilise the widespread student anger over the National Service Act. The balloting process for conscription was being conducted under a veil of secrecy; the Act itself criminalised draft resisters, denying them the right of trial by jury; and it even sought to force university officials to divulge information about their students.

The SDS made no secret of its planned protest. Activists scrambled to distribute leaflets calling for an open meeting on the campus lawns to raise support for an action in Martin Place the following day. It was a well-attended, loud and angry meeting, which passed a unanimous resolution to stage a sit-in in front of the Commonwealth Offices. These details were accurately reported in the morning papers. Even the most rabid right-wing rag acknowledged that the SDS leaders had called for non-violent protest and advised students not to resist when police dragged them away.

As editor of the student newspaper, *The Tribe*, Anna convened an urgent meeting of her reporting and editorial team in its offices. They had much to do if she was going to remake the whole paper. Pierre Villiers was there with the photographer Dave Blatch and the most reliable members of her small team as she explained her intention to pull apart the planned edition so as to make space for coverage of the expected confrontation with the prime minister.

They all knew it was a bold decision. She was breaking the long-established slow rhythms of *The Tribe*, but one of the key campaign promises she had made when she was elected editor was that under her leadership the paper would become more relevant and report big events when they happened, not weeks later.

She gave an editor's pep talk that sounded, even to her, like a footy coach before a big match. This was their first opportunity to really prove they could do it, but everything had to go right for them.

'For God's sake, try to behave like reporters not protesters,' she pleaded. 'If we get ourselves arrested, we'll be buggered.'

She looked pointedly at Pierre, who ran his hands back through his long hair and winked at her.

'What is it?' she demanded.

'Well, we should remember that having fun is half the fun.'

'Very true, comrade. Except you won't have much fun in jail. And we won't have your story on the front page.'

'We'll be careful,' said Blatch. 'But that doesn't mean the cops won't target us.'

Anna nodded. 'So, just in case, I've got a contingency fund for bail and the SDS have a group of friendly lawyers who'll appear for anyone who's arrested. They know our deadline, so our people will be treated as a priority. But nothing will happen until the following morning and, if the courts drag things out, we'll still be in trouble. We'll have to have all our copy and pics ready to go by Thursday arvo. So just don't do anything silly.'

Pierre gave an ostentatious salute. 'Righto, boss.'

As the meeting broke up, she took him aside. 'We're all right, aren't we?' she asked quietly.

'Sure. What do you mean?'

'*Righto, boss?* You finding it hard to take orders from a woman?'

Pierre looked surprised. 'Oh, c'mon, Anna! You know better than that. I find it hard to take orders from anyone.'

'Okay,' she said, still uncertain. 'I had to ask.'

Pierre just smiled. 'Got a little present for you,' he said, pulling a tiny glass medicine vial from his pocket. It was filled with white powder. He put it in her hand. 'Peace offering.'

'What is it?' she asked cupping the vial in her palm.

'Speed, very pure. You might need it over the next few days.'

She pocketed the thing and kissed him on the cheek.

'Offer accepted,' she said and went back to her office.

•

Anna had run for editor of *The Tribe* on a ticket backed by Students for a Democratic Society, but their support came with a price. Having delivered her the votes to take over the paper, the SDS acted as if they had won a beachhead in the Union Building and *The Tribe*'s offices became the de facto headquarters of their campus activism.

Anna had no real problem with that. As a founding member, she understood their desire to occupy ground in the middle of the university. It had been her idea to convert *The Tribe* into a journal of the New Left, so she could hardly object when they wanted to turn their principles into action. The SDS borrowed its tactics from the US anti-war movement and its philosophy from Tom Hayden, that movement's most charismatic leader. Anna admired their revolutionary verve.

She used her first edition to republish Hayden's 'Agenda for a Generation'. The 1962 statement seemed to mimic the high-blown rhetoric of the preamble to the US Constitution: '*We are people of this generation, bred in at least modest comfort, housed now in universities, looking uncomfortably to the world we inherit . . . Beneath the stagnation of those who have closed their minds to the future, is the pervading feeling that there simply are no alternatives, that our times have witnessed the exhaustion not only of Utopias, but of any new departures as well.*'

The exhaustion of utopias . . . That was an idea Anna understood well. She had been raised by communist parents and spoon-fed The Party's utopian ideals from her earliest days as a red-diaper baby. By her early teens in the Junior Eureka League, those beliefs were giving her bad indigestion. Eventually she spat them out completely and decided that the old left had destroyed itself by letting Stalinist murderers drag them around by the scruff of the neck. Her conclusions had threatened a serious rift with her father.

For years, as he rose higher in the ranks of the Australian Communist Party, Frank Rosen had patiently stated and restated his case for reforming it from within, but, as Anna's understanding became more sophisticated, she grew more and more impatient with his arguments. World events made her case for her. Any foot-draggers who had not rejected the Soviets after Hungary, she told Frank, surely had no choice after the savage crushing of the Prague Spring in 1968.

Although it was not clear to Anna at the time, Frank Rosen had always been sympathetic to his daughter's arguments. He was one of those leading the push for reform, but the CPA's Stalinist faction fought them at every turn. Once Anna understood the role he was playing, she admired his determination, but she never forgave The Party for its downright hypocrisy. She warned Frank that no matter how hard the communists might try to reinvent themselves by recruiting from the vanguard of the anti-war movement they had nothing to offer idealistic young people.

But Anna never had the heart to tell him what she truly believed: that The Party was doomed to die a slow and ignominious death, and Frank Rosen with it. She wondered sadly if that was how she would one day have to sum up her father's legacy. Perhaps silence was better? No, Frank would hate that. He would rather a fierce dialectical debate over his coffin than any sentimental nonsense.

Searching for alternative ways of thinking and organising, Anna found that Tom Hayden's manifesto and his considered rhetoric best encapsulated the apathy and malaise that allowed bad things to happen unchallenged: *'Feeling the press of complexity upon the emptiness of life, people are fearful of the thought that at any moment things might be thrust out of control. They fear change itself, since change might smash whatever invisible framework seems to hold back chaos for them now.'*

As editor of *The Tribe*, Anna embraced what Hayden called the 'synthesis of politics and culture'. She was using the paper to push the cultural boundaries on sex, gender, race and drugs. Sexual freedom was about a woman's right to control her own body and naturally linked to the right to access contraception and abortion, personal freedoms constrained or suppressed by politics. She argued in forceful editorials that only political change would allow people to live freely.

Anna believed there was a broad but hidden consensus for change, and she opened up her pages for uncensored discussions—of homosexuality, of the emergence of the Black Power Movement among young Aboriginal people, and of a broader critique of Australian racism. She published consumer reviews of LSD tabs and buyers' guides to the marijuana market. She created space for writers, poets, filmmakers and cinema reviewers—and on their behalf she openly challenged censorship laws. On these issues of personal politics, Anna gave *The Tribe* an edge it had never had, but, above all this, she made opposition to the Vietnam War the central theme of its coverage.

•

The following afternoon, Anna was in the middle of the heaving street protest outside the Commonwealth Offices in Martin Place. Over her shoulder she had slung a tape recorder, and in her right hand was a microphone that she waved as if it had magical powers to protect her. When she saw that the police had removed their numbered badges she knew things would get rough.

At 5.15 pm the protesters linked arms and surrounded the prime minister's waiting limousine. Someone grabbed Anna's arm and tried to draw her in, but she pulled away, sure this provocation would bring a swift response. Moments later, a flying wedge of police charged from the building's entrance. The linked students ran towards them, and Anna found herself caught between the two groups of rushing bodies. Before she could react, she was roughly pulled out to one side. Stumbling backwards, she turned and saw Pierre.

'Stay on your feet,' he yelled and hauled her behind a column of the building. They braced themselves against the concrete, facing one another.

'This'll be ugly.' But there was something eager in his expression, exhilarated.

'Where's Dave?'

Pierre pointed. 'There!'

Dave Blatch was crouched next to another photographer in the lee of the column on the other side of the building as tumbling waves of people broke around it. In the space between the office and the black limo, a police line pressed forwards, tightly packed and flailing their batons at any human target. Then the ranks of protesters broke. A melee erupted, a battle for the space around the official vehicle. Students threw themselves onto the bonnet and banged at the windows.

As police tore demonstrators off the limousine, Anna watched Blatch capture the violent action in a sequence of shots. Isolated protesters were knocked to the ground and pummelled with billy clubs, others were rocking the limo from side to side. Those the police managed to cut out from the herd were dragged away and thrown into the back of paddy wagons. A young, red-faced man with long blond hair, sticky with blood, ran at the police screaming: 'You cowardly cunts!'

A group of police charged the fellow, knocked him over and beat him until a young woman rushed over.

'Don't hurt him,' she cried. 'He's bleeding.'

Anna watched as a constable, no older than the young woman, thrust her hard against a tree trunk. She slid down onto her bum, barely conscious. Prisoners jumped around inside a locked paddy wagon, screaming slogans, and it began to rock wildly. Other police dragged battered, limp bodies along the ground by arms or hair. Gradually the police got the upper hand and gained control of the space around the vehicle. Anna heard shouts behind her; she saw the doors of the Commonwealth Offices open and there was the prime minister, standing grim-faced in the doorway, transfixed by the chaos in front of him.

'It's him!' she shouted to Pierre, who stumbled across the gap to tell Blatch. The photographer spun around, snapping shot after shot as the prime minister was rushed out in a phalanx of police and bodyguards. Peering around the column, Anna and the prime minister were face to face for a moment. Somehow she caught his attention and he stared at her with a puzzled intensity she would later describe as *lascivious*.

Anna felt a dark thrill, part righteous, part malicious. She wished him no actual harm, but she was proud of her own role in making the prime minister experience chaos and directly confronting him with the consequences of his decisions.

Then he was inside the limo, and—as protesters swarmed around it, screaming and beating on the windows—he was driven away through the chanting mob: '*End conscription! End conscription now!*'

They found out the next day that the former fighter pilot had refused to be snuck out the back; a Blatch snapshot caught the fixed smile on his scarred face as he salvaged a public relations victory: one man refusing to bow to an angry, disrespectful mob.

As Anna watched the PM's escape, two students on the edge of the crowd threw down test tubes and crushed them with their heels. She quickly caught an acrid stench and her eyes began to burn. Whatever the gas was, she knew it was a stupid and dangerous escalation. People panicked, pushing each other aside to get away, and as it drifted out over the blue cordon and the police sniffed it in the air, they began beating their targets with renewed ferocity.

With the rest of the cabinet ministers still stuck inside the Government Offices, the police were desperate to clear the streets for the convoy of waiting Comcars. Now the prime minister was secure, the confrontation degenerated into a free-for-all in which press credentials counted for nothing. A *Herald* journalist was knocked down, his arm fractured, his spectacles shattered. Tape recorders and microphones were ripped from the hands of reporters.

Crouched low behind her column, Anna saw a cop snatch the camera from the hands of the photographer working alongside Dave Blatch. He smashed it repeatedly on the pavement and was about to lunge at Blatch's Nikon when Pierre intervened, grappling with the rogue copper in an ugly, twisting dance.

Blatch managed to scurry away and Anna pulled him down next to her. Together they watched Pierre disappear into a knot of blue uniforms, shouting all the while that he was a journalist.

•

It was still dark when Anna drove into the empty university the next morning; *The Tribe* would be printed that day for distribution overnight. She parked at the Union Building, used her master key to get through the security entrance and climbed two flights of stairs to a pair of large orange doors, across which had been painted in swirling, psychedelic lettering *The Tribe*. Anna unlocked the door and stepped inside the empty newsroom. She switched on the low-hanging fluorescents and the familiar tantalising scene flickered in front of her: dormant typewriters and telephones, piles of copy paper, newspaper archives, tattered armchairs and the ping-pong table, one bat resting aslant a ball. On every other flat surface, ashtrays overflowed with crushed cigarettes and the nubs of joints, so recently smoked that the sweet resinous stench of dope hung in the air.

The walls were haphazardly decorated with political posters. Her own contribution was the framed front page of the June 1968 edition of *The Black Dwarf* with its defiant headline: WE SHALL

FIGHT, WE WILL WIN, PARIS, LONDON, ROME, BERLIN. Tariq Ali himself had signed it and sent it to her as a gesture of solidarity.

Since she became editor, Anna had made sure to get here before the sun every second Thursday, which required both discipline and sobriety, neither of which came easily to her. It was her job to produce and distribute twelve thousand copies of the student paper every fortnight and she took the job more seriously than anyone who knew her might have predicted.

Anna made tea and toast in the kitchenette, careful to avoid contact with the petri-dish experiments being conducted in unwashed mugs and bowls. Things had clearly gotten out of hand again and she made a mental note to get a bit fascist about it at the next meeting.

Balancing her mug in one hand and heavily Vegemited toast in the other, she made her way over to the long, sloping table where each page would be roughly pasted up. She was pleased to see that the typeset galleys had come in on time. They included copy for each of the news stories, articles and poems, printed up in sixteen-inch lengths. The headlines were in too, all sized for the page and ready to be pasted into the final layout. Stacked in separate piles were the cropped photos, the artwork and the ads.

Anna's task now was to go through 'the book', with its scaled-down versions of each page, so as to make sure the subs had got it right and it was delivered to the compositors' room at Quality Press. It had to be there by midday to meet the deadline for the presses to roll that night.

Anna picked up the large photo she had chosen for the front page and examined it again. A young man, his teeth gritted in a rictus of pain, was being bent backwards by a police sergeant. The cop was a burly, middle-aged man with cropped white hair; his victim a nice-looking boy, neatly groomed and conservatively dressed. The cop's left hand gripped the boy's throat, thumb and forefinger tightening around his larynx. The boy's eyes were shut, the sergeant's hat was tipped drunkenly forwards, his own eyes half-closed and his mouth very close to the boy's ear. Such tender violence, she thought and, looking closer at the photo, she imagined the cop whispering something in the boy's ear: 'I'm gonna fuck you, son . . . I'm gonna fuck you hard.'

The latent sexuality in this male-on-male assault seemed so flagrant that she wondered again if she should have referred to it in the headline, as Pierre Villiers had demanded. Pierre had written a vivid firsthand account of the clash and was so incensed by the violence of the state apparatus that he wanted the photo to carry an equally provocative banner: *FUCKED BY THE PIGS!*

Anna smiled. Of course Pierre would want that, the bloody Trot. His general view—*And fuck the university establishment too; if they fuck with us, we'll fuck them right back!*—was a sentiment he would repeat often and loudly at editorial meetings. It was not that she disagreed with him—the vice chancellor and his cronies were conservative prigs—but she was much more of a pragmatist than Pierre. Her main goal was to keep the paper going. A shutdown, as a result of flouting censorship laws, would be disastrous.

She had moved *The Tribe* to the forefront of the anti-war movement at a time when the conscription regime was being progressively hardened, when the military-industrial complex was calling the shots and when the war showed no signs of slowing. She knew they had to play a long game, not a brief and glorious charge at the ramparts, and she laid her headline over the picture: POLITICAL PANIC EDITION.

She thought it worked well enough. Beneath the large photo, she arranged the second smaller strap- and by-line:

THE BATTLE OF MARTIN PLACE
Witnessed by Pierre Villiers

That should keep her star reporter happy. He might be a Trot, but he never rejected the bourgeois conceit of recognition.

She glanced at the poster Pierre had stuck high on the wall. Leon Trotsky, the man himself, stared out benignly across the newsroom, masquerading as a cool hipster with a wild mop of flyaway hair, wire-rimmed glasses and chin beard. Pierre's hero hadn't exactly shunned recognition either, but the old Bolshevik had learned the hard lesson about the futility of popularity without power.

After biting into her drooping toast, Anna wiped a smear of Vegemite from her chin, licked it from her fingers, and moved on to the inside pages where there were more strong pictures of police brutality. Filling much of page three was Dave Blatch's startling picture of the prime minister in motion, the faces of his bodyguards registering their anxiety that this could all go terribly wrong. The headline said it all: POLICE STATE ON THE RUN.

She arranged the RESISTANCE AND REPRESSION headline across the top of pages four and five, and added a shot of her Trotskyite reporter being hauled away by police. Just as she had feared, Pierre had been one of the thirty protesters arrested. He faced the ubiquitous charges of resisting arrest and assaulting police. Pierre had not been bailed out until Thursday morning, but he had managed to hold onto a small notebook and pencil and had spent much of the night in the lock-up compiling his account of the action.

Eventually Anna stepped back from the pages to look at her handiwork, laid out on the slanting desk. She sipped her lukewarm tea and nodded with satisfaction. Then she moved on to the rest of the paper.

11

ANNA WAS FINISHED by 11 am. She always managed to work faster when she was alone. As predicted, no one else from *The Tribe*'s editorial team had made it in yet. Mrs Kent, the stolid middle-aged woman who managed the paper's advertising for a percentage of the profits, had come in to check that all her ads were properly placed, and she stayed to help Anna pack each of the pages into hard cardboard covers for delivery to Quality Press.

'Thanks for the help, Elaine,' said Anna when the boxes were packed and ready to go. The older woman pushed a shank of blue-rinsed hair back behind her ear and sat on a desk to light a cigarette.

'No problem, love,' she said. 'It's a good edition, that one. Keep it up and the metros'll be recruitin' ya next.'

Anna laughed. 'That'll be the day.'

'Oh, you'd have to rein in your red-ragger bullshit, I reckon,' Elaine advised, squinting through a veil of smoke. She meant it kindly.

'Can you really see me doing that? This means something to those poor bastards facing the draft. The establishment owns all the big papers. They'd never take a stand on anything that challenges the status quo.'

Elaine looked at her shrewdly. 'Well, love, you know my son's in Vietnam? He doesn't like it much, but he doesn't like your protesters either. Reckons they're a bunch of spoilt kids who'll always figure out a way to stay out of danger.'

'That's just smart, isn't it?' Anna replied. 'To stay out of a war you don't believe in.'

'Well, I'd have to think about that, love. It's okay for some, I s'pose, those with the means to figure it out anyway. Look, I'll leave you to it. I've got to go book you some more advertising. Keep those profits rolling in for the worker's collective.'

Elaine Kent crushed her cigarette in an ashtray and made for the door.

Anna called out after her: 'What's your son's name?'

'Clark,' called Elaine as the door closed behind her.

Anna smiled and shook her head. Was she taking the piss? She liked Elaine Kent for her laconic ways, but would she joke about her own son like that? Either way, Anna hoped Clark really was bulletproof.

•

She was back in her office reading through her correspondence when Pierre poked his head through the doorway.

'*Bonjour, la classe,*' he said brightly.

'Ah, *la tête de merde.*'

Pierre pondered this. 'That might actually translate, you know.'

'I should hope so.'

'Why so cruel? This is about getting up before dawn, isn't it? I recognise the symptoms.'

Anna looked at her watch. 'This is about wondering if you were ever going to turn up. It's nearly twelve.'

'Right on time, then.'

With the help of two volunteers, they carried the boxes down to the loading bay and carefully stacked them into the back of the old panel van, which some friend of Pierre's had loaned to the enterprise. Pierre's job was to haul everything to the press in Glebe, where the final pages would be compiled and printed. It was his turn to work on the stone, watching over the compositors with Anna's 'book' as his guide. That was the last thing she handed him.

'Good luck. It's going to work well.' She leant into the window to stress the point. 'Don't let anyone fuck it up.'

'I'm the stone sub. Trust me.'

'I do.' Anna gave him a one-armed hug through the window. 'Just don't fuck it up.'

She watched him drive off and went back upstairs. In the last hour the newsroom had transformed into a zoo for exotic human animals. A cloud of marijuana smoke hung over the ping-pong table where two freaks with tangled hair down their backs were playing in slow motion. A few people were at their desks speaking loudly into phones or tapping valiantly at typewriters.

She noticed that the more languid types had occupied the battered armchairs, rolling joints and talking nonsense with great intensity. Most of that nonsense was being drowned out by Iron Butterfly. Someone had just put 'In-A-Gadda-Da-Vida' on the turntable, an endless droning track she hated. Anna looked at her watch: seventeen minutes to go. She stepped into her office and closed the door.

She discreetly pulled out Pierre's gift and tapped a small quantity of powder onto the desk. She quickly snorted it through a drinking straw and winced at the burn. Her eyes watered and she sniffed, relishing the metallic taste in the back of her throat. When after a few moments her head miraculously cleared, she reached for a pile of material from the contributors' box and started reading.

In this way, the day passed quickly until most of the staff and hangers-on had drifted off to other pursuits. Anna had been thinking it was time to pack it in herself when one of the volunteers, a young, gay Arts/Law smarty, cracked open the door and put his head in.

'Excuse me, Anna. You've got a visitor.'

'Who is it?'

'A gentleman caller, don't know him.' He winked. 'Very butch.'

Anna stared back at him, irritated. 'I'm not expecting anyone. Did he say what he wants?'

'Says he wrote an article. Want me to send him in?'

'I guess so. Thanks.'

Moments later the door opened again and she saw him for the first time. Her impression was simply of a strong presence entering her space, then she registered physical details. The man standing in front of her was striking in several ways. He was tall and well made, but not in the standard way. He had the appearance of a trained athlete, as if something had tempered him and left an easy physical confidence.

These were qualities that Anna normally found intimidating, even repellent. She had learned from schooldays to associate that form of confidence with the Australian version of machismo, which she despised, but her instinctive distrust was offset by his appealing smile and the intelligence she read in his startling green eyes.

She stood and offered her hand: 'Anna Rosen.'

'Marin Katich.'

She felt strength in his hand and let it go quickly. Why was that name familiar?

'Katich?' she asked. 'Is that Yugoslavian?'

'Croatian.'

She sat down, gesturing for him to do the same. 'I've never heard the name Marin before. It's unusual, in a nice way.'

'It means "of the sea"'. He sat down opposite her and leant forwards, elbows on the desk. 'But what's unusual these days? I don't imagine anyone blinks at Rosen anymore.'

'Only at the Royal Sydney Golf Club.'

'Those rich bastards would blink at Katich, too.'

'They don't have bylaws to keep Croatians out.'

'Yeah, well, I can't really see you playing a lot of golf.'

'Strangely enough, my father plays golf . . . On public courses.'

Marin smiled, resting his chin on his fists. 'Got to love the workers' paradise, eh?'

Sarcasm? Anna felt a little warier. No trace of an accent. Born here, then?

'So, what can I do for you?' she asked.

'I sent you an article about three weeks ago, but I never heard back so I thought I'd drop by and say g'day.' He spoke so quietly that she found herself leaning forwards to hear him better.

'A lot of people send us articles. What was it about?'

'Vietnam,' he replied. 'About flawed thinking in the protest movement.'

'Wait,' she said, suddenly remembering why the name was familiar. She reached into the drawer beside her and pulled out a typed manuscript. She looked at the title page. 'This is you then? M.A. Katich?'

She handed him the manuscript; he glanced at it and passed it back.

'That's me.'

'I'm surprised.'

'Why?'

'I had in mind a much older man.'

'Someone like B.A. Santamaria, you mean?'

Sarcasm again.

'Yup,' she said. 'Catholic Right, in any event. Are you saying that's not the case?'

'I was brought up a Catholic. My old man is pretty religious.' Marin had returned to soft, measured tones. 'But I don't belong to any party. So, tell me—did you read the whole thing, or just chuck it in the Do-Nothing Drawer after a page?'

He smiled again as he said this. It was a nice smile. She smiled back at him.

'That's not the Do-Nothing Drawer. That's the I'll Come Back to It Later Drawer.'

'So, did you read it all?'

'Not all of it,' she admitted. 'But a fair bit. That's why I didn't bin it. It's well written.' She looked at him cautiously. How tough could he get, she wondered, if push came to shove? She decided to give a little. 'Now that you've prompted me, I'll definitely go back and read the whole thing. How's that?'

'That's good. But be honest—what did you think about what you did read?'

All right then, since you ask. In for a penny . . .

'If you really want me to be honest, you come across as an apologist for US military aggression in Vietnam.'

'What makes you say that? I don't support the Americans, let alone apologise for them.'

'That's the implication I got.'

'Look, in 1963, the bloody Americans assassinated Diem, a democratically elected president! They put the generals in power just because it suited them better, and that was Golden Boy Jack Kennedy who did that. They're as corrupt as the Soviets as far as I'm concerned.'

Anna felt herself being drawn in against her better judgement. She was still buzzing a little from the speed and had the fleeting thought that maybe the drug was playing a role now.

'Well, Ho Chi Minh led the fight against the Americans,' she said. 'Maybe you should be praising him instead of branding him a dictator.'

Marin leant back in his chair. 'But that's exactly what he was. Surely you don't buy that Uncle Ho bullshit, do you? Where do you stand on freedom of speech, freedom of expression, freedom of religion, the right to vote? Uncle Ho was against all of those things. Oh wait, I remember where you stand on freedom of speech. You've got a special drawer for that, haven't you?'

Anna slammed the drawer shut. 'That's nonsense. I explained that to you.'

'Well, it's out of the drawer now. Pandora's drawer. You should have kept it shut.'

'Ho Chi Minh was fighting for national survival against the most powerful military-industrial complex in the world.' Anna had raised her voice. He was getting under her skin. 'What do you expect? Those are not exactly perfect conditions for democracy.'

Marin let out a long breath. 'Don't be naïve,' he said, marshalling his arguments. 'Ho's got plenty of history behind him. He wasn't conjured up out of thin air. He was a Moscow-trained revolutionary. As for *national survival*, that saintly old coot purged all the non-communist nationalists in the early fifties, so bad luck for them. Then he orchestrated the mass murder of landlords and a host of others he designated traitors with a stroke of the pen, so bad luck for them, too. And all that was done in the name of land reform. Ring any bells? Where've we seen that before? There's no way this bloke was ever going to transform into a democrat sometime down the track.'

'His people loved him, Marin, that much is bloody obvious.'

'Oh, *his people*? Well, that's if you ignore the million of them who voted with their feet in 1954 when he set up his people's-fucking-dictatorship. A million of them moved south. What do you think they were running away from, for heaven's sake?'

Anna knew this of course, but she wasn't prepared to admit that this Katich fellow was mounting arguments she'd used against her own father.

'Oh, come on,' she said, choosing the more complex path. 'Those people were stampeded to run south by a massive CIA fear campaign. You should check your own version of history. The Pentagon orchestrated the whole thing. "Operation Passage to Freedom"—does that ring any bells for you?'

Marin hit the edge of the desk with both hands. 'Of course it does, Anna. But I prefer to look at facts and documents, not slogans. Do you seriously think a million people would pack up their homes, leave their property, their land, the graves of their ancestors and turn their families into refugees just because of American propaganda? Whole villages full of rational people did this. They ran away because they'd seen what his so-called fucking "land reform" really meant—murder and starvation.'

Anna didn't like it when he slapped the table. She thought of telling him to fuck right off out of her office. Instead, she heard him out and took him on. No one argued about this stuff anymore, but she knew that they really should.

'Don't underestimate the CIA,' she admonished him. 'Do you know they dropped pamphlets all over the north with maps of Hanoi showing the concentric rings of destruction from an atomic blast. I've got one of the damned things around here somewhere. They wanted people to think that if they stayed put they'd all be nuked. This was 1955. Ten years after Nagasaki and Hiroshima. I'd have believed them.'

Marin put his elbows back on the desk and leant in again.

'I don't doubt that,' he said, calm again. 'I don't trust the fucking CIA, and I don't like the fucking Yanks generally. But what really burns me up is seeing those kids marching down the street chanting "Ho, Ho, Ho Chi Minh . . . The Viet Cong is going to win." I just want them to think about who it is they're chanting for. Not to mention they're out there raising money to send to the bastards.'

Anna looked at him. Who the hell was this guy? Reasonable on the surface, but didn't he know people were dying? The most important thing now was to stop the war. She looked at the green eyes burning away in his otherwise impassive face. Didn't he know you have to choose sides at some point?

'Well, you might not like what they're chanting, but it's true.' She realised now that she really wanted to convince him. 'The Viet Cong and the NVA are going to win the war, and our boys are being sent over there to die for nothing. Worse than that, they've been sent over there to prop up a corrupt military dictatorship. You said as much yourself. The dictatorship will fall the minute the US pulls the plug, and they *will* pull the plug sooner or later. You must know that.'

Marin sighed. 'I do. I think you're right about that, and when it happens you'll get another massive wave of refugees running from the communists. Look, the Americans have fucked this up, just like the French fucked it up before them. And they're doing it on a far grander scale—'

Anna cut him off impatiently. 'There's nothing grand about napalming children, about massacring whole villages, about the rape and murder of women and children by insane all-American boys.'

'You're right. A far *bigger* scale, is what I meant. But they're not the only ones with blood on their hands. That's the point of my article. Those kids out there marching should have at least some idea about the real nature of the man whose praises they're singing. Who it is they're backing. How all this is likely to end up. There's been a long, long history of murder and massacres in those Vietnamese villages. Ho's communist cadres killed hundreds of thousands of people in those same villages.'

'Oh, right,' said Anna angrily. 'Now you're quoting Nixon. The "Bloodbath of '54". I've been paying attention. Hasn't it occurred to you that Tricky Dick has the resources of the whole CIA to write his own version of history?'

Marin put his head in his hands for a moment and then looked up.

'Nixon will use whatever he can to advance his own arguments. All I can do is examine the evidence. And the evidence is there in Ho's own words: he wrote it down in party documents and directives. You know his famous slogan, don't you? "Seek an understanding with the rich peasants and liquidate the landlords." Liquidate them! That's pretty clear, isn't it? Uncle Ho's just following his big brothers, Stalin and Mao. You know what Mao said, right? "The execution of one such big landlord reverberates through a whole county and is very effective."'

Katich reached over the desk and picked up his manuscript. He held it up.

'The evidence is here—the firsthand accounts of witnesses and defectors from inside the Party, people who saw fresh corpses every day. Landlords with death sentences pinned to their chests. Local people who saw the wives and children of the dead men locked away to starve in their homes. Anyone who dared help them was arrested and punished. So, tell me—if you find your friend is a murderer, how long can you keep him as a friend?'

Anna paused and looked down at her hands. That was pretty much the line she had used herself about the Stalinists. But she could also make the opposing case; she'd heard it made back to her often enough. Who are those witnesses? Defectors, you say? They've got a vested interest in lying. And what about the documents? You know how easy it is to confect documents, don't you? The French, the CIA, MI6, the tsarist secret police, for Christ's sake! You've heard of *The Protocols of the Elders of Zion*, haven't you? Want to start up a pogrom? Just get your secret police to counterfeit an inflammatory document first . . . On and on and on. She'd heard all the excuses before.

In the end, she was inclined to believe much of what Marin Katich was saying about Ho Chi Minh. That didn't lessen her anti-war convictions one bit. So what if his article muddied the waters? They were pretty muddy to start with. All of this went through her mind before she decided on détente.

'All right,' she said. 'You've convinced me to run your article. You're entitled to put these points, to make this argument on the grounds of free speech, at the very least. It won't go in this issue. It's chock-a-block. But I will put it in the next one. Deal?'

'Deal.' He put out his hand.

She reached across and shook it for the second time. The electricity she felt at his touch surprised her.

'Now . . .' she said, opening the drawer on the other side of the desk and pulling out a plastic bag filled with dark green herb. 'I need a joint. Want to join me . . . Marin A. Katich?'

'That's right. Your short-term memory's okay. So, what do you call *that* drawer?'

'That's the Drawer of Happy Outcomes.'

12

THE GEAR SHE HAD was strong and they were thoroughly stoned when Anna challenged Marin to a game of table tennis. They played eleven hypnotic games back to back, a fierce competition that she won six to five. When Marin threw himself into a tattered armchair, Anna was still standing at the table, precision bouncing the ball on her bat and flipping her wrist as she did it.

'Where'd you learn the play like that?' he asked.

'I used to go to youth camps when I was a kid. I was the age champion.'

'Youth camps?'

'The Junior Eureka League. It's for young communists. They train us up in ping-pong, then infiltrate us back into society to wreak havoc on political opponents. Break their spirit.'

'Funny. I already know who your dad is—it's not exactly a state secret.'

'It was very nearly a secret from the state, but anyway we won that referendum. Listen, are you hungry? I've got a bad case of the munchies.'

Marin suggested a place he knew in the little enclave of Middle

Eastern restaurants in Surry Hills. 'If you like Lebanese, it's not too far.'

He convinced Anna to ride there on the back of his motorbike. He kicked the black monster into life and they roared off helmetless down City Road and up Cleveland Street. Anna clung onto him, despite her misgivings. His body was hard under the T-shirt and moved with supple ease as he slipped at speed through miraculously appearing holes in the traffic. She was exhilarated but disturbed at the same time by her sudden dependency on the man and the machine. She would have to learn to drive one of these things herself.

At Au Za'atar, Marin greeted the owner like an old friend, calling 'G'day Mo' to a thickset man who responded with a bear hug.

'This is Anna,' said Marin when Mo released him.

'Nice ta meet youse,' said Mo, looking her up and down with his heavily bagged eyes. 'Hungry?'

'Starving.'

'Is Fatima cooking?' asked Marin.

'Yeah, man.'

'How about the mezze, then?' said Marin. 'And if you've got any of your wine out back, that'd be great.'

Mo clapped a hairy arm around Marin's shoulder and winked at him. 'I'll do my best, man, since you bring your girl here. Sit down. Sit.'

Mo returned, bearing a jug of wine and a comically suggestive smirk, and plonked the jug and two glasses on the table.

'Wine for your "girl", eh?' said Anna as Marin poured.

'The food makes up for it. Trust me.'

'I'm imagining poor Fatima locked in the kitchen. Does he keep her in purdah?'

'Fatima's his mum. He's still eligible, so watch yourself. I saw the way he was measuring you up there. He's wondering how you'd look with a bit of meat on your bones.'

'Remind me not to have any of those sweet pastries.'

'Fatima makes the best baklava in Sydney—let's see if you want to stick to that.'

They gorged themselves on plates of vine leaves, spinach pies and kebabs with hummus, baba ghanoush and tabouli on flatbread. Mo came back from time to time like a dutiful suitor to light Anna's cigarette, to refill the wine jug whenever it got low and later to pour them muddy Lebanese coffee.

'What's Au Za'atar mean?' Anna asked him.

'It means "at the beginning", said Mo, with a huge grin. 'Like the beginning for you two, yes?'

Anna avoided the question and instead ordered baklava with their coffee. They were still talking avidly when Mo quietly started turning out lights and putting chairs on the tables. Disturbed by the activity, Anna checked the time.

'Christ,' she said. 'I've got to get to the printers in Glebe. The paper'll be coming off the presses soon.'

'That's no problem. I can take you.'

'You don't need to. I'll catch a cab.'

'No, I'd like to see that.'

She looked at him warily before agreeing. Marin thanked Mo and paid him before she had a chance to object. It was only when Anna stood up that she realised how much the wine had affected her. She asked Marin to wait while she slipped into the bathroom.

Anna had a pee, then pulled the little vial from her pocket and tapped out two lines onto the ceramic cistern. She took a banknote from her pocket, rolled it up and snorted one of the white crystal mounds, wincing briefly. Her head cleared and the sense of inebriation was gone. In the mirror, she saw an intense young woman, not uninteresting. Perhaps they could be friends.

Anna laughed out loud. Yes, definitely still stoned. Don't be fooled. She bent and turned on the tap, scooped up a mouthful of cold water and splashed her face before coming back out.

'I left a line of speed for you in there,' she whispered, handing Marin the rolled banknote. 'Better go in quickly before Mo finds it.'

Marin gave her a disbelieving look.

'You're mad,' he said. But he took the note and disappeared into the bathroom. Moments later he was back, still sniffing.

'That's some after-burn,' he said, handing the note back. 'Here.'

'Keep it. That's my share for the dinner. I don't like blokes paying for me.'

'Have it your own way,' said Marin, pocketing the note. 'Shall we go?'

•

The ride to Glebe was faster than she could have imagined, and impressionistic. Leaning into corners, whipping past cars and trucks—*vap, vap*—lit and unlit shopfronts, dark shapes of late-night people—*vap*—neon and street lights and traffic lights, accelerating through orange. Then, in no time at all, they had arrived.

She took him into Quality Press through the near-empty compositors' room. Most of the workers had clocked off. The presses were running and their noise filled the space. Two compositors were still there in a back room, drinking beer from longneck bottles.

'G'day Anna,' one of them called out over the racket. 'Want a beer?'

'No thanks, Pete. How'd it go?'

'Yeah, no dramas, love. What about your mate?' Pete held up a bottle.

'No thanks.' Marin waved it away. 'Already had a few.'

'Knows when to stop? Lucky man. Could be a keeper, Anna.'

She made a face at him. 'Where's Pierre?'

'Out the back. Watching the run.'

'Okay. See you, Pete.'

•

They found Pierre bent over, thumbing through a warm copy of *The Tribe* fresh off the presses, his face almost hidden by strands of long hair. The noise was deafening this close to the machinery and he didn't notice them until Anna tapped his shoulder. Pierre looked up from the paper and smiled when he saw her, pushing the hair away from his glasses. Then, without warning, his expression changed. He had realised she was not alone.

'This is Marin!' she said loudly. '*MAR-IN*!'

'Okay!' Pierre yelled back. He quickly scrutinised Marin, sizing him up in a primal way, and didn't offer a handshake. Instead he turned back to Anna.

'It all looks good,' he shouted. 'I'll leave you to it.'

Anna was puzzled. As Marin wandered off and picked up another copy of *The Tribe* from a wooden table nearby, she cupped her hand and spoke directly into Pierre's ear.

'Don't you want to go for a drink?' she asked him. It had become a tradition to sit together in the late opener the Fairfax subs frequented and go through the paper with a fine-tooth comb over a beer and a few frames of pool.

Pierre glanced back over at her companion. 'With him, you mean?'

Anna looked over at Marin and saw him at that moment through Pierre's eyes. 'Yes, with him,' she said, though she hadn't thought about it until that minute.

'No, thanks,' Pierre said abruptly. He grabbed his satchel, shoved the paper into it, threw it over his shoulder and stalked off without another word.

Anna watched him go, annoyed by the show of petulance. She looked across at Marin, who smiled and shrugged, and then went over and spoke to the men supervising the loading of the bundled papers into the waiting distribution trucks. After a while she came back.

'It's all under control here,' she said to Marin. 'I'm heading to the pub to go through the paper. Want to come for a drink?'

'Sure. Looks like your boyfriend's taken off, anyway.'

'He's not my boyfriend!' she shouted over the presses.

'You might want to tell him that.'

At the Australian Hotel, they ordered beers while Anna went through the paper. Then they played a few games of pool, which Marin won. When it became very late and she was thinking about calling it a night, he asked, 'Do you want to have an adventure?'

She gave it a moment's thought before responding.

'Sure, why not.'

•

The stars seemed just out of reach as they stood there, still a long way from the summit of the bridge. Anna identified the Southern Cross and felt she had never been so close to it. Ahead of them, the arch flowed up towards the centre of the bridge, its highest point. The curvature was so pronounced that it had its own horizon; she couldn't see the summit, but the route was clear—a stepped path up the spine of the arch, steep and narrow with low railings on either side.

Marin beckoned, striding ahead. 'Come on, then.'

Anna felt momentary resistance to traipsing after him, but soon began climbing again. She moved cautiously because the smooth surface on either side of the path created the illusion she might slide backwards, like a child trying to climb a slippery-dip. After a while, the horizon changed shape. Anna thought they had reached the top, but then she saw that some great thing spanned the whole width of the arch and was blocking their path. In silhouette, it was a horned beast crouching in front of them.

'What is that?' she demanded when Marin stopped.

'Our last obstacle,' he said. 'It's one of the cranes. There are four of them. See the two over there on the other side?'

'God, they're huge.'

'They're basically giant cable cars with massive electric motors to haul them up and down the arch.'

He showed her the tracks on either side of their path housing steel cables glistening with oil. As they got closer, Anna saw that the horns were fixed cranes extending from the machine's roof on either side. Attached to the cranes were floating cradles, which swayed above the harbour in the breeze and tapped the monster's steel flanks.

'You okay?' Marin asked her.

'How are we supposed to get around that thing?'

'Simple enough. We climb down into the cradle, go past the machine and back up the other side.'

'Hang on—they look really wobbly.'

'It's safe as houses. The riggers do it every day. These things have been here since the bridge was built.'

With that he stepped over the handrail and moved slowly along the back of the machine to the outer edge of the arch.

'We do have to be careful, though,' he said as he reached the edge. 'It's two hundred feet down to the roadway and another two hundred to the water.'

Anna felt her legs go weak.

'I don't think I can do this.' Her voice sounded small in the vastness.

Marin walked to the edge, took hold of a rope and swung himself down into the cradle. He disappeared for a moment, then his head and shoulders reappeared and he called to her.

'Anna, look—we're nearly there. Come over here. No more surprises. I promise.'

He helped her down into the painters' cradle, which was still swaying a little from his jump.

'This time, really don't look down,' he advised.

She did. The vertiginous drop to the water was so terrifying that she froze, fiercely gripping his arm.

'Okay, well, you've seen it. Now slowly turn your back.'

He faced her towards the steel wall of the machine and enveloped her with his body, slowly edging them past the stalled beast. He then helped her clamber back up onto the arch and to the safety of the central pathway.

Still breathing hard, Anna saw that this time they really were near the top. Marin climbed up beside her and sat down.

'Not so hard?'

'Bloody terrifying.'

'I'll tell you now what once happened to my old man.'

'In that thing?'

'Yeah, years ago. There were four of them going down in the cradle and the gears started freewheeling. Suddenly they just dropped out of the sky. The ropes were smoking. All of them screaming blue murder. They fell eighty feet before the crane driver realised the winch had popped its brake. When he yanked it back on, the cradle tipped over and they were all hanging on for dear life. A miracle no one was killed. When they pulled them back up, Dad climbed out, went straight down on his knees and said a prayer. No one raised an eyebrow. Just patted him on the back.'

Anna sat staring at him before she spoke.

'You know what?'

'What?'

'I'm glad you didn't tell me that before.'

•

The summit was a wide, flat place with high flagpoles set in the middle and a metal railing to keep summiteers well back from the edge. They were now on equal footing with the city's tallest buildings, whose signs glowed like a line from an incomprehensible poem: *Occidental, Plessy, Clyde, AMP.*

The harbour below was a relief map laid out at Anna's feet. The white curves of the Opera House sails rose from the construction site on Bennelong Point. She still marvelled that the parochial morons in the state government could have commissioned such a thing. Utzon's dream was so clearly at odds with their crippled souls. Like the products of evolution, it was a brilliant accident.

Beyond the Opera House were islands, coves and inlets. Bays and beaches marked out by phosphorescence on the tips of small waves. At the furthest reach, she saw The Heads, the north and south cliff faces at the harbour's entrance. And, beyond them, nothing but the dark ocean.

Anna felt the stiffening breeze on her face, the first signs of the promised southerly buster. She tasted the sea on it and thrust her arms up high as the cool air rippled around her. The halyards on the flagpoles began to whip around noisily and she heard the distant bells of harbour buoys rocked by the swell.

Elated, she turned to Marin and moved into his arms.

'Thank you,' she said simply. 'I do get it.'

'My pleasure.'

'Do you bring all your women up here?'

'You're the only one. The only one who'd come, that is.'

He laughed and she thumped him on the chest.

'Tell me more about your father,' she said.

Marin stared out over the harbour.

'This was the first thing he saw when his ship came in. The bloody great "Coat Hanger". Ivo was an engineer, so he understood he was looking at something special. But you know how it goes—he soon found out that his qualifications didn't count for anything here. They weren't going to let him build any bridges. Working on this one must have seemed like the next best thing.'

'What year did he get here?'

'1948. He was trying to get as far away from the communists as he could.'

Anna laughed at the irony. 'Now you're fraternising with the enemy on his beloved bridge.'

Marin's expression clouded. 'This is none of his business.'

Anna scrutinised his closed face again, looking for clues. 'You mean you wouldn't dare tell him about me.'

'I mean it's none of his business.'

'But I'm one of those nasty subversives.'

Marin's face opened again. 'That must be part of the attraction.'

She put her arms around him and looked into his eyes. 'That's a big transgression. They're right about us Rosens, you know. We're a dangerous mob.'

He smiled at that. 'Bomb throwers, eh? They say the same thing about my people.'

'Something in common, then?'

'As long as you don't blow up the bridge,' he said.

'No, I've always liked the old thing.'

'Besides . . .'

'Besides what?' she demanded.

'It's not as if I'm actually *sleeping* with the enemy.'

Anna studied his face again. The enigmatic Marin Katich. She made up her mind at that moment and reached up to kiss him.

After a while he dropped his hands to her waist and she felt their warmth in the gap between her singlet and jeans. He kissed her neck below her ear. When he pulled at the bottom of her singlet it seemed natural to raise her arms so he could slip it over her head. He pulled off his own T-shirt and she held him flesh to flesh.

Passion took them slowly to the floor, their limbs folding as they crumpled down. She unbuttoned her jeans and he pulled them off, peeling them from her ankles like a shedding skin. She felt the steel deck, cold beneath her. Kneeling silently before her, he stripped off his remaining clothes. The chemicals in her bloodstream made everything raw. Round steel rivets pressed into her back and she arched up. Still he was silent as he moved over her. She pushed back, taking the weight of him on her hips.

His eyes glistened with the lights of the city. She saw beyond the surface reflections and found him at last, crying out from the bottom of her throat as the southerly screamed across the harbour and over their bodies.

THE LETTER

13

SCHEVENINGEN, THE HAGUE

15 DECEMBER 2005

A TEMPLE GONG woke Anna from a dreamless sleep. She silenced the alarm and padded over to the window. A mass of low clouds was rolling in from the North Sea and she felt the chill, even in the centrally heated room. She called up the front desk and reserved a bicycle, then she showered, dressed for the weather and went down to breakfast.

A long buffet table was set up at one end of the dining room. Anna was ravenous after skipping dinner. She walked the length of the buffet, filling her plate with prosciutto, pastrami, smoked salmon and oily herring with horseradish. She piled on soft cheeses and thick slices of black bread, ignoring as she did so the surprised glances of other guests. She imagined them whispering: *Where does she put it? Does she have hollow legs?*

Above the bar at the end of the great room the trompe l'oeil stage curtains now framed a slide show, showing black-and-white photos of Scheveningen in the late nineteenth century. Anna attacked her plate of food, pausing from time to time to watch the projected images of ghostly, languid women in ankle-length dresses floating under parasols along the Strandweg, mostly accompanied by narrow-shouldered men in bowler hats and boaters. Others rode by on bicycles and in carriages. Fishermen mended their nets or trimmed the triangular sails of their flat-bottomed herring boats. On the beach, barefoot children gave donkey rides to the sailor-suited *kinder* of the aristocracy.

All these folk, Anna realised, even the youngest children, must surely be dead by now. Their orderly world was gone, too. She wondered how many of the children were Jews? Did they grow up in this pleasant city only to be wiped from existence during the Nazi occupation? She pulled out her notebook and wrote: *The past is not a foreign country. The icy blade of memory keeps it close.*

The Kurhaus was Scheveningen's last grand hotel, and within its walls an attempt was being made to create a simulacrum of the old world. Waitresses in trim grey uniforms and orange silk scarves glided between the tables with silver coffee pots. She called on them three times to refill her cup before it was time for her to go.

•

Anna was hit by chill air the moment she wheeled her bicycle outside. On the closed skating rink, a man in felt shoes was sliding around, using a steel-bladed rake to scrape loose ice into a neat pile to shovel off the edge. She wrapped her scarf around the lower half of her face and tracked cautiously across the damp marble forecourt, where she found Pierre already waiting with his own vintage machine.

'*Buongiorno,*' she called.

'*Ciao, bella*, I was about to text you.'

She rolled her bike up beside him.

'Have you had breakfast?' she asked. 'They have quite a spread there.'

'I stopped for an espresso,' he said, patting his diminished paunch. 'Best to avoid old habits. Shall we go?'

Anna sensed that Pierre was being artificially jolly, but he was avoiding eye contact and she wondered if her revelations last night had stirred old and deep grievances. She touched his arm.

'I'm sorry, Pierre.'

He leant over the handlebars and looked up at her. 'It's one hell of a secret to keep all these years,' he said. 'A bit of a shock, is all. God knows what Rachel will make of it. But, look, I know you're determined to get in and speak to Katich, and I'll do what I can to help you.'

'Thanks.'

'My advice, for what it's worth . . .' he said, pausing for emphasis. 'Don't do it. Go back to Sydney.'

'Can't do that,' said Anna. 'I have to confront this. I need to hear from him what he says about these charges. I've got to know what happened. I just have to know. We thought he was dead, Pierre. He was meant to be dead.'

'Yeah, I figured you'd say that. You were always bloody relentless. That hasn't changed. Come on, then,' he shivered. '*Brrr*, it's way too cold to hang about here. Let's go see where they've got him locked him up. It's not far.'

Pierre launched himself expertly into the traffic and Anna followed, wobbling at first until she got the feel of the unfamiliar gears. It was still heavily overcast, but the rain held off. They put their backs to the sea and crossed the tram tracks, heading into the suburbs of Scheveningen.

Anna warmed up as they pedalled though quiet neighbour-hoods of solid brick houses with attics in their red-tiled roofs. The inner streets were cobbled and bracketed by corridors of leafless elms with antique lampposts standing at regular intervals. Two horses clopped towards them and the riders steadied their mounts as the bicycles passed.

'See up ahead?' said Pierre. 'That's the prison.'

Anna rode up alongside him. Shielded on its fringes by prosperous neighbourhoods, Scheveningen prison had been virtually
invisible until they abruptly encountered its high outer wall.

'I can't believe they built it here.'

'It's been here for a long time,' said Pierre.

He dismounted next to the wall. Strung along the top, high above
them, Anna could see strands of electrified wires. Every hundred
metres or so there were swivelling surveillance cameras set to cover
every inch of the wall.

'Ah, this is what I was looking for,' said Pierre.

He had stopped in front of a bas-relief set into the wall, depicting haggard men and women chained to a gnarled tree and ringed
by barbed wire. A date, *1940–45*, had been etched below it.

'It's a memorial to the Dutch resistance fighters jailed here
during the occupation,' Pierre explained. 'The famous "Soldiers
of Orange". Older folk still call it "The Orange Hotel". Most of the
suspects had a short stay—they were tortured, then taken out into
the sand dunes and shot.'

'No Jewish memorial?' asked Anna.

'No. You'll find the locals aren't so keen to talk about that side of
things. They want us to believe the Anne Frank mythology—that
kindly Dutchmen hid all the Jews away in secret rooms. But I'm
sure you know a bit about this.'

Anna nodded. Pierre was right: a higher percentage of Dutch
Jews were killed in the Holocaust than any other country in Western
Europe, seventy-five per cent.

'It should be a national scandal,' she muttered.

'Eichmann loved Dutch efficiency,' said Pierre. 'Like I said, they
don't exactly embrace the dark side of their history.'

Dutch efficiency. That had been the most shocking revelation for
her as she researched her family's history. In 1942, the mayor of The
Hague ordered his bureaucrats to scour the city's records to locate

all ten thousand Jews registered as living there. Only a lucky few escaped being rounded up. The vast majority were brought here, to this very prison, where they were processed and then packed onto Dutch trains heading east.

Anna was silent as they rode around the perimeter until they came to the first break in the wall, a massive steel gate with the address 1256 Stevinstraat, and a small sign: *Penitentiaire Inrichting Haaglanden.*

'*In-rish-ting* means institution,' said Pierre. 'As in, the Penitentiary Institution for the region of Haaglanden. For such a wealthy city, the outer boroughs are surprisingly some of the poorest in the country. There're lots of migrants locked up here, a lot of Muslims. It's a pretty tough regime.'

Anna was puzzled. 'I don't quite get the set-up. How do they keep those inmates separate from the war crimes unit?'

'The war criminals are in a prison within a prison,' said Pierre as he climbed back on his bike. 'Come on, we'll ride around to the front and you'll get a better idea.'

They cycled almost a kilometre up the busy Stevinstraat, with the prison on one side and the wild dunes on the other, until the wall took a right-hand turn, and they followed it around into another quiet street of neat houses, some built right up to the wall. A few hundred metres further along they came to an old fortified entrance that she recognised from the news footage. It resembled the gatehouse of a seventeenth-century castle, with two stone towers standing on either side of a great wooden gate; each tower was buttressed and topped with a crenulated battlement.

'This I know,' she said. 'It's where the reporters do their pieces to camera.'

'Yeah. From that raised roadway.' Pierre pointed up at it. 'When they first brought Milosevic here, this whole street was chock-a-block with satellite trucks. But you see how it is? The gate and the wall block out everything. Some of the big networks rented houses on the other side of the road and put cameras up in the attics to see over the wall—from up there you can actually see the top floors of the war crimes unit. But all the prison windows are blocked, so it was a waste of money, really.'

They climbed up to the raised street, from where Anna could see the roofs of larger buildings inside the complex.

'See the metal roof slightly higher than the others?' said Pierre. 'That's it. It's four storeys high. Someone once asked the commandant how secure it was to keep Milosevic inside a normal prison, and he explained that if Milosevic managed to escape from the war crimes unit he'd find himself still in prison and among the general population of criminals. Not much of an incentive for him with all the Muslims locked up in there.'

'My problem is how to break in, not out,' said Anna, wondering for the first time if this was the closest she would get to Marin Katich.

'You know they don't allow journalists inside,' said Pierre. 'You're going to have to find another way.'

She noticed a malicious glint in his eye.

'Go on,' she urged.

'It's nothing.'

'Oh, come on. What is it?'

'Well, they do allow conjugal visits.'

14

WHEN THEY GOT BACK to the Kurhaus, Anna thanked Pierre and watched as he cycled off, dwindling into a blur in the icy drizzle. The man at the reception desk stopped Anna with the news that there was a message waiting for her and she was surprised to find it was from the lawyer Willem van Brug, the public defender whose job it was to represent one Tomislav Maric.

Anna had rung van Brug's secretary before she left Sydney only to be informed, in a brusque exchange, that if she wished to see van Brug she must make a formal written request 'in the correct manner'. The woman ended the conversation with the admonition that more notice would have been appropriate. Under the circumstances, she said, there was no guarantee that the lawyer would be able to fit Anna into his busy schedule, besides which he was away on another case in Amsterdam and might be there for some time.

Anna had sent off the required email with no optimism, assuming that her request would be a low priority. Hence her bewilderment when she read the message announcing that not only was van Brug back in town but that he was available to see her immediately. She called his office to confirm and thought again about Dutch efficiency.

Anna waited only a few minutes for the number 1 tram, which would take her back to the city centre. It was empty until a group of business types bustled aboard after a few stops, each carrying the same conference briefcases. She saw in their faces the defeated expressions of people whose expectations of a seaside working holiday had been cruelly dashed by Scheveningen's harsh winter.

The tram whispered around a corner into the long, straight stretch of Scheveningseweg. Near the city centre, she climbed reluctantly from the warm capsule onto the frozen streets of the old town, and when she paused to get her bearings coldness seeped through the soles of her boots, numbing her toes. After a brief search, she managed to locate the office of Brinker–van Brug Advocaten in an unfashionable back street. It was on the ground floor of a building that was one in a long row of dishevelled nineteenth-century terraces. Nothing Anna had seen near the centre of the city was truly dilapidated, but she realised that Willem van Brug was clearly not at the prosperous end of his profession.

Inside she found a strait-laced, middle-aged woman waiting behind a desk.

'Anna Rosen to see Mr van Brug.'

'*Goedemorgen mevrouw Rosen*, I am Hildegard. If you will please wait here. Meneer van Brug will not be long. Would you like coffee, perhaps?'

Anna accepted the offer gratefully, a little surprised at the gracious welcome from a woman who had previously tried to fob her off. She hung up her coat and scarf, and took a seat in the waiting room. Soon she was savouring richly brewed coffee poured from an elegant pot into a china cup.

It wasn't long before a very tall, dapper man came bustling though the door and hung up the long coat he had draped over his arm. The man exchanged a few words with Hildegard before turning to Anna, bent at the waist.

'Ms Rosen?'

'Anna.'

'I am Willem van Brug. Good morning to you.'

The lawyer produced the words in an odd staccato, standing stiffly with his hand stuck out in front of him. In the moment it took Anna to put the cup back down on its saucer, van Brug bobbed upright. He reminded her of one of those toy birds that dip their beaks in a cup of water. When Anna got to her feet, he returned to the dip mode.

'Good morning to you,' she said, grasping the proffered hand briefly so that he could spring back to his prodigious height.

'I see Hilde has made you coffee so, please, if you will join me in my office.'

Van Brug moved swiftly to open his door and Anna noticed that, despite his impeccable appearance, the lawyer was still wearing bicycle clips on his trousers. She gathered her cup and saucer and stepped inside, taking the chair opposite his desk. Hildegard entered discreetly with more coffee and biscuits, and whispered something to van Brug, causing him to disappear under the desk. Moments later he bobbed back up, holding the offending bicycle clips in two fingers. Hildegard plucked them from him as if they were something just fished out of a sewer.

'*Dunk u*,' he muttered.

Anna saw a hint of affection in the woman's eyes as Hildegard withdrew, quietly pulling the door shut behind her. While the lawyer took a moment to sip his coffee, she noticed he was younger than she had first thought, with clear blue eyes and the smooth face of a man in his early thirties. Unearned years had been added by his manner of dress: a three-piece houndstooth suit tailored to fit his angular, narrow frame. His rose-coloured tie was matched by a silk handkerchief, neatly arranged in his top pocket. He put his cup down and smiled at her.

'Thank you for coming so promptly.'

'I beg your pardon?'

'I thought I might have difficulty locating you.'

'Oh,' said Anna with a frown. 'Sorry, but I'm confused now. I was told you were away on another case, so I was waiting to hear if you could find some time to talk to me.'

'Ah . . .' Van Brug gazed at her with lawyerly caution. 'Hilde did not mention that. Are you not here to collect your document?'

'Document? I'm here to talk to you about Tomislav Maric.'

Van Brug held up his large hands in a calming gesture. 'I see. I see,' he said. Then he picked up a biscuit and dipped it absent-mindedly into his coffee, sucking on it for a moment.

'Mr van Brug . . .'

'Call me Willem.'

'Willem,' Anna corrected herself. 'Some days ago, back in Australia, I found out through The Registry that you are representing Tomislav Maric, so I made an appointment to see you at the earliest opportunity. To be quite clear: I am a writer and I'm here working on a book about his case.'

Van Brug took a moment to think about this new information, then waggled a long index finger in the air before reaching down into a low desk drawer.

'Then I have some interesting news for you,' he said, producing a large manila envelope. 'Early this morning I went to Scheveningen prison to see Tomislav Maric and he did instruct me to pass this on to you, Anna Rosen. No one else was to read it.'

He held out the envelope two-handed, as if fulfilling some sacred duty. She sat looking at it.

'I'm lost for words,' she said.

'I imagine that is something of a problem for a writer. Now, Ms Rosen, I have more to tell you and I must say that this development was also surprising for me. Maric, we may say, has been a difficult man to represent. Very difficult. I can't remember a defendant who has been less interested in his own defence. Until now he has refused to say anything much to me at all. Except for rudimentary communications, he has been completely uncooperative. Of course, I am still being paid for my work on his behalf, but I am not at all comfortable with the arrangement. I have offered to stand aside, but even this he has refused. I was—what is the phrase?—at the end of my wits. Then, this morning, everything was different. This document he has asked me to pass to you without reading it and I have done that reluctantly. Honestly, I do not even know if I am acting against the law, but I do it only to establish some trust with him. If nothing changes, he will go to trial facing the most serious of charges with no effective legal defence and, no matter what he has done or not done, I think that is wrong.'

After his long speech, the lawyer paused and took up his coffee cup again, watching Anna with undisguised curiosity. She looked at the envelope, suppressing a strong desire to rip it open immediately.

'I will do what I can to help,' she replied.

'So, Ms Rosen,' van Brug said as he stared into her eyes. 'Why does he wish to see you?'

Anna gave a small involuntary jerk. 'He does?'

'It will not be easy to arrange, but I am very curious still as to why he wants to see you.'

'I knew him in Australia when we were both young. We were at university together. I sent him a message when I learned he was in prison here. But I haven't seen him for more than thirty years and until just now I had no idea that he would agree to see me.'

Van Brug nodded. 'I am very interested to hear that. This is a most curious story. Curious indeed. So, Mr Maric once lived in Australia. That, I did not know. I have tried to ask many times about his past and he has refused to tell me anything. Does that mean he may still be an Australian citizen?'

Anna suddenly regretted being incautious. The existence of the mysterious manila envelope had been so distracting that her tongue had run ahead of her thoughts.

'Mr van Brug . . . Willem,' she began cautiously. 'Are you bound by some duty—client legal privilege, we would call it in Australia— to keep your communications with Mr Maric confidential?'

'I am, most certainly. You can speak to me freely. I am only interested in representing him to the best of my ability.'

'Thank you,' said Anna. 'I think the best thing would be for me to read whatever is in this envelope, to find out what Mr Maric has said and then we can sit down and talk.'

'Well, it happens that I have to go to meet with one of my colleagues for a short time. I am happy for you to remain here to look at whatever it is Herr Maric has sent you. I will be back in less than an hour and then perhaps we can talk. Is that acceptable?'

'All right,' she said quietly. 'That's kind of you.'

'My pleasure,' van Brug replied, manoeuvring his ungainly figure out of the office. 'I will close the door so you can have some privacy.'

Once he'd left, Anna stared again at the envelope for a moment, and then quickly tore it open. She pulled out the bundle of pages within and began to read.

So, you found me, for better or worse. I never thought I would see or hear from you again. I imagined it from time to time, how it would be, what I would say to you, but what good was that? I've been dead for so long that I came to believe the world was better off without

Marin Katich. There were many reasons why he should no longer exist so I just let him go. I won't go into all of that now, but please believe me when I say that his resurrection will be painful and it will be dangerous. I have to tell you that I am not the man you once knew, certainly not the young man in the photograph you sent me. I have it in front of me now and I barely recognise him. He is no longer me. I'm no longer him. I've seen too many bad things. I've done too many bad things, the kind of things that burn in your soul like a knife whose tip is searching for your heart.

It's strange, you know, I've just read back these few lines and you could be fooled into believing that a completely rational person had written them, as if all the turmoil in my head can be put down in words that make sense of it all, but that's not true. I'm like that fellow who's trying to untwist the last strands of the man inside him. Gerard Manley Hopkins, right? I've been groping in the darkness for such a long time, Anna, but maybe it's possible that writing this down will help—and this photo, this damned impossible photo, feels like a tiny crack of light. While it does, I'll keep writing.

First the photo. That it could even exist seemed incomprehensible, almost supernatural, but then I remembered that our 'friends' had us under surveillance at that time. The fact is we were never free of them from the time we met. Of course by the time the photo was taken, they were under orders from the stuttering spider. Moriarty. That poisonous creature in his funnel web of secrets, he was behind everything. He was the one who stole my life away. So much of this was hidden from you, but I know from your book (thank you for leaving me out of it) that you worked out for yourself that Moriarty had a long connection to my father, going way back to when ASIO and the Croatian Brotherhood were bonded in what they believed was an existential fight against communism. Anyway, that connection between Ivo and Moriarty was at the heart of everything that happened, the events that tore us apart.

Of course it's more complicated than that. I had my own role to play, my own responsibility in all of this, and if it is possible for us to meet face to face I will make my confession to you. I still feel terrible guilt about leaving you without a word, but by then I was caught in Moriarty's trap. I don't know what you've already put together, but there was so much I could never tell you, for my own peace of mind as much as anything, since this is one of the many scores I have to settle with the world. Above all, I owe you the truth.

Looking back, it's almost beyond belief that the same spider burst in on us three decades ago just as I had begun to tell you the full story. I've puzzled on that over the years. How the hell did Moriarty know that I was there in that room? There can only be one explanation. He must have had you under surveillance.

It was thirty-three years ago. That's hard to believe, isn't it? But I remember it all so well. You were staying in that hotel—The Wellington, The Wello. For all that I've suppressed or locked away, I never forgotten a thing about that night, not a single detail. It was pitch darkness when I climbed up the drainpipe, a cold, rusty Jacob's ladder up to the roof. I crept across it and climbed over a wall into your balcony. I could see you sleeping inside, your face pale on the pillow, lit by the electric clock. I felt like an intruder, some kind of stalker. I knew I had no right to be there. I was a dark creature from another dimension, from a world you would never know, and would reject if you did. I honestly believed you would hate me if you knew what I had become and I was sure you would try to stop me doing what I had to do—what I thought I had to do—to avenge my brother. See, I knew for sure they had murdered him and who could let that go?

I almost turned and ran at that point, but instead I stood there and did the breathing exercises they taught me when I was a kid, the same ones I used to calm myself when I was bent over a rifle. Then I went in to you. I swear I wasn't expecting or imagining what happened between us. My only idea was to explain everything, one act of contrition. It seemed like the only chance to do that. It would have been a last act of decency the night before I killed Bijedic. I don't know if I'll ever be able to fully explain to you what really happened the next day . . . I could have easily killed the bastard, but I didn't. You were always sceptical of things that made the world seem less rational, so you probably won't believe me when I say that, from beyond the grave, my brother played a role in staying my hand. I swear to you Petar was with me that morning.

Not that leaving that evil bastard Bijedic alive did me any good. I was a marked man from then on. I brought the world down on my own head and that was the end of my life in Australia; I was done, broken. Every security agency was after me—and not just in Australia. All this was my own fault. I'm not asking for and I don't deserve anyone's sympathy, least of all yours. I was lost in the wind and I knew I could never see you again.

I believed that was true until today. Now I'm sure this is the one chance to settle my debt to you. So, if you really are bent on coming here, I'll do my best to help you. You'll still need to convince the prison authorities to let you in, and I don't like your chances. I know how resourceful you are, so maybe you'll pull off a miracle, but I should warn you that even if you do somehow manage it you won't like what you find, not about me and not about this place.

I can't begin to describe what it's like in here. No matter how much they try to disinfect the stench of the men it never goes away. This is the place where the 'civilised' world locks away its monsters, although they're careful not to call us that. Even the very worst are presumed innocent, and the UN, bound by its farcical liberalism, confines its alleged monsters in this fortified, heavily surveilled motel, furnished by Ikea. It's purgatory with pottery classes and yoga and Dutch healthcare and apples from New Zealand. Since everyone in here is on trial, all life is governed by the rule of law; or, put another way, this perverse little world is ruled by lawyers and, lawyers being lawyers, the prison authority—The Registry—adheres strictly to a set of regulations to protect the rule of their law. You must think that I'm babbling. The truth is I'm totally out of practice at communicating complex ideas. It's like trying to run with atrophied muscles.

I'm going to the trouble of explaining this to you because if they know you're a journalist, The Registry will throw every obstacle in your way. Those allowed in from the outside world to see inmates include prison guards, doctors, a psychiatrist, family members (all dead, in my case) and, of course, lawyers. No journalist from anywhere in the world has been allowed to meet a single one of the war criminals under indictment. That is the wall in front of you. Not the one built to keep the monsters in but a wall of regulations built to keep people like you out. God forbid the public should hear directly from the alleged monsters before their cases are decided. That would sully the purity of their law.

I want to help you find a way to break down that wall. I think it's possible to do it, but you will have to think like a lawyer and find a loophole in the regulations. I know of one such loophole: Rule 64. You should ask Willem van Brug to explain it. I have told him this may be the only way to get you in. You will know by now that van Brug is incredibly frustrated because I have told him so little. He knows virtually nothing about me. He certainly has no idea who I really am and so I'll leave it to you to decide what to tell him. For what it's worth, he seems reasonably intelligent, and I think he is a good man.

Finally, I will give you one argument to make the case that allowing you to meet me will not interfere with the administration of justice, which is their biggest concern, but could actually facilitate it. I have to admit that my argument is the same one used by every man in here, bar the insane. In my case, it just happens to be true.

I don't claim to be a good man, I don't claim to have a clear conscience, but I did not do the things they're accusing me of. I am not guilty of the crimes they have indicted me for.

15

ANNA HAD REGAINED control of herself by the time Willem van Brug returned to his office. She could not say which of the competing emotions had overwhelmed her as she read the letter: anger, frustration, grief, longing, fear. All of them had combined in greater or lesser parts to undo her and she found herself weeping uncontrollably at the loss she had suffered all those years ago and the incomprehensible futility of it. She knew that the passage of time would have made this so much easier to cope with were it not for Rachel. She had stopped and stared at the line about his family: *all dead, in my case.* Marin Katich had his long-held secrets and so did she. Now, after more than three decades, he wanted to unburden himself. But Anna remained determined to keep her biggest secret.

If van Brug noticed that his wastepaper bin was now stuffed with damp tissues he gave no sign of it; he simply sat down at his desk and asked, 'Well, Anna, are you prepared to tell me what's in the letter?'

'I can tell you,' she said calmly, 'that he claims to be innocent of the charges that have been laid against him.'

She looked to van Brug for his reaction, but his expression was unreadable.

'What is it they say in the movies?' he said after a moment. 'Stop the presses.'

'He says he knows that's what everyone says.'

'*Ja*, that's true, they are all innocent men, even when the trail of blood leads to their doorstep. Did he name any witnesses or other evidence that we might use to prove that he is innocent?'

'Not in the letter.'

Van Brug shrugged, as if this came as no surprise. 'Still, this is the first word I have heard from him about how he intends to plead. It's a first step. What else did he say?'

Anna had already considered what she should pass on to the lawyer at this point. 'Much of the letter is personal and nothing to do with the allegations against him,' she responded cautiously. 'He did mention a Rule 64 and he said he had spoken to you about it.'

Van Brug did not answer, Instead, he reached again into a drawer in his desk and produced a printed document, which he handed to her.

'Here you are,' he said. 'These are the regulations governing prison visits by media representatives. It is generally forbidden for journalists to enter the prison, but you will see that I have highlighted Rule 64, which Mr Maric pointed out to me. It says that you can seek special permission from the Registrar. Now, you are lucky in a way because it happens that he is an Australian, born in Sri Lanka. His name is Prometheus Singarasa.'

'I've heard the name,' Anna said, flicking through to the highlighted page. 'I didn't realise he was Australian.'

Van Brug nodded. 'That may or may not help. They are very strict about their rules. Now I have given this much thought because Prometheus knows very well that I have been unable to get Tomislav

Maric to cooperate with me to prepare his defence. Now here comes this woman, Anna Rosen, and things start to change. You are the new factor in this equation and you may be the one to change the attitude of Mr Maric. So, I have a radical proposal for you.'

When the lawyer paused, it seemed like a courtroom trick to allow suspense to gather around a proposition. Anna waited for him to make his point, tapping one finger on his desk in the rhythm of her pulse.

'Go on, I'm listening,' she said, louder than intended.

'Well, all right, here it is . . .' He paused. 'I think you should join the defence team for this case.'

Anna was genuinely shocked. 'Are you serious?'

'Yes, I am. The idea is not so crazy. Many lawyers have experts and researchers working for them. The prosecution has whole teams of such people. I think you will still need to convince Prometheus Singarasa to allow you to do this. As the Registrar, he has the discretion to do so. I think this is a much stronger argument than simply asking him to bend the rules to allow in a journalist who is writing a book. It will be much harder for him to stand in the way of Maric getting a proper defence. If you agree, I will write to him immediately.'

Anna thought about it for a moment. 'But they already know that I'm proposing to write a book. I've sent them emails about it.'

'Well, if that does come up, you can argue that there are no rules to stop lawyers or even judges writing books about the cases they've worked on once they are over. I am sure that more than one of the lawyers on both sides of the Milosevic case will be writing books. I know for a fact that documentary film crews have been running around behind the scenes, filming during the trial. The producers are not permitted to talk to Milosevic, of course, but some of these lawyers have themselves become celebrities. I am sure publishers are working on those book deals now, ready for the trial to end.'

Anna had begun to grasp the significance of the opportunity van Brug was offering her. It was not something she would ever have considered herself. Her journalist's mindset kept her on the riverbank watching the floodwaters go past. Now she was being offered the chance to leap in. If she said yes to van Brug, she would no longer be a mere observer. She would be part of a team trying to defend Marin Katich against allegations that he had committed crimes so heinous they sickened her. But what if he really were innocent of them? She came to a quick decision.

'I'll do it on one condition.'

'What is that?'

'If I find evidence that he's guilty, I won't keep it from the prosecution. And if he confesses to me, I'll offer myself up as a witness against him. I won't be bound by the constraints of legal privilege. You must accept that.'

'I do. I had already considered that possibility. I will explain to Mr Maric that those are your conditions. The same would have applied, I am sure, if you spoke to him as a journalist.'

Anna jumped to her feet, full of pent-up energy. 'Well then,' she said. 'It seems we are destined to see a lot of each other, Willem.'

The lawyer stood up too, towering over her and bending again to offer his hand. She shook it vigorously.

'*Ja*, Anna, that is good,' he said. 'You will find that I am, by nature, a cautious man. Most people who know me will find this a very—how should I say it?—a very uncharacteristic decision. Even now, I am a little nervous at being so bold.'

'Well, I don't want to exacerbate your nervousness,' she said. 'But there is one more thing you need to know before we go any further.'

'What is it?'

'His name is not Tomislav Maric.'

•

On the way back to the hotel, Anna bought a pack of cigarettes at a kiosk. In her room, she cracked open the window to the freezing mist rising off the North Sea. She sat smoking at the open window, looking around at the velvet-covered chairs, the antique chest of drawers, the unopened minibar and the oil paintings. Her long black coat, hanging over one of the chairs, was the only item she owned that did not seem out of place. The few clothes she hadn't already worn were still bundled inside the Briggs & Riley suitcase, and they didn't amount to much. She had packed too lightly and wondered if, with judicious dry-cleaning, she could make it through to the January sales. She picked up the Blackberry and tapped out a message to Pierre.

Hi mate, looks like I'll be here for longer than expected. If your spare room is still on offer I'll take it. Anna x

Pierre replied almost immediately.

Stay as long as you want! Koppelstokstraat 174, Geuzenkwartier. It's not far. Leave the money trap NOW. I'm here. I'll make supper. You bring wine.

Anna confirmed the plan and rang reception. She checked the time. It was the middle of the night in Sydney. Later she would have to ring Rachel to explain why she would not be home for Christmas. She shivered, threw the cigarette out the window and pushed it closed.

The melancholic mist pressed against the glass. Anna stared into it and saw sections of the pier emerging and disappearing in the diaphanous swirl. Then she caught her own reflection in the glass—a wan face, drawn and anxious. She drew a curtain on this unwanted apparition and busied herself with packing.

Near the end of the short day, the taxi dropped her at what the driver said was the nearest off-licence to Pierre's apartment. It was over the road from the Scheveningen boat harbour, which was still shrouded in sea mist and growing darker by the minute. The street was empty, the mist foreboding, and she quickly entered the warm, well-lit store for refuge. The Pakistani proprietor regarded her sourly, but his expression seemed to brighten when she chose two pricey bottles of chablis. He even came out into the cold to direct her to Koppelstokstraat, which was indeed only a short trundle away.

Koppelstokstraat was part of a multi-street complex of modern, red-brick terraces designed to mimic the charm of the city's older neighbourhoods but failing, Anna thought, the character test. The street was packed with colourful, miniature cars squashed into every available parking space. She tried to imagine the inhabitants, famously the tallest people in Europe, folding themselves into these tiny vehicles. Many of the identical houses had one or more bicycles leaning unchained near their front doors, a sign that there was little to disturb the comfortable lives of the people inside. It was safe, clean and middle-class, and so very unlike a place that the Pierre Villiers she once knew would have chosen to live.

She found 174 easily enough and Pierre answered her buzz.

'Come on up,' he called, and the door opened to reveal a steep, narrow flight of stairs. Anna banged her suitcase awkwardly upwards, silently cursing her old friend for his lack of manners—that, at least, was consistent with the man she knew. She emerged at the top into a spacious, warm and, she had to admit, tasteful apartment full of Danish furniture, bookcases and modern art. Pierre was in the kitchen at the other side of the room, stirring something in a steaming frying pan under a roaring range hood.

'My word,' said Anna.

'Oh, fuck it,' said Pierre, downing tools and rushing belatedly over to her. 'I should have come down and helped.'

Anna put down her bags and hugged him with genuine affection before she detached herself to make a theatrical gesture at the room.

'Who'd have guessed,' she said. 'You live in a grown-up's house.'

'What did you expect—a squat?'

She laughed. 'No, but it's so . . . perfect. It's like you went and got your teeth fixed without telling anyone.'

'I don't know whether to be pleased or aggrieved.'

'Definitely pleased,' she said gently. 'It's lovely. Thank you so much for getting me out of that stuffy hotel.'

'I'll show you to your room in two secs,' he said, rushing back to the kitchen. 'Just need to turn this down.'

Anna followed him across the room and placed the wine bottles on the bench.

'Oh, nice,' said Pierre, squinting at the labels. 'Premier Cru!'

He opened the oven. 'Roast tomatoes,' he said, then closed it and stirred the pan. 'And fried eggplant. I'm making pasta.'

'I'm officially impressed.'

Pierre threw a handful of salt into the pot of water and clamped the lid back down. 'All under control,' he said. 'Let's take your gear up.'

There were two bedrooms upstairs and Pierre ushered her into the front one. It had a dormer window to the street and an antique desk beneath it.

'You can work here,' he said. 'It's nice and quiet. There's wi-fi, I'll give you the password, and through there an ensuite bathroom. Clean towels and everything.'

Anna looked around like a prospective tenant. 'It really is perfect, Pierre. Thanks again.'

'Comfy bed,' he said, pointing at it awkwardly. 'Firm mattress. Look, you make yourself at home. I'll finish cooking. You can give me your news over supper. I hope you don't mind eating early.'

'No, I'm starving. I'll come down soon.'

Pierre lingered for a moment at the doorway. 'Like old times, eh?' he said. Then he turned and rushed back down the stairs.

•

As Anna unpacked, setting out her toiletries in the bathroom, hanging her clothes and making the room hers, a familiar, trippy song came floating up from the living room. 'Solid Air'. She knew it straight away. John Martyn. She had first heard it when she was working in the Canberra press gallery. That was way back in February 1973. Soon after that, she joined the manhunt for Marin Katich, and then he came to her at night in her hotel room . . .

Only a few nights ago at the Kurhaus bar, when she had confessed to Pierre the secret of Rachel's conception, she had omitted from her account that it happened on the night before Marin's planned assassination of the prime minister of Yugoslavia. Now Pierre had chosen to play a song from those days about a friend who knows you and loves you, who would follow you anywhere—even through solid air. Was it deliberate or serendipitous? The thought put her on edge as she went back downstairs.

She found him flipping through his record collection. 'Have you got something else?' she asked. 'I'm not into seventies nostalgia.'

Pierre looked hurt. 'I love John Martyn,' he said. 'But sure, any preferences?'

'Classical?'

Anna relaxed when he chose a collection of Chopin preludes. Pierre threw her a box of matches.

'You light the candles,' he said. 'Supper's ready.'

•

Anna watched as Pierre effortlessly put the meal together. He tipped the cooked pasta into a large bowl; threw in handfuls of parmesan; splashed oil; mixed in the spicy roast-tomato-and-eggplant sauce, and added salt, pepper and some of the reserved pasta water to keep it moist. She knew where he had learned these sublime skills. Pierre's first wife, Chiara, was Italian, a volatile woman who was never far, in Anna's estimation, from an emotional crisis. Given her husband's peripatetic former life as a correspondent, it was remarkable the marriage had lasted as long as it did.

Pierre had been living in Chiara's apartment in Rome when Anna first met her. It didn't go at all well. Anna's easy bond of friendship with Pierre was immediately threatening to a younger woman already anxious about where she stood. Anna was philosophical about it—after all, what wife would welcome the company of a woman who could finish her husband's sentences in his native language, who was aware of his every foible, who understood, better than she did, the experiences and the culture that had made him?

'Pasta waits for no woman!' said Pierre, placing a bowl in front of her and refilling her wineglass with a flourish.

Anna took a mouthful of his creation. 'Oh,' she cried. 'Incredibly delicious. What did I do to deserve this?'

Pierre started to eat, followed it with a gulp of wine and putting down his fork.

'I was just thinking of Chiara,' Anna said. 'She taught you so well.'

'Some things, that's true.'

Pierre resumed eating and drinking, and Anna let him go until it was clear he wasn't going to add to the comment.

'Do you miss her?'

Pierre put down his fork again and took up his wine.

'Things went wrong from the moment I moved us to Zagreb,' he said. 'She hated it there. I mean, really hated it. She thought the people were charmless, crude and rough. And the politics! Well, as the city went onto a war footing—you know what it was like—that was the last straw. She said she knew now what it must have been like living in Italy when Mussolini came to power. One day she packed up and ran back to Rome. We tried to keep it together for a while.' Pierre shrugged. 'The end was inevitable.'

His glasses had steamed up and Anna watched him take them off to rub them clear with his napkin.

'Well,' she said, 'you'll always have pasta.' Then she held her tongue, brought up short by her own insensitivity.

'And you,' said Pierre, his eyes swimming imperceptibly behind the thick lenses. 'You'll always have Rachel.'

'I deserved that.'

'When are you going to tell her who she really is?'

'I better tell you what happened today,' said Anna. 'And then you can give me your advice. I met up with Marin Katich's lawyer after I left you this morning—Willem van Brug, you may know him?— and he may have found a way for me to get into the prison to meet him.'

'He doesn't even know who he's representing.'

'He does now.'

Anna explained van Brug's plan for her to join Marin Katich's legal team and her own conditions if she discovered proof of his guilt. She said she hoped Pierre might help her to set up a meeting as soon as possible with the Registrar, Prometheus Singarasa, and that she felt she should be the one to break the news to him that there was no such person as Tomislav Maric.

'I'll get you in to see Prometheus, that's no problem,' said Pierre. 'It would be pointless me going to him at this stage. They'd just think I sat on this information in breach of my duty. But you know what's going to happen next, don't you?' he went on sharply. 'Every man and his dog will descend on Scheveningen. Every Australian tabloid, every news and current affairs show. And they're bound to find you, the world's leading expert on the Katich family, for fuck's sake. You won't be able to move an inch without a camera on you. And, back home, Rachel will be watching her mother, refusing to comment, working on the legal team of an Australian fucking . . . Nazi fucking . . . war criminal. How on earth are you going to explain that to her?'

'I'm going to call her tonight.'

'And tell her what, exactly?'

'I'm not going to lie to her, Pierre,' said Anna. 'I'm going to tell her that I'm writing a book about this man, the son of the Australian Nazi I already wrote a book about. She'll get that!'

Pierre stared at her, his face a study in incredulity. 'You're not going to lie to her?' he exclaimed. 'Are you serious? Not telling her the truth is a fucking lie!'

'Marin wrote me a letter,' she said quietly. 'Van Brug passed it on to me.'

'Show it to me, then.'

'I won't,' she said emphatically. 'There's too much in it that's personal. I won't show it to anyone. But in the final line he says that he is not guilty of the war crimes they have charged him with. He says he didn't do it.'

'Oh, fuck,' said Pierre, angrily. 'You're obsessed with this man! Do you still love him?'

She saw the naked emotions roiling in Pierre and wondered if she'd made a terrible mistake coming to stay with him. But of all the people she knew, he was the best equipped to help her.

'Don't be ridiculous,' she said. 'I haven't seen him for more than thirty years. I'm still a journalist. I'm on the inside of this story. No one else will have a clue. And what if he's telling the truth, Pierre? What if he's innocent? This is Rachel's father we're talking about. Do you seriously expect me to tell her he's a war criminal if that might not be true? I owe it to her to find out the truth about him.'

Pierre poured himself another glass of wine and drained it with sudden violence.

'Oh, right, I get it now,' he said, regaining his composure. 'You're going to reinvestigate his case, aren't you. You're going to listen to his bullshit and go running back to Bosnia.'

'That's where we'll find the truth,' she said simply.

Pierre stared at her, lost for words. His glasses fogged again.

'Don't expect me to come with you,' he said finally. 'You're on your own this time.'

'Don't you want to know what really happened?' she asked. 'Aren't you curious? We were there.'

'That was thirteen years ago.'

'We saw his funeral.'

'I was pleased he was dead.'

'But he wasn't, Pierre. We know that now.'

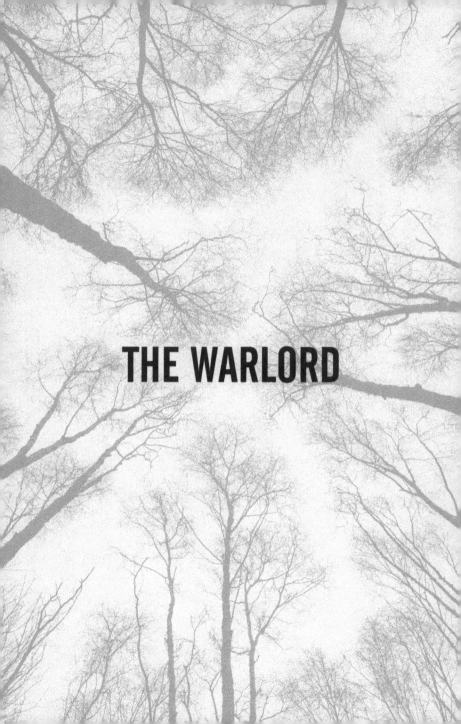

THE WARLORD

16

VUKOVAR, CROATIA

19 NOVEMBER 1991

ANNA EASED OFF the handbrake when the vehicles around her began to move forwards, all jostling for position as they ran up the precarious steel ramp onto the deck of the makeshift ferry. It was really a floating pontoon, being dragged backwards and forwards through the river's strong current by a tugboat. As she came up fast towards the boxy Zastava van in front of them, Pierre thrust a palm onto the dashboard.

'Stop!' he cried.

Anna hit the brakes hard, halting a body length from the van. She turned to her passenger. 'Bloody hell, Pierre.'

'What?'

'You promised not to do that. I hate backseat drivers.'

'This is not the backseat,' he said. 'It's the death seat.'

'Fuck, I swear it's only . . .'

A hard whack on the bonnet interrupted their bickering. Through the windscreen, she saw a sinewy man with the cruel features of a storybook pirate. He was yelling and gesticulating wildly. Anna shrugged at him and turned to Pierre.

'He wants you to move closer to the van,' he said.

Anna was about to state the obvious, but she held her tongue and began edging the car forwards.

'That wasn't a direct translation, was it?' she asked.

'No, there were some references to your mother.'

Anna smiled, even as the abusive pirate continued to yell and wave her closer and closer until she nudged the van's bumper. Only then did the fellow move on to his next victim.

Pierre opened his door a crack and said, 'I'm going to pop over and have a chat with that army officer we saw back there. Might learn something.'

'I'll leave you to it,' said Anna.

She watched in the rear-vision mirror as he made his way to the pea-green military vehicle with the red star on the bonnet, which had been bumped into the second last row. The driver was a major in the Jugoslavenska Narodna Armija. Pierre had been curious as to why a JNA officer of that rank was travelling alone.

As she watched him greet the officer like an old comrade, Anna found herself marvelling, as she often did, at how completely Pierre had managed to embed himself into the Balkans and become fluent in its dialects. He was the only person she knew who had predicted the collapse of communism and who understood that the process had been well underway in Eastern Europe long before the fall of the Berlin Wall.

He had relocated to Zagreb in the mid-1980s and there set himself up as freelance journalist. She recalled that, back in university, he had been obsessed with John Reed, the socialist writer and poet who had travelled from New York to Moscow in 1917, where he witnessed the Bolshevik Revolution and wrote his own firsthand account: *Ten Days That Shook the World*. Reed had been there for the beginning. Pierre would be a witness to communism's great unravelling.

As that became the story of their time, Anna had returned again and again, with Pierre as her guide, to cover it. They were here now because of the siege of Vukovar which, with its terrible reminders of Stalingrad, seemed set to become another pivotal moment in history.

Anna climbed out of the car and walked to the chains that hung loosely across the front of the barge. It was a clear morning and the low sun felt good on her face. The pirate continued to fill up every inch of available deck space, lashing everyone indiscriminately with his sharp tongue as he pinioned the motley collection of vehicles into neat rows. The army vehicle Pierre was now leaning on, chatting to the major, was some kind of Fiat. Jammed together on the ferry were blunt-ended Yugos, a few Zastava vans, a collection of blackened trucks of uncertain origin, and a late-model black BMW with Belgrade plates and tinted windows. The beemer looked sleekly arrogant in this poor company. Anna knew that carpetbaggers would be among the first on the scene after a ceasefire, and she imagined the hidden occupants would soon be rolling through the ruined streets of Vukovar in climate-controlled comfort with a boot full of deutschmarks, cigarettes, whisky and black-market pharmaceuticals.

Pierre's old Golf had also been carefully prepared for entry into the war-torn city. Before they set off, they gaffer-taped a single word onto the white bonnet—AUSTRALIJA. To reinforce the message that they were harmless neutrals from Down Under, Anna also stuck an Australian flag on the inside of the windscreen. As a final touch, Pierre taped a toy kangaroo onto the dash in the hope that the marsupial might be a charm exotic enough in Eastern Slavonia to put trigger-happy guards at ease. They carried a laissez-passer from the JNA commander, General Zivota Panic, but some of the troops they had encountered at roadblocks on the Serbian side of the river had lacked either basic reading skills or a clear appreciation of the chain of command.

Anna looked out over the Danube. It was wide at this point and turbulent after the recent storms. She judged the strength of the current by the speed at which a half-submerged log swept past, bobbing around like a drowned man in the swirling water. The river marked the border between the republics of Serbia and Croatia, a border that had become an arbitrary line when the Serb-dominated JNA, the Yugoslavian National Army, crossed it in August to crush the rebellious Croats in Vukovar who had been demanding independence from Belgrade. Only the previous day, after a shockingly bloody three-month siege, the last defenders in Vukovar had laid down their arms and surrendered. Anna and Pierre had been trying to get into the city for weeks, and now was their best chance.

On the other side of the river, Anna could see a muddy landing where a handful of vehicles were waiting to come back. The high dirt walls of the embankment concealed what lay beyond. Somewhere to the north of them was the ravaged city. Anna thought of the horrors she had seen on TV screens, mostly filmed by the besieged inhabitants, and she felt a shivery, bowel-loosening sensation. She clutched at the camera hanging around her neck as if it might provide strength or purpose, or both.

She had overturned her life to come here, and left her daughter behind in the care of her parents. Rachel had just started her last year of high school. The HSC was on the horizon with all the pressure that entailed, but Anna told herself that Rachel would be fine, that she was a resilient girl and proud to have an adventurous mother. Anna had no clear idea how long she would be away. She only knew that this war, which she had forecast in the books she had written, had drawn her inexorably back to a country whose brutal history she was viscerally connected to. It twisted and squirmed inside her like a living thing. She thought again of Rachel: it had given birth to a living thing! The daughter she loved more than anything in this world.

Anna had stayed in Vukovar once before. She had boarded with a Serbian family during a research trip many years ago. One summer's day, the family had taken her on a picnic to a sandy beach on the Danube. She remembered the father. *Andrej?* Yes, that was his name. She remembered Andrej teaching his young son, Vlado, an impossibly beautiful boy, to cast a fly with a wooden fishing rod. She hadn't stayed in touch with them, and could not recall their family name; but now, so close to their warm and pleasant home, she wondered what had become of them, and whether they had survived the conflict.

•

A burly man joined her at the chains. He wore one of those shirts with a little crocodile on it and she wondered if that was his spirit animal. The man lit a harsh-smelling cigarette and stared bleakly over the water. After a while he turned and held the packet out to her. She shook her head.

'You go to Vukovar?' he said in English.

'Yes.'

'You want my advice?'

'Would it matter if I didn't?'

'Don't go there.'

The man threw his cigarette into the river, turned and walked back to the black BMW. He stared at her for an uncomfortably long time before climbing in and slamming the door.

•

A battered tugboat, its bruised white flanks stained with rust, bumped so hard against the barge that Anna nearly lost her footing. She looked up into the wheelhouse and saw the captain, an unshaven man with the coarse features of a heavy drinker. She visualised a bottle of *slivovic* just out of sight below the level of the window.

The pirate leapt onto the bow of the tug and yelled a stream of abuse at his skipper. Anna got the gist of it—*Watch what you're fucking doing, you fucking son of a whore!* The pirate wasn't about to take the blame for shoddy seamanship. Under the hard eyes of his passengers, he swiftly fastened the ropes fore and aft and the tug pulled the ferry out into the river.

Pierre joined her at the car.

'Shall I take over the driving?' he said.

'Oh, come on, Pierre.'

'No, seriously,' said Pierre, using his serious voice. 'The major reckons there are multiple checkpoints from here. I'll have to do a lot of talking.'

'Okay.' She handed him the keys. 'I'll take the death seat.' She nodded in the direction of the red-starred Fiat. 'Who is he, then?'

'Army intelligence, I reckon. He's not saying, but he has the vibe.'

'The vibe, eh?'

'I know the type,' said Pierre. 'You can almost smell it, like the old KGB cadres in the Soviet army. You talk to them and they always learn more than you do.'

'Did you learn anything?'

'Yeah, watch out for Chetniks. He reckons they're out of control.'

They made the crossing without further incident. The pirate dropped the chains and ran up the hill ahead of the cars. Pierre gunned the Golf up the muddy bank to a maddeningly situated tollbooth where people were forced to fish out cash to pay the pirate while their handbrakes strained on the forty-five-degree incline. The cars ahead slewed in the mud and the Zastava almost slid back into them.

When Pierre finally got to the booth, Anna suddenly sang out: 'Don't do it! Don't do it!'

Pierre's hand stopped in mid-air, a twenty-deutschmark note fluttering in his fingers.

'What?' he demanded.

Anna replied with a loud chorus from 'Don't Pay the Ferryman'.

'Oh, fuck,' said Pierre. 'Not funny.' He shoved the note into the pirate's hands and accelerated past him up the hill.

'Chris de Burgh,' said Anna. 'Prog rock at its best.'

'Just don't freak me out every time we get to a roadblock.'

'I thought we could use a musical soundtrack.'

'Sorry, I'm a bit on edge. It's hard enough dealing with these loonies as it is.'

'I know, it's freaky, isn't it?' Anna said. 'The Danube as the Styx; that pirate as Charon.'

'Next stop Hades?'

'Feels like it.'

•

It was grey and cold when they reached the southern outskirts of Vukovar, passing slowly through the Serb lines. Out the grimy window, Anna saw massed formations of JNA tanks and armoured vehicles and thousands of listless troops held in reserve. They passed vast dormant artillery positions arrayed in flattened corn-fields. From such places, at the height of the bombardment, twelve thousand rockets and shells were poured into the city each day.

'I stayed here once,' said Anna, thinking again of the gentle family and their angelic son.

'It was a beautiful place, wasn't it?' said Pierre. 'I used to come here a lot. The closer we get, the sicker I feel.'

Pierre managed, almost miraculously, to talk his way through checkpoint after checkpoint, employing Serbian dialect and self-deprecating humour to underline the fact that the two of them posed no threat. At the final checkpoint before the destroyed centre, Anna caught a sulphurous whiff of the madness that had engulfed the city.

Pierre pulled up at a boom gate adjacent to the roofless shell of a bombed-out building. In its rubble-strewn courtyard, two men were twirling around on a battered motorcycle that spewed black smoke into the fetid air. The riders whooped as it kicked up dust and stones in the tight turns. A crew of armed thugs in ragtag outfits watched on, shouting encouragement and tossing around liquor bottles like drunks on a hunting trip. None of them ducked when the passenger on the spinning bike began shooting his pistol into the air.

'Jesus!' Anna cried.

'Chetniks,' said Pierre. 'Looks like they've been boozing since the surrender. Hey,' he warned when she leant down to the bag at her feet, 'don't touch the camera. It'll make it worse.'

A man with a hawk's beak of a nose above a thin moustache unslung his weapon and came towards them. Clamped onto his head was a conical black *subara* with a silvery badge on the front. As he got closer, Anna saw on the badge the Chetnik emblem—the Serbian crown and twinned eagles above a skull and crossbones. Bandoliers of bullets crisscrossed the man's chest. A gingery fur stole was draped over his shoulder, an obsidian-eyed fox biting its own tail. The Chetnik levelled his Kalashnikov at the open window and barked a question. When Pierre tried to hand him their papers, the fellow unleashed a long torrent of abuse in which Anna recognised one phrase.

Popushi mi kurac!

Suck my dick!

Pierre responded sharply to the insult and the Chetnik's intoxicated eyes widened for a moment until, to Anna's surprise, spluttering laughter erupted from his broken-toothed mouth. Now that it seemed he was no longer about to be shot, Pierre rapidly explained something.

At first Anna was relieved when the Chetnik lowered his weapon, but then he stuck his ugly mug through the window. As the fellow scrutinised her, his toxic breath filled the cabin. Anna held her own breath and stared straight ahead as he reached across Pierre into the car. She stiffened, but it turned out she wasn't his object after all. The Chetnik plucked the stuffed kangaroo off the dash and shoved it inside his tunic, so that its furry head stuck out above the bandolier, the fox and the marsupial competing for pride of place. Then he raised the boom and waved them through.

Pierre drove on slowly, glancing in the rear-vision mirror as the checkpoint receded. Anna put a hand on his trembling arm.

'He told you to suck his dick, didn't he?'

'He did.'

'So, what the hell did *you* say?'

'I said, Sure, but I'd have to take my teeth out first.'

'Fuck,' Anna laughed. 'That's high-risk humour.'

'It just came into my head.'

'We lost the poor old roo.'

'I told him where we come from the kangaroo is a talisman against evil.'

'Should have brought a boot full of them.'

Pierre drove on slowly towards the centre. He weaved around piles of masonry and the burnt-out shells of passenger vehicles. One skeletal red car had been blown through the window of a pharmacy. They passed a long row of eighteenth-century baroque houses with arched verandas, built when the city was an outpost of the Habsburg empire. It was now bombed beyond repair.

'*Barokni Grad*, the Baroque Centre,' said Pierre. 'Completely fucked. They're killing history as well as the people.'

Soon the road became impassable and Pierre pulled over.

'We could try another way, but I think we're close,' he said. 'We'll walk from here.'

Anna got out, and a few metres from the car she almost stepped on what looked like a bundle of old clothes. Under a layer of dust and rubble was the body of a man. She had seen dead people before and had prepared herself for what she would find in this place; but it is one thing for death to exist in the imagination and another altogether to have it in front of you. The dead man lay face down, his feet twisted at unnatural angles. On his scuffed slip-ons, she noticed the Bata brand. The old fellow was wearing shoes made in Vukovar.

Patches of waxy skin on his ankles, on an exposed arm and on his upturned cheek brought back her earliest memories of a dead animal—a formaldehyde-drenched rat put on her school desk one day during science class. Every kid had got one of these pale, cold things splayed belly-up, spread-eagled, limbs pinned back, ready to be dissected. The stench had stayed in her olfactory memory and she fancied she could smell it now. Her eyes pricked with tears. She went to raise her camera, but she found herself immobilised and cold, as if the blood had stopped moving in her body. She felt hollowed out.

'You all right, Anna?'

'Yeah, it's just . . . He looks like garbage someone tossed in the street.'

'Do you want to go back?'

'His head!'

'It's horrible. Let's go,' Pierre said.

'Not yet.'

Anna forced herself to see the body through the camera lens. The old fellow's yellowish-grey hair ended in a bloody tonsure, where the top of his head had been neatly removed like a breakfast egg. She took a series of shots working around the body, including a close-up of the imitation Fair Isle pattern of his jumper and ending where a piece of metal had torn through it into his back.

They walked on silently. Anna lit a cigarette to stifle the smell of death. The rattle of unseen automatic weapons was the only sign of life. It prompted another childhood memory: of cracker night in Sydney, when the explosions in suburban neighbourhoods near and far were a cause for tingling excitement rather than fear.

An ancient couple came shuffling towards them. The old man wore a beret. In one hand, he carried an overnight bag. He used the other to help his wife, who was hobbling along with the aid of a stick. As the couple moved past Anna's camera, blind to its lens, rain began to fall. Up ahead was a multi-coloured cluster of Yugos, blown apart where they'd been parked. Rainwater pooled in their crushed and rusting bonnets and roofs.

More civilians emerged from basement shelters, seeming not to notice the rain. Their synthetic winter clothes were quickly drenched. Further on, a skinny man, naked but for blue underpants and white socks and seemingly oblivious to the cold rain, was being prodded along by a Serb soldier. Long, filthy hair forced its way out under the soldier's helmet like a fungal growth on a dying tree. Other young soldiers watched impassively. Some, Anna noticed, had surprisingly delicate faces under their shining bell-end helmets.

The rain was easing when Pierre diverted her into a narrow lane. It was full of bodies. Dozens of dead civilians had been laid out in lines, some wrapped in blankets, some in sheets of clear plastic. A man was inspecting them, delicately lifting the edges to peer at one face after another. He told Pierre that pigs and chickens had been eating the abandoned corpses.

Anna stepped carefully around the desecrated dead; to steady herself, she put out a hand towards the broken cement wall strung with electric wires. It was just a lane between buildings, and she imagined it was a shortcut kids used to take when walking to school.

They heard boisterous shouting ahead and soon came into a large square where a gang of Serb militiamen had gathered for a spontaneous victory party. Most had strips of white cotton tied to their epaulets to identify them. As what? she wondered. Liberators? Murderers? The privileged few who should not be shot on sight?

Whatever they were, these carousers were on multiple highs, mugging for a Scandinavian TV crew, which was filming their celebrations.

Anna noticed there were women among the fighters and she approached a sharp-faced platinum blonde with a hunting rifle slung over her shoulder and a khaki beret set at a jaunty angle. As Anna began to photograph her, the woman greeted a tough-looking, angular young man and gave him a long kiss. Then the pair paraded for the camera, arm in arm. Anna thought they must see themselves as romantic heroes, like volunteers in the Spanish Civil War. She wondered what Orwell would have made of this lot.

Another man stared silently into her lens, striking the studied pose of the hardened veteran and taking a long drag on his cigarette. He was strung about with trinkets and charms, like a murderous Christmas tree. He handled his still-warm weapons with fingerless gloves.

Another young woman, not much older than Rachel, rushed over to get her photo taken. She was slim under her bulky camouflage vest and sported a red beret and large-lens purple sunglasses, like a model in a fashion shoot. Her sensuous lips parted to reveal a big gap in her front teeth. As Anna snapped a close-up, a line from Chaucer's Wife of Bath's Tale came to her: *Gat-tothed I was, and that bicam me weel*. Quickly bored, the lusty creature pirouetted before the TV camera, which had bustled over, drawn in by her strange magnetism.

'This will be a Serbian town,' she told the camera in drug-affected English. 'It'll be ours. No more Ustasha. No more fascists. Fifty years we were waiting and hating each other. Waiting and hating.'

When someone put a boom box on top of a wrecked car, the young woman stopped talking and danced without inhibition to a folk tune, swinging a Kalashnikov in her arms like a lover. A man with a shotgun gyrated his hips and green grenades on his belt clanked in syncopation. More bearded Chetniks joined in, including a *Mad Max* extra with live mortar rounds on his back.

One of them broke away and made for Anna.

'I'm from Nis,' he told her. 'Take my picture. Chetnik, Seselj's party. Heard of it? We're doing the liberating. The fucken army's doing nothin.'

Behind the man from Nis, a Croatian flag was splashed with fuel and set alight. Pierre pulled Anna over to the side of the square where three young men in blue jeans and ski jackets sat slumped against a wall catching a sleep, she might have thought, if it were not for the bullet holes in their heads. Anna reeled away. It was hard to think of them as men. They could have been Rachel's schoolmates. Down a side street, Anna saw more bodies lying in clumps, dragged from their cellars, she imagined, and very likely dispatched in the street by the same Chetniks who were now chanting a song under their ominous black flag with its piratical skull and crossbones.

Slobodane, Slobodane, salji nam salate, bice mesa, bice mesa, klacemo Hrvate.

When she asked Pierre to translate, he said: 'You don't want to know.'

She urged him again and he relented.

'Slobodan, Slobodan, send us some salad, for there will be meat, there will be meat, when we slaughter Croats.'

•

There were frequent volleys of gunfire coming now from streets near and distant, and she knew 'cleansing' continued even as the murderers danced and sang. Pierre took Anna by the arm.

'We've got to go,' he said. 'Before they realise we're witnesses to this.'

As they tried to leave, a red-bearded man leapt in front of them. He sculled from a bottle of brandy and threw up a two-fingered victory sign.

'We fight because they kill kids,' he yelled. 'You seen a two-year-old kid dead and pigs is eating from his chest? You ever seen that? No? We only fight. To the last bullet.'

A grinning man appeared behind them, slid a dagger across his own throat and then, egged on by his drunken girlfriend, he put the blade between his teeth. Anna saw that they really wanted her to photograph them—to be captured in this moment of delirium, to perform and to pose, anything for the cameras. It seemed that the blood and the killing were stimulants; there was something darkly sexual about it. She continued to capture these images, appalled by what they revealed about a hidden corner of human nature and yet somehow excited herself to be recording a truth so raw and repulsive. She leant in close to Pierre.

'You're right, let's get out of here,' she said. 'We should try the hospital—the Red Cross should be there by now.'

•

Keeping the Danube to his right, Pierre navigated the Golf through the broken city to Vukovar Hospital, which he knew to be north of the centre, close to the river. They found it surrounded by tanks and roaming packs of troops still looking for people to kill. Pierre cleared their passage with a JNA officer and they drove on into the hospital grounds, coming first to a pulverised wing that had once faced the distant artillery positions. All the windows on that side were burnt and blackened sockets. They passed it slowly, following the road to a cul-de-sac at the hospital's entrance, where the abandoned wrecks of two shrapnel-wracked ambulances sat slumped on their axles.

From the scorched remains of an ornamental garden the twisted black corpse of a tree rose above the deceased vehicles.

Anna could not imagine how the hospital had continued to function during the bombardment that caused this wreckage. Pierre explained that they had shifted all the operating theatres and beds into the basement.

In the aftermath of the siege, the hospital was still in chaos. When scores of family members had come to find their wounded relatives, the military had forced them to wait outside, and now they milled anxiously at the base of the stairs, unable to get answers from the armed men who were coming in and out of the hospital unhindered. Anna had learned the previous day that the Red Cross was negotiating with Serb commanders to allow them to send in a convoy to evacuate the hospital; she guessed these civilians were considered a hindrance.

Anna and Pierre were able to walk into the hospital simply by flashing their media credentials at the armed guards at the entrance. They followed a pair of women in white coats down a set of stairs into an underground corridor crowded with beds and drip stands. Dozens of men, the walking wounded, limped about among the nurses and doctors tending them. The long corridor was the basement's main thoroughfare and its low ceiling was strung with water pipes and electrical wiring. Off to the left and right were makeshift operating theatres and emergency rooms, and beds had been pushed into every spare corner.

Anna found an English-speaking doctor who was busy examining a bearded man in a brightly patterned ski jumper.

'One moment,' he said in an exhausted voice. His patient's arm was swathed in plaster, shattered bones held in place by a metal brace. When the doctor found time for her, Anna learned that a serious problem had developed.

'The army want to separate fighters from civilians,' he said, drawing deeply on an American cigarette from the pack Pierre had gifted him. 'They say the ones here cannot be evacuate by

Red Cross. They say they must keep them as POWs to make exchange for Serb prisoners.'

'But there was a deal with General Panic,' said Anna. 'It was negotiated as part of the surrender.'

The doctor gave a Balkan shrug, suggesting he'd seen too much to believe that civilised rules might apply at this time, in this place.

'You must know more than me,' he said. 'I do know Red Cross convoy is held up outside city. They cannot enter.'

He looked around to see if anyone was listening, then lowered his voice and leant in closer to her.

'Also, Chetniks came in here to tell us they will kill anyone who tries to evacuate Ustashi. That's what they call all the fighters—fascist Ustashi.'

'Do you know any of the fighters?' asked Pierre. 'We'd like to talk to them.'

The doctor looked around in the crowded corridor.

'That man there in the blue robe,' he said, gesturing to a young man leaning on a set of crutches. The man's grubby pyjamas were cut off halfway down his left leg to accommodate a plaster cast. 'He's Frenchman who came here to fight with the city's defenders. A brave man, maybe he will talk to you.'

•

They agreed that Pierre would do the talking. Anna's French was passable, but his was fluent. After a friendly greeting the man identified himself as Jean-Michel Nicholier from Vesoul, a town in central France near the Swiss border. Pierre had lived in Switzerland as a boy and, when he explained that he had been to Vesoul, the young man was delighted by this slim connection to his life in France. Anna studied Nicholier as he chatted with Pierre. He was good-looking with a frank, expressive face, a ready smile and large brown eyes. He had an elfin quality, which seemed misplaced in a man who had been caught up in the most vicious street fighting since Stalingrad. His bright face darkened when Pierre asked him about the Serb militias.

'They arrived in the villages,' he said. 'They killed all the men. They took all the women with them.'

'Did you see that?'

'Yes for sure, for sure, in the small villages on the outskirts of Vukovar. When they reached the city, we had nothing left to defend ourselves with. I rang my mother in Vesoul. I told her: "We need help! We need help! No one is listening to us." The world left us to be crushed like animals.'

'And what will you do now? Do you want to go back to France or stay and fight for the Croats?'

'I'll go to Zagreb first and see if it's okay, and, yes, perhaps then I'll return to France and spend some time with my family because they don't have any news of me. But then I'll come back to the front. I volunteered to be here for better or worse.'

'It seems like it's for worse in Vukovar,' said Pierre.

Nicholier nodded and smiled again, but Anna saw that his smile concealed a great deal.

'It's a slaughterhouse,' he said and shook his head slowly. 'Slaughterhouse, slaughterhouse.'

•

As they were talking, two Serb soldiers pushed their way into the crowded corridor, shoving Nicholier aside roughly as they went. The first one gave the Frenchman a hostile glance. The second soldier—unshaven, angry, gripping a short-barrelled automatic weapon in a tight embrace—stopped and stared at Nicholier before muttering something to the friendly doctor, who quickly came across and told Anna and Pierre, 'He said you have five minutes only.'

Anna turned to Nicholier, deciding to trust her French.

'Do these ones scare you?'

'No, I'm not scared. They are soldiers. I consider myself a soldier. But of course I know there are stupid people on both sides.'

'What do you think will happen to you? Will you be evacuated?'

Nicholier laughed and his face lit up again with surprising insouciance.

'I hope so. I hope for evacuation. The Federal Army are supposed to arrange this. If it goes well, they say that tomorrow we should leave for Zagreb. So, tomorrow I will go . . .'

Anna was reluctant to blunt his optimism. She was trying to think how best to warn him that things were not going well on that front when he interrupted her with a question of his own.

'And you? Where are you from?'

'Australia.'

'You know there was an Australian fighting with us? He was famous among the defenders. He was the commander of a small group who would go out and destroy Serb tanks. That is how we held them off for so many months.'

'Do you know his name?'

'No, but many volunteers don't use their real names. This man had a *nom de guerre*. They called him *Cvrčak*.'

'Cicada?' she said, reverting to English.

'*Oui, la cigale* . . . Cicada, cicada.'

Anna felt a sudden chill that came from deep within her belly and seemed to spread out through her limbs. Pierre was oblivious to her change of mood. He was staring anxiously over Nicholier's shoulder and she followed his gaze to see the angry Serb soldier now shoving his way back through the crowded corridor, moving in their direction, shaking his head.

'Anna!' said Pierre.

She ignored him, holding the Frenchman's attention. 'This man, the Cicada,' she asked. 'What did he look like?'

'Anna! We've overstayed our welcome.'

Nicholier looked at Pierre, confused.

'What did he look like?' she persisted.

'A big man,' said Nicholier. 'He had green eyes.'

At that moment the soldier shoved Pierre out of the way and grabbed the Frenchman's shoulder.

'Is he still alive?' cried Anna.

'I don't know.'

Nicholier's eyes were on Anna's, as if he understood this was no normal question. The soldier pulled him back down the corridor and he stumbled, trying to stay upright on his crutches. The doctor, who had been hovering nearby, came and took Pierre's arm.

'You should leave here, my friend,' he said. 'While you can.'

17

VUKOVAR, CROATIA

14 SEPTEMBER 1991

AN EARTHQUAKE woke Marin Katich. Windows rattled in their frames. Plates, cups and cutlery shivered and clattered on the wooden table. A faded tourist picture went askew on its hook. It showed the old monastery from the other side of the Danube. In his flimsy cot, Marin felt rumbling vibrations through the floor. Across the room the two boys threw aside their blankets and ran to the window.

Peering through it, the dark-haired one cried: '*Jebi sa!*' Fuck it! Fear raised the boy's voice a few octaves.

The lad next to him leant forward, a hand on his friend's arm, with strands of dirty blond hair hanging over his face all the way to his gaping mouth.

'Get back from the window!' Marin yelled, for he had identified the sound now. As he struggled out of the cocoon of his sleeping bag, he felt a stab of sadness. They were just kids, volunteers who'd come in with him last night on the almost empty armoured bus. The boys had huddled together as the bus took heavy fire on the cornfield road. He knew only that they had grown up together and were still pupils at the same school. Their names were Vinko and Mirko—but he couldn't tell one from the other.

'Th-they're on t-top of us!' The second boy struggled to get the words out.

As Marin made for them, the boys turned and sprinted into the next room. From the edge of the second-floor window, Marin saw a huge metal shape moving below and recognised the profile immediately. *T-55*. A main battle tank. Above the roar of its massive engine the tracks were clanking and squealing as one side braked for the fast right-angle turn into Slavonska. Other tanks were queued up behind it, braking and jostling for space so as to make the same turn. Their hatches were down.

The house was on the corner of Slavonska Street and Trpinjska Road, the main route into the city. Trpinjska was jammed with armour as far as he could see. He understood immediately that he was looking at the main thrust of the Serbian assault on Vukovar. The seemingly endless column of armoured vehicles was moving slowly, turrets swivelling as their long guns searched for targets.

Over the mechanised roar, Marin heard a racket from the next room. Boys shouting. A window thrust up. He rushed to the doorway to find the dark-haired boy at the open window, a long tube on his shoulder. An RPG loaded with a conical rocket. The boy was in the firing position, sighting down, knees bent, braced for the shot. Behind him, his friend shoved shanks of hair back over the top of his head to clear his eyes before shouting: 'Now! Now!'

Marin threw up his arms. 'No!'

At that moment the dark-haired boy depressed the trigger and a puff of black smoke spat out the back of the firing tube into the startled face of the blond kid. Then came the explosion in the tube and a ball of flame and super-heated air shot out the back, completely enveloping the boy's head. The boy screamed and went reeling crazily across the room, his face seared by the blowback in the confined space.

Marin saw the rocket spear out of the tube. A forty-five degree shot into heavy armour at such close range was unlikely to be effective. He ran forwards.

Krump!

The air vibrated with the force of the explosion. Through the window he saw a ball of smoke and flame rising above the turret of a T-55 that was halfway through its turn into Slavonska Street. Marin grabbed the shooter by the collar and hauled him back into the room. The boy went sprawling to the ground and dropped the weapon. His friend was screaming, hands up to the blackened, cooked skin on his face.

'Get down and shut up!' Marin shouted.

He crouched and scuttled sideways across the floor, pulling down the injured boy, who had severe burns on one side of his face that had welded his left eye shut. The kid was useless now, and a liability.

Marin grabbed the uninjured boy by the shoulders. 'Which one are you?'

'Mirko.'

'Okay, Mirko. Wrap something around Vinko's face quick as you can and try to keep him quiet. We have to get out of here.' He had no idea how long it would take the tank crews to figure out where the attack had come from.

There was a stash of arms in the room. He grabbed a Kalashnikov, slung it over his shoulder, and filled his coat pockets with loaded mags. There were RPG rockets in an open box—high-explosive warheads, but not shaped-charge rounds that could penetrate the armour of a battle tank. The boy's shot would have caused superficial damage only.

He heard the hydraulics of the turret mechanism as the tank reacted in the street below. They had very little time. Mirko was trying to stifle his mate's screams. Then Marin saw two Zoljas leaning against the wall. That was a weapon that could do some damage. He grabbed one for himself and threw one to Mirko.

'The RPG's no good,' he hissed. 'Take this Zollie.'

'I don't know how to use it,' said the boy, his young face contorted with remorse.

Marin hauled him up. 'We have to get out NOW!'

Together they hoisted up the injured boy. Vinko was whimpering in shock. His face was wrapped in a heavy metal T-shirt on which two screaming demons fought over a bell: *Hell's Bells*. Marin was struck by the weirdness of it. *AC fucken DC! In Vukovar!*

They hauled Vinko out of the room and down the stairs, barely making it beyond the first flight when an explosion rent the air behind them. One of the tanks had fired point blank at the offending window. The shell exploded on the inner wall, taking out part of the roof along with it. Marin's ears rang and his head pounded as he dragged the boys towards the back door. Rubble and plaster rained down, making pale ghosts of them.

The boys staggered like drunkards, but they didn't stop moving. They made it out of the house as a second explosion brought down the rest of the roof and blew a cloud of debris through the doors and windows. Marin imagined the hot breath of a monster at their backs. Moving at a fast hobble, they made it through the backyards of half a dozen homes while the tanks continued to reduce the corner house to a pile of rubble.

Marin's biggest fear was infantry. He expected to be hunted down by foot soldiers, but there was no small-arms fire and he had seen no troops on the ground when he'd first looked through the window. It didn't mean, however, they weren't there somewhere.

They came to an open field and he led the boys into it. There was a stone barn at the far end, a copse of trees and a low wall. He dragged them over the wall where the boys slumped down, exhausted. Mirko's wide eyes were glassy and unfocused. The injured Vinko was silent, mercifully deep in shock. Marin set the two Zolja rocket tubes against the wall, took the AK-47 off his back and crawled to a gateway to look back into the field.

Still no Serb infantry. He was puzzled. Perhaps they were waiting in reserve, expecting the Croats to retreat at the sight of the massed tank assault. If so, it was a bad mistake. Back on Trpinjska Road sporadic explosions continued.

Marin took out a cigarette pack, shook out two and lit them. He put one in Mirko's mouth and watched as the boy dragged hard on it, coming to his senses. Both of them were useless to him now: one was out of the game, the other would have to take care of him. Little wonder military planners valued weapons that maimed, not killed; each injury tied up a number of opponents.

'Mirko,' he said, holding the boy's shoulders, looking into his red-dened eyes. 'Do you think you can manage to get him to the hospital?'

'Yes. They told us it's through the cornfields, back towards Vukovar.'

'Go now. Leave that Zollie. Take no weapons. You see any Serbs, act like you're civilians caught in crossfire.'

'Okay.'

'Go! Go! Your mate is badly hurt. He needs you.'

•

When they disappeared into the cornfield, Marin took stock. He had the two Zoljas, the AK and plenty of ammo. He picked up one of the anti-tank weapons and hefted the heavy tube, examining the firing mechanism. It was simple enough, and he quickly worked out that it was designed to telescope out to nearly twice its length, bringing up the front and back sights. He knew these Zollies were single-use weapons: once you'd fired off the rocket already inside it, the tube was useless.

Marin sat with his back to the wall and lit another cigarette, listening to the distant rumbling of tanks. He had arrived the night before to join the defence of Vukovar, and now, this very day, the city was facing a massive attack. He supposed he was seeking redemption. When he was young, not much older than the two hapless boys struggling through the cornfield, he had seen men die as sacrificial lambs for the cause of liberating Croatia. It was almost twenty years since he had joined his father's ill-fated military mission into Bosnia. He had not signed up back then because he was inspired by the cause that had driven his deluded companions to their deaths. Instead, he had insisted on going as a replacement for his damaged brother, knowing that Petar would surely have died if he had gone with the others. For most of the twenty volunteers it turned out to be a suicide mission; Marin had been the only survivor. In running battles, he had used his skill as a sniper to kill men from a distance. Yes, they had been his enemies and would surely have killed him if they could have, but their ghosts were unforgiving. They never let go of him.

•

Vukovar was completely different to the Bosnian fiasco. The people here had done nothing more than dare to seek independence from Belgrade's totalitarian rule. The city had been under siege and a mere handful of defenders faced overwhelming odds: the entire force of the corrupted central state had been mobilised to crush them. The merciless man responsible for that, the president of Yugoslavia, Slobodan Milosevic, sat at the heart of power in Serbia. Although the edifice of the Yugoslavian state was crumbling, Milosevic still controlled immense military power, and he had chosen to direct it against the Croat rebellion in Vukovar. If the independence movement was destroyed there, he reasoned, it would evaporate throughout the rest of Croatia, sending a message in blood to other fractious republics.

Milosevic's power resided in the so-called Peoples' National Army (the JNA), which was made up of tens of thousands of professional troops and conscripts drawn from every part of Yugoslavia. Its vast mechanised divisions included many hundreds of tanks and artillery battalions. It was a force that had been amassed decades earlier, designed to resist a Soviet invasion. As well as the armoured divisions, there was an air force of MiG fighter planes, ground-attack aircraft and helicopters. Added to this formidable array were newly formed Serbian paramilitary formations, and Marin knew that these men, led by such criminals as the psychopath Arkan, would give no quarter, would obey no rules and would treat Croatian civilians—men, women and children—as enemies to be slaughtered.

Marin believed that the fate of Vukovar and its people was a cause worth fighting for; even worth dying for. He understood that this was the fight for which he had been raised from infancy. No matter what he thought about his father's motives in inculcating this idea in him, no matter how much he distrusted Ivo, and no matter that the old man had succumbed to the darkness in his soul, Marin reasoned that he was not like his father; that he was not, in essence, his father's son. He longed to find in this war the kind of clarity that his whole life had lacked. He longed for a purpose, something pure to believe in. Here he had found it.

•

Marin crushed the cigarette and pulled out his city map. He saw that his instincts had been right. An unchecked armoured assault down Trpinjska Road from the north would soon threaten the city centre. But the map showed a canal running behind the fields, which should provide cover much of the way back to the road.

He had no idea where to find the other defenders, but he resolved to do whatever he could. There was no time to waste. He strung the two Zoljas over his shoulder, checked the Kalashnikov, and ran in a crouch to the canal. Once in it, he moved quickly towards the road.

But as he got closer, a massive explosion rocked him. A torrent of flame and smoke rushed into the clear sky. Marin climbed the bank, lifted his head above the edge and saw a burning tank in the middle of Trpinjska, its turret half blown off. A blackened, smoking creature emerged from a hatch like a charred chrysalis and rolled off the hot steel deck to the ground, writhing there until a burst of automatic fire tore it up.

Marin could see that caught behind the destroyed tank were six others now backing and turning, tracks squealing. They were twitching, as live animals do in response to danger. Their long guns shivered, their machine guns sprayed blindly into the nearest buildings.

From the ground floor of a house behind the tanks came the flaming arc of a missile. It hit the last tank and up it went. Marin heard an explosion and a secondary blast as the tank's munitions detonated, incinerating the crew inside. He registered horror at their fate, but felt at the same time a surge of elation that the defenders were holding their ground.

Then a man darted out into the street and threw a package into the moving tracks of one of the tanks now trapped between the burning wrecks. As the fellow turned to run, the package exploded too soon and his flimsy figure was catapulted through the air. But his sacrifice was not in vain: the makeshift bomb shattered the tank's track and the remaining length of it wheeled off as the thing tried to back away, its metal tread buckling and screeching until it juddered to a halt.

Two men ran onto the road and dragged the body of the first attacker back into a house. Again Marin was surprised at the absence of infantry to defend the tanks. The Serb commanders must have thought this would be a picnic. They had counted on the opposition melting away at the mere sight of the tanks.

'You there! Stay where you are!'

Marin turned slowly, cursing himself for his carelessness: he had been caught, completely vulnerable. It was too late to bring his weapon to bear. His back tensed. Facing his inquisitor, he raised his arms away from the AK. The man had a short-barrelled automatic weapon slung on his back and a walkie-talkie in his right hand. He wore a neat grey uniform. A patch on his shoulder read *Policija*—so, paramilitary police.

'Move slowly, friend. I don't want to shoot you if I don't have to.' The man spoke calmly. 'Who are you?'

'Illija Lovric,' said Marin, using the alias he had lived under for years, the name of an old comrade who had died on the Bosnian mission in 1972. He carried false papers under that name. He could have reverted to Marin Katich, for this was perhaps the one place it would be safe to do so, but he didn't want to exist here under the shadow of his father's connections to the wartime Ustasha. Marin knew that hundreds, perhaps thousands, of sons of the diaspora had come here to join the fight for Croatian independence and he had seen that many of them identified strongly with the old Ustasha, its ideology and its imagery.

'When did you get here?' the man asked.

'I came in last night from Zagreb.'

'The Cornfield Road?'

'Yes.'

'How was it?'

'Hot,' said Marin. 'We took heavy fire.'

'That'll be the last transport. You got here just in time. We can use those Zollies. Come with me.'

Marin glanced back to the Trpinjska Road. The surviving tanks were in retreat, rapidly backing out around the smoking hulks of the disabled machines.

'Come on!' the policeman repeated. 'The boys have stopped them here. The attack has split into side streets. We have to hit them in Slavonska.'

Marin climbed back down into the canal. The man clapped him on the shoulder and stared into his face for a moment. Marin saw no hint of fear in the man's eyes, but he caught a spark of something like ironic humour.

'Good man,' the policeman said. 'No stupid questions. I like that.' Then he turned away, walking fast down the canal. Marin kept pace by his side. 'Name's Blago Zadro. I'm in charge of this zone, if anyone is.'

Zadro was a short, slim man—in his forties, Marin guessed, roughly the same age as himself. The policeman had a perfect Roman nose, bow-shaped lips and neatly combed dark hair. He looked more like a French actor than a military leader—a quirky lead perhaps, playing the role of a municipal mayor during the Nazi occupation, an unlikely man forced to rise to the occasion. The Motorola crackled and Zadro spoke into it, telling someone that he was on his way to Slavonska Street. He told them that the tanks must not get through. They must be stopped at any cost.

Zadro led them towards the sound of a battle. Close now, they climbed to look over the edge of the canal. This was Slavonska Street. At the far end, perhaps three hundred metres away, a disabled tank was smoking and crackling with secondary explosions. Were it not for the burning tank, Slavonska would have seemed like an ordinary suburban street with a single row of two-storey houses on either side. As Marin had already learned, behind those houses was farmland; there were patches of forest and cornfields left to grow high during the long summer. Most of the houses were white with steep red-tiled roofs and narrow front yards fenced in and gated. They were the simple homes of ordinary folk in the Borovo district: farmers, shopkeepers, mechanics, shoe factory workers.

Marin knew that many of the men had sent their families west to stay with relatives in safer towns, and then stayed to defend their own neighbourhoods. Their cars were still parked on either side of the street—nothing fancy, mostly locally built Yugos. In a gap between vehicles, he saw three men crouched behind a Second World War vintage howitzer. It had armour plating around the short barrel and was sandbagged, but it was still exposed in the street.

'Brave boys,' said Zadro. 'Our Borovo artillery is from ancient history.'

The telltale roaring and clanking started up again at the end of the street.

'Here they come,' cried Zadro.

Marin saw the long barrel of a gun emerge first as a tank crawled from behind the burning wreck. As soon as it cleared the obstacle, the tank spat a ball of flame and the heavy body of the machine rocked back on the recoil. Again, Marin thought of it as a living thing, a great beast bracing itself for a shock. The wall of a white house exploded twenty metres beyond the men cowering behind the howitzer. The moving tank gathered itself, fired again, and another shell flew over the heads of the crew into the disintegrating white house. Rubble rained on their backs, but the men at the gun moved methodically, without panic, aiming and firing down the centre of the street at the oncoming tank. They missed by a wide margin and, as they scrambled to reload, the tank fired again, hitting a small yellow car, which flipped and tumbled away behind the defenders.

It was a duel fought with fierce intensity. The howitzer fired and missed again, and the tank continued to rumble towards it, its machine gun raking the street ahead. Another tank now made its clanking way around the smoking wreck and Marin saw that the lopsided battle would soon be over. He began to climb out onto the street, but the policeman hauled him back by the collar.

'Wait!' Zadro yelled.

As Marin rocked back onto his haunches, two men with RPGs on their shoulders rose from the front garden of a house adjacent to the approaching tank. From close range, both fired into the tank tracks. Behind the smoke rising from the dual explosions, the men ducked back inside the house. The turret gun wheeled towards them and blew a huge hole through the front wall. Marin hoped the men had had the sense to relocate.

They had stopped the tank's forward motion. The driver tried to reverse, but it was crippled. The howitzer's crew re-set their gun and fired again into the vulnerable moving turret. This time an explosion enveloped it in flame.

A third tank cleared the wreckage. Two of them now came fast down the long straight road in staggered formation. The brave howitzer had drawn them out and both fired at it on the run. One shell passed high over the crew, the other struck close by, raising a torrent of concrete and shrapnel that knocked the howitzer onto its side and sent the men sprawling to the ground.

'Now!' shouted Zadro and hit Marin hard on his shoulder. As he scrambled onto the street, looking for a firing position, the surviving crew of the maimed tank came tumbling out of its damaged turret. Marin saw a man run into the street firing full automatic bursts at the escaping tank crew. Several of them went down.

'Go!' the man shouted to him. 'I'll bring the tanks this side. You kill them.'

Marin reached cover beside the now-abandoned tank and went down on one knee. He put one Zolja down and telescoped the other into its firing position. The two tanks bore down fast on his position, tearing up the street. The air seemed to vibrate from the tremendous power of their engines and a tremor of fear passed through Marin's body.

He yelled at the top of his voice, allowing a primal scream to escape from him, like a physical thing. The tanks' machine gunners fired steadily to the left, drawn that way by the lone fighter, and it gave Marin a moment to prepare. As he drew a bead on the first behemoth, he was startled to see a tiny orange vehicle come hurtling out of a side street and swing into its path. It was a Zastava 750, a toy car, someone's absurdist statement. Marin paused in disbelief. He thought of the man with shopping bags, who stopped a tank in Tiananmen Square, but there was no mercy here. With a sickening, grinding scream, the great beast accelerated right over the top of it.

As the tank tipped back down from the orange wreckage and the crushed remains of the driver, Marin fired. The missile hit it sweetly, tore through its armour and caused a massive internal explosion. He took shelter as steel shrapnel rained down.

He felt a hard thump on his arm and looked up to see a gibbous-eyed man with a crazy grin. It was the fellow who had risked his life to give him cover.

'Fire and move!' the man yelled. 'Follow me!'

Marin scooped up the second Zolja and ran after the man to the left side of the street and through the door of the nearest house. He followed his guide to the back of the house and outside again. The man stopped and leant in close. His breath smelled incongruously of peppermint.

'Another turtle to fry!' he said, before haring off through the backyards with their torn-down fences. They came out of a house behind the last of the tanks that had ventured into Slavonska Street. The panicky machine was rapidly backing out of the killing zone. The loss of three tanks, all smoking hulks, had halted the assault. But Marin had no intention of ending the lesson here.

He telescoped the Zolja and knelt by the front gate of the house. The tank was about one hundred metres away when his missile ploughed into its vulnerable rear. A column of flame, perhaps fifty feet high, burst through the turret hatches. The machine was a giant Roman candle—and yet it kept rolling towards him. He heard men screaming inside. A low hatch flew open and two blackened, wretched creatures scrambled from what had become a slow-moving coffin.

Marin dropped the empty tube and ran towards them, but his companion was nearer, weapon already at his shoulder. He shot down the flailing men with two short bursts, whooping for the sheer joy of it. Then he walked over to the crumpled bodies in their still-smoking uniforms and put a bullet in each of their heads. The flaming tank rolled on past them, crunched into a parked car and stopped.

'We need to go,' the man said. 'We can't stay here.'

Marin stared at him. 'We could have taken them prisoner,' he said.

'Are you crazy? Did you see what their mates did to poor old Tunic? Crushed him like a bug in his little Fico. They would have killed us without blinking.'

'They might have had intel.'

'It was a mercy killing. You burned them up; I ended their misery. Anyway, no use crying over spilt blood. We have to report to Blago. You know him?'

'Yes.'

'The command post is not far. I'll take you.'

He followed the fellow into the house and they made their way back down the passageway through the backyards. Marin's battlefield euphoria had gone. He was silent, brooding on the killings. His dreams would be full of the screams of burning men. His own ghosts were restless, clamorous. They seemed to be speaking all at once. He could make nothing out except their remorseless anger. Then the man beside him brought him back to reality.

'You're a strange one,' he said. 'What's your name, new guy?'

'Lovric,' said Marin. 'Illija Lovric.'

'You're not from Vukovar, I think. Not with that accent.'

'I grew up in Australia.'

'Oh! I always wanted to go to the Australian Open.' The man stopped, clapped Marin on the shoulder, took his right hand and pumped it briskly. 'I'm Jure. Jure Rebic, from Split. Not so far as Australia. No kangaroos there. It's only famous for a rabbit.'

'Sorry?'

'The greatest rabbit on the tennis circuit.'

Marin puzzled about this for a moment, and then it came to him. 'Ivanisevic?'

'Goran, yes, of course, the great Zec. I could have been his manager, but I had some trouble over a little South American import business . . .'

Rebic paused and, when Marin looked at him in confusion, he put a finger up to one nostril and gave a loud sniff. 'Ha!' he cried. 'Got your attention now. Colombian marching powder works real good in battle. Keeps you running, fast as the rabbit, faster than bullets. You need anything, *anything*, come see me.'

'I've got no money.'

'Ah, money's useless here anyway unless you've got dollars or deutschmarks. You got them?'

Marin shook his head and Rebic laughed.

'Okay. Get me a ham—liberate a good Dalmatian ham, I'll give you a gram. Just don't tell Blago. He's not a real cop, but the uniform might give him ideas.'

'Not a real cop?'

'Hell, no. He's a politician. They made him a cop so he could train up the locals as a military outfit. Belgrade has the army, Zagreb has the cops. That's how they did it, under the noses of the fucking Serbs. Mind you, we're still outnumbered a million to one.'

•

The command post was in an innocuous house on a quiet street that had not yet been visited by tanks. The place was full of men fresh from the battlefield. There was a pub over the road—the Mustang Bar—and someone had procured bottles of bourbon. A bottle was tossed to Rebic as the two of them entered, and he passed it straight away to Marin.

'The Australian first, boys,' he announced. 'This is Illija Lovric, our new comrade. He deserves a drink. Got here last night and destroyed two tanks this morning. *Ziveli!!*'

'*Ziveli!*' said Marin.

He took a nip from the bottle and passed it back to Rebic. There were shouts of approval and welcome. Several of the fighters came up to greet him, among them a big man, so tall that Marin found himself looking up at him; there were few men in that category. The giant wore a camouflage jacket over a Hawaiian shirt and old blue jeans; a black pork pie hat was moulded onto his large head. He clapped Marin hard on the shoulder and addressed him in English.

'You don't look much like no koala bear,' he said in a low growl that Marin realised could easily turn threatening. But the giant only smiled and gripped his hand. 'I'm Zjelko. What will we call you? Maybe Bondi Boy? I bin to that beach. Many years ago.'

'Illija.'

'That's no good. That's any old name.'

Marin thought for a moment and opted for the truth: 'When I was younger, they called me *Cvrčak*.'

'*Cvrčak!* That works too good. We love insects. My little band of brothers, see, we're the "Yellow Ants" *Zutri Mravi*. You join us, yes? Kill some more tanks. Jure is one of us. We call him Rambo.'

•

Marin watched Blago Zadro move among his men. He still clutched the walkie-talkie in his right hand and he waved it like a wand, bestowing praise on one man, offering heartfelt commiserations to another who had lost a close friend, brotherly love to the next, a kind uncle's smile to the one after that. Marin realised his first impression of the man had been right. Zadro had the unfeigned charisma of a natural leader. A politician, Jure Rebic had said. That was true enough, but there was something simple about him. Zjelko the giant told him that Zadro had no military training at all, far from it; before all this started, he'd been an ordinary worker at the Bata shoe factory, but not an ordinary man, as it turned out. He had been shrewd enough to devise a strategy to stop the tanks.

'Brothers,' said Zadro, addressing them all. 'These days will be the hardest. Some more of us will die, but today we have pushed back their attacks, we are destroying their tanks. You see how much material damage they have done to us, but we showed them our strength, we showed them our courage and we showed them that we know how to fight for our homes. These are our homes here. We have placed our flag and no one will take it. This will never be someone else's land. Now come. Come, Zjelko, bring your Yellow Ants, and bring over the Rats. Let's have our picture taken for history.'

'Where's my hat?' said Zjelko, throwing his huge arm over Zadro's shoulder. Someone tossed him the hat, another brought over a bottle of Jack Daniels, which quickly passed from hand to hand.

'Come on, Rambo.' Zadro drew them into a tight group in front of the bar. 'And you too, handsome,' he called to Marin. 'One picture. A group picture.'

Marin found himself welcomed into this band of men whose courage could not be doubted. He felt he was finally home.

'Here we are,' Blago laughed, calling the camera in closer. 'Get the shot. The brigade of the Mustang Bar, the Mustang Ustashi from Trpinjska. Ha ha ha ha!'

18

ZAGREB, CROATIA

JUNE 1992

A SUMMER RAINSTORM swept through Trg Bana Jelacica in the early evening, just as Anna was crossing the square. She paused at a sheltered tram stop, pulled out her little umbrella and silently congratulated herself as it blossomed over her. A tram—blue with a cream top—hummed up to the crowded stop. The number 11 to Dubrava looked shiny and new, washed clean by the rain. It was brightly lit inside and she saw the passengers as if they were on display behind glass, a collection from a gloomy, drab and utilitarian species. Zagreb was a city at war and Anna sensed its inhabitants had become deeply suspicious of one another.

Posters of President Franjo Tudjman seemed to be plastered everywhere she looked, staring grimly at her from the wall of the tram shelter and down from prominent places around the square. The intended message: *This man, you can trust*. Anna found the image both bland and repulsive, yet she knew that a team of propagandists must have chosen this face with its frozen wave of white hair, its cold blue eyes half-hidden behind outsized spectacles, its tight, downturned mouth. It was the face of a strongman to reassure doubters that violence, pain and loss were necessary sacrifices.

Anna had her own reasons to despise this Croatian messiah. Tudjman was an unrepentant Holocaust denier: a historian who claimed the estimated number of six million murdered Jews was founded on exaggerated data and on biased, emotional testimony. Exaggerated! Emotional! She would have liked to put him in a room with her mother. In the same way, the good professor Tudjman had sought to diminish the numbers of people murdered by the wartime Ustasha in their own concentration camps so as to relieve modern Croatians of the need to feel collective guilt. It seemed that every time Anna came back to Zagreb, the urge to deny, to forget and to rewrite history had become stronger.

Throughout the square, the red, white and blue flags with the chequerboard emblem, once so dearly embraced by the Ustasha, hung damp on high poles. In the crisp light above the flow of black umbrellas, and above the crisscross of electric tram wires, Anna read the neon signs high on the baroque buildings that walled in the open space—Kerametat, Kras, Varteks, Chromos, Zagrebacka Banka, Kuca, Evropska Moda. The signs seemed to have their own significance. Money was flowing into this newly declared independent state. A giant screen on the Chromos building advertised in psychedelic colours the eight million Kuna lottery. Anna felt she understood the subliminal message: money will flow to all you citizens, as if via a drip-feed, provided we all embrace the helpful mafia, which has agreed to control the flow of capital.

Anna felt the beat of corruption like the pulse of the city. On the way here she had passed the crass steel-and-glass structure of the Hotel Dubrovnik and found the street outside it packed with new-model black beemers. Hulking black-suited drivers and bodyguards gathered close to the vehicles, smoking and gossiping as their bosses caroused inside.

She was early for her meeting with Pierre and decided to stop for an aperitif at a bar with a dripping outdoor awning. A young, black-eyed waiter, his dark hair in a crew cut with a geometrically correct flat top, fiddled with his bow tie as he apologised. They were not serving out here in the rain, but by all means sit. She did so with a small display of petulance and pulled out her notepad.

In front of her, in the centre of the square, was the statue of a horseman in a hussar's outfit, sword upraised. Floodlit in the rain, man and beast shone a slick silvery-grey and were reflected in pools on the ground, swirling in a neon rainbow. Anna knew the horseman to be Ban Jelacic, the nineteenth-century nationalist for whom the square was now named and she was fascinated to make his acquaintance. The last time she was here the horseman had been conspicuously absent and the square called Trg Republike. That had been the case since 1947, when the communists tore the statue out like a rotten tooth and denounced Ban Jelacic as 'a servant of foreign interests'.

When the newly elected President Tudjman had declared Croatia's independence less than two years ago, he brought Ban Jelacic galloping back into the square to ride forevermore on his granite plinth into the bright, autonomous future he had dreamed of for Croatia but failed to achieve. The Ustasha had briefly achieved the dream of an independent state with Hitler's help, but it collapsed along with the Third Reich. And now came Tudjman. Anna imagined a time in the not-too-distant future when statues of the revanchist historian would be erected in the squares and plazas of Zagreb—no horse, no sword, nothing anachronistic, but swathed perhaps in the handmade Italian suits preferred by populist demagogues.

As the rain began to ease, a gang of youths ran hooting across the square. They were dressed in the exported costume of young black Americans—baggy singlets, basketball shorts hanging down past their knees and oversized trainers. All orange and black, they skipped between the arriving and departing trams.

Anna noticed the giant screen had changed to an ad for cigarettes featuring *Hravatskoi Sam* as the indigenous Joe Camel. She made a note to herself about the intersection between globalism and nationalism and got up to leave, reflecting grimly that she had agreed to meet Pierre at the Sheraton's American Bar.

•

Anna took a seat at the bar as the night's entertainers were setting up in the corner. The sign on the bass drum read: *Domingo—The Band.* They were tuning up by the time Pierre slid onto a stool beside her and she nodded at the retro-garbed players, raising her eyebrows at him.

'It seemed like the most convenient place,' Pierre said defensively. 'I'd have asked you to the apartment, but Chiara . . .'

'What?'

'She's convinced we have a past.'

'We do,' said Anna. 'Just not the one she imagines. Is this going to be a problem?'

'It's her problem.'

'We'll be away for a while. She's okay with that?'

'This is what I do,' Pierre said dismissively. 'I can't pick and choose who I work for based on her paranoia. Let's have a drink.' He ordered beers with *slivovic* chasers.

It had been seven months since she and Pierre had ventured into Vukovar. Anna had gone home to her daughter and her safe life in Sydney where she had endured terrible memories and nagging thoughts about the large, green-eyed Australian who called himself The Cicada. A week ago, Pierre had called her with news that a man answering that description with the same *nom de guerre* was now in command of a large militia of Croat and Muslim fighters, and in control of a swathe of strategically vital territory west of the besieged city of Mostar. It had not been hard to convince her editor to send her back.

Anna tossed down the liquor and asked: 'Have you heard anything new?'

Pierre winced, as if the question contained an implied rebuke. 'Your pimpernel is damned elusive,' he replied. 'Not a single picture of him that I've been able to find. What's confirmed is that he goes by *Cvrčak*, he's a big man and he's got green eyes.'

'It's got to be him, hasn't it?'

'I haven't found anyone who says he's Australian, but I wouldn't have let you come all this way if I didn't think it was likely. How's my goddaughter, by the way? She's doing the HSC this year, isn't she?'

'Rachel sends her love. She's staying with my dad. She loves being with him,' said Anna, aware that she was the one who sounded defensive now. 'Rach'll be fine . . . So, what's the plan?'

'I've found someone who's agreed to help us. You'll have to pay him a modest fee.'

'Shit,' said Anna. She hated sounding like a penny-pinching freelancer, but she was already paying Pierre a daily rate and even though Leon had agreed to fund the trip, the magazine operated on the thinnest of margins and she was restricted to a shoestring budget. On the other hand, she knew that false economies in a warzone could put lives at risk. If she had to dip into her own pocket she would do that, and argue the toss with Leon later.

'Who is he?'

'Adin Genjac, he's a local journo,' said Pierre, all business now. 'Works in Mostar for *Oslobodjenje*.'

This was a positive. Anna knew the paper's reputation for fearless reporting. It was being published daily from a nuclear fallout shelter close to the frontlines in Sarajevo.

'All right,' she said. 'How well do you know him?'

'Mostly by reputation. I've met him once or twice. He's smart, he's funny, but the downside is we're going to have to go to Mostar and pick him up.'

'You can still get in?'

Pierre nodded. 'You can from the south, yeah.'

'There's a "but", right?'

'The Serbs are still shelling the shit out of the place.'

'Why do we need Genjac?'

'He has an in,' said Pierre. 'He knows some of the Muslims fighting with The Cicada's outfit, and he's a mate of the military commander in Mostar. He also knows where to find them and the safest way to get there. That's something I just can't do for you, Anna. The roads are dangerous, the situation's fluid. The lines are shifting all the time. We need local knowledge.'

'Okay, I get it,' said Anna. 'Let's book him.'

Pierre smiled at that. 'I already did,' he said, without a trace of embarrassment.

Anna knew better than to be annoyed at Pierre's presumption. She trusted his judgement and, still affected by jet lag, she was relieved that he had accomplished so much while she was travelling.

'Good one,' she said. 'When do you want to leave?'

'Tomorrow morning. We'll drive south, head down the coast to Split, overnight there, and then up to Mostar the next morning. Can you be ready to go at 5 am?'

'Of course.'

'That was never your strong suit.'

'You've got it the wrong way round,' Anna replied with feeling. 'The short-term memory loss must have been permanent.'

Pierre didn't laugh but instead stared hard at her. 'One thing I never forgot is how big a fuckwit Marin Katich is. Are you sure you want to go through with this? Last chance to back out.'

'Are you serious? I twisted Leon's arm to pay for this trip. An Australian warlord with his own army in Bosnia? That's a big story if we can make it stand up.'

'I can see the front cover,' Pierre drew his thumb and forefinger in a straight line through the air. 'Anna Rosen's *Heart of Darkness*: A Love Story.'

'Give it a rest, Pierre.'

'Mistah Katich, he dead,' he responded with an inappropriate grin.

Anna felt like knocking him off his stool, but then the band started up noisily with an ABBA song, in which a fellow called Fernando was asked repeatedly if he could hear the distant drums and if he remembered the roar of guns and cannons. The singer was terrified, but ready to die if she had to.

Pierre began to sing along, laughing like an idiot. Finally caught up by his infectious mood, Anna joined in.

•

They made it to Split late afternoon the following day, settled into the simple hotel Pierre used whenever he visited the Adriatic port town, and went out for a meal at the Boban restaurant. They were shown to an outdoor table overlooking the harbour under a bruised purple sunset.

'Boban,' said Anna. 'The name's familiar.'

'It should be,' said Pierre. He paused to ask the waiter for a bottle of wine, before leaning in to talk quietly. 'The place was named in honour of Rafael Boban, commander of Pavelic's Black Legion. There's a lot of nostalgia for the Ustasha these days. That's why I booked here. We might learn something. Also, the seafood is pretty amazing.'

Their waiter was a short, thickset man wearing a white apron. His name was Davor, as Pierre elicited when he returned with an unlabelled bottle of local white. After a brief discussion,

Davor returned with a plate of fresh fish and when Pierre chose the flounder-like rombo Davor congratulated him on his good judgement.

'This'll be something,' said Pierre. 'They do it in a wood-fired oven.'

'I guess we can put up with this,' said Anna, pouring wine for each of them. 'In the interests of research.'

The restaurant was full. While there were a few other women in the room, the clientele were mostly men, flashily dressed, loud and unrestrained in their machismo.

'It's owned by a Canadian Croat,' Pierre explained. 'There're a lot of people returning from the diaspora with dollars and deutsch-marks, especially here on the coast. They're buying up everything they can while prices are at rock bottom. A lot of the local Croats are seriously pissed off. They've got no money and these rich fuckers are flooding back like they own the place, which they will soon enough. Not to mention they're the ones who've kept the Ustasha legacy alive.'

'You're saying the Katich family would have fitted right in?'

'I'm saying if Marin Katich is commanding a militia a few hours north of here, the money's got to come from somewhere, right?'

It took some time before Davor returned, carrying a cast-iron pan with a heavy lid. He laid it on the table, removed the lid with a magician's flourish and a rich aroma rose with the steam. The rombo was in a mixture of garlic, potatoes and vegetables and some kind of spiced stock. As Davor filleted and de-boned the fish, he proudly described how it had cooked slowly in the pan, buried under red-hot cinders.

'Eat, eat,' he encouraged them when he was done. 'Enjoy.'

'Perhaps you'll have a drink with us later, Davor?' Pierre asked. 'Tell us the secret recipe.'

'Sure, sure—drink, yes,' said Davor, beaming. 'Secrets, no.'

Anna had rarely tasted anything so delicious, but she couldn't stop herself looking around and speculating on the nature of her fellow diners. They reminded her of the carpetbagger she'd run into on the Vukovar ferry, men who saw opportunities in a war that brought despair to the many. At the end of the meal, Davor brought to the table a bottle of herb-infused liqueur and Pierre convinced him to join them.

'Just one,' the waiter agreed, pulling up a chair. 'I have much to do before I can go home.'

'We're driving to Mostar in the morning,' said Pierre.

'Oh,' cried Davor. 'Then I should leave you with this bottle.'

'Good idea,' said Pierre, draining and refilling his glass. 'What have you heard?'

'Same as everyone,' said Davor. 'Serbs are bombing the city to rubble. Just like in Sarajevo, but no one is watching. Many people are dying, Croats and Muslims together. You will see. Maybe you will die if you go there.' He paused, sipped his drink and looked at Anna. 'Best pray to God. It is not a place for women.'

'I'm looking for a man I once knew,' said Anna abruptly. 'A Croat from Australia. He is fighting against the Serbs. They call him *Cvrčak*.'

Davor looked at her with undisguised curiosity. 'A man you once knew,' he repeated. 'And for this you risk your life?'

Pierre went to interrupt, but Anna put a hand on his arm to stop him as she held Davor's gaze. 'Do you know about him?'

Davor shifted uncomfortably. 'I can't help you,' he said and began to get up from the table.

'Do you know anyone who can?'

Davor paused and lowered his voice. 'The men at the table behind me. You could ask them, but they may not want to answer your questions. You should be careful.'

With that, the waiter stood up, cleared the remaining plates from their table and retreated to the kitchen. Anna looked over at what was now the only other occupied table in the restaurant. She had noticed that the two older men—in their sixties, she guessed—had been drinking steadily since they finished their meal and were locked in a passionate discussion. One of them, in particular, caught her attention because of his antique eyewear: a tortoise-shell frame with flipped-up blue sun-lenses. The man's lean, heavily lined face was darkly tanned and she imagined him spending long days in a poolside deckchair issuing orders to subordinates. The other, smoking a cigar he occasionally dipped into a liquor glass, was equally dark-skinned. He was a broken-faced, thickset fellow with a large gold crucifix sitting on his smooth chest inside an open shirt. Davor need not have warned her to be cautious. They were a dangerous-looking pair.

'Let me speak to them,' said Pierre.

'I'll come with you,' said Anna.

'Trust me this once, will you, Anna? Fellows like this have only one idea about women.'

'I don't give a rat's what—'

'I know you don't,' Pierre cut in. 'Look, you already gave the waiter a hint that this is personal. If these fellows are "connected", and Davor seems to think they are, how long do you think it would take for the news to reach the great *General* that his girlfriend from Australia is on the way up the mountain to meet up with him on the frontlines. You'll be a legend before you get anywhere near him, like some tragic character from a gypsy love song.'

'Christ, Pierre,' Anna said, her face red with indignation. 'Why don't you tell me what you really think?'

'I think you should go back to the hotel,' he said. 'Wait up for me. I'll see what I can find out from these fuckers.'

•

Anna left the Boban in a belligerent mood. She ignored Pierre's advice and headed to the harbour. It was a hot, still night and she wanted to find a place to swim, or at least to walk off her anger. She understood Pierre had a point about the old fascists at the restaurant. Probable fascists, she should say. But his suggestive jibes were starting to get on her nerves. Keeping the secret of her daughter's conception from her old friend had become a burden and she realised it may have been a mistake. She was sure Pierre would think and behave differently if he knew why she was so determined to track down Marin Katich.

She was asking a great deal of him, she knew that. After all, Pierre was putting his own life at risk and he didn't really know why; that was unfair. But while Rachel herself had no idea who her father was, Anna still felt she could not tell Pierre the truth about her motives. The promise she had held out to her editor of a powerful, revelatory story about an Australian militia commander in a hot zone of the Bosnian war would have to be enough for him, too.

She came out from a lane between some old buildings and found herself on the harbour promenade under a line of tall palm trees. It was well lit but eerily empty for a place that, were it not for the war, would have been full of tourists now, in early summer. She passed a moored yacht and caught the unmistakable sweet scent of marijuana.

On the brightly lit stern, a group of young people were smoking, drinking and laughing. One man in that company, puffing happily on a joint, leant over the rails and gestured to her, calling out in French that she should come aboard and join the party. The town is dead, he kept repeating—*C'est morte*—there's nothing to do here, nothing, come and have some fun. When Anna turned him down, he smiled wistfully and gave a sad, theatrical bow.

As she walked along the dark, empty docks, Anna found herself thinking about her would-be suitor on the yacht. His voice and manner had reminded her of Jean-Michel Nicholier, the young Frenchman she and Pierre had met in the bowels of Vukovar Hospital. Despite a negotiated agreement, the Serbs had refused to allow the Red Cross to evacuate wounded prisoners of war. Having told Anna about the Australian comrade who called himself *Cvrčak*—the Cicada—Nicholier was dragged away on his crutches by the Serb irregulars. Anna had reported his arrest to the Red Cross and made regular inquiries about the young Frenchman ever since. Only a few weeks ago, she had learned that his body had been found in a mass grave. Nicholier had been rounded up with three hundred other wounded men in the hospital who the Serbs identified as having fought with the city's Croat defenders. They were taken to a place called Ovcara, a farm in the southern outskirts of Vukovar. Left in the custody of paramilitaries, the men were systematically beaten, then split into smaller groups and shot. Their bodies were bulldozed into the earth.

Following the coastline immediately south of the docks, Anna found herself on a small empty beach. Thinking about the young Frenchman had filled her with sadness, and she thought a swim might wash some of it away. She made sure that she was really alone, stripped off her clothes and stroked out into the deep water as she liked to do at home. She swam until the harbour city was reduced to distant lights, then rolled onto her back and looked up at the stars. Floating there in the warm, velvety sea, she found herself blissfully suspended in a peaceful moment between the tormenting mysteries of her past and the dangerous path she was about to follow. But when her thoughts turned inevitably to Rachel, tears filled her eyes, and she turned and swam back to the shore.

•

When the sun rose the next morning, Split was far behind them and they were driving up into the mountains, whose limestone karst skeleton was a high wall between Croatia and Bosnia. Since she and Pierre had set off in the pre-dawn darkness, there had been a chilly silence in the car.

This was a hangover from the ill-tempered confrontation between them when Anna had returned to the hotel close to midnight. After she tapped lightly on Pierre's door, it had flown open.

'Where the hell have you been?' he blustered, wide-eyed with rage. 'I've been worried sick!'

Anna knew that Pierre's agitation mostly arose from his concern for her safety, but his opening line pressed too many buttons. 'For fuck's sake,' she cried. 'If I'd wanted a fucking husband, I would have married one.'

'You could have left me a note.'

'I didn't come back to the hotel, Pierre. I went for a swim.'

'Anything could have happened to you. How would I know?'

'You don't need to know what I'm doing.'

'There's been a lot of nasty shit happening in this town.'

Anna dropped her gaze and unclenched her fists, deliberately calming herself. 'Look, Pierre, I've been taking care of myself for over forty years. You were talking to those old Ustashi, or whatever they were. I admit I was annoyed when you told me to go back to the hotel, so I went for a swim, that's all.' Anna gathered herself then and asked in a quieter voice, 'Did they tell you anything?'

Pierre had smoothed his frazzled hair, stood back from the door and gestured for her to come in. 'I only got one thing,' he said, sitting on the edge of his bed. 'They didn't want to talk about The Cicada, claimed not to know anything much about him, except to say that they are hugely pissed off that he's fighting alongside the Muslims. They couldn't help themselves. It was obvious in the end that the Croat nationalists want that part of Bosnia for themselves. They hate the Muslims as much as the Serbs. If it was up to these guys, they'd be at war with both of them.'

•

Pierre was now motoring fast through switchbacks, climbing up and up the empty mountain road. Every now and then, they saw signs that normal life continued, as Anna knew it inevitably did, even close to catastrophic conflicts. An old woman in a headscarf, carrying a hoe on her shoulder, stopped and watched blankly as they passed. A draughthorse grazed beside the road. Tall, conical haystacks, propped up like tepees with long sticks, stood in patches of farmland. A cart carried men collecting firewood; one sat grimly atop the woodpile. Minarets rose like sentinels above many small settlements. In one village, an Orthodox church, intact on the outside, had been stripped and left as a shell while, nearby, blue smoke rose from an open-sided hut in which a man in shorts and a singlet tended a spitted lamb over glowing coals. From time to time, they saw children on the side of the road holding out jars of wild berries.

'We should get some,' said Anna as Pierre shot past them.

'I can't turn around,' he said irritably.

But Pierre stopped dutifully at the next village and they bought jars of blackberries and raspberries picked from the forest. Anna threw a handful of raspberries into her mouth, too many, and a thin line of red juice ran down from the corner of her lips. The children laughed at her comically bad manners, but when she dabbed the juice away with a white handkerchief it looked blood-stained and she thrust it quickly into her pocket. Pierre watched this small sequence and said to her gently, 'Don't worry. It's not an omen.'

•

They knew they were close to Mostar when they began to come across abandoned villages; then roadblocks appeared, manned by armed Muslim soldiers wearing patches of the army of the Republic of Bosnia and Herzegovina. At each checkpoint from then on they were guided to the next with warnings that the Serbs were close by, that sometimes the road was shelled, sometimes there were snipers. Sometimes people died randomly. Large signs taped on the bonnet and windows of Pierre's grimy old Golf identified them as journalists, but they both knew that these were mere talismans; they offered no guarantee of protection.

Then, without warning, they found themselves looking down on the city. Mostar was hunched below them, seemingly defenceless against any armed force that held these heights securely enough to plant artillery batteries. The buildings were so ravaged by the shelling that on this quiet, clear morning they appeared to Anna tremulous and vulnerable.

Pierre knew the city well enough to get them quickly to the sandbagged building in which Adin Genjac shared a basement office with other journalists. He parked close to the entrance and they went downstairs into a noisy newsroom, familiar to Anna in every way except for the fact it was underground and windowless. A dozen or more people, most of them smoking, talked intensely into phones or chatted to each other in small groups.

Pierre led Anna across the room to one such group, in the centre of which was a very tall man with thinning black hair tied into a ponytail. He had a crumpled, appealing face, which seemed to reflect his every emotion like fast-changing cloud formations, swirling from delight to disbelief to sudden annoyance and back to delight as he spoke and listened. When he saw them coming towards him, the man's large brown eyes registered both recognition and pleasure, and he broke away from the group, taking two strides to gather Pierre in a powerful hug.

'You made it, comrade,' he cried in his own language, then switched to English as he turned to Anna. 'And you are Anna! Genjac, Adin Genjac. Adi, if you like. I'm happy to meet you. Fucking Serbs are quiet for a moment.'

'Has there been a ceasefire?' asked Anna.

Genjac pulled a soft packet of cigarettes from the pocket of his brown T-shirt and shook out a few. He offered them around, and Anna took one, which Genjac lit for her.

'No,' he said, sucking so hard on his smoke she thought he might finish it in one long drag. 'They like to keep us guessing. Maybe they are too hungover right now. Soon they start drinking again. They like best to kill people when they are drunk. Sometime today they will begin again. They have many bombs. So, for us, right now, this is good. We could stay here, maybe drink some coffee, but I think we should go out quickly while the Serbs are sleeping, yes?'

When they agreed, Genjac quickly farewelled his fellow journalists and shepherded Anna and Pierre from the office in a manner that suggested they were now under his protection, in his town, in his hands.

When they reached the car he turned to Pierre. 'Maybe it's best I should drive,' he said. 'What do you think?'

Anna was already climbing into the front passenger seat. She dipped her head to see Pierre's reaction, catching his eye as he reluctantly handed over the keys and climbed into the back. He was a nervous passenger when she was behind the wheel and she was curious to see how he would respond to this latest relegation, but as she turned back to rib him about it Genjac gunned the engine and tore away from the kerb. The Bosnian took a fast left, drifting around the corner on squealing tyres, and then looked recklessly across at her, laughing as she fumbled to get her seatbelt on.

'Fast-moving target is best,' he shouted. 'To avoid snipers.'

'Where are we going?' she asked, matching his volume.

'Pierre said you want to go to the frontline. We start there. Later today, if roads are clear, we go to the town of Ljubuski, where is the headquarters of General Cvrčak.' Genjac looked over to Anna again. 'Stupid name, don't you think?'

Anna shrugged. 'Have you met him?'

'No,' said Genjac, accelerating fast into another corner. 'He's a very secret man, this big insect. Hides in the trees and makes a loud noise, ha ha!'

'Pierre says no one has a picture of him.'

'I take my camera today,' said Genjac. 'Maybe I'll win Pulitzer.'

Anna frowned, turned back to the road ahead and flinched as the car narrowly missed an old couple attempting to cross it.

'Watch it, Adin!' cried Pierre from the back.

Genjac uttered an expletive under his breath and was still grumbling when Anna tapped his arm.

'You're working for me today, Adin,' she said firmly. 'I'll pay for any pictures we use. But they'll have to be exclusive for my story.'

A sullen cloud crossed Genjac's face. 'You're the boss,' he said.

•

The Bosnian was forced to slow down when they entered the narrow streets of the old town. There were damaged and destroyed buildings on either side of them. Orange tiles blown from their moorings teetered from cracked roofs, waiting, it seemed, for a breeze to send them clattering into the street. Mosques were the most sought-after of targets; when they passed the blackened stump of an amputated minaret, Genjac slowed to a crawl and Anna saw on the ground beside it, wedged where it had fallen, the minaret's shattered spire, its severed end like a splintered bone. She felt a visceral outrage that four-hundred-year-old Ottoman treasures were now sport for drunken artillerymen.

'See what they have done?' said Genjac, his voice seized with emotion. 'They are murderers of history.'

From once-elegant Turkish houses and the ancient limestone shop fronts of the bazaar, piles of rubble spewed onto the cobble-stone street. Genjac steered around them until the road ahead was too narrow for the car. He backed it into a space between two buildings facing out—for a quick getaway, he explained. But the skies were clear and not even the crackle of small arms interrupted what Anna felt, given the level of destruction all around her, was a perverse, unnatural stillness.

'We walk from here,' said Genjac. 'The bridge is close.'

He led them around a corner into a street that ran alongside the Neretva River on its western bank and high above the emerald waters. Up ahead, Anna saw the unmistakable high arch of *Stari Most*, the Old Bridge, with its fortified limestone towers on either bank. For a moment, she forgot to be scared.

'I've never seen it,' she said to Pierre, bumping along beside him like some tourist. 'It's beautiful.'

'One day I'll tell you why Suleiman the Magnificent had it built,' he said. 'But right now I can only think about the Serbs up in those hills.' He called to Genjac, who was blithely striding ahead of them. 'How safe is this street, Adi?'

'It's not at all safe,' Genjac replied. 'But it is quickest way.'

'It's very exposed. Are there snipers up there?'

'I hope not,' said Genjac. 'Our boys are dug in above the bridge on the east side, sometimes they hold the ridgeline, some-times the Serbs. No one's shooting at us yet, so maybe this is a good day.'

Pierre glanced at Anna, who shrugged.

'He must know more than that,' he said to her, before calling again, 'Are you taking the piss, Adi?'

'Maybe, maybe not,' said the Bosnian. 'We could crouch down and crawl along the wall, but I'm too old for that, my back won't let me. I came this way yesterday and no one shot me.'

They reached the famous footbridge without incident and Genjac asked them to wait while he crossed it to find someone. Close to its entrance, Anna found a middle-aged woman with dyed orange hair clambering through the wreckage of a salon. She watched the woman picking her way through the mess, stuffing anything salvageable into a bag: a dust-encrusted brush, a pair of scissors, plastic containers of hair products, scarred bottles of nail polish and other, unidentifiable, items. The woman had to climb over an obstacle course of red leather make-up chairs; they were sprawled across the vinyl floor, bent-legged and misshapen beyond repair. She attempted to haul upright a hairdryer beneath whose dome, Anna imagined, generations of local women had had their perms set. Such quotidian destruction contained its own kind of sadness, an ordinary sadness for the end of everyday life.

The woman spoke no English, so Anna called on Pierre to translate. He crunched over broken glass and called through the opening that had once held a plate-glass window, now shattered into thousands of tiny, angular particles. Somewhere in those fractured pieces, the woman told them, was the handpainted sign *Sabira Salon*. It had been blown apart, along with her livelihood, by the shell dropped through the ceiling.

As they were talking to the woman, Genjac appeared with two Muslim soldiers in tow and interrupted Pierre's translation. 'We must go,' he said. 'These men will take us across the bridge to the front lines.'

Anna reached out to shake the hairdresser's hand and the woman lurched sobbing into her arms. The two women were caught like that in a tableau of despair when the first shell came whistling through the air and exploded on a rocky outcrop on the other side of the bridge. Anna felt a tremor of fear run through the hairdresser's body before the woman pulled away, dropped her bag of salvaged items and ran clumsily up the street, away from the bridge, slipping on the cobblestones as she went.

As Anna bent to pick up the bag, a second shell whistled in and exploded with a terrible roar, much closer. Genjac suddenly gripped her shoulders.

'Anna! Come on!' he shouted. 'Mortars!'

His face was a mask of fury or terror, she couldn't tell which. He tore the bag out of her hands and tossed it aside. The Muslim soldiers were already running back over the bridge. One of them had hold of Pierre's arm, dragging him along and he turned, crying out to Anna. She sprinted after him onto the bridge alongside Genjac. It was steeper than she had imagined, much steeper, and she felt as if she was in one of those dreams in which you run and run and make no ground. She stumbled and almost fell on her face trying to keep up with the Bosnian. Another shell exploded and then another, and her ears rang from the concussions.

As she scrambled over the highest point of the arch, clouds of dust from the explosions rose above the hill in front of them. Below her, she saw Pierre and the soldiers sheltering in the stone fortifications at the other end, waiting for them. Running downhill, Anna heard a louder whistling, more like a scream. She instinctively threw up her arms as an intense flaming light blossomed in front of her. From the heart of the flame a terrible force erupted and she felt herself flying backwards into a dark void.

•

Anna was aware only of a ceaseless, circular chanting in the dark. Then came colour and scent—saffron robes, oil lamps, incense. She looked up into the open eyes of the sleeping divinity. Her fingers held on lightly to the sacred white thread. In this way she drifted above the pain until at last, against her will, she was drawn back down to it, down to the clamour of voices in a large room and to a strange booming. Her right eye opened, blinking in the fluorescent light, darkness still on the left. The ringing pain in her head came dully at first, then it rushed to the surface, blurring her vision.

'Anna.'

A voice she knew. She tried to sit up. There was a tube in her arm, a drip stand beside her. A figure leant in, blocking the light.

'Anna.'

She turned to the voice. A familiar face, eyes swimming behind thick lenses. 'Pierre,' she said, and then winced as the pain focused into a sharp point. She lifted her hand and found the bandage over her left eye, wrapped tightly around her head. A sudden panic.

'Don't worry, your eye's okay,' he said. 'They had to stitch you up below it. You were lucky.'

A crashing boom came in the distance and then another, much closer. She felt it in her chest and it seemed to shake the walls. Then another, further away again.

'They're still shelling,' said Pierre. 'You're safe here. We're under-ground. How are you feeling?'

'My head hurts.'

'Is it bad?'

She nodded.

'The morphine's wearing off. We could ask for more painkillers. Do you remember anything?'

'Running, an explosion . . . Then nothing.'

'You caught a piece of shrapnel and got knocked down. We thought you might have fractured your skull, but the X-rays are clear. You have a concussion. Are you following me? You're okay. I haven't called Rachel yet.'

'Don't. Not yet.' She looked at him and the gears slowly engaged in her mind. 'How long?' she asked.

'You've been out for six hours.'

She touched the bandage again, thought of asking for a mirror, and then she remembered. 'Genjac?'

Pierre's face tightened. 'Not so good. But he's alive.'

Anna struggled to push herself up. 'I want to see him.'

Pierre put a hand on her shoulder, gently restraining her. 'You can't. He's back in surgery. They're trying to save his leg.'

She sunk back into the pillow. Her head pounded in time with her pulse and the pain finally assailed her defences.

'Morphine,' she said. 'Please.'

•

Anna was alone when she woke again. The ward was quiet and dark, emergency lighting only. The shelling had stopped. So, she thought: night then. The drip was still in, but empty, and her mouth was terribly dry. Her head still pounded, but it was bearable now. She put her hand to her cheekbone and touched the bandage, sharper pain.

Genjac!

They're trying to save his leg.

She found a water bottle beside her and drank half of it in one go. Inevitably, she had to pee.

No sign of a nurse. She carefully stripped the adhesive bandage from the needle in her arm and eased it out, put the bandage back and held it there to stop any bleeding. She eased her legs over the side and stood. Leaning against the bed, she waited for the worst of the dizziness to pass. Her clothes were neatly folded on a wooden locker at the end of the bed. She stripped off the hospital gown and dressed slowly: T-shirt, jeans and the light jacket with many pockets. She sat on the locker and her head pounded when she bent to pull on her boots. She found paracetamol tablets, swallowed four of them and left the ward slowly, her limbs stiff and sore.

Anna found a bathroom and examined her face in the cloudy, black-spotted mirror. She lifted the edge of the head-wrapping and uncovered her bloodshot left eye and her bruised, swollen cheekbone. A smaller bandage concealed the stitches, so there was no way to assess the likely scar. She removed the outer bandage, unravelling it like a turban. She looked less of an invalid with it off. Sunglasses would cover most of the damage in daytime.

Anna limped back into the corridor and found a nurse dozing in an armchair. The woman woke with a start. She understood enough to lead Anna to a makeshift recovery room, in what must have been a storage place for documents. Institutional filing cabinets had been pushed aside to make space. Pierre was sprawled on a wheeled bed, snoring loudly. In the next bed was the unconscious figure of Adin Genjac. In a chair beside him a strikingly beautiful young woman was curled up asleep, her arms wrapped around a pillow. The nurse excused herself and left.

Genjac was barely recognisable. An oxygen mask was clamped to his pale face, concealing the ridge of his large nose, and his ponytail was trapped under his neck. His cheeks were hollow and without animation; he seemed older and frailer. His left leg was in a sling raised above the bed and encased from thigh to toe in a plaster cast, from which emerged a complex framework of steel braces, joints and screws. His right leg lay under the sheet and Anna traced its shape down to the raised tent over his toes. He had come out of surgery with both legs. She found herself weeping with relief.

Some sound from Anna prompted the young woman to open her eyes. Her voice startled Anna.

'You were with my father.'

Anna turned to the young woman, whose large brown eyes were immediately familiar, and said, 'We were running across the bridge. And then . . . He was taking us to the front.'

'You're crying,' said the young woman.

'This is my fault.'

The girl shook her head. 'Every day Adin goes to the front,' she said calmly. 'He does not go for you. This is his war. The Serbs have tried many times to kill him, but they cannot, *inshallah*.'

On the other bed Pierre stirred, woken by the voices. 'Anna,' he cried, sitting, and then stumbling over to her. 'You shouldn't be up.'

'I had to know how he was.'

Pierre led Anna to the bed he had vacated and made her sit down. 'You're in no shape to be wandering around.'

'I'm okay,' she said, prodding Pierre on the chest. 'Tomorrow we'll drive to Ljubuski.' When Pierre didn't respond, she mumbled, 'We will.'

Then she lay down, rolled onto her right side and fell asleep.

•

It had been difficult for Anna to persuade Pierre that she was in any shape to travel. He argued that she had nearly died and had taken a piece of shrapnel in the head, so she was likely still in trauma, and if it were up to him he would hire an ambulance and have her driven to the hospital in Split. She told him he was being ridiculously overprotective and that, in any event, Ljubuski was south-west of Mostar, and therefore on the way to Split. As to trauma, she had nothing more than a headache, manageable now with moderate painkillers. She put on sunglasses to show how much better she looked if you couldn't see her swollen black eye.

The truth was very different. She had hidden from Pierre that she was weak and dizzy, and that she found it hard to focus her thoughts, except on making this one argument: *They had made it this far and so should carry on.* Anna left Genjac's daughter Ena with half the US dollars she was carrying and promised to send more from Sydney. She sat by the Bosnian's bed and told him she had decided to continue to Ljubuski.

'You must do that,' he whispered.

Even in his weakened state, Genjac had insisted on passing on, with Ena's help, the names of his Muslim contacts in *Cvrčak*'s militia and writing a personal note for her to carry to them.

They had left the hospital during a morning lull in the Serb bombardment and Anna felt herself panicking as she stepped out of the basement into the open air. The thought that shells could rain from the clear sky at any moment was unbearable. She flinched as the lightning flash and the roar of the explosion replayed in her head like a single startling frame in a movie reel.

She made it to the car, climbed in and slammed the door, but felt as if a veil had come down over her eyes. Her breathing was altered, her heart began to race and it seemed she might lose a grip on herself, as if the moorings of her personality had been loosened and she could come undone at any minute. All of this she hid from Pierre, saying only in a strained voice: 'Let's get out of here.'

•

Looking back, Anna would remember the journey to Ljubuski as a series of impressions.

She had closed her eyes as they raced through the empty streets, refused to look at the blackened wrecks of the looming buildings and concentrated only on controlling her breathing. The symptoms only eased when they left the precincts of the city behind them and entered the mountains, but she knew now the extent of the hidden damage she had suffered and how much more fragile she was than she had imagined, how vulnerable to weakness.

They stopped at Medjugorje, a town whose name literally meant 'between mountains'. Pierre found them a small restaurant he had stopped at once before. They hadn't eaten a meal for more than a day and he was voraciously hungry. Anna drank strong, sweet Turkish coffee and picked at a Bosnian cake. She felt nauseous, her head seemed to be in a vice, and she swallowed another small handful of tablets as Pierre watched anxiously.

'Are you sure you can manage this?' he asked.

'I'm fine,' she lied. 'Just a headache.'

At least Pierre's mood had lightened and she knew that was all to do with putting the perils of Mostar behind them. He told her the strange story of the town they were in, about how in the years before the current conflict millions of Catholics from all over the world had made pilgrimage to Medjugorje.

In 1981, six local children had claimed to have had visions of the Virgin Mary. The children's stories might have been dismissed as youthful hysteria, but their dreamlike accounts were given currency by the Croatian parish priest, Father Zovko, and the town's fame quickly spread. Soon this purported miracle got the attention of the Yugoslavian communist authorities and agents of the state's secret police (the notorious UDBA) were sent to investigate. Father Zovko was arrested, tried and sentenced to three and a half years' hard labour for 'participating in a nationalist plot'. Nothing worried Belgrade so much as a revival of the religious fervour that had underpinned the wartime Ustasha movement.

In recent years, as the power of the central communist authority had waned, so had their grip on religion. Catholic pilgrims began to flood back into the town, where two of the visionary children, now adults, claimed to be the recipients of regular monthly messages directly from the Blessed Virgin. Her messages, received by both of them, were like punctual celestial telegrams: one on the second of each month, the other on the twenty-fifth.

'Unbelievable, every single month?' said Anna, pleased to have her thoughts diverted. 'What a curse. It must be like having your period.'

'A bloody Mary?' Pierre ventured.

When Anna rewarded his crude joke with a smile, her first moment of levity since she was blown up, Pierre went on.

'That's not all. Eventually the pilgrims themselves started reporting strange hallucinations. They would see the sun spinning in the sky and changing colour, or a halo of light around the sun full of crosses and hearts.'

Anna automatically stared up at the sun, twin reflections of it in her dark polaroid lenses.

'Careful now,' said Pierre. 'A whole bunch of dim-witted pilgrims got permanent eye damage doing that.'

'I'd like a sign from God,' said Anna. 'Wouldn't you?'

'You're still alive,' he said. 'I've had my miracle.'

•

They drove on from Medjugorje and eventually entered a long valley with mountain ranges on either side. The town of Ljubuski sat in a bowl of mountains, close under the Butorovic Range at its northern end. From the outskirts of the town, Anna could see a jagged, broken-toothed structure emerging from the highest peak and Pierre explained she was looking at the ruins of an ancient fortress. In the fifteenth century, Croatian pioneers built the original town on the mountain and it thrived until their defences were overrun during the Ottoman invasion. The Turks had fortified the town with high battlements and made it a border garrison, establishing it as the Western edge of their empire.

Over the years, Anna had heard different versions of the history of this region from both Croat and Serb nationalists, for whom the Muslim invasion seemed like recent history. Such people often referred to their Muslim neighbours as 'Turks', even though they were in fact ethnically identical Slavic people.

Here, in the region of Herzegovina, of which Ljubuski was one of the largest towns, Croats were in the majority. Most Croat nationalists regarded Herzegovina as the homeland of their Catholic faith, so one of the most surprising things about the warlord *Cvrčak* was that he had so strongly allied himself with the local Muslim Bosniaks, going so far as to recruit thousands of them into his militia.

About Ljubuski, Anna had learned the following facts in preparing for this journey: There were fewer than thirty thousand people in the surrounding region, of whom about seven thousand five hundred lived in the town itself; three quarters of the town's population were Croatian; twenty per cent were Bosnian Muslim; and one per cent were Serb. She wondered how many of that one per cent had remained; she guessed that some in that category must have married Croats or Muslims, and they might still be here.

As they drove into the centre of the town, Anna saw large numbers of armed men in the streets. Some wore camouflage, but many were in black fatigues reminiscent of the Ustasha's Black Legion, which she assumed was no accident. Pierre drove slowly past clots of these men who, when she looked at them closely, seemed unkempt and ill-disciplined. They bore their weapons haphazardly and took no pride in their appearance, from their dirty uniforms to their unwashed, straggly hair. She thought, perhaps fancifully, that many of them looked like criminals; they had the sullen expressions of street thugs looking for a mark. Some stopped in their tracks and stared with open hostility at the outsiders whose car marked them clearly as journalists. She saw the faces of lean, angry, rat-faced men, and felt waves of antagonism emanating from them.

'I've got a bad feeling about this place,' she said.

'Yeah,' said Pierre. 'Something's not right, that's for sure.'

They parked in the main street of what otherwise appeared to be a neat, respectable and even mildly prosperous town; it had the usual mixture of elegant old baroque buildings and ugly, shoddily built communist-era office blocks and apartments. They approached a café where a group of soldiers were drinking beer at a table beneath a pair of red Coca-Cola umbrellas, their weapons leaning against the wall beside them or lying at their feet.

At a closer table sat a wiry man with a much larger mate, both basking in the sun, sipping espresso from tiny cups. The thin one had straggly blond hair to his shoulders and a deeply lined brown face. He wore an outsized mauve singlet and tie-dyed jeans, and might have been a roadie for a hard rock band were it not for the bandolier of cartridges around his emaciated waist. As they walked past him, the man called out, pulled from his belt a sawn-off shotgun and aimed its twin barrels at Pierre's chest.

'Hey!' yelled Anna. 'Put it down!'

The thin man and his fat mate laughed, as if this were the funniest thing they had heard all morning.

'Hey!' cried the thin man, waving the weapon about. '*Hey!*'

Anna saw that the scrawny outlaw had a collection of women's watches and bangles on either wrist.

'Keep moving,' said Pierre.

But when they reached the dishevelled group of black-uniformed drinkers, the closest soldier looked up at them. The man was slumped low in a plastic chair, feet on the table, lazily rolling a cigarette.

'You are here for the news?' he asked in English.

Pierre looked puzzled. 'What news?'

'The killings.'

'I don't know what you mean.'

'Don't lie!' said the soldier and he sat up, no longer lazy but intense, like a switch had flicked inside him.

'I'm not lying,' said Pierre.

Anna read pure hatred in the man's face, and something more. Could it be grief?

'Fuck off out of here!' the soldier cried. 'Go, before you get a bullet for your troubles. You people are no better than flies on shit.'

•

A careworn old man in a crumpled grey suit directed them to the militia headquarters. It was not far, he told them nervously. As they walked the prescribed route, the vice around Anna's head returned. She had stupidly left the pain medication in the car and had no other choice than to bear the migraine as it tightened its grip. Now the pain was affecting the peripheral vision in her damaged left eye, in which she had begun to see flashes of coloured light.

They entered a long driveway. At the end was a solid and once-elegant building in need of a paint job. Anna imagined it had once been the villa of a wealthy family until being transformed by the communists into a municipal office of some sort. It was surrounded by overgrown gardens. Ahead was a circular courtyard in which several vehicles were parked on one side. There was a wide portico over steps going up to the front door, and above it hung the familiar red-and-white chequerboard flag. A group of black-uniformed men sprawled listlessly on the steps. As Anna got closer, she saw that there were multiple bullet holes in the windscreens and doors of three of the parked vehicles, one of which sat lopsided on flattened tyres.

The pain in her head and the flashing in her vision were becoming more intense. Several of the soldiers looked up as they approached. One of them—a bearded man, with his head down and the butt of his Kalashnikov between his feet—did not raise his eyes. An older soldier appeared in the doorway—an officer with grey hair slicked back and a holstered automatic at his waist. Pierre called out a greeting to him.

'What do you want?' the man asked gruffly.

'We've come from Australia. To meet the general.'

The man looked at each of them; his face expressing surprise and disbelief.

'Come inside,' he said, and they followed him up the stairs and into a room with desks and maps and telephones. It was strewn about with many weapons including, Anna saw, a heavy machine gun, boxes of ammunition, boxes of hand grenades and mortar shells. Then she noticed high on the wall a large coloured poster with slogans in Croatian at top and bottom. It was the photographic portrait of a heavily bearded man in camouflage uniform with a black forage cap. He wore the shoulder boards of a senior officer. Anna was uncertain what rank they designated, but something like general was surely possible.

She walked over to it, transfixed. Her head was pounding now, the pain was almost crippling. Looking closely, she saw the unmistakable green eyes. There was no question.

This was Marin Katich.

'You have come to see the general?' asked a voice from behind her, speaking in American-accented English.

'Yes,' said Pierre.

Anna turned to a man standing in the doorway, which had opened from a large office. He was dressed in a uniform similar to the one worn by the bearded Marin Katich. He was tall and athletic, smooth-shaven and bareheaded with short, steel grey hair. A good-looking fellow, some might say, and Anna may have agreed were it not for his disturbingly protuberant eyes.

'All the way from Australia?' the man asked.

'Yes,' said Pierre.

The man looked to Anna, still standing by the wall poster. He paused for a moment, as if considering his next move.

'I am General Rebic,' he said, reaching out to shake her hand. 'Jure Rebic. And you are?'

'Anna Rosen,' she said, stepping back. 'This is my colleague Pierre Villiers. We are journalists.' She pointed to the poster. 'Please can you tell me where we can find this man?'

'You know him?' asked Rebic.

'Many years ago, yes.'

'Please,' said Rebic. 'Come into my office. We can talk there.'

Rebic directed them to chairs, then sat on the edge of his desk in front of them.

'I'm sorry, I have bad news for you,' he said in the sonorous tone of a sympathetic priest. 'I will be blunt. The general is dead.'

Anna swayed back in her chair as if she had taken a blow. The flickering light at the edge of her vision darkened and she saw Rebic as if at the end of a tunnel. Her head seemed to be splitting apart, but through the pain she still managed to hear Pierre's next questions.

'What happened to him?'

'You saw those destroyed vehicles as you came in? The general was in the lead car. They were ambushed. Most of his staff officers were with him. It happened yesterday. Nine killed. I was lucky to be here, or I too would be dead.'

'Ambushed by who?'

'By the Croatian army at a roadblock they set up to trap him. It was a terrible act of betrayal by his own brothers in arms.'

Anna stood up and the dark tunnel narrowed. The pain was overwhelming. She felt herself toppling.

THE MEETING

THE MEETING

19

SCHEVENINGEN, THE HAGUE

21 DECEMBER 2005

ANOTHER BITTERLY cold morning found Anna Rosen outside the walls of Scheveningen prison. It had taken nearly a week in the slow Christmas season to get the permissions she needed from the registry of the International Criminal Tribunal for the former Yugoslavia. Now she shivered, pacing up and down in front of the giant fortified gate. Her long black coat swished with each turn, her boots clicked on the cobblestones. She was waiting for Willem van Brug. She clenched her jaw to stop her teeth chattering, an exaggerated effect that she reckoned was more due to agitation than the chill. The lawyer was not late. She was early. This morning she would see Marin Katich for the first time in thirty-three years. An absurd phrase of her father's kept repeating in her head: *Nervous as a cat in a room full of rocking chairs.*

The previous day, Anna had taken the familiar number 1 tram and got off at World Forum. It was a short walk from there to the imposing building at Churchillplein 1, an appropriately severe, brutalist structure, which housed the ICTY. She entered via the glass box of the security office, which had been grafted onto the entrance. X-rayed and wanded, she was directed inside to a young, tough-looking Nepalese guard behind a desk in the foyer, to whom she explained that she had an appointment to see the court Registrar, Prometheus Singarasa. While she was waiting, Anna chatted with the guard and discovered that he was a Gurkha.

'My dad fought alongside Gurkhas against the Japanese in New Guinea,' she told the young man. 'He brought back a kukuri knife and put it up on the wall. I remember him showing it to me when I was a little kid. He kept it sharp as a razor.'

The young man was surprised.

'They must have been good friends to give him a kukuri,' he said.

'I guess so,' said Anna. 'He did say he was glad they were on his side—but, friend or foe, they'd slit your throat in the dark if you forgot the password.'

The Gurkha man was still laughing at this when a short, elegantly dressed man walked up to introduce himself. Prometheus Singarasa was as handsome as a Bollywood star. He had perfect hair, an unlined face and shrewd brown eyes.

'Good to finally meet you, Anna,' he said, his Australian accent both obvious and unfeigned. 'You won't know this, but you're one of the main reasons I ended up in The Hague.'

'Ivo Katich?' she said.

He nodded. 'I went to work for the DPP just out of law school and got involved in drawing up his indictment. Pity he never made it to trial.'

'Yeah,' said Anna. 'He should have died rotting in prison.'

'We were pretty confident of a conviction, that's for sure,' said Singarasa, 'and we were ready to go. Anyway, the Katich case gave a whole bunch of us war crimes experience. That's why there're so many Aussies here—the perfect line in your CV. So, welcome. Sorry it's taken so long to meet you, I was at a conference in Belgrade.'

'Your office told me,' said Anna. 'I'm sure I've been a nuisance calling them every day.'

'You're here now so come on, I'll take you in.' He touched her elbow and led her through a second set of security doors to a lift. 'It's a bit of a rabbit warren. The ICTY grew like Topsy and took over the whole building. It's ugly, I know. Used to be the HQ of a big insurance company, but that was good because they had big disaster-proof bunkers for storing their documents.'

The lift arrived and Singarasa pressed 3.

'First two floors are the judges' chambers,' he explained. 'The Registry's on the third, along with the investigators.'

'That's where Pierre works?'

'That's right,' he said. 'And the investigators John Ralston and Bob Reid are there. Both Aussies. Both former NSW homicide detectives, actually; you should meet them. Bob's here, I can introduce you.'

'I do hope to meet them both, Prometheus,' Anna said as the lift opened, 'but not today.'

Singarasa gave her a quizzical look as he led her into the corridor.

'It's complicated,' she said. 'I'll explain later.'

•

Singarasa showed her into a large corner office with windows on two sides. Anna accepted his offer of coffee. She had relaxed somewhat when she learned of his involvement in the Ivo Katich case, but that also meant he knew a great deal about her journalism and that familiarity could work against her. She knew that without his agreement, she was sunk.

As the senior legal officer of the war crimes tribunal, Singarasa had the authority to allow her to join Tomislav Maric's defence team. This he had already agreed to in principle after a written request from van Brug, but he had insisted that Anna must sign an agreement not to publish anything about the case until it was concluded: no journalist articles, no public commentary, no book.

He had wanted to meet her to formalise the arrangement face to face. When the coffee came, he handed her the written agreement. She read it quickly and looked up.

'Should I sign it now?' she asked.

'You realise that it's completely binding?'

'Yes.'

'The Maric case could go on for years.'

'I know.'

'You won't even be able to talk about the indictment.'

'Yes, I know it's sealed,' she acknowledged. 'Why is that?'

'I can't tell you.'

'Is it something to do with the witnesses?'

Singarasa gazed at her impassively for a moment, making a calculation. 'Look, Anna,' he said at last. 'I'll tell you this much *off the record* because it may be relevant to the case. Several potential witnesses to the events in the indictment have recently died suspicious or unexplained deaths.'

'What? Is Maric a suspect?'

'I really can't tell you . . .'

'How many potential witnesses? Can you tell me their names?'

Singarasa shrugged. 'Van Brug will be given this information in due course.'

'A mystery, then?' said Anna.

'Yes,' said the Registrar. 'I know you're good at them.'

'Okay, where do I sign this thing?'

'Before you do,' said Singarasa, 'I'm curious. Why do you want to do this? What is it about this case? It won't be the most high-profile trial. He's far from the biggest war criminal here. Why are you so interested?'

Anna composed her face and appeared to consider his question. 'I'll tell you what I know, Prometheus,' she said. 'Provided you let me sign this first.'

Singarasa's shrewd eyes widened, he had not expected such a response. 'Now I really am curious.'

'Do you agree?'

'If you were anyone else, I'd say no,' he said. 'But all right, I agree.'

'Good,' said Anna. She signed both copies of the agreement and gave them to Singarasa to countersign. He did so, handed over her copy, and watched as she put it into her briefcase.

'So?' he said.

'Okay,' she said, pausing to take a breath. 'There is no such person as Tomislav Maric. The man you have locked up is Marin Katich. He's the son of Ivo Katich and he was born in Sydney.'

The Registrar looked startled, his unflappable demeanour deserting him.

'Oh my God,' he cried, running both hands back through his perfect hair as he calculated the implications. 'Ivo Katich's son?'

'Yes.'

'That's just . . . Well, it's unbelievable.'

'I know, Prometheus,' said Anna. 'It's a lot to take in.'

'He's Australian?'

'Unless he gave up his citizenship. But I've no reason to think he did.'

'His Croatian papers?'

'Forgeries, I imagine. Not so hard to find a new identity during a war. Remember he had a *nom de guerre* in Bosnia. Maybe he knew the real Maric well enough to obtain his birth certificate.'

'You know what's going to happen, don't you,' said Singarasa, his voice rising, 'when it comes out that Ivo Katich's Australian son is locked up here, waiting to face a war crimes trial?'

Anna responded in a deliberately neutral tone. 'I know exactly what's going to happen,' she said.

'I'm going to have to put out a press release about this,' Singarasa said. 'And then every Australian tabloid, every journalist under the sun, will be camped out here. They'll be chasing after me, they'll be after Pierre, and every other Australian working at the tribunal. Ralston's away right now, thank God, but there's Bob Reid in the investigations unit. His wife, she's a lawyer. Christ, there are so many of us.'

'I know all that,' said Anna, locking her eyes on his. 'That's why I need to get in to see him as soon as possible. In the meantime, you don't have to say anything at all. First you're going to have to find the proof that what I've told you is true and that will take some time.'

Singarasa nodded glumly, then picked up the signed agreement from his desk. 'Bloody hell, Anna, did you trick me into this? You know you won't be able to say anything, no interviews. That would break the agreement and you'd be locked out forever.'

'Prometheus, that's the last thing in the world that I would do.'

'I'm trusting you, Anna. I'd lose my job if you talked.'

'You can trust me,' she said and she meant it.

•

Anna's face was pale in the winter sun and would have been paler still were it not for the faint touches of colour she had begun to apply before abandoning the effort, staring at herself in the bathroom mirror as if she were mad. She was thinking about Rachel when she spotted the lawyer's gangly, long-limbed stride in the distance. She had resolved to say nothing to Marin Katich about their daughter, but she was worried she might suddenly lose her composure and blurt it out.

'*Goedemorgen*, Ms Rosen,' said van Brug, and Anna looked up in surprise, wondering how he had managed to cover the ground so quickly.

'Good morning to you, Willem, and please call me Anna.' She reached into the briefcase slung over her shoulder. 'I have brought something for you. My book on Ivo Katich.'

'Ah, thank you,' said van Brug, taking it carefully in his gloved hands as if handling a precious artefact. '"Australian Nazi"—I can see how the family would not have welcomed the publication. I will read it with great interest.'

The lawyer took a moment to secure the book in his own briefcase.

'Now,' he said, 'there are several security points before we reach the meeting room, so I must remind you that you cannot be carrying any weapons or contraband, and no recording devices. We are permitted to take with us documents or books as required, so this one is not a problem.' He patted his briefcase. 'And note-books and pens. This is understood?'

'Yes, it is.'

'Good, good,' he said, dipping his long face to one side.

'Is there anything else, Willem?'

'I was wondering if you are perhaps a little nervous?'

'No,' she said. 'I'm anxious, of course, that it goes well, and about where to start talking after all this time.'

'I know you don't want me in the room for this first meeting, so I will take you in, make some excuse and leave you alone. I will go back to my office to wait, but I will expect a full briefing after, yes?'

'Of course.'

'And tomorrow he must also speak to me,' said van Brug. He had already made this clear, but wanted it confirmed. 'There is much to do.'

'I will do my best to convince him.'

'You must,' he said. 'Now, I have told the commandant two hours for this first meeting. Do you think you will be that long?'

'I don't know,' she said. 'I imagine that will be up to Katich.'

'If you send me a text when you do know, I will come and pick you up outside the gates.'

Anna agreed and then shivered. She had been standing still for too long in the icy air and her face, only partly protected by the high astrakhan collar, had gone numb.

'Oh, I'm sorry,' said van Brug. 'You are going blue from the cold. That was thoughtless of me. Come, it's warm inside.'

Their bags were X-rayed and they passed through the airport-style metal detectors. Then, accompanied by a guard, they walked into a courtyard past the prison hospital. Ahead was a high razor-wire fence and behind it a modern-looking four-storey block—the purpose-built UN detention unit. Here was a second round of security screening, more X-ray machines, handheld metal detectors and bag searches before they entered a communal meeting room where two colourfully dressed African woman were seated at a table talking to a black man with cropped white hair. The man glanced up at Anna and she saw his bloodshot, malarial eyes pierce through her façade of normality. She felt a griping pain in the pit of her stomach and hoped she wouldn't have to make a dash for the toilets. Van Brug pointed out a closed door at the end of a hall-way—a special room, he explained, for conjugal visits. She glanced at him, suspecting some peculiar attempt at humour.

Then they came to a guard sitting outside one of several small rooms in the same corridor. Beyond the guard, through a thick glass window, she saw a dark figure sitting behind a plain wooden table, smoking distractedly. Somehow she recognised the shape of him. Van Brug inadvertently moved between her and the man in the room, but as the lawyer talked to the guard she managed to catch fleeting images of what lay ahead: an ashtray full of butts; a haggard man, thinner, but still powerful; burning eyes; strands of grey-streaked hair falling across his face; and something else, something intangible. Had she caught in his restless shifting some trace of the old Marin Katich?

The lawyer was saying something to her.

'Sorry, Willem, I wasn't listening.'

'You can go in,' he said. 'The guard will stay here. You have two hours. Don't forget to text me.'

She went through the door and shut it behind her. Marin Katich looked up at her, a burning cigarette poised mid-air in between tobacco-stained fingers, a wisp of smoke, expressionless green eyes. Anna stood still, her back pressed against the closed door. Some time passed before she spoke.

'Can I have one of those?'

The green eyes blinked. 'I thought you'd given up,' he said.

'That's funny,' she said.

'Not really,' he said.

Remaining seated, he shook a cigarette from the pack and held it out. She walked towards him unsteadily, took the offered smoke, bent as he lit it for her and then straightened, stepped back and drew on it, swaying a little.

'Christ, that's made me dizzy,' she said.

'You lose the taste for it, I suppose.'

'Do you mind if I just put it out?' She leant down and ground it into the ashtray without waiting for his answer. 'Seems like a waste. These are probably like currency for you.'

'Not really,' he said. 'You can get them from the commissary. Everyone smokes in here. It's like a Balkan café.'

'It sounded a lot worse in your letter.'

'A café full of psychopaths.'

'Where should we start?'

'You could take your coat off and sit down.'

'I can't . . .' She paused again. 'Give me a moment.'

'At least stop pacing around. You're making the guard nervous.'

'Look!' she said, louder than she intended. 'I just don't know who the hell you are.'

'Now you're making *me* nervous.'

'Fuck,' she said. 'Okay, I'll sit.'

Anna pulled up the chair, hung her coat on the back of it and sat.

'That's better,' he said.

'Not for me.'

In the long silence that followed, Marin lit another cigarette.

'I'm just so fucking angry with you,' Anna said finally. 'That's why it's so hard to sit still.'

Marin nodded.

'Okay,' he said. 'I get it. Why don't you start by asking questions?'

'No, you don't get it! I thought you were fucking dead, mate!'

'They wanted me dead,' he said, 'and once they thought I was, I had to stay that way.'

'Who is *they* in that sentence?'

'Those who betrayed me. It's a long story. Is that where you want to start?'

'For fuck's sake. I have no idea where to start. Don't answer a question with a question. Up until last week, as far as I knew, you'd been dead for thirteen years.' Anna automatically touched the tear-shaped scar under her left eye. 'Thirteen years!' she repeated. 'Thirteen years ago, I came looking for you in Bosnia and almost got myself killed.'

Marin stared at her, incredulous; a long piece of ash fell into his lap. 'What are you talking about?'

'It happened in June 1992. I was in Mostar looking for a man who called himself *Cvrčak* and I got blown up by a mortar shell.'

'What!' he exclaimed. 'A mortar shell? How badly hurt were you?'

'It's a bit late to be fretting over my welfare, isn't it?'

'No, it's just . . .'

'What, Marin? *Unbelievable?* It's very hard for me to accept that you didn't know about this.'

'Anna, you have to believe me, I have no idea what you're talking about. This is . . . Not just unbelievable, it's incredible. I didn't think anything could surprise me, but this . . . You have to tell me what happened to you.'

'I was lucky,' she said. 'No serious damage. They patched me up and we drove to Ljubuski the next day. Went to your headquarters. That's where your man, Jure Rebic, showed me the bullet-riddled car you were supposedly in. That was a nice touch.'

'Wait, you met Jure Rebic?'

'He was very convincing.'

'I'm sure he was. He's one of the world's biggest liars—'

'Fuck this! Don't tell me you didn't put him up to it! You must have heard I was coming. That whole scene had to be a set-up. It's all too—'

'Anna!' said Marin with a sudden intensity. 'I know you're angry. You've got every right to be, but please, just stop interrupting for a moment and listen.' He pushed back his chair, stood and pulled up his T-shirt.

Anna winced at what she saw. From high on the left side of his chest and down over his belly to the beltline, his flesh was crisscrossed with ugly ridged scars, evidence of rough battle-field surgery. He pulled the shirt back down, sat and lit another cigarette.

'They took eleven bullets out of me, along with my left lung,' he said and smiled wryly. 'Yeah, what an idiot to be chain smoking with one lung, right? That man you met, Jure Rebic, he was respon-sible for this. He's the one who betrayed me. He's the reason I was in that car. He sent us into the trap. My best officers, all of them, were slaughtered. It's only by a miracle that I survived.'

Anna stared at him across the table, looking for the truth in the eyes she had once known intimately. They were red-rimmed and bloodshot, but whether that was from tiredness or emotion was impossible to tell. Time and distance and bitter experience had turned them into the eyes of a stranger—but in them she also saw Rachel.

'Tell me about Rebic,' she said.

'It started in Vukovar,' he said. 'That's where I met him.'

20

VUKOVAR, CROATIA

16 NOVEMBER 1991

MARIN MOVED FAST in a crouching run down the sunken road alongside the cornfield. An Osa tube bounced on his left shoulder. His Kalashnikov, hot from the recent engagement, was in his right hand. The skinny kid Ante Lovren was running in his peripheral vision, a missile held tight to his chest with a yellow glove. Jure Rebic was ten metres behind them, jogging with his sniper rifle at port arms. The deadly clatter of a heavy machine gun came in their wake. Tracers streaked over their heads.

Marin turned and saw that Rebic had slowed down.

'Keep up, Rambo!' he cried. 'They're on our tails.'

Rebic stopped and waved him on. 'Go on! Don't stop!' he shouted. 'If they come after us, I'll make them pay.'

Now Marin stopped. 'They'll outflank you, Jure.'

'Fuck off, you stupid insect, and get that Osa home,' said Rebic. 'We can't afford to lose it.'

Marin knew Rebic was right. They were down to their last few missiles; they were no longer being resupplied and the tanks kept coming.

•

Rebic had woken him that morning with a report from a forward observer that a turtle—a T-84—was moving slowly towards their positions on the Trpinjska Road. A lone tank was unusual. The Serbs had recently changed their tactics, now sending tanks in groups of four to zigzag across the street, laying down smoke, firing into the walls of houses, pumping them full of tear gas and then ploughing into them. It was a demolition strategy to destroy concealed firing positions. Behind the tanks would come armoured personnel carriers, raking the streets and houses with heavy machine-gun fire.

Thanks to a lull in the bombardment it was a quiet morning, and they made a quick decision to go after the lone turtle. They lay well ahead of it, hidden on the edge of the sunken road. Rebic crawled into position with his rifle. Like Marin, he was an accomplished sniper; it was his job to take out the driver's periscope, and then Marin and Lovren would rise quickly from the side of the road, load the tube and fire the missile.

Rebic hit his mark. But when Marin rose with the Osa, he immediately drew heavy fire from multiple positions ahead of the tank. An ambush. The lone tank was a decoy.

Bullets ripped through the air and tore up the ground in front of him. Marin and Lovren dropped down and returned fire. Attackers rose and moved forwards. Marin clocked them as Chetnik paras, *Beli Orlovi*, White Eagles. He knew they were in for a fight. The regular army was now using paramilitary troops like these to spearhead infantry operations.

The Chetniks were well organised and weaved their way towards them, keeping up cover fire as they came. When Marin saw they were in danger of being overwhelmed, he signalled for a fast retreat into the sunken road.

With Rebic now covering them, Marin and Lovren ran to the basement that served both as barracks and operational HQ for the Yellow Ants. Marin secured the precious Osa and pulled together a squad to go back for Rebic. They found him sauntering back down the sunken road as if he were returning from a football match.

'They're brave, but stupid,' said Rebic, bug eyes popping with excitement. 'I got their officer. Blew the fucking eagle right off his *šajkača*. Splashed them with his brains. They'll have to wash him off their stinking uniforms. They ran around like headless chooks after that.'

Marin watched the Yellow Ants gather around to hug Rebic and pat his back. He was a bloodthirsty bastard, Rambo, but he was fearless.

•

When they were back safe in the basement, the bombardment began again, explosions loud and close. Pavlovic miraculously produced a smoked ham; he said it was the last one from his mother's house. They sliced it up, shared it around and ate it on dry biscuits, washed down with warm *gemnist*.

'Hey, Lovren,' said Pavlovic, holding up a bottle of mineral water and peering into it. 'Where'd you get this fucking Jamnica? Spoils the wine. It's salty as a nun's nasty.'

'Scrounged a case of it from a basement like everything else, you ungrateful sod,' said Lovren. 'And don't be blaspheming! My sister's a nun.'

Pavlovic winked at him. 'How do you think I know what it tastes like?'

When Lovren jumped up and lunged at Pavlovic, Marin caught him and pushed him back down.

'Save it for the Chetniks,' said Marin. 'There're plenty of them. Anyway, I didn't know your sister was a nun.'

'She's not,' said Lovren. 'But that's no excuse for blasphemy.'

An explosion rattled the building above them.

'You think God's going to help us out of this?' asked Pavlovic. His edgy, animated body got moving and his arms waved about. 'We're fucking trapped here.'

'He sent us a ham, didn't he?' said Marin.

'My mother smoked that ham,' said Pavlovic. 'Not God.'

'Well, praise be to your mum,' said Marin. 'It's a fine ham. She wouldn't have wanted the Chetniks to make a banquet of it.'

'God abandoned us when he killed Blago,' said Pavlovic and there was muttering among the Yellow Ants, some agreeing.

At the back of the room, where he lay on a pile of flour sacks, Jure Rebic suddenly opened his eyes.

'Pavlovic, you fucking numbskull,' he said, roused to anger. 'God didn't kill Blago Zadro. He was just too reckless for his own good.'

'Too fucking brave,' said someone.

'Sure,' said Rebic. 'But it was a fucking Serb who killed him, and you should save every single bullet to kill one of them. That's God's message. An eye for an eye.'

'How many of them are there?' said Pavlovic, hunching his shoulders. 'How many bullets do we have left?'

After an especially loud explosion, Rebic crept up the stairs, propped open the door and scanned the street with his riflescope.

'Hey, Pavlovic,' he yelled.

'What?'

'Isn't your mother's house just over the road?'

'Yeah. Why?'

'Because there's a huge hole in the roof,' said Rebic. 'And I'm looking at a dozen hams hanging in there, that's why, you lying cunt.'

They crowded up the stairs, to be sure that Rebic wasn't joking, but sure enough, the absence of tiles now revealed a row of pinkish hams hanging in the rafters.

Pavlovic had tears in his eyes. 'I was saving them for my mum,' he said. His comrades took pity on him.

'That's nothing but a feast for Chetniks,' said Rebic. 'No way your mum's coming back for those.'

When it was safe, a party of heavily armed scroungers climbed into the roof and retrieved the hams. They ate well that night, laughing like fools, until Matic broke one of his molars on a piece of shrapnel nestling deep in the ham.

•

The men's morale was boosted by their feast, but Marin knew that Pavlovic had been right. They had very little ammunition left and only one missile for the Osa. They couldn't destroy tanks with hams. He knew they could only hold out for one or two days more.

Looking around at the small band of men in the shelter, Marin had a powerful sense of déjà vu. It took him back to Bosnia in 1972 and the hours he'd spent trapped in a cave on Mount Radusa. Huddled inside were the remnants of the twenty Croatian insurgents who'd come to start a revolution against Tito. Now they were trapped like rats and they knew that they had no choice but to split up and run from the soldiers sent by Belgrade to destroy them. Those men had finally turned on each other and degenerated into a barely sane, demoralised rabble. Marin had been just twenty years old when he'd taken his brother's place on that doomed mission. And he had been the only survivor.

Now, twenty years later, Marin felt a deep responsibility for the men under his command. He wondered what Blago Zadro would have done. Would he have asked them to fight to the last soul, to defend their neighbourhoods to the end? He found himself cursing Zadro for his crazy-brave recklessness.

Poor Blago had been out in the open on the street, heedless of danger, directing an attack on a group of tanks as he had done so many times before, issuing orders on his Motorola, which turned out not to be a magic wand after all. A raking burst of machine-gun fire from an unexpected direction cut Zadro down and that was it. He was gone, quick and simple. It was the end that Zadro himself had long expected and perhaps even welcomed. But his men had been shocked to find that he was mortal after all, and many of them felt as if they'd been suddenly orphaned.

The Yellow Ants and the Desert Rats had got together at the Mustang Bar that night to mourn and to drink and sing in his honour. They made up songs about Zadro, the Bata shoe factory worker who became a national hero. They carried a speaker outside and turned it towards the enemy in a display of defiance, to show that their spirit was unbroken. During the long night, they heard the Chetniks, close by in their own lines, getting more and more drunk as they tried to drown out the Croats with their own contemptible, mocking songs. Close to dawn, Marin took Jure Rebic up to a sniper's position inside a partly destroyed roof. Eventually, a drunken Chetnik popped his head up to shout abuse at the Croats, and Rebic put a bullet in his face. Marin and Jure each took a slug of *rakija*, and had then gone back down to their men before the mortars began to fall.

•

Now Marin went to a private space with Zadro's old Motorola. He knew what he had to do. They'd been under siege for eighty-seven days: eighty-seven days of the Serb bombardment; eighty-seven days of hunting and killing tanks; eighty-seven days of being hunted and killed themselves. The survivors had done everything that was humanly possible, except dying. It was time for them to retreat from Borovo. When Marin got through to *Jastreb*—the Hawk— their commander in the centre of the destroyed city, he got no argument but only praise and God's blessing. It was Jastreb who gave the order: break out if you can, take as many men as possible, Vukovar is about to fall.

Marin took Jure Rebic aside first and told him the score.

'Where will we go?' said Rebic.

'I've got a plan.'

21

SCHEVENINGEN PRISON, THE HAGUE

21 DECEMBER 2005

ANNA STARED across the table at the man she knew and didn't know.

'Jure Rebic was my loyal deputy,' said Marin. 'Or so I thought back then. He was a brave fighter, a natural leader in his way. We broke through the Serb lines and got all our men out of Vukovar.'

'So, you told Rebic you had a plan. What was it?'

'The siege had held up the Serbs long enough for the Croatian forces to regroup and prepare. That was the real purpose of Vukovar's sacrifice. After that, Milosevic was never able to take another Croat city. I knew the next war would be in Bosnia. So Rebic and I took the men who still wanted to fight and we travelled south to Ljubuski. Well, you've been there, so you know there are very few Serbs in that part of the world. Ljubuski had been a stronghold in our history. I thought it could be again. I wanted to repeat what Blago Zadro had done and recruit and train a force to be ready for when the Serbs pushed west to take Mostar.'

'Your father was born in Ljubuski,' said Anna. 'This is what puzzles me. He was a vile racist and a murderer. I found plenty of evidence of that . . .'

'You don't need to convince me.'

'So you say,' said Anna sharply.

She felt they were getting to the nub of it now. No matter what noble motives Marin Katich ascribed to his actions in Vukovar, he was still responsible for the depredations of an Ustasha-style militia in Bosnia. She had seen for herself the black uniforms and the type of men who wore them.

'But you then go back to his town, to *his* heartland,' she said. 'The place where he learned to be a racist.'

'No,' said Marin. 'You're wrong about that. Ivo joined the Ustasha at university in Sarajevo. I think he was like one of those young jihadists seduced by Al-Qaeda, ready to train suicide bombers or fly planes into buildings. He was indoctrinated, like they were, by religious extremists—not mullahs, in his case, but priests. I came to realise that my father was mentally ill, clinically ill. It was a form of madness, Anna, the madness that can be directed or channelled into a cause. But you have to understand, no matter what else you may think of me, I'm not mad. I'm not my father. I'm nothing like him.'

Anna pushed her chair back and stood up, as if her legs were powered by pistons and not under her control.

'What is it?' asked Marin, alarmed.

She waved his question away, pacing around the small space. An unstoppable train of thought had taken her straight from Marin's objection that he was not his father to the hotel room in Canberra in 1973 when he had cried out:

Please don't look at me like that?

Like what?

Like you see something of him in me.

She was back in her room in The Wellington Hotel. It was as vivid as an old film reel. Her heart was pounding wildly. She lost control of her breathing and the incipient panic made her want to run out of the interview room.

Rachel!

She silently repeated her daughter's name. She had an overwhelming urge to run from here, to fly back home and hold Rachel in her arms as if she was still a child—but instead she continued to pace the room. Anna had feared this moment but she had never imagined it would affect her in this way. So much time, so much energy, had gone into thinking about it in the abstract. Now it was real and she felt wildly conflicting impulses. She would tell this man about his daughter. No, that's the last thing she would do!

As she paced about, Anna was conscious of him staring up at her in utter confusion. He could not have known that she was trapped in the past, transported to that room in The Wellington Hotel where he had appeared like an apparition after vanishing from her life two and a half years earlier. In the moments before Moriarty had burst in on them, she had told Marin that the doctors had discovered while she was in hospital that she was pregnant. The young Marin, his voice shaking with emotion, had demanded to know what had happened to the baby. Now her own words rushed back into her head:

What do you think happened? I waited. I even reached out to your father for the first time, but he refused to talk to me. I waited as long as I could Marin, but you had disappeared into thin air . . .

Anna had always regretted her decision to terminate that pregnancy. It was why she had gone ahead and had Rachel.

She looked now at the desolate middle-aged warrior tensed up and rigid on the wooden chair, turning an unlit cigarette between his stained fingers. It remained true that she had no idea what he had become. Whatever picture was forming seemed to change as rapidly as clouds in a high wind, threatening to blow away at any moment. There were just too many unanswered questions.

'Are you all right?' he rasped.

'It's just . . .' She stopped herself and started again. 'Oh, fuck. I'm just trying to get it together, okay? Give me a moment.'

Marin said nothing. Eventually, she sat back down, put her elbows on the table and leant towards him. For a time she stared into his face, looking for something in those familiar but elusive eyes.

'I've waited long enough,' she said finally. 'I can't do this anymore. Your war stories can wait. Everything else can wait. I want you to tell me why you disappeared in the first place. I have to know.'

'1970?' he said.

'Yes.'

THE DEMO

22

THE TRIBE, SYDNEY, AUSTRALIA

18 SEPTEMBER 1970

ANNA WAS WORKING in her glassed-in editor's office at *The Tribe* when Pierre Villiers burst in and threw a pile of copy onto her desk.

'Fuck this man!' he cried.

'Who?' said Anna, genuinely perplexed.

'Bob-fucking-Dylan man.'

'What about him?'

'He's pro-war, that's what,' said Pierre. He spat a wad of masticated gum into the rubbish bin as if expelling some rancid thing. Anna picked up the bundle of fax paper.

'What the hell is this?' she asked.

'It's a piece by A.J. Weberman,' said Pierre. 'We'll have to run it; but fucken hell, it's a bummer.'

'Weberman? Never heard of him.'

'Weberman's the underground's Bob Dylan investigator,' said Pierre, unaware that over his shoulder a large, dark-complected figure had just appeared in the doorway. 'Runs a course in New York called Dylanology. Got caught going through Dylan's rubbish bins with his students.'

'That's a low act.'

The voice came from behind Pierre. Anna looked up at the figure in the doorway. She felt a flush of warmth and noticed at the same moment Pierre's grimace when he recognised who it was.

'G'day,' she said to Marin Katich, who walked straight in and took a seat, his presence immediately altering the vibe between her and her deputy editor. 'I wasn't expecting you.'

'I was on campus. Thought I'd drop by.' Marin caught Pierre's eye. 'How are you going, mate?'

Pierre responded with a sullen nod. 'I'll take those back,' he said, retrieving the bundle of papers from Anna's hands. 'I've got to get on with this.'

'Hang on,' said Marin. 'Who's this bloke going through Dylan's garbage?'

'The gonzo journalist A.J. Weberman,' said Pierre, somewhat pompously, as if he alone was hip to this.

Marin looked puzzled. 'Gonzo?' he queried.

'It's a big thing in the States,' Anna explained. 'The journalist puts herself or himself in the centre of the story, completely subjective reporting, immersive, no need to pretend you've got no stake in the outcome.'

Marin smiled at that. 'Hasn't that always been your guiding principle here?' he asked mischievously.

'More an aspiration,' said Anna.

'Come on,' said Pierre. 'Gonzo's way more radical than that.'

Anna judged Pierre had sensed the chance for sport at Marin's expense.

'It works best,' he went on, 'if you ingest some mind-altering substance and infiltrate yourself into somewhere you don't belong,' he said, turning to Marin. 'If it was you, for example, I'd slip you a tab of acid, dress you in cheesecloth and sandals, and send you off to report on the Moratorium.'

'I'd be up for that,' said Marin. 'So what? This Weberman bloke dropped acid and climbed into Bob Dylan's rubbish bin?'

'I didn't say that,' said Pierre. 'But I wouldn't put it past him. Weberman used to be Dylan's biggest fan; now his schtick is that Bob's sold out, turned into a rich, secret conservative who doesn't believe any of the shit in his old protest songs.'

'Wow,' said Anna.

'Yeah, Dylan's been captured by the military-industrial complex, hostage to its agenda anyway. So Weberman starts up the D.L.F.— Dylan Liberation Front—to free Bob from himself.'

'That part's cool and funny,' said Anna. 'But saying Dylan's pro the Vietnam War? He's just taking the piss, isn't he?'

'You ever seen Dylan at a protest?' said Pierre.

'Joan Baez says he's not into politics,' said Anna. 'I can dig that.'

'Hang on,' said Marin. 'This Weberman might be onto something. Dylan did an interview two years ago and this fella asked him if artists had a responsibility to use their influence to stop the war. Dylan turns around and says, "I know some very good artists who are *for* the war." The interviewer nearly fell out of his chair.'

'Trust you to know that,' said Pierre.

'Why wouldn't I?' said Marin. 'I'm writing a thesis on hypocrisy.'

'I've never heard of Dylan saying that stuff,' said Anna.

'It was an interview for *Sing Out* magazine,' said Pierre.

'So,' she said, 'you're agreeing with Marin?'

'I'm not taking pleasure from it like he is,' said Pierre.

'It doesn't make sense,' said Anna. 'He wrote "Masters of War", for fuck's sake. He's got to have been taken out of context.'

She looked at Marin, but saw he was staring hard at Pierre.

'Taking pleasure?' said Marin. 'That's total bullshit, Pierre. These are just facts. Dylan lets his guard down sometimes. He told the same interviewer about a painter, an old friend of his—apparently this painter's all for the war. So much so, he's ready to go over there himself to join the fight. And Bob says, "Well, that's something I can comprehend." No wonder he's not marching.'

Pierre winked at Anna and stood up, tucking the Weberman article under his arm.

'Don't you know someone like that?' he said and turned to walk back into the newsroom. He stopped at the door and called back at Anna. 'By the way. Don't forget there's a meeting of the V.M.C. tonight, at Bob Gould's house.'

'Oh, bugger,' she said. 'I'd completely forgotten. What time?'

'Starts at six, supposedly,' said Pierre, glancing at Marin. 'But it'll probably get going later than that and drag on for hours, as usual.'

Pierre left them to think about that and drifted back into *The Tribe*'s crowded newsroom, brandishing the Weberman diatribe and ready to plot the downfall of that famous Nixonian reactionary, Bob Dylan.

When he was out of sight, Anna stood up and held Marin in a tight hug. She put both hands on his buttocks and pulled him closer, went up on her toes and whispered in his ear: 'I had a different idea for tonight.'

Marin kissed her.

'Why don't we meet for dinner,' he said. 'Once you've finished with the Moratorium revolutionaries.'

'They're not—'

'I know,' Marin interrupted her. 'It's a broad coalition. Of course it is, but you're meeting at Bob Gould's, right?'

'Yeah. So?'

'So he's a paleo-Trot, isn't he?'

Anna didn't bite. She was well aware that the fabled broad coalition had been rapidly disintegrating in the months since Moratorium One. The union movement had lost interest. Frank Rosen's faction of the Communist Party was trying to gain control of the Vietnam Moratorium Committees. So were the Trotskyites and the Maoists, with notably less success. Meanwhile, the right-wing of the Labor Party was on a unity ticket with the conservatives in their hatred of the French Socialist–inspired idea of 'contestation'. They were anxious to stop a radical vanguard, out of their control, successfully mobilising mass action for change.

'How about dinner at seven-thirty?' she said. 'Over the road from my place.'

Marin pulled a face. 'That veggie joint?'

'The Toucan, yeah,' she said. 'I thought you liked it.'

'No, I love it,' he said, kissing her again. 'See you there.'

•

Marin left Anna at *The Tribe*, ran down the stairs, kick-started the big bike and roared out onto City Road. He had some free time after handing in two big essays, and he wanted to get home to Leichhardt while his father was still on shift on the Bridge and Petar was still at school. Twice in the past week, Anna had asked him about his mother and her questions had lodged in his mind like a splinter. He was in the habit of not thinking about the woman who had walked out on him and Petar, but when he did it was like a sweet sickness. None of his memories of her made sense.

He parked the bike in the driveway of his house, closed the gate and yanked on the roller door until it went up with its usual tortured scream. In the back of the garage were stacks of mouldering boxes. They were full of old toys and adventure books and other belongings the brothers had grown out of. He found many things in them: his and Petar's school reports; forgotten sporting pennants and trophies; exercise books full of childish compositions; drawings and paintings. He sorted through this musty old stuff, oddly discomforted by nostalgia for his disturbing childhood, until he at last found what he was looking for: a shoebox full of photographs.

Marin sat there among the scattered relics of his childhood and flicked slowly through the photos. Most were school class portraits, or sports photos of Petar and him playing cricket and rugby, or snapshots of awkward birthday parties. Buried among this dross, he found a single photo of his mother. He had hoped it would still be there, having somehow escaped Ivo's purge. It had been taken one summer when Petar was an infant. She was holding the chubby toddler on her lap while he, Marin, was standing beside her, bare-chested in a pair of khaki shorts. She was a beautiful woman with calm green eyes. Her arm was over his shoulder.

There had been no warning to the boys that she was going, and since then no phone calls and no letters. Questions to his father went unanswered and soon the boys were forbidden to speak her name. Marin's parents had had plenty of arguments that he had witnessed as a child, so he knew there had been tensions; but there had been no final confrontation, no dramatic departure from the house. From one day to the next, she had simply vanished.

As he grew older, Marin began to harbour dark fantasies about what might have happened to her, and with Ivo's black moods murder became the dominant fantasy. Only once did he confront his father directly, Ivo so drunk that he was barely coherent, yet he had given Marin his only account of what might have happened: 'She's back with the fucking communists! Back in Bosnia! She betrayed us, Marin, betrayed us all.'

Marin carefully tucked the photograph into a pocket and packed away the boxes. He left a note on the fridge, vaguely explaining that he would not be home tonight.

•

At 7.30 pm, he was in the Toucan Café on Glebe Point Road, immediately opposite Anna's apartment. From where he was sitting, he had a view through the bay windows of her room under the slate witch's hat. Anna had left a desk lamp on and he could see the top of the big cedar wardrobe and the globe of the rice-paper lantern hanging from the ceiling. It was strange looking into the room from the outside.

He had a mental image of Anna hunched over her typewriter in her silk dressing gown, enveloped in smoke from a hash-enhanced rollie, puffing on it as she banged away at an essay, or an editorial for *The Tribe*, or an overwrought anti-war speech. He thought about her energy, her maddening enthusiasms, her passion for ideas and her private gentleness. He felt a fluttering sensation in his stomach, anxious to see her walk in through the door, anxious to know she was real—anxious, for no reason, that he might lose her.

Marin ordered a soy-milk banana smoothie with wheat germ. He grimaced when it arrived and wished he had arranged to meet at the pub down the road; no way to change that now. At eight o'clock, there was still no sign of her and he walked outside to have a smoke on the pavement, staring uselessly up into the empty room, as if some activity might suddenly begin there. He went back into the restaurant and a few minutes later the waiter came over to tell him there was a phone call for him. It was Anna, apologising for being late. She'd been held up in a meeting.

'I'm so sorry,' she said. Relieved just to hear her voice, he told her not to worry about it. 'I'll be able to get away soon. Will you wait for me?'

'Maybe at the pub?'

'Or at my place?' she suggested. 'Rob in the apartment at the back has a spare key. He's home now and I rang him and asked him to give it to you, so if you want to go in . . .'

'Sure.'

'I'll make a nice supper for us later.'

•

The front door of the Glebe house was always unlocked, so Marin entered and climbed the stairs, up past the handpainted eye above the first-floor iridology studio, up to the apartment at the back of the house on Anna's floor. Through the door, he heard classical music. He knocked loudly.

It opened a crack and a pair of bloodshot eyes peered out of the gloom. 'Yeesssss.'

'I'm Anna's friend,' said Marin. 'She told me she rang you about a spare key . . .'

'Oh. Oh, right, so *you're* Marin.' The door opened to reveal the shiny, inflamed, pockmarked face in which those intense, red-rimmed eyes were set. It was an unhealthy visage framed by an unruly mop of greasy black hair.

'I'm Rob. Come in. Come in. Would you like a cup of tea, a glass of sherry? Something stronger?'

'No, thanks, I'm fine.'

'Now don't be shy. Anna said I should be nice to you.'

Rob came out into the hallway and took Marin by the arm. 'She said she'd be some time, and I told her I'd take care of you. Don't make a liar of me. At least come in while I find the key.'

Marin saw now that this odd creature was wearing a red silk dressing gown loosely knotted around his waist and, evidently, nothing else but a pair of Chinese slippers. Marin reluctantly allowed himself to be guided through the doorway and, now that he could hear the music properly, he was struck by its beguiling quality.

The hallway was dimly lit and painted as deep a red as Rob's silk gown. There were pictures, mostly old oil paintings in gilt frames, hung along it at intervals. Marin glimpsed an untidy bedroom with rumpled satin sheets, gold like the picture frames. The hallway opened into a large room dominated by an upright piano and huge bookcases, more than half of which appeared to be stacked full of long-play records. One shelf held a spinning turntable and at either end of the room were large speakers that filled the space with a sound so perfect that he had the sensation of sitting in the middle of an orchestra.

Marin stood still for a moment, mesmerised by it. 'What's this music?' he asked.

Rob paused, gathering the silk gown tighter around him and retying it. His head tilted to one side and his hands fluttered up as if he were conducting the invisible orchestra. 'Sublime, isn't it,' he mused.

'It is.'

'It's Mahler's fourth symphony, the third movement. It's hard to believe this came out of the head of a mortal man. Sit, sit and listen.' Rob gestured to a pair of faded wing-backed chairs on an oriental carpet. 'I'll get you a drink and find those keys.'

Marin sat down and relaxed in spite of himself. The symphony swelled with an enthralling beauty, but at the same time he heard undertones of something darker. It immersed him and directly engaged his emotions. He had never experienced classical music in this way.

Rob returned and put a large glass of whisky in his hand. 'I thought you might prefer this to a cup of tea,' he said. 'I hope you don't mind if I leave the volume high?'

'No, no, I like it.'

'That's good, then. It needs to be heard like this, loud and present, not as background sound, especially if you're listening to it for the first time. Now, I'm still trying to find where I put that key,' said Rob and slipped out again.

Katich sipped the whisky, which was surprisingly smooth, and he felt its warmth suffuse him. He became aware of themes in the music coming and going like tempting glimpses of a familiar tune, lifting the spirits for a moment then giving way to a slow, harmonious peace that made him imagine drifting to sleep in some sheltered place. Then, without warning, it turned menacing, a sudden storm gathering with clashing instrumentation and a drum beating a relentless slave-galley rhythm.

Rob came back into the room at that moment, carrying his own glass of whisky and the bottle. He put the bottle down on a side table, folded himself into the opposite wing-backed chair and took a long drink. He caught Marin's attention with a languid gesture of his hand.

'Mahler once described this section in a letter,' he said. 'He wrote that it's as if the sky goes dark and horrible, suddenly ghastly, like being overtaken by an attack of panic on the most beautiful day in a light-filled forest.'

'That's a good description,' said Marin.

'But wait for it all to change,' said Rob as the cacophony reached a climax. 'We're about to ascend to heaven.'

Rob carefully arranged the silk gown over his knees, unsuccessfully protecting his modesty, as he fished out of a pocket a packet of Marlboro Red. He tapped one out and reached across to offer it to Marin. 'They don't let fags into heaven,' said Rob with an ironic wink. 'Best to bring your own.'

They sat silently, drinking whisky and smoking, as the movement turned from sinister to ethereal; Marin understood what Rob had meant by the ascent to heaven. The highest shimmering strains of the violins became higher and higher still, accompanied by sparse notes on the harps until the flutes chimed in, creating the sensation of slow, slow flight.

'It's almost an out-of-body experience,' said Rob as he leant over to refill his companion's glass. Already light-headed from the whisky, Marin nodded, drank some more and looked down. He was thinking of the photograph in his pocket. His mind had gone back to the day it was taken.

They were on a summer holiday. He was shirtless, having run back from the surf, and his mother was sitting in the shade breast-feeding baby Petar. In that moment, the harsh sunlight filtered by the gum trees, she was like a Renaissance Madonna. He felt tears welling up in his eyes and put a hand to his forehead to cover them.

The music had done this to him, somehow recovering that memory of innocence in a shadowed forest. How had Rob described it? *Suddenly ghastly, like being overtaken by an attack of panic on the most beautiful day in a light-filled forest.* Then it came to him. Someone else was there, the person behind the camera. Of course, it had to be his father. Ivo had taken the picture. He was there all along. The thought sent a chill through Marin, drying his tears even as the music reached its final note of yearning joy and sadness.

As the note died out, Rob resumed his disquisition.

'It's coming to the end now,' he said as the orchestra picked up the strands of an earlier tune. 'One of the strangest endings to any symphony, a poem sung by the soprano. She has sat still, patient, in front of the conductor through the whole movement. Imagine all of that emotion filling her up and now she stands to sing.'

Marin looked up as the woman's voice filled the room with a ringing, joyful sound, an antidote to the earlier menace.

'It's German,' said Rob. 'Do you understand any of it?'

'No, I don't speak German.'

His father did, of course . . .

'It's a song Mahler wrote before he even started work on the Fourth Symphony. *Das himmlische Leben*—'The Heavenly Life'—a child's vision of paradise as a garden in which your every need is provided for: fish that swim happily into nets, deer that run down the street, overflowing fruit bowls and so on. Listen,' said Rob, holding up a long finger. '*No worldly turmoil is heard in heaven. We all live in sweetest peace.* That's what she's singing.'

Rob was conducting again with small and subtle movements of his left hand and he shut his eyes. Then he returned to reality and refilled his glass, offering the bottle again to Marin who waved it away.

'I've had enough, thanks.'

'Some critics hate this song,' said Rob. 'They say it's too mawkish, but I think they just don't get it. There's nothing mawkish about Mahler's heaven. Alongside the beauty, there's malevolence and danger: *John lets out the little lamb. Herod the butcher lies in wait for it! We lead a patient, innocent, patient darling little lamb to its death!* Do you see? Herod, the mass murderer, the slaughterer of the innocents, he's right there among the children in heaven. What should we make of that?'

Marin looked at him for a moment before answering. 'Evil is everywhere. It's a part of life.'

Rob looked at him thoughtfully.

Marin heard the song finish and the weighted arm of the turntable slid off and began jerking. Rob jumped up and placed the arm carefully into its cradle, then turned back.

'Bravo, Marin,' he said. 'That's rather a deep answer. I think you've understood this music better than many who've heard it a thousand times.'

Now the spell of the music was over, Marin stood up from his chair. 'I better go,' he said. 'Anna will be home soon.'

Rob reached into his pocket and produced the key. 'Oh yes,' he said. 'You'll need this.'

'Thanks,' said Marin. 'And thank you for explaining the music. You're a good teacher.' He gestured to the piano. 'Is that what you do?'

'No, no,' Rob laughed. 'I teach linguistics.'

'Oh, I don't know much about linguistics.'

'No, nobody does,' said Rob. He shook Marin's hand. 'It was nice to meet you, Marin. Not many people would sit and listen to music they have never heard before with such attention. It really did engage you, am I right? Come back again when you have some spare time.'

'I will,' said Marin, doubting it.

•

It was after ten o'clock when Anna got back home. Marin was lying on the couch in the sitting room, reading in the pool of light from an angled lamp. It was an unseasonably warm night and he had opened the doors to the balcony. She leant across the back of the couch and ran her fingers through his hair.

'Oh, hello,' he said, putting the book aside and sitting up.

Anna kissed him, threw down her satchel and slumped into the old armchair opposite the couch. 'Sorry I'm so late. That meeting was a nightmare.'

Marin raised his eyebrows. 'That's the problem with revolutionary committees,' he said. 'It's never more than one or two steps down the track before they start the purges.'

Anna laughed. 'Oh dear,' she said. 'I wish that was just a joke.'

'It's no laughing matter,' said Marin with mock solemnity, retrieving the book he'd been reading. 'Especially if they come searching and find stuff like this in your bookcases.'

Anna recognised the cover: a man sitting in a dark room, his face deliberately scratched out—Francis Bacon's *Man in Blue V*.

'*Darkness at Noon*,' she said. 'Imagine you zeroing in on that.'

'I just didn't expect to find an anti-communist classic among the usual suspects.'

'Well, most of Orwell's books are there too,' she said. 'Have you read *Homage to Catalonia*?'

'No, I haven't.'

'It's Orwell's memoir of the Spanish Civil War. If you're interested in Koestler, you'd better read it. There's a connection between the two of them. Koestler was in Spain at the same time as Orwell. Sent there by the Soviets as a spy. Did you know that?'

'No, I didn't,' said Marin, impressed again by the depth of her knowledge.

Anna explained how Franco's security police had Arthur Koestler under surveillance, tumbled that he was a Soviet spy and threw him in prison.

'Koestler was sure they were going to execute him,' she said. 'That's why *Darkness at Noon* feels so real. He knows exactly what would have been going through Rubashov's head as he waited to be dragged down into the cellar.'

'I just read those last pages again,' said Marin. 'Do you remember? Rubashov insists they let him take a piss even though he knows they're about to put a bullet in his head.'

'It's hard to forget,' said Anna. 'Then, when the executioner is behind him, he smells the oiled leather of the man's gun belt and all he can think is: where's the Promised Land? The poor bastard knows he's been duped. No Promised Land; nothing but desert and darkness.'

Marin stared at her with frank admiration. He loved her mind, the way it worked.

'You know,' she said. 'Despite what you might imagine, it was my father who gave me that book. He was the one who taught me to question everything.'

'Yet he stayed in the Party,' said Marin. 'After Budapest, even after Prague.'

'That's right,' said Anna. 'He could have walked away. That's what I did. But he's a reformer. He believes the only way to change things is from within.'

'He's got his work cut out for him.'

'That's true,' she acknowledged. 'So . . . you met Rob, then?'

Marin saw amusement in her eyes. 'I did.'

'And?'

'And what?'

'Rob usually makes an impression.'

'Oh, he made an impression all right,' said Marin. 'He's a cross between Bertolt Brecht and Frank Thring.'

'The red silk gown?'

'Yeah, that and nothing else.'

'I always avert my eyes.'

'He translated a nice German song for me. It was quite a performance—the soprano, a glass of scotch and a pair of low-hanging hairy balls.'

Anna laughed again and stood up. 'Well, if you can put up with a few eccentricities, he's worth it. He's a genius, actually. Now I bet you're hungry. Come on—I'll make something to eat. I'm starving.'

As Anna busied herself assembling a salad in the small kitchen, Marin straddled a chair and watched her bend to light the oven grill.

'Do you want a hand?'

'No, no, it's fine.'

'Can I just grab your bum then?'

'Don't you dare.'

He reached out, but she swung around and threw the lit match into his lap.

'Hey!' Marin yelled. 'Fuck!' He jumped up, flapping his hands at the flame.

'I warned you,' she said as she lit the gas and slid a tray of bread under the griller.

'That was dangerous,' said Marin.

'You were playing with fire,' she said, coming back to sit on his lap. 'And I was protecting my dignity.'

They kissed until he smelled something burning. 'Speaking of fire . . .'

'Oops, the toast!'

Anna jumped up, pulled the tray out, flipped the smoking bread slices and pushed it back in.

'See what happens when you distract me,' she said, handing him a bottle of wine. 'Here, open this.'

Anna grilled cheese and tomato on the toast, sprinkled it with tabasco and salt, and set it on the table with the salad as Marin poured the wine.

'Not exactly gourmet fare, I'm afraid,' she said.

'You're wrong. The tabasco makes all the difference.'

They ate and drank until the hunger pangs subsided. Marin refilled their glasses; he watched as Anna picked at the salad for a while until she detected his mood had changed.

'What is it?' she asked.

'I've got something to show you.'

'Okay,' she said, still fishing in the salad bowl, her fingers on an oily lettuce leaf. He pulled the photograph out of his pocket and held it out to her. Anna wiped her fingers clean and took it from him, holding it carefully by the edges.

'Your mother?'

'Yep, that's her. I found the picture at home.'

'She's beautiful, Marin. Will you tell me about her now?'

'Her name is Samira.'

Anna pointed at the chubby little kid.

'And that's Petar?'

'Yes, just a toddler then. He was five when she left.'

'Look at you—little tough guy. Is it really true that you have no other pictures of her?'

'Petar has some that he found in the house years ago.'

'But your father tried to destroy them all. That's terribly cruel.'

'She left him, Anna. And she left us. We were just kids. Would you forgive that?'

Anna felt a surge of indignation. 'She must have had her reasons,' she said. 'There's always more to stories like that.'

'Maybe, but she never wrote to us. Never made contact in all these years. How do you explain that? Is that how mothers behave?'

'No, that's horrible. But I would still want to speak to her and hear what she had to say.'

'All these years I've thought about her as if she's dead. That's all I can do.'

'But you still kept the photo.'

'Yeah, but I only went to find it to show you.'

'Do you think you'll ever want to go and find her? To ask her all those questions?'

'She went back to Bosnia with some man. I don't even know his name.'

'She was still young. She may have had other children. You could have half-brothers or -sisters over there.'

'I don't want to think about that.'

'Don't you think something will always be missing if you never know?'

'Maybe it's best not to know.'

Anna pondered this. 'Her name—Samira—is that a Catholic name?'

'I wondered if you might ask that.'

'Why?'

'It's a Muslim name.'

'You're kidding! Your mum's a Muslim?'

'Not a practising Muslim. She was quite secular, as you'd imagine since she married a Catholic. And she's blonde with green eyes, same as mine. Who could tell if it weren't for the name, but I do remember her telling me years ago that her father used to go regularly to the mosque.'

'Your grandfather.'

'I don't think of him like that.'

'But he is.'

'It's too hard to think about.'

'And what about the man she ran away with?'

'I don't know and I don't care.'

•

On Friday morning, the day of Moratorium Two, Marin woke to find Anna already up and in her battledress, although he knew she would vehemently object to such a militaristic description of her costume. Somehow *peacedress* just didn't trip off the tongue.

He was looking at her through the bars at the end of the brass bed. His gaze moved up from the laced ankle boots to the tight black jeans and the denim jacket embroidered with a large peace symbol and freighted with multifarious buttons and badges. Then up to the Palestinian keffiyeh around her neck and the woven band around her forehead. She was the very model of the modern militant.

He interrupted her preparations: 'You off for a job interview?'

'Oh,' said Anna 'You're awake.'

'An extra in *Zabriskie Point*, maybe?' he said.

'Smart-arse.'

'Can't you just come back to bed?'

Anna jumped up beside him, knees bouncing on the mattress so the metal frame rattled, a reminder of the long night. She leant over him.

'Come on,' she said, 'You knew what you were signing up for.'

'I'm not complaining,' said Marin. He reached up, grabbed two handfuls of the keffiyeh, pulled her down and kissed her.

She jumped back up, smiling down at him. 'We can come back to this later, can't we?' she said. 'Tonight, when it's over. Keep the spare key. I promise I won't be late.'

'I'll probably have to bail you out first.'

'Don't worry,' she said. 'We've got contingencies for that. But I won't do anything silly.'

He wanted to say: *It's not you I'm worried about.*

'Okay, see you later,' he said. 'Take care.'

'Of course,' she said.

That was the only false note, and it seemed to hang in the air after she blew a kiss from the doorway and left.

•

Marin levered himself off the creaking bed, went to the bay window and leant over her desk to look out. He saw her on the street below: lithe and full of energy, a colourful, captivating presence moving swiftly past the dull morning commuters at the bus stop. He noticed the gold, woven peace sign on her back was glowing in the morning sunlight and it seemed to him in that moment like a moving target. She turned the corner onto Parramatta Road and was lost to him.

He went into the little kitchen and found it cluttered with last night's plates and wineglasses. He filled the Atomic coffee machine, which looked, as the name suggested, like a bomb. He washed up, emptied the ashtrays and got things shipshape as the Atomic sat quivering on the gas burner until a wild burst of steam shot out of its safety valve.

Marin drank his coffee black and bitter, and smoked a cigarette while he thought about what to do. He thought about the Moratorium and how it was all going to shit. The Maoists and the Trots were at each other's throats, and the Anarchists were at war with both of them. The Anarchists, at least, he felt some sympathy with. Sure, they were against the war, but they also opposed the Stalinist regime in North Vietnam and they liked to rile up the other rads with the chant: '*Ho Ho Ho Chi Minh, chuck him in the garbage bin.*'

Down in Melbourne, Albert Langer's lunatic Maoists at Monash Uni, infamous for collecting money to send to the Viet Cong, now had the student council in permanent session passing revolutionary motions. Here in Sydney, the nutters wanted everyone to dress up in black pyjamas and carry NLF flags. Marin understood that the hard left was no longer satisfied with marches and speeches. They wanted a serious confrontation with the police army, the imperialist state and the bourgeoisie.

Nor did the state seem any less crazy to him. Government ministers were ramping it up with hysterical rhetoric about Moratorium 'mob rule'. Billy Snedden, the minister in charge of conscription, had condemned protesters as 'political bikies pack-raping democracy'. Others had warned that the new social movements behind the Moratorium were bent on destroying society by weakening the cement between its bricks. As if to remedy that in single-armed combat, Attorney-General Tom Hughes had set upon protesters outside his house with a cricket bat.

For all this headline-grabbing nonsense, Marin knew the outcry from the federal politicians was just piss and wind. He was more worried about their state counterparts. Here in New South Wales, the premier, Bob Askin, had given his police free rein for Moratorium Two. Askin told the press he'd been too lenient ahead of the first big demo in May; he had changed the Summary Offences Act to make it easier to arrest demonstrators, urging his judges and magistrates to make an example of these 'lawless minorities'.

Late last night, Marin had learned from Anna that the police commissioner had refused, at the last minute, to approve the Moratorium organisers' applications for the marchers to use city streets. The police were now demanding that tens of thousands of protestors confine themselves to narrow footpaths. When she told him this news, Marin responded that Blind Freddy could see that both sides were spoiling for a fight and that an ugly, violent confrontation was inevitable. Anna had not welcomed his advice; she said she had enough to think about without that kind of negativity.

The conversation had started badly and, when it threatened to get worse, he shut up and kept his darkest thoughts to himself. Marin's biggest fear was that the police would target Anna as a key activist and organiser, and that, as the daughter of a senior communist, the target on her back was even bigger. He decided she would need an angel looking over her shoulder.

•

In the late afternoon, Marin was moving among the crowd of spectators at Railway Square, waiting for the marchers coming down Broadway from the university. He could see them now snaking towards him, a tight-packed mob incongruously resembling a medieval army behind its banners and under its forest of flags. Marin had dressed in a black suit with a white shirt and tie, like an office worker out to gawk at the demo, or one of the many journalists who were buzzing around the crowd as purposefully as worker bees. He saw that the media people, especially those carrying cameras, appeared immune from the rules about staying off the street. They hovered unchallenged behind the rows of hundreds of blue-suited police whose job was to keep people pressed onto the sidewalk. Marin watched a TV crew dip into the crowd and question a group of bystanders. A young woman with shopping bags in each hand giggled and leant into the outstretched microphone. 'I'd march,' she said. 'But I wouldn't be game enough really.' A young man nearby with a pockmarked face and hair to his shoulders sought out the camera: 'I'm here because there's a Moratorium going on,' he said in the voice of a man twice his age. 'And I don't believe in it and I want to show my disapproval when it comes by.'

This unexpected exchange caused a flurry of activity from other TV reporters, who fretted they might miss a defining moment. A supercilious-looking fellow in a tweed jacket plunged into the crowd and thrust his wind-socked microphone in Marin's direction like a blunted bayonet. When Marin turned away, the camera's eye settled instead on a middle-aged woman, stern-faced with a stiff perm held in place by a chiffon scarf.

Tweedy asked her why she was here.

'To see that it's carried out orderly,' she said, her downturned mouth barely moving. 'Just to see what the young ones have got in mind.'

'Do you support the Moratorium?' asked Tweedy.

'I do,' she said.

Now they could hear the repetitive chanting of the approaching demonstration: '*One, two, three, four . . . We don't want your fucking war!*'

Marin felt the arousal of the crowd. People bent towards the road, craning their necks, policemen tensed, photographers ran down the road, kneeling like supplicants before the oncoming marchers.

Tweedy turned away from the little group that had gathered around his camera and stood alert. Marin imagined his ears going up like a retriever. But two men in his vicinity refused to be ignored. Marin had seen them emerge, half-cut, from the nearby pub and make a beeline for the posh-accented reporter with the leather patches on his elbows, evidently spotting the sure signs of a wanker.

The taller of the two, a horse-faced tough with dangerous smile and a black tooth, grabbed Tweedy's arm.

'One of my mates was shot in Vietnam, mate,' he said, eyes moist. 'You reckon that's funny, do ya? You reckon these marchers care, do ya?'

His drinking companion jumped in: 'You couldn't be a bigger clown if you tried!' He had a pudding-bowl haircut and a beer belly that put his shirt under strain at every button. Marin saw that the pair had worked themselves up for a fight with the first pacifist they came across and it might have gone south for Tweedy at that moment but for the intervention of a big man with an impressive Roman nose who pushed in front of them.

'What about the Czechs?' he demanded of Tweedy. 'Only Vietnamese people suffer? Why not one of you people got one placard Freedom for the Czechs!'

'Not *my* people . . .' Tweedy began, before being pulled out of danger by his cameraman. The reporter pedalled backwards holding the microphone like a defensive weapon.

The first marchers had reached the crowd on the footpath and were forced to push on through, into what had now become a serious bottleneck.

ONE, TWO, THREE, FOUR . . . WE DON'T WANT YOUR FUCKING WAR!

•

Marin stepped out onto the road ahead of the crush, moving alongside Tweedy and his crew as if he too was part of the fourth estate. He scanned the crowd searching for Anna. As the body of the demonstration hit the bottleneck, it was obvious that this many people could not be funnelled through such a narrow space. When individuals spilled onto the road, the police began cutting them out like rogue cattle, roughly pinioning and manhandling them into the back of waiting wagons. Shouts of outrage, screams and cries came from the milling crowd.

In the uproar, voices were indistinguishable, but Marin guessed that Horse Face and his mate had found their real enemy. There were scuffles and flurries of violence, which worsened when the police—in squads, in pairs or on their own—elbowed their way into the disintegrating march to rip flagpoles out of the hands of protesters. Marin heard them shouting that they were confiscating weapons, that flagpoles were potential spears or pikes.

He saw a tug of war between a policeman at one end and a young woman at the other, fighting to keep hold of her red-and-black anarchist flag. The flag was finally ripped off the pole, and the woman wrapped it around her neck and threw up a fist to the cheers of those around her.

Then Marin heard a familiar voice on a loudspeaker: 'STAY ON THE FOOTPATH! STAY COOL! DON'T BE PROVOKED. SLOW DOWN AND STAY ON THE FOOTPATH!'

He spotted Anna up above the crowd. She had climbed onto a big green box built to house telephone junctions. One arm was wrapped around a light pole and the other held a megaphone. She was directing the marchers into the narrow space on the footpath. He found it strange watching her from a distance in this role; regardless of his own political views, he felt a surge of pride, but he was careful to keep out of her sight. He knew Anna would not thank him for being here and would probably flip her lid at the idea of being stalked by an overprotective boyfriend.

'STAY OFF THE STREET! THEY WILL ARREST YOU IF YOU SET ONE FOOT ON THE STREET! THE COPS ARE TRYING TO PROVOKE US! STAY OFF THE STREET! DON'T LET THEM! DON'T FALL INTO THEIR TRAP!'

The police were still wrestling flags from the hands of protesters, but he saw that Anna and other marshals had restored some order. Most of the protesters managed to avoid arrest, edging through the bottleneck to continue the long march up George Street.

Marin skipped ahead of them, running with the media. He passed department stores, office blocks, a cinema, cafés and other small traders and then, on either side of the street, he saw the Yugoslav travel agencies his father had branded as treacherous communist fronts. Further on, in the forecourt of Sydney Town

Hall, a large body of police and empty paddy wagons were waiting, ready to arrest any radicals who might try to occupy this prime protest real estate, where only a few months earlier protesters had gathered during Moratorium One to make their speeches and burn their draft cards.

By mid-afternoon, protesters began to pour into Wynyard Park. One large group had walked over the Harbour Bridge. Others came down King Street, some from Circular Quay, or to Wynyard itself on buses and trains. The numbers swelled and Marin heard estimates from journalists, who claimed some mystical ability to estimate crowd sizes—fifteen thousand, said some; twenty thousand, said others. They all agreed the police would halve those estimates.

The large numbers of police around the park were determined that no one should leave the tight cordon in which they planned to contain the growing crowd. Marin tried to keep Anna in sight as she moved from place to place, speaking to other organisers. He found a marshal with an orange vest and a Moratorium armband, and learned from him that when the whole group had assembled the protesters would defy police instructions en masse and march down the centre of York Street back to Town Hall to occupy its forecourt and stairs.

There was no traffic in York Street. The police had closed it at either end. As a result, there was no ostensible reason why the marchers should remain on the footpaths. Marin realised this was what the police and the premier had wanted all along and had planned for: a fig leaf of legality to crush the demonstration. They would provoke a violent confrontation to send the message to the cautious middle class that they should stay away from this radical movement.

As people continued to make their way into the little park— spilling out of buses, walking in from side streets—it filled up like a packed peak-hour train, and Marin sensed a claustrophobic edginess. He watched a middle-aged woman with three kids in tow; she was searching for a way out, and being rebuffed by police. They happily let people in, but not out. He looked around at the faces in the burgeoning, restive, hemmed-in crowd. Many looked tired and pissed off, or simply confused. A smaller group were hyped up, ready to go. He had the odd thought that they were like replacement troops sent to the trenches, nervously waiting for the order to go over the top.

He glimpsed Anna from time to time, bent in urgent talks with groups of worried organisers, and he was trying to keep her in sight when a troupe of Viet Cong swept in front of him, performing for Tweedy's camera. They wore black outfits, the dark stripes of their headbands stark against white grease-painted faces. Painted tears of blood tracked down from their blackened eyes and blood dripped from the corners of their mouths. They moved in slow circles, stalking an imaginary enemy with invisible machine guns before dying sequentially, each with their own artistic variation, silently screaming and writhing on the ground.

Without warning, people around Marin began to move, as if some hive mind had activated them. Up ahead, banners were unfurled, hand-drawn signs unrolled, fluttering flags raised. The march was forming. As Marin pushed his way through the press of people, someone held up a large photo of Uncle Ho and began a chant:

HO! HO! HO CHI MINH! HO! HO! HO CHI MINH!

Marin pushed past the chanters and saw through gaps in the bodies joining the march that hundreds of police were running into position as a superintendent raised his megaphone.

'REMAIN ON THE FOOTPATHS! DO NOT WALK IN THE STREET!'

In the no man's land between the roiling crowd and the agitated cops, photographers ran, crouched, shot, ran, crouched, shot, twisting between the opposed forces. Tweedy was there with his TV crew and Marin broke through to stand with them.

'This could be bloody!' Tweedy said to him, journo to journo, a strange light in his eyes. Marin looked at the lines of cops. Many were raw-faced country boys, conscripts in the police army, bussed in for the big day, on shift since dawn. Most were as tired and confused as the protesters, but some of them wore faces set in righteous anger.

ONE TWO THREE FOUR, WE DON'T WANT YOUR FUCKING WAR! ONE TWO THREE FOUR, WE DON'T WANT YOUR FUCKING WAR!

The head of the march moved slowly forwards and the super-intendent issued a formal warning:

'YOU ARE IN VIOLATION OF THE LAW!'

ONE TWO THREE FOUR—

'YOU ARE INTERFERING WITH VEHICULAR TRAFFIC!'

—WE DON'T WANT YOUR FUCKING WAR!

Marin saw a rippling movement along the frontline of police, the hive mind again, as they unhooked their numbered ID badges and shoved them into pockets. Then he saw Anna emerge, small, fragile, defiant, from behind the wide Moratorium banner. She stepped forwards with her megaphone pointed at the cops.

'DON'T OBEY ILLEGAL ORDERS! OUR FIGHT IS NOT WITH YOU!'

A roar came from the crowd. He watched a police sergeant point her out to subordinates, an unheard order issued with fierce inten-sity. A chant went up from the Maoist cohort.

PIGS! PIGS! PIGS! PIGS!

The march was now well into York Street, ten people wide at its ragged head and winding back into the tight mass of demonstrators in the park.

The first flying wedge of police broke onto it like an angry wave. There was a sudden uproar of screaming and shouting. Distorted, amplified voices broadcast orders over loud hailers. In the violent confusion, skirmishes and one-on-one brawls erupted through-out the street—but still the body of the march pressed forwards, pushing more people into the melee. Marin quickly lost sight of Anna and ran to search for her. A cop grabbed his arm and he spun around and yelled the magic word: 'Press!' To his surprise, he was immediately released and ran on.

On the side of the road, two cops had knocked an elderly man to the ground. One aimed a kick into his ribs. Marin saw a familiar long-haired, bespectacled figure run into the fray. It was Pierre Villiers, the first time he had spotted him that day. With an inchoate shout, Pierre grappled with the cop who was kicking the grounded man. The second cop hit Pierre full in the face with his baton. His smashed glasses flew off and blood burst from his nose as he staggered back. The two cops had left their elderly victim on the ground and were dragging Pierre away when a tall, heavily built fellow forcefully intervened, using his elbows and arms to free Pierre. The cops started in on the big fellow, but then they stopped, recognising his famous face. Tom Uren, the Labor MP, a figurehead in the anti-war movement—too risky to take him on. The cops left off and moved on to the next battle. Uren helped the old man up from the ground and took him, bloodied and shaken, back into the park.

Pierre picked up his broken specs and was staring at them trans-fixed when Marin grabbed his arm.

'Hey!' he yelled. 'Where's Anna?'

Pierre put on his bent specs and peered at the blurry figure in front of him. Blood from his nostrils bubbled over his lips and dripped from his chin. Marin saw his eyes were wild and muddled.

'You!' said Pierre. 'What the fuck are *you* doing here?'

'What are you on, mate?'

'Peyote, man, and this is some bad fucking trip.'

'Have you seen Anna?'

'No, fuck, man,' said Pierre, stepping back suspiciously. 'You're not you, are you? Who are you?'

Marin took Pierre by the shoulders, trying to shake some sense into him.

'Shut up, you stupid stoner,' he shouted. 'They're after Anna!'

'Fuck, man,' said Pierre, sending a spray of blood onto Marin's white shirt. 'Tell her to watch out for the blue devils! They're all fucken dead, man. You see them? Zombies! Fuck, man. It's the day of the fucken dead.'

Marin left him babbling and ran towards the small band of protesters at the head of the march, who were struggling with police to keep hold of their banner. Still more people pressed on from the park, filling the street; it seemed that the sheer weight of their numbers would overwhelm the police. Marin saw that a small group of young cops had removed themselves from the street brawl and were sitting on the roadside, distraught, hats off. Others were forming up for a second flying wedge.

Then he saw Anna. She was walking along the edge of the disintegrating march, megaphone up, calling on the protesters to link arms, to stay strong, to not respond to violence, to keep moving. The second wave of cops was almost on them, yet still she exhorted the marchers: 'ON TO TOWN HALL! THEY CAN'T STOP US! WE HAVE TO OCCUPY THE TOWN HALL.'

'Anna!' Marin cried, sprinting towards her. But he was too late.

The blue wave hit Anna from behind. He saw her buckle and go down. Though panicked bodies were flying in all directions, Marin tore his way through. But when he reached the place where he'd seen her fall, she was gone. Through the police ranks, he saw two cops dragging her away. He shouldered his way through the police, crying 'Press!' over and again into the faces of young cops until he had forced his way behind them. Up ahead, two cops were pulling Anna into a side lane where the paddy wagons were waiting out of sight. He was running again, shouting as he went. He reached the darkened lane and turned into it, his eyes adjusting, and finally spotted them at the far end of the lane, behind the wagons.

One of the cops had hold of Anna's arms. The other had his face pressed close to hers, and Marin saw the man's contempt, both wrathful and sexually charged. The cop said something that caused Anna to buck violently, though her arms were pinioned. She screamed her revulsion back at him. Marin yelled as he sprinted down the lane between the police wagons, but his voice was drowned out by the clamour of screaming and sirens from the street. He saw the angry cop grab at Anna's T-shirt and tear it up to her chin, exposing her breasts. She reared back, spat in his face. Then, with a sudden violent movement, the cop cracked her hard across the top of her skull with his baton, once, twice.

She was limp in the arms of the second cop when Marin hit the assailant with the full force of his right shoulder. 'Like a freight train'—that was the description later given in a witness statement by the second cop, who now let go of his unconscious prisoner, dropping her as he drew his own baton.

Marin's momentum took the first cop into the brick wall at the end of the lane where he pinned him, raining swift, savage jabs into his ugly, predatory face, bouncing the man's head against the brick wall again and again. Such was his rage that he barely felt the blows from the second cop flailing at his back. But when a wild baton-strike hit his neck, the pain finally cut through. He let go of Anna's tormentor, whose body slid slowly down the wall.

Marin turned to ward off the attack from the second cop, grabbing the baton with his left hand and swinging his right elbow into the man's face. The cop dropped to the ground.

Marin bent over Anna. He gently pulled down her T-shirt and listened to her heart. It was beating fast. Her breathing was hard and ragged. When he pulled up an eyelid, he found her pupil contracted. He rolled her onto her side and kissed her forehead.

He was kneeling there, whispering to her, when they came and hauled him to his feet. Many rough hands were on him as his arms were bent back and the cuffs went on.

23

THEY WERE WAITING for him at Darlinghurst Police Station. He was dragged from the back of the stifling wagon and left standing for a moment, manacled under streetlights as cool air dried his sweat. His eyes were wide, uncertain and fearful. His suit was ripped, his white shirt was bloodstained and there was a bruised welt across the back of his neck, which made it hard to stand up straight. Then the reception party came pouring out of the station and he was shoved into a gauntlet of clubs, fists and boots.

He ran awkwardly, arms cuffed behind his back, shoulders hunched, turning this way and that to take the blows. He was driven by blows into the green fluorescence of the lock-up, an open space heaving with arrested protesters. He saw in the faces of the cops that they didn't give a fuck if there were witnesses. He's resisting arrest, trying to escape, whatever it takes to justify the brutality. The other prisoners automatically stepped back from the pariah, making space as he was herded through them with whips and scorns, like a dangerous animal.

'SCUM! DOG! FUCKEN WOG! DEADMAN!'

The rumours were unclear as to his exact crimes. Cop-killer, attempted cop-killer—however the fuck it ended up, whatever the final charges, he'd put two of their own in hospital! Two! He was a mythical demon, deserving the full treatment. Have to show these fucken hippies: *You fuck with us? THIS is what happens!* The prisoners stayed silent, holding out their hands to be printed, answering questions respectfully, fearful of being targeted themselves like this martyr, whoever he was.

Marin was in a whirlpool of violence.

Bouncing around in the back in the cage of the wagon, gagging on the repellent stench of hosed-out vomit, he had known without doubt that what he'd done had torn him loose from his life. Nothing would ever be the same. He had started the day in one place and now he was in this other place, this dark place. It was a simple, terrifying fact.

They hauled him down a corridor too narrow for the beaters. They flung open a door, pushed him through it and ran him head-first into a wall. A door slammed behind him. He was alone. It was not a cell. A desk, two chairs. An interview room.

A thin stream of blood ran into his mouth. It was salty sweet and sickening. He spat it onto the floor in disgust. Every part of his body seemed to be throbbing. He wanted to throw up, but forced it down. He lowered himself painfully into a chair and let his head drop to rest on the desktop, hands still pinned behind his back. He fell into blackness, spinning down into the whirlpool.

•

'SIT THE FUCK UP!'

Marin opened his eyes, ready to obey any order. He forced his beaten body upright. A heavy-set man in a dark suit was standing over him. One look at the man told him this was a veteran of bad shit. A detective, he assumed, from some hard-core division.

There was a large book under his arm. A phone book. Residential. A to Z.

The big man sat down opposite Marin, stared at him for a long moment before pulling a face. 'Marin *Kat-ich*,' he said.

'Yes.'

'Fuck kind of a wog name is that?'

Marin sat tight-lipped.

'Think you've got the right to remain silent, do you, dickhead?'

Marin bit his cheek, tried to keep his face neutral.

'We'll see about that,' said the detective, distractedly. He didn't look up, but flicked instead through the phone book until he got to K.

'Quite a few of you cunts in here. *Kat-ic* with an I-C. *Kat-ich* with an I-C-H. None with the initial M.'

'I live with my dad. His name's Ivo. I.P. K-A-T-I-C-H. Stanmore. Can I call him?'

'What do you think this is, a fucken hotel? Get reception to put a call through, you reckon?'

'No.'

'No. Good answer. You think I'm here to ask questions, do you?'

'I don't know.'

'I'll use your poofter name, shall I, *Mar-in* . . . No answer to that? Eh . . . *Marianne, Marie*, whatever the fuck they call you in Wog World. I'm not here to ask you questions, girly. I don't care about your fucken answers. I'm here because of the two young coppers you put in hospital. One of those blokes is still in a coma, right. You better hope he wakes up, or it's murder . . . Got anything to say about that?'

'They were beating a woman,' said Marin quietly. 'They were going to rape her.'

'Oh, *Marianne*! That's a bad answer. No one's going to believe your bullshit. You know that, right? They're gonna throw the fucken book at you, girly. You know what it's like, having the book thrown at you? Do you? No? Let me show you.'

The detective was quickly on his feet. He scooped up the phone book, braced his legs and swung it two-handed, like a square cut on a rising ball, into the side of Marin's head.

WHAM.

'That's what it's like. That's for being a stupid fucken wog.'

WHAM.

'That's for the young bloke in hospital.'

WHAM.

'That's for the other one.'

WHAM.

'That's so you know this will never stop.'

WHAM.

'There's a special hell in jail for blokes who attack coppers. You're fucked, mate.'

•

Marin came around on a hard bunk in a dimly lit cell. He was nauseous. The pain in his head was crippling. Someone had removed the cuffs while he was out. He lowered himself onto the cement floor and crawled to the open stainless-steel toilet, gathered his arms around the rim of the bowl and threw up until he had totally emptied himself. He crawled back to the bunk, climbed onto it and passed out again.

The next time he opened his eyes, it had been a loud noise that brought him around. The cell door had opened and clanged shut. Violent nightmares had drawn his body into a foetal position. Without moving, he watched a man coming towards him with a wooden chair. The man put the chair down close to Marin and sat. He was lean and thin-faced, with sharp, intelligent eyes. He wore a crumpled linen suit that looked like he'd gathered it up from the floor that morning. Marin saw the signs of a heavy drinker: a once-handsome face now haggard, bloodshot eyes, a slight tremor. Marin tried to focus on the man, but his head was splitting. He was in so much pain in so many parts of his body that he could barely move. His mouth was so dry that his tongue felt swollen in it. He tried to talk, but all that came out was a loud groan.

'B-B-Bloody hell,' said the man. 'They really d-did you over, didn't they?'

'Water . . .'

'Here,' the man said. He carefully opened the lid of a green, military-style canteen and handed it across. When Marin tried guzzling it on his side, water ran out of his mouth. He painfully forced himself to sit up and took a long drink.

'Slowly,' said the man. 'You'll be sick. I b-brought these. Take a c-couple now. Two more in a few hours.'

Marin was handed a small bottle labelled *Codeine*. He tapped out three of them and swallowed them down. He gripped the canteen hard, staring at the man.

'Not the strong stuff, I'm s-sorry. Best I can do for now.'

'Who are you?'

'You can call me T-Tom. I'm a friend of your father's.'

'I've never heard of a friend called Tom.'

The man gave a frozen smile that never touched his eyes. 'He won't have spoken about me. I'm one of those special friends you don't t-talk about.'

'What do you mean?'

'The kind of friend you call when you're in trouble. And believe me, son, you're in a serious p-p-pickle.'

'Are you a lawyer?'

'Do I look like a lawyer?'

Marin looked at him for a moment and decided not to answer. 'Do you know what happened to Anna, Anna Rosen?' he asked. 'I have to know how she is.'

'Don't worry about her. W-worry about you.'

'I don't care about me. What do you know about her? How is she?'

'Stop f-f-fretting, Marin. She's fine. Believe me. She was taken to c-casualty. Her father came and took her home.'

'You know that for sure?'

'I know that for sure, Marin. Like I said: Don't worry about her.'

'How do you know so much? How do you know about her?'

'It's my b-business to know things.'

'You say you're a friend of my father, but Ivo knows nothing about Anna.'

'He knows what I've told him.'

'What does that mean? If you're not a lawyer, who are you?'

'That's not important right now. Take a b-breath.'

'It's important to me.'

'Take a fucking breath, son. You need to listen to me or your life is about to go down the g-gurgler.'

'My father . . .'

'Shut the fuck up and listen. That policeman you attacked is in hospital. He's got a c-c-cracked skull, a broken jaw, serious concussion; you're lucky you didn't k-kill him. The other fellow's not so b-bad. But you beat the shit out of two c-cops, Marin. What do you think's going to happen next?'

'He tried to tear off Anna's T-shirt.' Marin mimicked the cop's actions, dragging up an imaginary T-shirt. 'He exposed her breasts! He was all over her. He was going to rape her.'

'I'd be angry too, son,' said Tom. 'But exposing a girl's t-tits, even if you could prove it, is not rape.'

'Anna spat in his face,' cried Marin. 'She spat in his face, and he smashed her skull with his baton again and again while the other cop held her arms. That's what happened. That's why I hit them.'

'I'm not saying this prick is a g-good man. I'm saying he's a *police-man*. Are you with me? He'll have a dozen w-witnesses. All of them p-p-policemen! They'll all testify that your attack was unprovoked, a vicious unwarranted attack on a young police c-constable doing his very best to protect the community and restrain a violent r-r-radical she-wolf. Are you following me?'

'That's not what happened. Anna will tell them. She'll give evidence against them.'

'Don't be so fucking naïve. I thought you were smart. She was out c-c-cold when most of this happened, accidentally hurt while resisting arrest. You think any j-jury will believe d-differently? Don't you get it, son? It doesn't make a b-blind bit of difference what really happened. It's what all those upright, honest *policemen* say under oath in c-court. That's what matters.'

'There must be other witnesses. And Anna'll have wounds, medical reports. That's real evidence.'

'You need to understand how angry the police are. You've put t-two of their men in hospital. Beat one almost to d-death. Let me explain some simple facts. Do you know what they see when they look at you?'

'No.'

'What the judge will see? What a jury will see?'

'No.'

'A fucking r-radical wog who's f-fucking this pretty little Jew communist . . .'

Marin was up and braced, his fists clenched.

'Sit down!' barked Tom. 'Sit, I said!'

'Who the hell are you?'

'I'm your f-fucking saviour, son! Believe in me. Now sit or I'll walk out now.'

Marin slumped back down onto the bunk, shaking his head. 'What sort of man talks like that,' he demanded, and Tom responded with a remorseless grin.

'I'm t-telling you the hard truth, son. So shut up and listen! It's not what I think. It's what *they* think. The police. The p-prosecutors. The j-judges. The juries. The fucking juries . . . Have you got the faintest idea what sort of c-c-country you live in? We're barely out of the Stone Age. You spend a few years at university now, maybe you think everyone's n-nice and civilised? You've stepped outside the sheltered workshop now, son. This is the real world you're in . . . And your name is what? Ma-rin Katich? Croatia, you say? *Croats!* They're all fucking bomb-throwers, aren't they? Violent types? Why'd we let 'em in here in the first place if all they want to do is kill each other? We know these fucken people. Short fuses, hot-blooded b-b-bastards. And look at this one, will you? Big cunt, isn't he? That poor fucking copper's half his size. I wouldn't do their job for quids. And what about this sheila he's screwing? Half his luck. Anyway, he's f-fucking her, so she'll say anything to get him off. Plus, she's a fucken commie, isn't she? And a Jew. Can't trust any of them. Fuck 'em all. Lock him up. Throw away the key . . . Are you with me now, Marin? Are you hearing me?'

Marin was silent, indignant, fuming.

Tom glared back at him. 'You better lose that f-fucken attitude quick smart or you're on your own. Are you hearing me?'

'Yes.'

'Good. Now, if you're ready to really listen, I'll answer some of your questions.'

'Who the hell are you?'

'All right . . . First, I've known your f-father for many years. We share certain interests. Political interests. Your father and I . . . Well, you could put it this way: we're on the same side. From time to time, we help each other out. There's a bigger picture to all of this. I'm not going to go into all the d-details right now. Let's just say that we're allies. He wants to see the end of the communist dictatorship in Yugoslavia. He wants Croatia to be free again. We want to see the end of c-c-communist dictatorships all over the world and, above all, we want to make sure the bastards don't t-take root here in Australia.'

'We?'

'What?'

'You said "we", Marin said.

'I'm not alone. I'm p-part of an organisation. A government organisation.'

'ASIO, you mean?'

'Look, depending on what happens next, you'll learn all of this in time. You have to be p-patient. But understand this: we have the same enemies, your father and I. Real enemies. Existential enemies. I'm talking about the r-real evil in this world, the source of it. This is not some game played by uni students. This is a game with consequences for all of us. And right now it has consequences for you.'

'What have I got to do with this?'

'You're a smart young b-bloke, Marin, I know that much about you. We've been following you. I've read your essays. That piece you wrote for *The Tribe*. How the hell you got them to publish that, I'll never know. That surprised a few of us.'

'You've been watching me?'

'Let's just say we've been k-keeping half an eye on you. Your father's a good friend. Of course we'd have some interest in his s-son. But I wouldn't say we were "watching" you that closely, at least not until you took up with Anna Rosen. You just tumbled into the n-net there. If I were a fisherman, I'd call it by-catch. We're f-fishing for one species and another gets caught by accident.'

'You're watching Anna? What, bugging her phone? Following her around? Got informants in the anti-war movement, have you? *The Tribe?*'

'I'm not going to go into all of that, but obviously the R-Rosen family tree is communist from its very roots. Each time it b-bears fruit we take an interest, of course we do. What else would you expect? Even they understand that. We're just doing our j-job. But, then, as I said, you entered the frame. That really took us by surprise, I can tell you. But I do understand the attraction. She's quite something, that girl.'

'Don't you fucking talk about her like that!'

'But we have to talk about her, Marin. We have to talk about Anna because now we're getting to the heart of the matter.'

'What the hell is this? You want me to spy on her? You can get fucked!'

'Okay, Marin, you need to get something into your head right now. You've come to the most important c-c-crossroad in your short life. Today, you either grow up or you d-disappear from the world altogether. The police prosecutor is ready to throw the book at you. They're r-racking up a collection of charges against you: intent to cause grievous bodily harm, m-maximum sentence twenty-five years in prison; assault police officer in the execution of his duty, maximum sentence seven years; threaten injury to resist lawful apprehension, m-m-malicious wounding, and on and on it goes. They are out to get you. The Police Commissioner himself has asked the prosecutor to consider attempted murder. Are you starting to see the position you're in?'

'Yes.'

'No matter what the final number of ch-charges is, they intend to prosecute you to the full extent of the law and, believe me when I say this, you will go to jail for many, many years. That is the truth. Do you d-doubt it?'

'No, no, I don't.'

'I said earlier that I'm your saviour. Or, at least, I c-could be. What if I told you that I could make all of this go away?'

'I'm listening.'

'I should add that everything I'm about to say I have d-discussed with your father. I have his complete agreement.'

'Can I speak to him?'

'No. You're going to have to make this decision on your own. Trust me or don't trust me. It's not going to work any other way.'

'What do you want from me?'

'The first thing that you're going to do is w-w-walk away from Anna Rosen.'

'What?'

'You're to leave her and not look back. You have to s-sever ties with her completely and not tell her why.'

'I'm not doing that! Fuck you!'

'Say that one more time and I will walk away right now. I'll be the one who doesn't look back, and you can sit alone in a p-prison cell for the rest of your pathetic life wanking off while you think about her fucking other men because, I promise you, she will move on . . . You want me to go? I'm out of here.'

'No, no . . .'

'Marin, you have to understand. It was over from the m-minute you beat the shit out of those c-coppers. There's only one way to get you out of this. We have to cut a deal with the prosecutor and the j-judge. Even the fucking p-premier will have to sign up to this. And when it's done, you will be working for us. You will be under orders.'

'Working for you? What does that mean?'

'It means you're being recruited, son.'

'You want to turn me into a spy?'

'It's not as simple as that. You won't be on the b-books anywhere. You won't be c-clocking into an office. You'll be what we call an "asset". You probably won't meet anyone else in the organisation apart from me. That's how it will w-work. This is a long-term thing. The m-moment you cease to cooperate, those charges will be re-activated and you'll be hauled in like a fugitive and thrown into the deepest d-darkest cell we can find. Do you understand?'

'Yes.'

'Good. When they let you out of here, you will set up a m-meeting with Anna Rosen and tell her that it's all over between you. You've had enough of her r-radical bullshit. You can't stand it anymore . . . Say whatever you need to say and then walk away from her and don't look back. Do you agree?'

Marin refused to look up. His eyes had filled with tears and he felt them streaming down his face.

'Marin! Do you agree?'

'Yes.'

'You will tell her nothing else. You will tell her n-nothing about me, nothing of this m-meeting. Do you agree?'

'Yes.'

'After that, you will go to your f-father's house and wait. I will contact you there. Is that c-clear?'

'Yes.'

'When you get to your father's house, there will be a l-letter. It will be an official envelope. Many young men have received the same letter. In it will be your d-draft papers.'

'My what?'

'Your d-draft papers, son, your n-number just came up.'

'What are you talking about?'

'Marin, listen to me. This is part of the d-deal to get you out of here. We will use it to m-mollify the prosecutor, judge, the premier. It's the only way. You'll be d-drafted into the army. You're going to Vietnam.'

24

SCHEVENINGEN PRISON, THE HAGUE

21 DECEMBER 2005

Vietnam! Was this a sick joke? Anna stared across the table at the man who had infiltrated her life so very long ago. She had known so little of the truth about him back then that she had come to think of him as an imposter. But this . . .

Vietnam!

It was as if he had finally led her to an uncrossable bridge. She could not stay still. She scrambled to her feet and stood behind the chair, gripping it.

'No!' she said. 'You have to stop.'

She could not have described her own conflicted feelings, she could not pin them down: bewilderment and sadness; sympathy and contempt. She stared at Marin. In his face she saw helplessness and resignation, but what did she really know about his true nature? What did he know of it himself after all these years of fighting and killing?

And now he had played Vietnam like a bloody trump card. She shook her head.

'I just . . .' she began. 'I can't take in any more of this right now.'

He looked at his watch.

'Our time's nearly up,' he said. 'They'll be here soon to take me back.'

Anna drew in a breath. *Our time's nearly up.* He said it as if they'd just been discussing the weather. *Yes, it's cold outside. It's terrible this time of year in Scheveningen. Make sure to put on your coat. Don't forget your gloves.*

How the hell was she supposed to respond to his revelations? All of it, everything he had told her, seemed to have bubbled up from the unquenchable well of male violence. He couldn't know, he could never know, that she was trying to find a way to deal with the fact that her daughter's father came from the bottom of that well.

'Fuck, Marin,' she said. 'You really have no idea.'

'What about?'

'You've had decades to think about this, but I'm hearing it today for the first time. And, honestly, I'm finding it . . . excruciating. That's the truth. I don't know how you thought I'd react, but I'm not going to fall on my knees in gratitude to you for saving me from a rapist by beating him half to death. And the rest of it . . . Moriarty . . . Fuck, Moriarty! I just need time to think. It's all too much.'

'I understand.'

She smiled faintly at that.

'I'm not sure you do,' she said. 'I'm not sure you have the tools to do that. But I do know one thing. You're telling the truth, as you understand it. And I do thank you for that.'

•

From the moment Marin began telling his story, it was obvious to Anna that he was saying it aloud for the first time. There was a vividness to the words that poured out of his mouth. She knew very well that old stories, especially about moments that have irreversibly changed you, tend to be told over and again to different people in the course of your life, subtly altering with each retelling until they begin to sound scripted and to lose their impact. By contrast, Marin's account seemed unrehearsed, except perhaps in his mind, and even as he told it he appeared to be reliving each moment as if it had just happened. She believed him when he said he had never told this story to another soul.

Tom Moriarty was perhaps the only other person living or dead who could have put their two stories together, but Moriarty didn't count as a soul, not in her mind. If she was wrong and that fucking monster had a soul she only hoped it was burning in endless flames. She sometimes wished that she did believe in hell because that's where Moriarty belonged. He was an emissary of the devil, Mephistopheles, in the form of a dissolute spy.

As she had listened to Marin, she had soon stopped taking notes. She didn't need them. His story was indelible and now his memories were wound together cinematically with her own. It had been like an out-of-body experience, watching yourself through the eyes of another. She remembered bouncing on the bed the morning of the demo; she remembered warning him that he'd signed up for this; she remembered the passion of the night before; she remembered kissing him and telling him to wait for her; she remembered looking back at him from the door; and she remembered everything she had done that day.

It was a long time since she'd thought about it, but Marin's story put her back into the terrible embrace of those two cops. The would-be rapist was again pressing against her. She remembered screaming at him. She remembered picking up on his hatred of women and throwing it back in his face. She couldn't recall her words, but the sense of it was clear. He was a pathetic, inadequate excuse for a man, a limp creature whose resort to violence was proof of his sexual inadequacy.

She had pushed every button imaginable and set off the unexploded bomb inside him. Not that she blamed herself. The two cops had had her pinioned and helpless, under threat of rape at the back of a dark lane, a violation both hideous and primal.

Anna turned and saw that the prison guard was at the door. Marin got to his feet.

'I've been told that van Brug will be here tomorrow at midday,' he said. 'Will you be with him?'

The guard entered the room and walked over to Marin. 'He must come with me now, Madame,' said the guard.

'Yes,' said Anna. 'I'll be with him.'

'Good,' said Marin. 'I'll see you then.'

Marin put out his hand. She shook it briefly and let it go.

•

Anna texted Willem van Brug before she left the prison and was surprised when an early-model VW Beetle, letterbox-red, pulled up beside her at the fortified gates. The lawyer reminded her of a praying mantis as he emerged from the car, all elbows and limbs, and rushed around to open the passenger door for her. A bicycle was racked onto the VW's roof, creating the illusion that an invisible trick cyclist was using it as a ramp. She tested how securely it was attached before climbing in.

'I am training later at the velodrome in Alkmaar,' van Brug explained as he restarted the motor, which sounded oddly like her mother's old sewing machine.

'Listen, do you know Koppelstokstraat in Geuzenkwartier?' she asked.

'*Ja*, it is not far.'

'Could you head there? That's where I'm staying. There're a few restaurants close by. If you've got time, we can stop for lunch. I need a drink.'

The lawyer seemed lost for conversation as they drove down the Strandweg past the Kurhaus, the pier and glimpses of the North Sea, which she decided was not quite so ominous under a bright winter sun. The familiar Tibetan gong chimed and she checked her Blackberry, prompting a rapid text exchange.

Pierremob: So, how'd it go?

AnnaR: Ahhh!

Pierremob: ??

AnnaR: Talk later. With lawyer.

Pierremob: Rachel come up?

AnnaR: NO!

Pierremob: Singarasa making Katich statement today!

AnnaR: Fuck!

Pierremob: Back at 6. See you then?

AnnaR: Yes.

Things were going to get messy much faster than she had hoped.

'Fuck!' she cried, startling the sedate lawyer who was driving with the caution of a man twice his age.

'Has something happened?' he asked, trying not to take his eyes off the road.

'The fucking Registrar,' she said. 'He's putting out a press release on Marin Katich today.'

'*Godverdomme!*' van Brug exclaimed.

'What?'

'God damn it,' he said.

'Yep,' said Anna.

•

Concerned about the security of his bicycle, van Brug suggested a seafood place he knew near her neighbourhood and where he could park out front to keep an eye on it. It was in The Haven, on the edge of the boat harbour where the herring fleet took refuge behind a double sea wall. There were small lighthouses on either side of the calm channel in from the North Sea.

Anna liked the idea of havens, but when she had last come here to buy wine it had been as mist-shrouded, dark and foreboding as a New England port town in a Stephen King novel. Now it was cold and bright and the fishy fragrance of the fleet wafting shorewards on the sea breeze carried the promise of a fresh catch.

The lawyer was relieved to find a table at the window. He ordered black tea and a *flutje* of Grolsch for Anna, who had decided to start with a beer. She was disconcerted when the tiny glass arrived, raised an eyebrow at van Brug, and immediately ordered a second one. The lawyer seemed not to notice, sipping his tea as he examined the menu.

'I can recommend *Gegrilde Makreel met saffraasaus*,' he said without looking up. 'Or *Tonijnsteak met groenten, frites en terikay-kisaus*. Would you like me to translate?'

'Grilled mackerel with saffron sauce, or fish and chips?'

'Tuna steak with fresh vegetables and potato chips,' said van Brug. 'Yes, correct and with teriyaki sauce. So, a bit Japans.'

'I'll have the mackerel and some oysters to start,' said Anna. 'Will you have some with me?'

'No,' he said. 'I cannot eat live animals.'

Of course you can't, she thought—no live animals, no booze, no cigarettes, no drugs, no speeding, no jokes. The most interesting things about this man were the idea of him racing around a velodrome and his Dries van Noten suits which, she had to admit, were really sharp. If they were going to spend time together, she was going to have to get him to lighten up.

'Is that someone checking out your bike?' she asked suddenly, and his head jerked sideways to peer through the window.

'I see no one,' he said after a moment.

'Just kidding,' she said. 'Let's talk about Marin Katich.'

•

Anna began briefing him on the morning's meeting, deliberately avoiding Marin's revelations about September 1970, which she was happy to have an excuse not to think about. She stuck to issues relevant to the war crimes case, about which they would have to go into much more detail at tomorrow's meeting. It was clear to her now, she told him, that Jure Rebic was at the heart of this and that he was the key to unravelling the truth or otherwise of the war crimes allegations against Marin Katich. She set out what she had learned about Rebic: Katich fought alongside him during the siege of Vukovar; they escaped just before the city fell to the Serbs and took their surviving men south to Bosnia; Rebic became Katich's deputy in the five thousand strong militia force they had put together in Bosnia and their headquarters was in the predominantly Croat town of Ljubuski. The militia had been comprised of Bosnian Muslim and Croat fighters, and Katich had it incorporated into the structure of the Bosnian army command, taking orders from the Muslim-led government in Sarajevo.

Anna paused her narrative when a dozen *fine de claire* oysters were brought to the table. She squeezed lemon onto one and watched the frilled edges shrivel in reaction. 'They're alive all right,' she said, and, noticing the lawyer's almost imperceptible grimace as she sucked one from its shell, cried: 'Oh, that's delicious.'

She scooped one up and offered it to him over the table. 'You really don't want to try?'

'No, for me this is *onsmakelijk*,' he said, his face crumpling like a child's. 'Distasteful.'

Anna shrugged and sucked down another, taking a swig of beer. 'I thought everyone in Northern Europe ate oysters in winter,' she said, continuing to work her way through the dozen. 'You know, when I was a young journalist in radio, we would sometimes finish the morning shift, go down to the harbour and buy a sack of Sydney rock oysters, just like these *fine de claire*, except we eat them in summer when they're spawning. That's very much frowned upon here.'

'This is the convict manners, *ja*?'

Anna drank some beer and smiled at him. 'Oh good,' she said. 'You're fighting back. Anyway, the case. Like I said, Rebic is the key to all of this. We know that on 15 June 1992, General Cvrčak, that is to say Marin Katich, and eight of his staff officers were returning to Ljubuski in two cars when they were stopped at a roadblock and shot to pieces in an ambush from both sides.'

'This is in the foreword of your book,' said van Brug. 'I read this morning that you went to Ljubuski at that time to find Marin Katich and got there too late.'

'That's right,' she said. 'A day later, the shot-up cars were sitting in the courtyard of their headquarters. Jure Rebic was there— General Rebic, as he called himself then—and he was the one who told me that their commander, *Cvrčak*, had been killed. He said they were all grieving for him. By the way, the name Rebic knew Katich by was Illija Lovric. To this day, no one knows that he's really Marin Katich. They had a big funeral for *Cvrčak*/Lovric, buried him as a hero. But now we know he wasn't killed at all. He was carried away severely wounded, rescued by some of his Muslim soldiers, and he survived. I don't know how they managed to fool Jure Rebic.'

The lawyer looked puzzled. 'Why did they go to all this trouble to hide that he had survived?'

'They did it, Willem, because it was Jure Rebic who organised the assassination. If he knew Katich was still alive, he'd have sent people to kill him.'

'*Pleurislijer!*'

'What?'

'What a scoundrel!' said van Brug. 'And this is the story Katich has told you about Jure Rebic?'

'It is,' said Anna. 'And it's completely believable because of what happens next. Rebic assumes command of the militia. Remember, he was already calling himself General when I met him. The first thing he does is to purge the militia of all Bosnian Muslim fighters. They are gathered together, disarmed and disbanded. No doubt some of them, the most dangerous ones, were eliminated like those loyal officers killed in the ambush.'

'But why?'

'It's all about geopolitics,' said Anna. 'The assassination of Marin Katich was ordered at the top levels of the Croatian government.'

Van Brug was still puzzled. 'They wanted to kill their own man?'

'He was not *their* man,' she said. 'That's the point. Even though he's a Croat, General Cvrčak/Lovric was commissioned by the Bosnian Muslim government as part of their army. God, too many aliases—let's just call him Katich. Katich made speeches, broadcast on radio, about how it was the destiny of Croats and Muslims to fight together against the Serbs. More than thirty per cent of his soldiers were Muslims. What Katich didn't know, what he couldn't have possibly known, was that the Croatian President, Franjo Tudjman, had made a secret deal with Belgrade, with his bitterest enemy Slobodan Milosevic, to carve up Bosnia between their two countries. It was a shocking betrayal of the Bosnian government, whose backs were already against the wall.

'Tudjman and Milosevic had a clandestine meeting, can you imagine! They effectively agreed to stop fighting each other, and both turn on the Bosnian Muslims. Under the deal, the Serbs would keep the Bosnian territory to the east of Mostar and whatever they could steal in the north—don't forget they had Sarajevo under siege at this time. And the Croats would keep Herzegovina in the south, including Mostar as its capital and all the territory to the west of it—a Greater Croatia, with borders stretching right down to the coast. To achieve this land grab, all the Croats had to do was go to war with the Muslims and steal it from them. And what was the biggest obstacle to that? Marin Katich and his Croat–Muslim army!'

'So, this Jure Rebic,' said van Brug, 'he agrees to tear down this obstacle.'

'Exactly,' said Anna. 'This is why I believe Katich's story. Can you imagine what they must have offered Rebic? One Shakespearean betrayal and he could transform himself into one of the most powerful men in Croatia. There is much more to this story that Katich has not yet told me. We must get to the bottom of this with him tomorrow, but I know one thing for sure: the next step will be to find Jure Rebic.'

Their meals began to arrive. When the grilled mackerel with its aromatic sauce was placed under Anna's nose, she realised that, having skipped breakfast due to nerves, she was famished. She ordered a glass of German riesling while van Brug asked for sparkling water. The lawyer picked unenthusiastically at his over-cooked tuna before homing in on the *frites*, sprinkling on extra salt and eating them with his fingers.

After a while he paused, holding an extra long one mid-air. 'Before I forget this,' he said, putting the chip in his mouth and wiping his fingers. 'I found something interesting.'

Van Brug picked up his briefcase, opened it on his lap and produced a highlighted document, which he handed to Anna.

'This is the arrest document for when they picked up Katich from Rovinj. I have heard about this town before this. Many Dutch tourists go there in summer to fight with the *Duitser*, the Germans, for space on the beaches. Anyway, it makes sense why Katich ended up there. In the 1990s, Rovinj had a special hospital for wounded soldiers.'

He watched Anna begin to flick through the document and said, 'There is not much in there about the hospital. That's not the interesting thing. See where I have used yellow to highlight a name. *Ja*, do you see?'

'Jasna Perak,' Anna read.

'*Ja*, that is her,' he said. 'This woman, Jasna Perak, she was the representative of the Croatian government who was there with the SAS team that arrested Katich—Tomislav Maric, as they thought he was—in the middle of the night. I think she would also be a person to talk to, *ja*?'

'*Ja*,' said Anna, sipping on her wine. Her thoughts were going round and round, faster and faster, like a rider in a velodrome.

•

That evening, Pierre prepared them a light supper, while Anna built a fire in the living room. He had brought home a copy of the press release.

'The Katich is out of the bag,' he said as he handed it to her.

The release was headlined: 'Australian Facing War Crimes Trial.' It named Marin Katich as the Australian citizen; it stated that he had been hiding under an alias in detention after being arrested in Croatia and deported to The Hague under indictment to face trial for war crimes. Prometheus Singarasa was quoted: 'Mr Katich's true identity and his Australian nationality have no bearing on the serious nature of the crimes he is alleged to have committed. He was arrested in Croatia in August 2005, living under the alias Tomislav Maric, and was committed for trial for Crimes Against Humanity under a sealed indictment, which will now be amended to include his real name alongside various aliases he has used over many years.'

Anna read it one more time, then threw it into the flames. She watched it blacken, curl up and incinerate before she picked up her drink and joined Pierre in the kitchen.

He looked up from washing the salad. 'What are you going to tell Rachel?'

'It's the middle of the night in Sydney,' said Anna. 'I'll call her later.'

'That wasn't my question.'

Anna finished her wine, grabbed the bottle and poured herself another glassful. 'I'm going to tell her I won't be home for Christmas.'

Pierre put the salad aside, dried his hands and picked up his own drink. 'Fuck, Anna, really?' he said. 'Maybe you should fly home for Christmas, sit her down and tell her the truth. She has a right to know, doesn't she?'

'What? That her father's a fucking war criminal? And her fucking grandfather was a Nazi war criminal and a vicious anti-Semite?'

Anna drained her glass and filled it again.

'Steady on,' said Pierre.

'You're going to police my drinking now?' she asked.

'No,' said Pierre. 'Knock yourself out.'

Anna found herself, unexpectedly, on the verge of tears. She ran her hands back through her hair and sat down. She felt exhausted.

'I'm sorry, Pierre,' she said, softening her tone. 'Today was . . . You've got no idea the extent of this mess.'

Pierre moved closer, put his hands on her shoulders and looked into her eyes.

'Listen,' he said. 'I'm going to make us a couple of steaks. We'll go sit in front of the fire and you can tell me what happened, what he said. I'm obviously curious, of course I am, but just tell me what you're comfortable with, okay?'

'Okay,' she said and he went back to work in the kitchen. After a moment, she interrupted him. 'How's your memory of 1970?'

Pierre paused from spreading crushed garlic and salt into the steaks. '1970?' he said. 'When exactly?'

'September, the second Moratorium.'

'Yeah? We were both there . . .'

'Did you take peyote that day?'

Pierre looked startled. 'How on earth do you know that?' he said. 'Did I tell you?'

'No,' she said. 'It's true, then?'

'Yeah, I swallowed a button in the morning. I was completely off my dial. I was fully hallucinating when things got violent. It was absolutely terrifying, worst trip ever. I never touched the stuff again.'

'Do you remember seeing Marin Katich?'

'Fuck no. Well, I honestly don't know—at one point I saw Mahatma Gandhi walk into a brawl, like hovering just above the ground, and everyone stopped fighting. Did Katich tell you he saw me?'

'Yeah,' she said with a laugh. 'It's a long story.'

'I do remember thinking the cops were zombies come to kill us all.'

•

Anna kept drinking as she paced restlessly around the living room. There was so much to think about, so much to be done to get to the bottom of this. She paused from time to time to throw a log onto the fire. Staring into the flames, she thought about Pierre's hallucinations. She was relieved when little details of Marin's story checked out. There were so many details to be confirmed, so many people she needed to find and talk to, still so many unanswered questions.

But if there was the remotest possibility that Marin was, as he claimed, innocent of the charges in the indictment, she owed it to her daughter, *their* daughter, to find out the truth. Pierre was correct about that—as painful as it was for Anna to admit it, her daughter had a right to know the truth about her father and about who and what he was. But Anna also understood that she couldn't talk to Rachel until she knew what that truth was.

Pierre brought their plates in and set them on the coffee table with the bowl of salad and a freshly opened bottle of wine.

'Thanks for taking care of me,' she said.

'It's easy,' he said. 'I probably wouldn't make a proper meal if it was just me, so . . . Mustard?'

Anna shook her head. 'No, thanks,' she said putting her glass down. 'There's something that came up today with van Brug.'

Pierre spooned mustard onto his plate, anxious to start. 'What is it?' he said.

'When you lived in Zagreb, did you ever come across a woman called Jasna Perak?'

In spite of his hunger, Pierre pushed the mustard aside and looked up, intrigued. 'Jasna Perak,' he said. 'She was a spook, very close to Franjo Tudjman. Where'd you come across her?'

'She was with the team that arrested Katich in Rovinj.'

Pierre shook his head, the food temporarily forgotten. 'That's really surprising,' he said. 'Jasna Perak is seriously connected. She was an intelligence advisor to the president during the war. She was a founding member of the H.I.S., Tudjman's original intelligence service. They split it up a few years ago, took military intelligence out of it, and she ended up in the new secret service, the O.A. I don't know at what level, but she must be close to the top.'

'Do you know her?'

'Yeah, we used to talk,' said Pierre. 'I've still got her old mobile number.'

'Would you call and ask her if she'll see me?'

'In Zagreb?'

'Yeah,' said Anna. 'I'm going to have to go there.'

'It's almost Christmas,' he said.

'I'll take a present.'

THE GIRL WITH GREEN EYES

25

SYDNEY, AUSTRALIA

22 DECEMBER 2005

RACHEL ROSEN woke early. Leah was still asleep. Her back was towards her and Rachel leant across and kissed her lightly, brushing the pale skin above her shoulder blades. Leah, breathing deeply, didn't stir. Rachel sat up and examined her lover in the soft morning light. She had lost weight, her fine bones were more visible under the contours of her back, where her ribs and the underlying structure of her hips could be plainly seen. There had always been a fragility to Leah's beauty, but lately she seemed to have become more delicate, more vulnerable.

Rachel knew that the constant, carping pressure from her religious family was taking a psychological toll. Leah seemed distracted and on edge when they made love. There was an evanescent quality to Leah's happiness, as if it were slipping out of her grasp.

Her own mother hadn't helped. If only Anna had made more of an effort, Leah might have felt some comfort from knowing she had the support of another family. More than a week had passed since the disastrous dinner, and although Anna had rung to apologise again before she left for Europe Leah had still felt slighted and rejected. She complained to Rachel that Anna had obviously decided that her religious beliefs were an insurmountable obstacle and that she was an intellectual lightweight, unworthy of her daughter's love. These were Leah's impressions and nothing Rachel said could assuage them.

But Rachel had a very different view. She knew that, notwithstanding their fierce argument over Israel, her mother would never have deliberately hurt Leah's feelings. Anna generally enjoyed a passionate debate, accepted differences of opinion, even profound differences. No, something else had been in play that night. Anna had been profoundly distracted, disturbed even. Leah could not possibly understand this but, whatever the problem was, Rachel was convinced that it was nothing to do with her.

Rachel got up carefully, leaving Leah to sleep. She padded into the study, woke up the computer and checked the markets, which were predictably quiet and stable leading up to Christmas. She walked through the living room, where the lights on the little tree were blinking frosty white and then multi-coloured. A handful of wrapped presents nestled beneath it. She remembered how the tree had offended Leah's brother Eli, who had come to see them as a peacemaker. Eli was the one member of Leah's family who wanted a reconciliation between his parents and their wayward daughter. Rachel was grateful for his efforts, but even free-thinking Eli, when he saw the stunted pine with its elegant decorations, had accused Rachel of being 'a Christmas-tree Jew'.

She went into the kitchen, switched on the radio and began the process of making coffee. She was barely paying attention when the news bulletin began with its familiar musical sting.

Our top stories today: A man facing war crimes charges in The Hague has been revealed to be an Australian citizen . . .

The Hague? That's where Anna had raced off to to see Pierre, who worked for the war crimes tribunal. What the fuck? Rachel pushed the coffee aside and stared at the radio.

Police have charged a Sydney man with sending text messages inciting violence during the Cronulla riots on the eleventh of December . . .

Rachel waited, tensed up, both hands flat on the kitchen bench.

The New South Wales Government has lodged an action in the High Court against the Federal Government's Work Choices legislation.

Another musical sting and then at last the newsreader was back with details of the top story. Rachel turned up the volume:

An investigation in The Hague has revealed that a man who has spent four months behind bars awaiting trial over war crimes committed during the conflict in the former Yugoslavia is an Australian citizen. The man was arrested in Croatia and jailed in The Hague in August under the name Tomislav Maric, a false identity. Authorities in the War Crimes Tribunal have discovered that his real name is Marin Katich, an Australian citizen, born in Sydney . . .

Rachel's eyes widened. *KATICH!* It was a name she had known since she was a child.

Marin Katich is believed to be the son of Croatian-born Ivo Katich—

Ivo Katich, thought Rachel, the subject of her mother's book.

—who in 1987 was due to face the first war crimes trial in Australian history, charged over atrocities committed in Yugoslavia during the Second World War. That trial was abandoned when Mr Katich was found to be unfit to stand trial.

And now his son! What's going on? What was Anna up to? Why hadn't she heard from her?

Authorities in The Hague tribunal have confirmed that the war crimes indictment will be adjusted to reflect the true identity of the accused, Marin Katich, who is believed to have had a number of aliases. The Australian is expected to face trial at the War Crimes Tribunal for the former Yugoslavia.

Rachel heard Leah calling from the bedroom.

'Can you turn down the radio?'

She switched it off. 'Sorry, darling, it was something to do with Anna.'

'What?'

'I'll tell you in a minute,' Rachel said. 'Do you want some coffee?'

'Oh, yes please.'

'Won't be long.'

Rachel finished filling the coffee machine, put it on the burner and dashed into the study. She rewoke the computer and flicked through to the news websites. It was the lead story on the *Sydney Morning Herald* site. She read it swiftly, looking for new details. Anna, she thought, why didn't you tell me? Obviously this was the reason her mother had rushed to The Hague.

One of the sites had a colour picture of a bearded man in a cam-ouflage military uniform. The caption read: *Marin Katich, Bosnia 1992*. Rachel recalled a grainy black-and-white picture of the same man in her mother's book. In the foreword of *Australian Nazi*, Anna had described how the Australian-born Marin Katich had been a militia commander during the Bosnian War and how she'd tried to track him down only to find he'd been killed in an ambush a short time before she got there. Rachel remembered that trip well. Her mother had been blown up and come back with that scar under her eye.

Rachel studied the man on her computer screen. This photo was not grainy at all. It was some kind of high-quality portrait.

'Rachel!'

Her ears were ringing. Her mind was racing. She tried to remember exactly what Anna had said to explain away her dis-tracted, sullen misbehaviour during the ruined dinner party. She'd got an email from Pierre in The Hague. 'Something is terribly wrong, darling'—that's how she'd put it. *Terribly wrong*. But what would be so terrible about finding this man alive? Surely that would be good news, or at least interesting news, not something terribly wrong. After all, Marin Katich was the man Anna had risked her life to go and find during the murderous conflict. Now he was alive—well, surely that was a whole new chapter in the story she had made her own.

'Rachel, where are you?'

Where am I? And the other question formed in Rachel's mind that she just couldn't let go of: *What else has Anna kept from me?*

She called to Leah, 'Coming.'

She needed to think about this calmly, methodically.

•

With an effort of will, Rachel settled herself. She took coffee and toast into Leah and told her a mostly true story about how Anna had tracked down an Australian citizen in the cells of the war crimes prison. She explained how the fellow had been charged under a false name and how it was an especially big story because the man's father had been charged in Australia nearly twenty years ago with war crimes in Yugoslavia that dated back to the Second World War.

Leah listened dutifully as she ate her toast. She was not at all inclined to celebrate the journalistic coups of the great Anna Rosen, but she did make a grudging acknowledgment.

'At least when she's tracking down Nazis she's not attacking her own people.'

Rachel decided not to respond to that. Repairing relations between the two women in her life was necessarily a long-term project and she was grateful, on this occasion, for Leah's lack of interest. It relieved her of any obligation to share her concerns about what Anna was up to. Instead, she helped Leah choose an outfit for the day from her side of the capacious walk-in wardrobe, whose meticulous order she always found comforting.

'Aren't you getting ready?' asked Leah.

'No,' said Rachel, chafing at her own deception. 'It's the stupid office Christmas party, remember? I don't have to leave till lunchtime.'

•

When Leah had gone, Rachel rang her assistant and told her she was ill and wouldn't make it to the office party. Then she gathered what she needed and took the lift to the basement car park where her black Audi was waiting. Rachel would never have admitted this to her mother, but, like the luxury of housing her vast collection of clothes in an architect-designed wardrobe, she found the car comforting—the smell of it, the embrace of its leather seat, the resonance of its engine. It was stupid, she knew, but being behind the wheel of this finely engineered machine gave her a sense of control.

She went fast and smooth up the ramp, out of the cool darkness into the glare and clamour of the city on a hot summer's morning. She navigated expertly through the traffic, barely thinking, clocking landmarks on the route she had taken so many times before: Hyde Park; William Street; the giant Coca-Cola sign; the sad carnival of Kings Cross; the splayed fountain making rainbows for junkies in the ratty park; then Potts Point; the electric gates to Anna's apartment; and the precious parking spot. She unconsciously drew a breath and climbed out.

Her mother had clearly left the apartment quickly. Anna had cleaned up their dinner plates and packed the dishwasher, but she had forgotten to turn it on and the kitchen stank of rotting fish. Rachel pressed the start button and the washer's swooshing and jugging filled the silence as she moved through the apartment. She threw open the tall windows in the living room for fresh air and poked her head into Anna's room: discarded winter clothes were strewn across the bed; shoes and boots were scattered across the floor.

She was most anxious to search the study. She sat in Anna's old captain's chair and powered up the computer and the dial-up modem, which Anna had steadfastly refused to upgrade. Rachel found something nostalgic about the modem's squealing handshake with the internet. She knew Anna's passwords and after a moment of agonising about violating her mother's privacy she went ahead and logged into her email account. There were many new messages, but she ignored them for now, scrolling back to the night of their dinner party until she found the one brief email Pierre Villiers had sent that night:

Have a look at the attached photos. Do you recognise this man? Call me!

One by one, the attachments opened sideways and Rachel flipped them upright. At first, she thought she wasn't going to learn much. She passed quickly over the first three images: two of a hooded and shackled man in an orange jumpsuit being led from a plane; the third a police-ID photo of man with a badly bruised face labelled with the name *Tomislav Maric*. She recalled Maric was the alias of the person now known to be Marin Katich. Then she opened the fourth attachment, a photo taken in a hospital room. The swelling and bruises on the man's face had subsided. It was in this photo that Rachel saw what she presumed had so disturbed her mother. The man's eyes were very clear in the photo.

Rachel's hands were trembling and she moved the mouse unsteadily, tapping the magnifying glass icon to blow the image up. She kept tapping it until the man's eyes filled the screen and, as they did, she felt a coldness spreading through her body, an icy wind of recognition, katabatic in its force, eroding her doubts. Rachel felt tears welling up in her own eyes and then she was sobbing, her chest heaving with emotions she could barely comprehend. She ran into the bathroom, wiped her eyes dry and stared at them in the mirror. The photo was not proof-positive of her suspicions, but at some deep level she knew.

When she had recovered sufficiently, Rachel resumed her search.

The filing cabinet was locked. After a fruitless attempt to locate the key, she went to the laundry and found a hammer and a crowbar in the tool box. It was not the kind of high-security cabinet in which sensitive financial documents were kept at her own office, so Rachel was soon able to jimmy open the drawers. Her mother's filing cabinet was ruined, but if Anna complained—a big *if* under the circumstances—she would buy her a new one.

Rachel searched the drawers systematically. Naturally the extensive files under K for Katich were of primary interest and she piled them on the desk. Then she found a box labelled *ASIO pics*. She was well aware that Anna had used Freedom of Information Laws to access her secret ASIO files. Years ago, Anna had shown Rachel some of the old surveillance photos of her dressed in full radical-chic mode in the 1970s. They'd had a good laugh about them.

Rachel opened the box, not sure what she was looking for, and found it immediately. Sitting on top of the pile—presumably this was no coincidence—were three photos, in a sequence, that had been taken at some distance using a telephoto lens. Written in pencil on the back of each of them was the date, *September 1970*. The two subjects of the surveillance were her mother, she guessed aged nineteen or twenty, and a strikingly handsome young man. Anna was running to him. She was pulling him towards her, clearly distressed. A close-up of the young man showed what Rachel had anticipated: he had unmistakably green eyes.

Rachel knew a good deal about the recessive gene involved. Throughout her life, so many people had commented on it. Her eyes were her most striking feature. She knew that she and this man were both in the tiny subset of humans, less than two per cent, who shared this distinctive green eye colour. But beyond that superficial marker there was a deeper sense of recognition. There was something familiar in his bearing, his facial expressions, his complexion. She knew enough to distrust these feelings. For as long as she could remember, she had longed to find her father, to fill the terrible gap that Anna had left her with by refusing to ever discuss the possibilities. Now here was evidence of her mother in the arms of a man who might well be him.

Father!

Above all, there was an overwhelming sense of relief that seemed to thaw the chill that had gripped her entrails. She knew other feelings were waiting at the edge that would soon come crowding in, but at this moment the lifetime of longing for an answer, her longing to know, seemed finally to be at an end.

My father is a man named Marin Katich!

She stared at the photos for a long time, trying to read something more in his face. It was not, she thought—she hoped—the face of an evil man. She opened up the news website on Anna's computer and found the image of the much older man in a camouflage uniform that she had seen this morning, the Marin Katich they were calling a war criminal.

She put the photo up against the screen and looked at them side by side—the man in his twenties, the man in his forties. The older one was harder, tougher—crueller perhaps? Was it cruelty she saw or was it that the uniform and the headlines about war crimes had created that impression?

Rachel resumed her search for answers in Anna's files, and as she worked her way through her mother's extensive notes and documents she gradually began to see how careful Anna had been. There were many references to Marin as the son of Ivo Katich, but nothing, save for the three photos, that indicated her personal connection to the younger Katich.

She reviewed in the files the documented details of the horrific crimes, crimes against humanity, which had been perpetrated by his father, Ivo Katich, when he was a senior officer in the Ustasha in Bosnia during the Second World War. The facts of those unspeakable crimes, which she had read years earlier in her mother's book, were now freighted with terrible consequence, and Rachel was no longer immune to them.

She remembered travelling to the Ravensbrück camp with her grandmother, Eva, together with Anna; she remembered her tears as Eva for the first time told them her story of life in the camp. As the granddaughter of a survivor, the Holocaust had been central to Rachel's identity for as long as she could remember. But now she would have to reimagine it all with a sense of blood guilt as the offspring of one of its perpetrators. She felt a profound shift in her soul. Tears formed again in her eyes, trailed down her cheeks and dropped onto the files she was reading.

When she felt able to work, Rachel took notes of every mention of Marin Katich, building the most complete picture she could. The photos had been taken in September 1970, so Anna and Marin Katich must have been together then, when Anna was at university, but there was no other reference to him in that period. The first actual reference in the Katich file was dated June 1972, when Marin was believed to have been part of an incursion into Bosnia, one of twenty armed insurgents who crossed into Yugoslavia on a mission to foment a revolution against the communist regime of Marshal Tito. There was no documentary proof that Marin was there, only strong rumours in the police and intelligence communities. If he had been among the twenty, Anna had noted, then he was the only survivor of that mission.

In September of that same year, Marin's younger brother, Petar, was suspected of having carried out the terrorist bombing of two Yugoslav travel agencies in the centre of Sydney. Again, there was no documentary proof. Petar had disappeared and Anna's notes showed that she believed he had been murdered by agents of the UDBA, the Yugoslav secret service. Then Rachel found typed notes about Marin Katich dated March 1973. The notes were incomplete and confusing, but they related to his involvement in a plot to assassinate the prime minister of Yugoslavia, a man called Bijedic, when he came to Australia on an official visit. Two names reappeared again and again: one was a Commonwealth policeman called Al Sharp; the other an ASIO officer with the unusual name of Tom Moriarty, beside which Anna had written: *Russian-born, Timur Morashev*. Rachel guessed that these two men, if they were still alive, would likely be in their late seventies. She resolved to try to find them.

The final reference to Marin Katich was in notes from Anna's trip to Bosnia in 1992. She had received information that Katich, or someone closely resembling him, had been commanding a large militia, headquartered in the town of Ljubuski in the region of Herzegovina in Southern Bosnia. When Anna got there, the second-in-command, an officer called Jure Rebic, had told her that the man she was looking for had been killed only days earlier, ambushed at a roadblock. This account, in dramatic form, became the foreword in later editions of Anna's book, *Australian Nazi*.

Rachel paused, thinking for a moment before she wrote down the name *Jure Rebic* and underlined it. Then she looked through her notes, reviewing the incomplete biography of the man she now believed to be her father. Rachel had realised why Anna's notes about him ended in 1992: she had thought Marin Katich was dead and so there was no need to burden her daughter with the fact of his existence. She knew her mother. Anna would have kept this secret forever to protect Rachel from the pain of that knowledge. But now, it turned out, he was alive.

26

SCHEVENINGEN PRISON, THE HAGUE

22 DECEMBER 2005

MARIN KATICH lay waiting for Zwolsman to come and unlock his cell. He thought about what he had told, and what he had not yet told, Anna Rosen. He had seen that Anna was repulsed by his history of violence. She drew away from him as if she wanted to cover her ears and shout. That was natural, and yet it caused him pain. It reminded him how far he had removed himself from the civilised world, remaining attached to it by only the most fragile skeins of memory.

One thread still connected him to that strange fellow Rob in Anna's Glebe apartment block, a man he had met once and never seen again, but who had nonetheless given him a gift. In the years Marin spent in Rovinj, slowly putting himself back together, classical music had been a balm almost as soothing as the morphine he had eventually forced himself to let go of. He had begun his listening where he had started—with Mahler's fourth symphony, a CD he picked up in the town market, and it moved him just as it had when he first heard it.

The composer had understood that, alongside the transcendence humans are capable of, there is evil too and that murderous impulses lurk in their souls. Marin believed that the violence from which he had never escaped had darkened his soul. The voices of the dead were constant reminders of that: they told him that he would soon join them.

The cell door rattled and clanged open. Zwolsman, unusually, came inside and stood close to the bunk.

'Mr K,' said the guard. 'Mr K, no longer Mr M . . .'

Marin sat up. 'What?'

'K for Katich.'

'So, it's out?'

'Since the news last night, you are the big celebrity,' said Zwolsman. 'I have breakfast early with the other guards. One of them, he picked up a butter knife and he says to me: "When you wake up Crocodile Dundee, tell him *this* is a knife!"'

Marin lifted his right hand and raised the middle digit. 'Tell him *this* is a finger.'

For some reason this appealed greatly to Zwolsman's sense of humour; he was still chuckling as he left the cell.

•

Later, waiting in the corridor to go down to the exercise yard, Marin was aware that he was the centre of attention. A number of the other inmates were openly staring, heads together, murmuring. The usual suspects—Mejakic, Borovcanin and Ademi—were scowling at him. Strangely, none of them confronted him. Milosevic was back in hospital and he was grateful for his absence.

He stood apart from them, alone until the Bosnian Halilovic came up and spoke to him quietly.

'So—*Marin Katich*,' he said. 'It may take a little time to get my tongue around that.'

'Take as long as you want,' said Marin, and the Bosnian produced a knowing smile.

'So, it turns out you are one of us,' said Halilovic. 'I can see why you wanted to keep that quiet.'

'Believe me, Adem,' said Marin, 'when I tell you I'm not one of anyone.'

Halilovic regarded him silently for a moment before responding. 'Marin, you were a commissioned Major General in the Bosnian Army,' he said. 'For me, you are a comrade in arms. For them'— he gestured with a movement of his head towards the muttering Serbs—'you're an even bigger enemy than you were before. A Croat in the Bosnia army—it was not unheard of but unusual, especially in a command rank. Did you have a reason?'

'My mother was a Muslim, she lived in Mostar,' said Marin. 'It was men like these who killed her.'

Halilovic nodded gravely and put an arm on Marin's shoulder: 'If you need help . . .'

'Thanks,' said Marin. 'You coming down?'

'Not today,' said the Bosnian. 'I've got a meeting with my lawyers.'

Marin went to join the group that was already heading down-stairs, led by Zwolsman. As was his usual practice, he entered the exercise yard and began walking to the far end, avoiding contact with the inmates from different floors who had gathered in small groups to talk or join some organised sporting activity. Marin was especially alert since being cut by the Gypsy and he took care to stay well away from other walkers.

Most of the men in the yard he recognised by sight, but he only knew the names of those on his own floor. He skirted a group of younger inmates playing a half-court basketball game at the near end of the yard, pausing only to watch a big black guy dunk the ball after a languorous lay-up.

It was a cold, clear day, colder for the absence of clouds, and there was a thin layer of ice on the ground in areas untouched by the sun. He stayed in the sun, trying to leach out of it what little warmth it had to offer. When he reached the end, he stopped and lit a cigarette under the high steel fence topped with razor wire. Beyond the wire was an overgrown, rubbish-strewn patch of wasteland. He put his back to it and looked up at the blue sky. He let his mind go back to when he was a boy floating on his back, drifting in the Towamba River on the far south coast of New South Wales, under the same sky. No one could take the sky away from him.

Marin smoked the cigarette down to its butt and flicked it through the fence. He stood still for a time, letting his mind drift as if he were still in the river. He didn't move until he saw a pair of men heading in his direction, then he put his cold hands in his pockets and continued the circuit, staying well ahead of the walkers.

The basketball players were noisier now, the score must be close because there was no trace of languor remaining in any of them; the game was being played in a frenetic scramble and spectators had gathered, egging on their champions. As he got nearer, Marin realised he would have to pass close behind the tight-packed group of men. He looked back, but the walkers were gaining on him so he hunched his shoulders and pressed on. The spectators were so enthralled by the game that none seemed to notice him edging behind them.

When he was near, a tall man holding a spare basketball turned towards him and called: 'Katich! Think quick!'

The tall man threw him the ball, a fast, hard pass. Marin reacted instinctively, pulled his hands from his pockets and caught it, immediately realising his mistake. The tall man was on him before he could drop the ball.

The man smiled grimly as he set to work. Marin felt a series of swift blows to the left side of his chest. It happened so quickly that he was still gripping the ball. The tall man grabbed it and bent close to his ear.

'Rambo sends his love,' he said before pushing him hard in the chest with the ball.

Marin staggered backwards, assailed by a sudden, overwhelming rush of pain. He saw the man moving away behind the crowd as swiftly as he had appeared. Marin clutched at the growing patch of warm blood flowing from the wounds. He tried vainly to staunch it as it seeped through his fingers. He pushed his way through the crowd and collapsed onto the basketball court. The last thing he saw was the face of the black man, staring down at him, wide-eyed.

•

When Pierre rushed into Anna's room that same morning she was sleeping off the effects of excessive drinking. She had woken in the middle of the night, parched and hungover, and swallowed aspirin with, it must have been, half a litre of water. Now Pierre shook her awake and she sat up blinking, red-eyed and startled.

'Katich has been attacked in the prison yard. Stabbed in the chest.'

'What?'

'He's still alive,' said Pierre. 'But critical.'

'Who did it?'

'They don't know. Our boys have called in the Dutch police.'

'They don't know?' cried Anna. 'In a prison yard? They don't have cameras?'

'It happened behind a crowd watching a basketball game. They found a homemade shiv, no prints on it.'

'Is he in the prison hospital?'

'Yes.'

Anna threw off the covers and got to her feet.

'I've got to get there,' she said, grabbing up her phone from the bedside table.

'I'll put coffee on,' said Pierre, 'while you get ready.'

Anna rang van Brug and learned that he had already been informed of the attack. He had tried calling her, but when the phone went through to messages the lawyer had sent her a text and moved quickly to make arrangements for them to visit the hospital. He offered to pick her up outside the apartment.

Anna had a one-minute shower, dressed fast, went downstairs and told Pierre what was happening. He handed her coffee and a croissant.

'It's too much of a coincidence, isn't it?' said Pierre. 'The morning after we go public with his identity.'

'It is,' she said, sipping the coffee. 'So, who are the suspects? Who'd want him out of the way?'

Pierre considered the question. 'Someone who hates him,' he said. 'Or someone who's got something to lose.'

'Jure Rebic?' said Anna. 'He already tried to kill him once, thought he'd succeeded. Now Katich has come back from the dead. Whatever happened in 1992, Rebic won't want him telling the tribunal about it.'

'If this was done on Rebic's orders, the odds are the hit man is a Croat,' said Pierre. 'I'll run your theory past our investigators.'

'Can you also ask around, see if anyone's got anything on Rebic? Who he is? *Where* he is?'

'I'll see what I can do. No promises on that, but I did get a reply from Jasna Perak in Zagreb. She says she's happy to meet you.'

Pierre handed Anna the printed email with Perak's details.

'Just remember that Jasna's a spook. She'll want something in exchange for whatever she tells you.'

Anna folded the printout and put it into her pocket.

'Thanks, brilliant Pierre, thank you,' she said. 'She must know Rebic, right?'

'You'll have to be very careful how you broach that,' he said. 'If Rebic was acting on Tudjman's orders to eliminate Katich back in 1992, it's possible Jasna was in the loop.'

Anna's Blackberry rang out its SMS tone.

'Bloody hell,' said Pierre. 'That fucking gong. You really should change that.'

'The alternatives are worse,' she said, reading the message. 'Van Brug's out front, I've got to go. Can I call you later?'

'Yup,' said Pierre. 'Did you call Rachel yet?'

Anna blushed. 'I didn't,' she said. 'I drank so much last night I just conked out.'

'At least send her a text,' said Pierre. 'She must be wondering what the hell's going on.'

'I will,' said Anna as she rushed to the door.

•

After navigating three security checkpoints, Anna and van Brug were sitting in plastic chairs in the dreary, utilitarian waiting room of the prison hospital. Also in the room were two middle-aged men in plain dark suits who turned out to be Dutch detectives waiting to interview Katich if and when he came around. Once Anna realised who the men were, she tried to engage them in conversation, but they refused to respond, except with monosyllables. Typical cops, she thought, with their ingrained habits of suspicion; they were the same the world over.

Sitting in a room filled with awkward silence, Anna had time to think after the morning panic. First, she cursed herself for not having asked Marin more about Jure Rebic when she had had the chance. Of course that was exactly what they had planned to do today, but someone, perhaps Rebic himself, was determined to make sure that he talked to no one. For a fleeting moment it crossed her mind, although she was ashamed to admit it, that life would be easier in many ways if Marin would go back to being dead.

That perverse thought prompted her to think about what, if anything, Marin Katich meant to her. After all, here was a man whose life had been turned upside down because he had stepped in to protect her. It had taken her thirty years to understand what had really happened that day, but she had finally learned why he had broken up with her and disappeared. At that time, on that day, she had been heartbroken; so what did she feel now? Her closest friends would ask her if there had been even the faintest spark when she saw him again for, despite the ravages of his life, he was still a good-looking man.

And what, she wondered, had gone through his mind when he had seen her again? With a flash of inspiration, Anna remembered Othello's contemplation on Desdemona: *She loved me for the dangers I had passed, And I loved her that she did pity them.* Could Marin have thought like that? Did he possibly imagine, as he told her his stories of war and death, that she might love him for the dangers he had passed? Had she fed such a delusion when she sent him the photograph?

She contemplated how she would truly feel if he never regained consciousness. She had repeatedly told herself that she was only here for Rachel, to discover the truth about her biological father, and the truth about the war crimes he was accused of committing. It was all for Rachel, she told herself again—but she wondered if she was protesting too much.

•

They waited for more than two hours like an estranged family brought together by tragedy. Eventually a tired-looking surgeon in a disposable scrub cap came in to talk to the four of them. The surgeon was lean, well-proportioned and almost as tall as van Brug. Anna could imagine the two of them in Lycra suits jostling for position in the velodrome. The surgeon had the face of an aesthete and long delicate fingers. He spoke in Dutch and van Brug translated.

'Mr Katich has come through some difficult surgery and they are hopeful he has a good chance of recovery,' said van Brug, struggling to keep up with the surgeon. 'But they have put him in a—what do call it . . .?'

'A medically induced coma,' the surgeon interrupted. 'I will continue in English for the lady. You are Australian, like Mr Katich?'

'Yes,' said Anna.

'I was saying that one of the knife wounds pierced his heart. Luckily only one chamber was damaged and we have been able to repair that. But he had what we call a pericardial tamponade, that is to say the wound caused fluid to build up in the pericardium, the sac around the heart, and this put pressure on the heart and it began to arrest. We had to do an emergency thoracotomy, but lucky for him we did not have to open his chest for the repairs.'

'What does that mean?' said Anna.

'We were able to spread the ribs under his arm to make the repairs; it means he should recover more quickly. To be honest, he was lucky in other ways: the bleeding might have been worse but, as you may know, he had already lost his left lung in what seems to have been a traumatic battlefield injury. Strange . . .'—the surgeon chuckled—'the missing lung made him harder to kill this time. Of course he is still in danger if there are complications—infection, further bleeding, cardiac arrest. He has chest tubes to drain air and fluid from the site.'

'How long will you keep him under?' asked Anna.

'Some days for sure, perhaps a week or more. It depends on his progress. So, as I said to the detectives, there is no point in waiting here. We will take your numbers and call if there is a change.'

'Can I see him?' she asked.

'Are you his next of kin?'

'No.'

'I'm sorry,' said the surgeon. 'They are strict here. Only next of kin.'

When they left the hospital, Anna asked van Brug to drop her back at Pierre's apartment. She intended to pack a bag and catch the first flight to Zagreb.

27

SYDNEY, AUSTRALIA

22–23 DECEMBER 2005

RACHEL ROSEN'S detective work in her mother's study had produced mixed results, but when she made her first breakthrough she found herself wondering if she'd actually absorbed some skills by osmosis from the obsessive journalist who brought her up. She had found in Anna's files a home number for Al Sharp, the former Commonwealth policeman her mother had been in contact with in 1973.

Sharp's wife, Muriel, answered the phone and gave her the bad news that poor old Al had died five years ago.

'It was the smokes that did him in,' said Muriel. 'If I told him once, I told him a thousand times.'

'I'm sorry to hear that,' said Rachel. 'My mum knew Al back in 1973, when he was working on a big case.'

'Oh,' said Muriel, instantly suspicious. 'Do tell.'

'She was a journalist.'

'Hmm.'

'Muriel,' said Rachel sharply. 'There was no hanky-panky going on. Someone was trying to assassinate the prime minister—'

'Not poor old Gough?'

'No, the prime minister of Yugoslavia. Do you remember Al talking about that?'

'It sort of rings a bell,' said Muriel, curious now. 'Tell me more.'

'There was another fellow working on this—Moriarty, *Tom* Moriarty. Do you remember that name?'

'Oh, I remember Tom all right,' said Muriel. 'He was a terrible scoundrel. He got drunk over here one night and tried to cop a feel. Al had to throw him out on his backside.'

'Do you know what happened to him? If he's still alive?'

'No, dear,' said Muriel. 'But there's probably a number for him in Al's old Rolodex. Do you want me to look for you?'

'That would be very kind.'

It took some time before Muriel came back on the line. 'The things you keep,' she said. 'I just remembered that Moriarty was with ASIO. Al never trusted that mob. He worked for them, you know, when he left the army. Hated it so much he transferred to the police.'

'Funny he kept in touch with Moriarty.'

'He did too,' said Muriel. 'There're a few numbers here. An office number. A home number and one for his son, young Don.'

Rachel took them all down and thanked Muriel, hung up and immediately started on the new contacts for Moriarty. The office number proved to be disconnected; the home number in Canberra didn't answer, but, third time lucky, she got through to 'young' Don, who sounded like a man in his sixties. She told him that she was researching her mother's life and had come across a number of references to Tom Moriarty and so was trying to contact him.

'Dad's in a nursing home in Canberra,' he said. 'The old house is closed up. He thinks he'll get back to it, but I can't see that happening. So how is it you know him again? Who's your mum?'

'She's a writer and a journalist, Anna Rosen.'

'Oh,' said Don. 'Of course I know her work. I read her excellent book on Ivo Katich. Dad had something to do with him, didn't he? From his time in the Organisation.'

'I believe so,' said Rachel. 'I'd love to have a chat with him about all of that. Do you think he'd be up for a visitor?'

'He has good days and bad,' said Don. 'His liver's pretty much given up the ghost, but he's got a mind like a steel trap. He does come alive when he's talking about the old days. I'm living on the south coast and I only get up there every few weeks, so I reckon he might be happy for a visitor. I'll give you the address, but I have to be honest: he's an irascible bugger. You might get there and find he's not interested in talking to you.'

'Thanks for the warning,' she said. 'I'll give it a go.'

•

By the time Leah came home that night, Rachel had resolved to tell her everything. She had realised during her day of rummaging through the secrets of her mother's life that she was in danger of repeating Anna's mistakes. She greeted Leah at the door with a loving kiss and a long hug.

'Come and sit down,' she said. 'There's something I need to tell you.'

Leah was immediately agitated. 'What is it?' she demanded to know. 'What's happened?'

Rachel embraced her again.

'It's nothing to do with my love for you,' she said, gently leading Leah into the living room, where the coffee table was laid with an open bottle of wine, glasses, crackers and hummus. Rachel poured them each a glass of wine and sat down opposite Leah.

'Did something happen at the office party?' asked Leah, ignoring the wine.

'No, I didn't even go,' said Rachel. 'Listen to me. It all started with the news on the radio this morning about this man in The Hague war crimes prison they've identified as Marin Katich.'

'I've been hearing about it all day,' said Leah. 'No one's mentioned your mother, but she's obviously involved.'

'She is,' said Rachel. 'Look, I didn't tell you this this morning and I should have. Something about that story really disturbed me, so I rang in sick to the office and went to mum's apartment. I spent most of the day there going through her files, looking for evidence or clues.'

'Evidence of what?'

'I think this man, Marin Katich, is my father,' said Rachel.

•

Leah first reaction was shocked disbelief. She didn't show much of what was going through her mind but simply went quiet, quiet and detached. Leah's silence only became more ominous as Rachel carefully took her through what she had found, showed her the photos from 1970 and prints of the recent pictures of Marin Katich. Leah broke her silence only to ask questions. Gradually, as each piece of the puzzle was laid out for her, Leah's questions became fewer and the stretches of silence longer. Eventually, she picked up the photographs and Rachel watched Leah staring at the man's eyes, as she had done herself, until she lapsed into a kind of depressive trance.

Rachel was worried when she saw this happening, but she had committed to complete honesty and she had to explain her next course of action, which was now clear to her. She would have to fly to The Hague and meet the man directly, face to face.

'I want you to come with me, Leah,' she said. 'We can do this together, or we can let it hurt us.'

Leah didn't answer, but instead stood up. There was a tremor in her hands and she grasped them together, pressing them into her chest.

'No,' she said. 'No, no, no, NO!'

She ran into their bedroom, threw open the cupboards and began shoving clothes into her suitcase. When Rachel reached her and tried to calm her, Leah stepped back. There were tears streaming down her face as she pushed Rachel away.

'This can't be,' she said. 'This can't be.'

'This has nothing to do with us,' said Rachel. 'Our love, I mean. You know who I am.'

'I don't,' said Leah. 'Not anymore. I have to go away to think. I have to go home.'

Rachel took Leah in her arms and found her stiff, resistant and changed, as if the essence of the woman she loved had suddenly drained away.

'Leah. Don't do this,' she whispered. 'We can get through this together. It's the only way.'

Leah pulled out of the embrace and took a step away from Rachel. 'This is not some movie, Rachel,' she cried. 'I'm not going to hold your hand as we drive over the cliff together.'

•

Leah slammed her suitcase shut and hauled it from the room, showing surprising strength as she carried it over the thick carpet before wheeling it down the corridor to the front door. She left it there and grabbed her shoulder bag from the living room.

Rachel stood in front of her, tears in her own eyes now. 'It doesn't have to be like this.'

Leah seemed to have drawn strength from the physical exertion with the suitcase. She stopped and drew on some hidden reserve of composure.

'Eli came to see me today,' she said. 'I had lunch with him. He came to invite us to Shabbat tomorrow. *Us!* Do you know what that meant to me after all this time? My parents! They found some forgiveness in their hearts. I fell in love with a woman, yes; but, she's a Jewish woman, so . . . Tell me, Rachel, what do you think will happen when they find out you're the daughter of a Nazi war criminal?'

When Rachel found no words to respond, Leah filled the silence with something like a final curse.

'Your mother is a *dybbuk*,' she cried. 'She's stolen your soul.'

Rachel watched Leah go. She stood speechless as the curse settled on her head. Whatever Anna's faults, she was not a demon. She had lied to Rachel and misled her about her origins, but she had certainly done so in a misguided attempt to protect her daughter from the truth. Nor was Rachel possessed by her mother's spirit. That was a stupid, primitive, kabbalistic insult. She had her own mind, her own motives. When she was sure that Leah was not coming back, she walked over to the pathetic little Christmas tree that Eli had so despised and kicked it over.

•

Before dawn the next morning, Rachel was behind the wheel of the Audi driving fast—not recklessly, but in a controlled fury— through the empty streets of the city. She hoped momentum would keep her thoughts from the terrible sadness and disappointment about Leah, and the persistent thought that her lover would be drawn back into the family cult. Her suitcase, packed with winter clothes, was in the boot. She had a lot of driving to do. She had booked herself onto the evening flight to London, with a connection to Amsterdam. Before that, she would drive to Canberra to talk to the geriatric spy, Tom Moriarty, then back to Sydney—a six-hour round trip.

Rachel followed the signs into the sickly, green-tinged underworld of the tunnel system and then up into the halogen-bright above-ground freeway, passing huge trucks one after the other.

Hers was one of the few cars on the road and she worked to get ahead of as many trucks as possible. Her mother had always told her that sleep-deprived truckies, breakfasting on coffee and speed, were the most dangerous creatures in Australia—more fatal, even, than snakes or sharks.

Rachel smiled at that memory since she knew that the younger Anna was no stranger to driving under the influence. But the smile faded as quickly as it had formed when she thought of the coming confrontation with her mother. Rachel had decided not to warn Anna that she was on her way to The Hague. She knew what she had to do and didn't want Anna to intervene. This was her thing now and, after a lifetime of secrecy, it was for her alone to decide what to do.

Rachel was well on her way when the sun came up over the gently rising green slopes of the Southern Highlands. She drove as fast as she dared, on past the Goulburn exits with their inevitable danger of speed traps, and then turning onto the Federal Highway and into the Australian Capital Territory. This always felt as though she was crossing the border into another country, one whose key industries were politics, bureaucracy and surveillance.

As she reached the city's outskirts, Rachel turned up the volume of her GPS navigator and followed its staccato voice. Close to the destination, she stopped at a café and bought two takeaway flat whites, an offering she hoped would be a treat to the old spy.

The sat nav got her to the front door of the nursing home a few minutes later. The place looked like a low-rise motel with scrubby bush plants out the front, rising out of a base of dark woodchips.

The woman at the reception desk summonsed a nurse to see if Tom Moriarty was happy to see her.

'He doesn't get too many visitors,' she said.

'Tell him I am the daughter of an old acquaintance of his,' she said. 'Anna Rosen.'

The word came back that he had agreed, and she was taken to a room with a view over the back gardens. The room had an electric hospital bed; the old man propped up on it by pillows was skeletal except for his swollen belly, which the buttons of his pyjamas strained to contain. He looked, she thought, like a pregnant woman in a famine. When he gazed up at her, she saw dark patches beneath his eyes and the general yellowish tinge to his skin.

'Come in, darling.' His voice was incongruously strong, coming from such a frail body. 'D-Don't be afraid of the yellow p-peril, it's not contagious.'

'I'm sorry?'

'The j-j-jaundice,' he said, waving a yellow hand in front of his yellow eyes. 'The old liver's shot, I'm afraid, and I'm p-pretty sure they don't plan to give me a new one. So, you're the d-d-daughter. What's your name?'

'Rachel,' she said, holding out the takeaway cup. 'I brought coffee. Are you allowed to drink it?'

'I should say so, after the b-bilge water they serve up here.' He reached out and wrapped his bony fingers around the cup, pulling off the plastic lid. 'A p-p-peace offering, is it?'

'Do we need to make peace?'

Moriarty didn't answer. Instead, he reached into the bedside drawer and produced a slim bottle of scotch, which he opened and shakily poured into the coffee, before holding it out to her.

'Want some?'

'No, thanks,' she said. 'You really want to do that?'

'Christ, you sound like my wife, God rest her soul. Look, my f-fucking liver's f-fucked, no matter what I do.' Moriarty took a swig from the bottle and screwed the lid back on. 'This is medicine for the sh-shakes. The c-craving gets bad and I can't think straight. You don't want that, do you?'

'No.'

'So, R-Rachel,' he said. 'That's a good Jewish name.'

'Yes.'

'M-Matrilineal, isn't it? Your mum's a Jew, ipso facto you're a Jew, no matter who your father is.'

'What's your point?'

'Well, your father's a C-Catholic, but they didn't call you Maria.'

'How do you know that?'

'That's why you're here, isn't it? I can't think of any other reason to have m-morning tea with a d-dying spy.'

'Yes, but how do you know my father's a Catholic?'

'Because I was there, at your c-c-conception.'

'What?'

'Not in the r-room! Ha ha ha, that's funny. Did you think I might be your f-f-father?'

'Not for a moment!'

'Oh, that's c-cruel.' He looked crestfallen. '*They f-fuck you up, your mum and dad. They may not mean to,* blah, blah, blah. No, I knew them both. There c-can't be many people who could say that. Perhaps they should have made me g-godfather.'

'What do you mean, you were there?'

'I was a s-spy, darling. I was hunting poor M-Marin. He had a hard life, that boy. I b-blame myself, I do. Bit of a g-guilty conscience. Now look where he's ended up. Anyway, stick to the t-timeline, Tom! Where were we?'

'My conception.'

'Yeah, wow, it was like something out of *Doctor Zhivago*. Very romantic. Someone should write a b-b-book. Anyway, I thought he might come to see your mother that night and sure enough he d-did. Middle of the night, over the b-balcony into her room, and Tom's your uncle.'

'I keep asking,' Rachel said, 'how do you know?'

'Oh right,' he said. 'Isn't it obvious? Listening device. I was next d-d-door with headphones on. All very exciting. I didn't have a st-stutter before that.'

'What!'

'Just kidding,' said Moriarty with a lunatic grin. 'I know no one wants to hear about their p-parents f-fucking; but if someone told me they knew exactly how I came into existence I'd want to know.'

'Why were you hunting him?'

'That's easy,' he said. 'He was a t-trained assassin and he was planning to k-kill the prime minister of Yugoslavia the next d-d-day. March 1973, the f-first foreign head of government to come visiting since Whitlam came to p-power and your dad was p-planning to knock him off. So, ask the rhetorical question.'

'How do you know that?'

'Because I t-trained him . . . Ooh! Aah!'

'What's wrong?'

'Here, quick, take the bottle,' said Moriarty, handing her the whisky. 'I need you to help me to the bathroom.'

Rachel steeled herself. Wrapping her arms around the corrupted old bag of bones, she helped him stagger to the bathroom.

'Give me the b-bottle,' he demanded and he put it on the floor beside the toilet, flipped up the seat, got onto his knees and emitted a tremendous retching sound before he threw up into the bowl, time and again until he was empty. Then he pulled the chain, straightened his back and called to her: 'Help me up!'

When Rachel got him to his feet, Moriarty flipped the toilet lid down again and sat there. Reaching for the whisky at his feet, he took a mouthful, rinsed his mouth and swallowed it. He turned his drained, yellowish face up to her.

'You'd make a shit nurse,' he said.

'Good,' she said. 'That's not on my career plan.'

'So,' said Moriarty, pausing to take another swig. 'Now we know each other a little b-better. Pull up a seat.' He pointed to the plastic chair sitting in the shower. Rachel carried it out from under the dripping rose, wiped it with a hand towel and sat down.

'So,' said Moriarty. 'What is it you do, darling?'

'I work for a hedge fund.'

Moriarty laughed, like it was the funniest thing he'd ever heard. 'Anna R-Rosen's girl in a hedge fund,' he said. 'That's made my day.'

Rachel took from her pocket the ASIO surveillance photo of Anna in the arms of young Marin Katich. She passed it to Moriarty, who bent forwards from his precarious perch on the toilet seat to take it into his hands.

'It was taken in September 1970,' she said.

'Now,' he said, staring at it, 'this is what I'm saying about g-guilty consciences. I made him do this, you see. Break up with your m-mother.'

'Why?'

'It's c-complicated.'

'I need to know, Tom.'

'Even your m-mother doesn't know.'

'Please tell me.'

'Official s-s-secrets, bullshit, bullshit,' said Moriarty, hitting the bottle again.

'You're dying, Tom.'

'Oh,' he cried. 'Flattery'll get you nowhere.'

'I mean . . .'

'I know what d-dying means, darling. Not much t-time to make amends, right?'

'If you like.'

Moriarty ran his hands over his face, then looked up. Rachel saw the whisky was taking a toll. He pointed a long bony finger at her.

'Those green eyes,' he said, the words slurring a little now. 'My Lord, I could have gone for them back in the day. Anyway, 1970. Your old man M-Marin, he was a tough kid. It's the M-Moratorium march in September and he comes across two cops in an alley, b-beating on your mother, she's his girlfriend by now, right. I guess he was looking out for her.

'It was an ugly, sexual thing with these cops, so Marin loses his b-bottle. Beats the shit out of the cops. Puts them in hospital. I know M-Marin's dad, Ivo—your grandfather, right? He c-called me up. Marin's in jail, looking at attempted m-m-murder.

'Back then I had a bit of sway in the Organisation. I p-pulled some strings. M-Marin is mine n-now. Quid pro quo, you break it off with Ana Rosen, right? It's that or life in j-jail. He had no choice. None. That photo, that's where he told her. So we take him away and put him through b-basic training—the army, Kapooka camp, then specialist t-training. We t-t-turned him into a sniper. Then it's off to Vietnam to work with the c-cousins. Operation Phoenix, you heard of it?'

'No.'

'The younger generation, eh? Bunch of know-nothings. Operation Phoenix. We go bush for weeks on end, t-track and kill the leadership of the V-Viet Cong. The f-fucking cadres. The worst m-murdering bastards in the country. They were the ones who liked to c-call all the f-fucking peasants into the v-village square to make 'em watch as they lopped off the arms of the local school teachers and let 'em bleed to death. We k-killed men like that and I've never lost a m-moment's sleep over it. Marin, though . . .'

Moriarty shook his head sadly. Rachel wondered if this was a parody of an old man who, looking back on his life, had genuine regrets.

'It f-fucked him up, right royally. He's the one p-pulling the trigger. We g-got him out when he started hearing voices. The ones he'd killed, you see, t-talking to him at night. That's down to me, isn't it? Tell your m-mum I'm sorry, will you? Will you d-do that?'

Rachel stared at him, said nothing.

'You b-better go now,' said Moriarty. There were tears forming in his sick eyes. 'I'm not f-feeling so good. Can you call a nurse? That red b-button in the shower. Can you hit it for me?'

Rachel got up and left him there. She didn't look back. Outside, she looked at her watch. Three hours back to the airport—she had plenty of time to think.

28

ZAGREB, CROATIA

23 DECEMBER 2005

SNOW BEGAN TO FALL as Anna walked along Ilica Street. It fluttered down from the still, dark sky, a multitude of white flakes illuminated by the high-strung Christmas lights. She stopped and put out a hand to catch a few and they nestled icy-white in the palm of her black glove until she bent forwards and licked them off like a child. The tolling of the cathedral bells, muffled by the snowfall, was joined by those of nearer churches. Anna knew this staid, old-aunt of a city well enough, but she had never been here for Advent and it seemed to have transformed itself now into a place of celebration, deeply at odds with her own state of mind. Yet she found herself moved by it.

Anna looked back and saw that fresh snow was already covering her tracks. She laughed at nature's clumsy metaphor and walked on, following the directions she'd been given to the Zagrebacka Uspinjaca, the old funicular. She climbed into the shiny blue box, already crowded with steaming, damp-faced, chattering folk in puffer jackets and woollen hats. Soon the automatic doors closed and the carriage jerked, then rose smoothly up the steep incline, the track hemmed-in by two sets of baroque buildings with red-tiled roofs.

In just over a minute, Anna was borne up into the upper town. The snow was heavier now as she made her way to St Mark's Square and began to recognise streets and buildings from past journeys, when she had first come to Zagreb to read the history of the Ustasha in their own documents. The pealing of the church bells, beautiful though they were, now reminded her that Archbishop Stepinac and his priests had held masses in April of 1941 to bless the declaration of the 'independent' Croatian state by the Ustasha's founder, Ante Pavelic, who was permitted to do so under the dominion of Adolf Hitler.

Anna had quoted at the front of her book the words used by the archbishop on that fateful day: '*The times are such that it is no longer the tongue that speaks, but the blood, with its mysterious links to the country in which we have seen the light of God.*'

Anna had been appalled when she first came across those words. What manner of man, let alone a religious leader, could see the light of God in fascism? And these days there was growing clamour from nationalists for the 'martyr' Stepinac to be elevated to a saint. She believed this country would never be free of its past until it truly remembered it.

•

She found the restaurant in a street close to St Mark's. It was a small, cosy place with an open fire. The maître de, a saturnine fellow called Branko, hung up her coat and led her to a table close to the fire, where a striking-looking woman sat smoking. Anna had a moment to see her in repose before they reached the table. The woman was roughly her own age, with bright red hair and plum-coloured lips.

She looked up, crushed out her lipstick-stained cigarette and rose from her seat.

'You are Anna,' she said, opening those lips in a wide toothy smile. 'I am Jasna.' She shook Anna's hand as firmly as a man.

'I have been looking forward to meet you, honey, a long time—can you believe it?'

'No,' said Anna. 'That's a surprise. Why is that?'

'Sit first, sit,' said Jasna and plonked herself back down as Branko seated Anna, flourishing a napkin like a magician and placing it on her lap. 'You must have a drink to melt the snow.'

Branko took his cue and filled up shot glasses for each of the women from the impressive-looking bottle already open on the table.

'This is the famous Travarica,' said Jasna. 'Do you know it?'

'No,' said Anna, but when she sipped it, she understood how it could have become famous. It seemed to warm her insides with a smooth, cold flame. 'Oh,' she said, 'that does melt the snow.'

'It is *rakija* from Dalmatia, where I was born,' said Jasna, beaming with pleasure. 'Grape brandy with many herbs infusing in it. I think you like it, yes?'

'Yes,' said Anna. 'Very much, but I'm curious about what you said. We don't know each other. How can you have been waiting a long time to meet me?'

'This is very simple, honey,' said Jasna. 'You know last year we get intelligence that this man *Cvrčak* is living in Rovinj. Our new EU friends, they are very pushy friends, good but pushy—you know this type, very anxious for us to round up some Croatian war criminals and send them to Hague. So I am in Rovinj with a team, you might call them a "snatch team", and I am watching this man—secret watching, you know? He has a pretty little boat from Venice, his business is to take tourists to the islands, and what I see painted in lovely big letters on the back is the name of this boat, can you guess?'

'No,' said Anna.

'It is called "Anna",' said Jasna.

Anna's ears seemed to be buzzing.

'Sorry?'

'Anna, Anna,' said Jasna. 'And now I find the real name of this big insect is Marin Katich, I find he's Australian citizen and now working on his legal team is another Australian citizen and her name is Anna! Wow! Coincidence?'

'Of course not,' said Anna.

'Good,' said Jasna. 'Nice to know I'm not idiot.'

Then to Anna's surprise she reached down beside her chair and produced a plastic bag full of loose cigarettes. She took one out, lit it from a candle and passed over the bag.

'You want one?'

Anna took one for herself, picked up the same candle and lit it. She exhaled smoke and downed the rest of her brandy, and the two women sat smoking for a moment like old companions.

'So,' said Jasna. 'He's old boyfriend?'

'From many years ago, yes.'

'And you are still interested, why?'

Anna considered lying to her or simply not answering. What was it Pierre had said? *Jasna's a spook. She'll want something in exchange* . . . She decided to give her something to establish trust.

'He's the father of my daughter,' she said. 'But he doesn't know that.'

'Oh, oh, oh,' said Jasna. 'This is real soap opera, isn't it?'

Jasna didn't wait for an answer but looked up, caught Branko's eye and nodded. 'We must talk,' she said. 'And we must eat! I have ordered for us already. Tonight I am your host. I cannot cook, which makes me sad, but this place makes me happy. Real Croatian food. We will have octopus salad and soup from Zagorje, this region is north of Zagreb, and from my own Dalmatia. Black cuttlefish risotto. Are you hungry?'

'I'm starving,' said Anna.

Anna was pleased she had trusted her instincts. She had understood that, since gathering intelligence is often about gossip, stories like her own must seem to a spook like tapping into the source. As the food came, course after extraordinary course, she told her story and explained how and when it intersected with Marin's, as she now understood it, unsparing of detail. Jasna ordered wine and then more wine, and anyone watching would have thought that these were two old friends, a little drunk and catching up on old times.

Eventually, Anna reached the moment she had been leading up to. So far she had brought Jasna along with her, only giving information and asking nothing in return; but once she had finished detailing the treachery and duplicity of Jure Rebic, it was time to take a risk.

'I need your help, Jasna,' she said bluntly. 'I need to find this Jure Rebic. I need to know what has become of him and where I might find him. Can you guide me in this?'

Jasna had eaten the last of her black risotto and Anna saw that the ink had stained her plum-coloured lips. Jasna now put down her fork, took a sip of wine and dabbed her lips with the white napkin. Watching these deliberate actions, Anna was worried that she had been too abrupt, too unsubtle.

'You haven't eaten your risotto,' said Jasna.

'I've been talking too much,' said Anna.

'So,' said Jasna. 'Now you eat and I will talk. Okay?'

'Okay.'

'I have my own soap opera to tell you. It is the Croatian soap opera. You know something of the wolves of the past, but not present, not *my* present, and not the wolves of the present.

'This story starts with Franjo Tudjman. We like to call him Croatia's George Washington, you know that, yes? Honestly, I used to love my dear Franjo. The slogan for his last campaign: "The President for President". So simple, huh? I wrote that slogan. This is the man who won the war, who gave us independence, gave us democracy. Who else would you vote for? No, for sure, it's got to be the President for President.

'For many years I worked with him, side by side. Helping fight the war, helping make Croatia free. Franjo, he is the one who did these things, our first president! He was not like a real boss to me, more like a second father. All this time he knows he has my loyalty, from the beginning and for many years. But let me tell the sad thing, honey: when you are on the inside like this, you start to learn things.

'All these years, I'm watching, I'm advising him on security, on intelligence. But, as time goes by, I learn that my idol has clay feet. The old story. He becomes powerful, too powerful. Somehow, without ever running a business, just being president, he becomes very rich. And he is powerful enough to pass a law which makes it illegal for journalists to investigate the personal finances of politicians. Can you imagine?

'So, I am asking myself: is this what we fought for? What so many of us died for? My brother, he died at Vukovar; my boyfriend, he died in the Krajina. And we did not spill their blood and that of others to fertilise—is that how you say it?—to fertilise the ground for a corrupt regime.

'Anyway, Franjo wins his second election, 1997. The President is president again, and do you know what the joke is being told all over Zagreb? I'll tell you, it goes like this: what is the biggest industry in Croatia? Answer: Fiat. And what is Fiat, you ask, for it seems so strange that some fucking Italian car company is the biggest company here in Croatia. No, Fiat is F...I...A...T...
Franjo i Ankica Tudjman...You get it? Franjo And Ankica Tudjman. Franjo and his wife are our biggest industry! And many men who are close to them become very rich. Men with connections, but no talent except for corruption. Some call this the "tycoon-isation" of Croatia. Some say we are now the Nigeria of Eastern Europe.

'Franjo has been dead now for six years, but this mafia state we have become, it all began with him. And why do I tell you this long, tragic tale? What has all this to do with Jure Rebic? I will tell you, honey. Who is the biggest mafioso in Croatia today, so long after the death of my dear Franjo? It is your old friend Jure Rebic! I'm talking about heroin, for he controls the Balkan Route; I'm talking about the trafficking in humans for sex trade of women and children; I'm talking about weapons smuggling; I'm talking about casinos and hotels; and I'm talking about the corruption of politics. But with all this power he is like invisible man. He is biggest political donor in Croatia, but I don't think a single voter would know his face. This is the man you want to find—but tell me, honey, are you prepared to die for this?'

Anna had been mesmerised by Jasna's speech. She had not expected anything like this, but nor was she going to be warned off.

'What if I found the evidence,' she asked quietly, 'that he is a serious war criminal? That he should have been indicted and sent to The Hague?'

'Honey, you didn't answer my question.'

'Jasna, you wouldn't have told me all of this if you didn't want me to go and find that evidence.'

'That is true; it would be great service to my country to get rid of this man. But it's no joke about the danger. I really don't want you on my conscience. It's like being in a Chinese restaurant and choosing your own fish from a tank. I can't eat it once its personal.'

'Will you help me do this or not?'

'You understand that he will try to kill anyone who threatens him?'

'I'll have to be careful. Will you help me?'

'I will do what I can to help you, honey. I will give you information. But when you go looking for this evidence, you will be on your own. You understand?'

'Yes.'

'Okey dokey,' said Jasna, as if there was nothing more to discuss. 'Dessert is coming. *Strukli* from Zagorje. You have left room for this, yes?'

29

THE HAGUE

24 DECEMBER 2005

RACHEL ROSEN repeated the journey her mother had made nearly two weeks earlier, though having travelled business class she was in substantially better shape when she came up the lifts in the morning from the train platform into the cavernous arrival hall at Den Haag Centraal. She wore a grey Burberry goose-down jacket like a suit of armour against the cold.

Pierre Villiers saw her coming and ran forward to greet her.

'Rachel,' he called.

She heard 'Wa-chel' and immediately smiled, turning to see the familiar shambling figure with his Coke-bottle glasses and messy hair—now streaked with grey, she noticed.

'Hello, Godfather,' she said and hugged him tightly.

'Oh,' said Pierre, 'I thought you'd have forgotten. I've been pretty useless at my duties.'

She laughed. 'The spiritual side was always a lost cause,' she said. 'But, here you are, so . . .'

'I've done what you asked,' he said, taking her wheeled suitcase. 'The car's outside.'

She had emailed him before she left Sydney, told him she was coming and why, and begged him not to say anything to Anna. Pierre had suggested she stay at his apartment and share the spare room with her mother—a chance, he said, for them to talk this through. Rachel didn't want that; she wanted to keep her distance from Anna until she had resolved matters for herself.

Then, during the stopover in Singapore, she had picked up a paper and read about the attack on Marin Katich. When she rang him for news, Pierre had told her that Katich had come through surgery but was in an induced coma.

'What's the news on my father?' she asked him now.

'You want to call him that?'

'I've been lied to all my life, Pierre,' she said harshly. 'I'm not going to resort to euphemisms now that I know the truth.'

'You know your mother only told me ten days ago.'

'Okay,' she said.

'They've brought him out of the coma,' he said. 'I made arrangements with the tribunal. I had to get the Registrar to approve it. You can visit as next of kin.'

Rachel was silent. Now it was real. She had half hoped some bureaucrat would refuse her request.

'Where's Anna?' she asked.

'I respected your wishes and didn't tell her you were coming. She went to Zagreb for a meeting. Now she tells me she's flying to Bosnia. She says she's on to some new lead on Katich . . . Your father, I should say.'

'He doesn't mean anything to me, Pierre,' said Rachel carefully. 'It's just something I have to understand.'

Pierre nodded and began moving. 'Let's go, shall we? Car's on a meter.'

Outside, the freezing air stung Rachel's face.

'I think it's going to snow,' said Pierre. 'White Christmas.'

Rachel screwed up her cold face. 'Anna texted me in Singapore,' she said. 'She said she wants to talk. But she didn't say anything about Zagreb or Bosnia. Still keeping secrets. Last thing she said was: "Happy Christmas".'

Pierre flipped the hatch and shoved her suitcase in. She folded her coat and laid it on the back seat. He waited for a tram to hum past before pulling into the traffic.

'I know you didn't want to stay at the apartment,' he said. 'But now Anna's gone, you're welcome to change your mind. I had the cleaner fix up the room.'

'Thanks, Pierre. I had booked a hotel, but actually I really don't fancy being on my own,' she said.

'Great. Shall we go home and drop your bags?'

Rachel considered the offer. It would be easier to have a rest, but she didn't want to break the momentum. There had been too much time to think on the long flight, especially after she read her father's war crimes indictment.

'He's awake *now*,' she said. 'Do you mind? I don't want to wait.'

•

Rachel looked up at the immense fortress-like prison gates. Finding that her hands were shaking, she shoved them deep into her pockets. She felt a terrible sense of dread, unlike anything she could remember.

For some reason, her grandmother entered her thoughts. The torments of Eva's life made her own concerns seem trivial and she rebuked herself for her own weakness, for her emotional fragility.

She struggled to control her breathing as Pierre ushered her through the various security zones. But each staring face she encountered—whether that of an armed policeman, or a prison guard, or a trustee sweeping the corridors—seemed to contain a particular vice: slyness, misogyny or desire. Pierre smiled reassuringly and explained where they were going, but she felt as if she were being led through the circles of hell.

Behind its own high-wire fence and many locked doorways was the prison hospital. Yet once she was inside, it was a familiar scene of wards and doctors and nurses; people she had been brought up to trust. But in one of those wards was the source of her dread.

Pierre spoke to a woman at the front desk, produced his ID and asked Rachel for her passport. The woman looked at the passport and scrutinised her with open curiosity before signing them in. Rachel barely comprehended the instructions the woman gave to Pierre, but followed him as he led her without ceremony to her father's bedside.

Marin Katich was in a partly raised electric bed, hooked up to a drip and a monitor, a chest drain emerging from under stained bandages. He was slumped into pillows. His eyes were closed and fluttering. He had broad shoulders and strong arms, but he looked sallow and haggard.

Rachel saw no sign of the vital, aggressive energy she had observed in his military portrait, nor of the bruised, angry resentment in the prison photos that Pierre had emailed to Anna. More particularly, she saw no hint of the handsome young man who had been forced to reject her mother.

She could not say what she felt on seeing him in the flesh for the first time. If she'd had to pick a word, it would have been *emptiness*.

'Katich!' said Pierre loudly. 'Are you awake?'

Her father's eyes fluttered open and a shaft of light through the barred window illuminated their startling green hue. She knew him then, and felt something beyond mere recognition.

'Do I know you?' he said. He was talking to Pierre and his voice was strong.

'I'm Pierre Villiers. The last time I saw you was September 1970.'

'What?'

'No, it's not a dream.'

'Fuck! *Pierre?* What are you doing here?'

'I'm not going to beat around the bush, Katich,' said Pierre. 'I'm here to introduce you to your daughter.'

Rachel stiffened; she had had no warning Pierre would do it like this.

'What did you say?' said Marin, his eyes flicked to Rachel and they stared at each other until her father shook his head. 'It can't be.'

'But it is,' said Pierre. 'This is Rachel Rosen and I am going to leave you two. You don't need me here. I'll be outside, Rachel.'

Pierre turned and strode out, his crepe soles squeaking on the polished vinyl floor. Rachel didn't respond, didn't turn to watch him go. She was fixated on Marin Katich: she saw tears glistening in his eyes.

'You're really my daughter?' he said, and Rachel nodded.

'Anna didn't tell me,' she said. 'She doesn't even know that I know. I found some evidence in her files, old photos and papers. But it was Tom Moriarty who confirmed it. I went to see him two days ago. He's in a hospice. He told me about the night you were with Anna in her hotel room. The night I was conceived.'

Marin's thoughts were still fogged by narcotics. 'Moriarty,' he whispered.

'Yes.'

'He was spying on us.'

'I know,' said Rachel.

'It's—'

'I know.'

'—incredible.'

'But true,' she said. 'That night was in March 1973, I was born on the twelfth of December that year. I got your eyes.'

'You did,' said Marin. 'I see that. I really had no idea—'

'Nor did I.'

'—you even existed.'

'No, Anna kept this secret from me my whole life. There's no way either of us could have known.'

Marin grimaced. He was obviously in pain. He made a move as if to get up and she flinched, thinking he might reach out to her. Instead he slumped back. 'What do you want from me, Rachel?'

She gripped her hands together so tightly her knuckles were white. 'I have to know who you are.'

'What did Moriarty tell you?'

'He's dying,' she said. 'He has a lot to confess.'

'He destroyed my life.'

'He said that.'

'So you know what I am,' said Marin, his voice strained with emotion. 'What he made me.'

'I do.'

'Why did you come?' he demanded. 'I must seem like a monster to you.'

'You do,' said Rachel. 'At least, you did, but now I see you and I just don't know. There's so much I don't understand. I've wondered about you my whole life.'

'I'm sorry.'

'I don't want your pity,' she said sharply. 'I want the truth.'

Marin tried to swallow. He choked before lapsing into a fit of coughing, as if the truth might kill him. He pointed to the bedside table as he struggled to regain his breath. 'Can you pass me the water?'

She put the cup in his hand, waited while he drank and took it back.

'I read your indictment on the plane,' she said. 'It made me sick. I locked myself in a toilet and threw up.'

Marin reached out his left hand, sought the morphine button and gave himself a hit. He waited in silence for it to take effect.

Rachel's patience ended and she cried out. 'Are you at least going to deny it?'

'I learned in prison that nothing sounds more false than an accused man protesting his innocence.'

'It's better than admitting your guilt.'

'Rachel, I am guilty of many things. It was your country, your government that made me what I am. They twisted and tortured my nature. They turned me into a killer. They left me haunted by what I had done for them. But they didn't turn me into a man who would kill civilians, women and children.'

'What about the indictment?'

'I just said that I have done terrible things in my life,' he said and his voice was hoarse. 'I'm prepared to confess to those things, but that indictment is a pack of lies . . . Rachel, if you're prepared to listen, I will tell you what really happened, but you'll have to sit down.'

Rachel brought a chair up and sat near the bed. It felt strange to be so close to this man. She noticed his large, coarse hands lying above the sheet. She listened as he told a story about a man named Jure Rebic. How they had met. The fighting in Vukovar, the escape from the siege, the trek to Bosnia, and how they had built together a Croat–Muslim militia in Herzegovina. As he continued, she sat silently, absorbed in the tale.

'We had five thousand men under arms when the fighting began and we were stretched over a wide territory. I have already told you that Rebic was a brave fighter. I felt I owed him my life and I trusted him completely. He assumed command of the eastern sector where some of the hardest fighting was. I gave him autonomy in that sector and that was a terrible mistake. Eventually, I began to hear stories that the men under his command were out of control, that he had built a prison camp where men had been tortured and women raped, and that his men had murdered civilians. At that time, we were engaged across many fronts in fierce battles. I was in command of forces around the city of Mostar, which was under siege, and I couldn't leave to go chasing rumours about Rebic, as terrible as they were. I spoke to him by radio and I sent him written orders to make sure no such atrocities were committed by men under his command. I ordered him to investigate the claims that prisoners of war had been abused and to deal with the perpetrators. I should have gone there immediately, but the Serbs were bombarding our lines and the civilians in Mostar.

'Rachel, I don't know how much Moriarty told you about me, but you should know that my mother, your grandmother, was living in Mostar at this time, not far from the Old Bridge, which we call *Stari Most*. Her name was Samira, Samira Begovic, and she was a Bosnian Muslim. I see that you're surprised, please wait and ask your questions later . . . You will come to understand that our identities are more complex than you can imagine.

'On one of the worst days of the bombardment a shell came down through the roof of my mother's house. Samira had refused to go to a shelter or even to her own basement. I found her body myself and that of her husband, and carried them out of the ruins. It is their practice that the bodies must be prepared and buried within twenty-four hours . . .'

Marin's voice seemed to catch here and Rachel saw that he was trying to stop himself from weeping. He clutched the bedclothes in his fist, fighting, it seemed, to contain his own raw emotions. He struggled to control his breathing and then continued.

'Can you imagine how hard it is to bury your mother and give her respect as shells are raining down? I was not in my right mind after that, Rachel . . .

'That is another story, but it took some time before I was able to travel to Jure Rebic's sector. The day that I did, his men were conducting an assault on a number of small Serbian villages. It was one of those days when the clouds are so low over the mountains that the colour seems to have leached out of everything. On days like that, the brightest colour is blood.

'I had only one bodyguard with me, a trusted man—Ante Lovren was his name. Why would I need anyone else when I was visiting our own troops? I came to a village which they had overrun and everywhere I looked were bodies. Old men, old women, children, all dead. Of course, the young men of fighting age were not there; they were long gone, recruited into their own armies. These were the families they had left behind—old women like my mother, old men like her husband. I was in a rage. I ordered the men to cease their operations and gather in the village square. I went looking for their officer, who they told me was a man named Mesic, the second in command to Jure Rebic.

'I found this man coming out of the basement of a house. He was hitching up his trousers. I ordered Lovren to take his weapons and hold him outside the house, and I went down into the basement. On the floor was the body of a young women, perhaps sixteen years old, she was naked. It was quite obvious that she had been raped, her throat had been slashed and she had bled to death. I wrapped her body in a blanket, carried her up the stairs, and told Lovren to bring Mesic and follow me.

'We went back to the village square where the other animals were gathered. I laid the body of the young girl in front of them. I had my men bring Mesic forward and made him look at the dead girl. I told him this was a field court martial and I pronounced on him the sentence of death. I shot him in the head right there and he fell next to the body of the girl.

'His men cried out, cringed backwards, thinking they would be next. I had Ante Lovren write down all of their names and told them that they would one day face the consequences of what they had done. I intended to strip them of their weapons and have them transported back to our headquarters in Ljubuski.

'But at that moment Jure Rebic himself arrived at the village. He found Mesic's body and he knelt down and began to weep. I told him what the creature had done and why I had had no choice, but he shouted that the dead man was his brother-in-law and the life of some Serbian slut could never be weighed in the balance against such a man. I told him to look around the village, that Mesic's men had committed a massacre here, and he screamed at me that they were following his orders, cleansing the region of terrorists and those who breed terrorists. I ordered Jure Rebic to hand over his weapons and told him I was stripping him of his command, effective immediately and that the men in the square would be taken to Ljubuski to face court martial.

'Rebic then pulled out his side-arm and cocked it. He called on his men to pick up their weapons. My bodyguard Lovren now had his weapon up, but of course we were outnumbered. I told Rebic that he would face charges of mutiny, but he laughed in my face and said that, had we not been comrades in Vukovar, he would kill me now. Lovren and I had no choice but to leave.'

At that point, Marin stopped and put his hands up to his face, as if behind his fingers he was still seeing the ruined body of the young girl. He reached for the water, took another drink and continued.

'Over the next two days, I called the officers of my general staff together to decide how to deal with Rebic. My biggest fear was that he would try to incite rebellion in other units. We travelled to different parts of the battlefield to make sure it didn't spread.

'What I didn't know was that we had a far more dangerous enemy than Jure Rebic. The Croatian president, Franjo Tudjman, had made a secret deal with Slobodan Milosevic, the very man who had tried to crush us in Vukovar. Tudjman agreed to stop fighting the Serbs in Bosnia and promised the Croat army would go to war against the Bosnian Muslims. Tudjman planned for his army to occupy a huge swathe of Bosnian land in the south and create a Greater Croatia, allowing the Serbs to pursue a Greater Serbia in the north.

'It was a betrayal so craven, so profound, that I could not have even conceived of it. I should have been more cynical. If I had understood better the nature of this man Tudjman, I might have been able to predict that the force I commanded, being forty per cent Muslim, would be targeted for destruction.

'I don't know exactly what happened next. Either Zagreb made contact with Jure Rebic, or he with them. What I do know is that it was Rebic who organised the ambush on our cars. I was coming back with seven of my staff officers from the meetings where we had determined to send an armed force to arrest him. We were attacked while driving back to our headquarters in Ljubuski. My officers were killed; I only escaped death by a miracle.

'I was secretly transported by loyal Muslim soldiers to the battle-field hospital in Mostar. Ante Lovren was with them, and it was he who sent word back to Ljubuski that I was dead. My men shaved off my beard and my hair and gave the hospital false papers for me, giving me the new name of Tomislav Maric. Under Rebic's command, meanwhile, every Muslim fighter in my battalions was disarmed and purged; and I know that many of them were killed.

'Until a few days ago, Jure Rebic still believed that I was dead too and no threat to him. As soon as he learned I was alive, he moved quickly. The man who stabbed me in the prison gave me a very clear message: "Rambo sends his love."'

Rachel had not said a word throughout her father's long saga. It seemed to her like something from another age. What he was, what he had done, was beyond her comprehension—he was military commander; judge, jury and executioner. But she found that she could not judge his Old Testament morality under such extraordinary circumstances as he had described. Above all, she instinctively believed that he was telling the truth and, if that was the case, the war crimes indictment she had read should have been brought not against her father but against Jure Rebic.

'Is there anyone still alive who can back up your story?' she asked simply.

Marin held her gaze as if trying to see beyond the question into her thoughts. 'I've been thinking about that,' he said. 'I lost track of most of my old comrades after the ambush, but there is this one man, the one of whom I spoke earlier, Ante Lovren. When Lovren joined us in Ljubuski, he was just a pimply young man who had been training to be a priest. This same Lovren was my most trusted bodyguard and, as I told you, he risked his life to help get me secretly to the hospital after the ambush. I believe it was Lovren who substituted another body in the coffin with my name on it. Being a Croat, he was not purged, but stayed on after Rebic took command.'

'Do you know if he's alive?'

'Yes, I saw him not long before I was captured in Rovinj. There is a medieval fortress town on top of a hill not far from Rovinj called Motovun, and I'd sometimes go there to have lunch and to play chess with an old friend. I was there one Sunday visiting a church off the main square called St Stephen's. I liked to look at the frescoes, but that day I heard a familiar voice. There, in front of the altar, the priest was conducting the mass and, when he turned to face the congregation, I recognised Ante Lovren. I asked an old lady and she said that, yes, it was Father Lovren and he was the priest of St Stephen's. I should have gone up to him there and then, but the long habit of secrecy stopped me. I left the church and never tried to contact him. But now I'm worried.

'Rachel, you must ask your mother to pass this information to the police. I know this about Jure Rebic: now that he has failed to kill me, he will try to silence anyone who can give evidence against him. I think Father Lovren could be in danger.'

•

Pierre took Rachel back to his apartment. He wanted to sit down and talk her through what she'd learned, but she excused herself, pulled out her laptop and went up to her room.

Half an hour later she came back down to find that Pierre had prepared lunch, and she sat with him and set out her plan. She explained to him why she wanted to be in Motovun for Christmas Day. Once he understood that there was nothing he could do to stop her, Pierre insisted on accompanying her.

30

MOSTAR, BOSNIA AND HERZEGOVINA

24 DECEMBER 2005

ANNA ROSEN was on a morning flight from Zagreb to Mostar while her daughter, unbeknownst to her, met with Marin Katich. Having booked an exit row, she found herself seated next to a Franciscan nun. It turned out that the Croatian-born nun had lived for many years in Canada and spoke perfect English; like the majority of the passengers, she was on her way to join a pilgrimage to Medjugorje.

'I have been there,' said Anna. 'A long time ago now, in 1992.'

'A bad time,' said the nun.

'For many people,' said Anna. 'Me included.'

'And you go back now?' asked the nun. 'To see the Virgin? She can provide great comfort.'

'Perhaps not so much to people of my faith,' said Anna. 'Although, she did give birth to the world's most famous Jew.'

The nun nodded and closed her eyes. Anna, seeing that she was clutching her rosary, turned away and picked up her book again, an old classic by Ivo Andric. Eventually she became aware that the nun had re-opened her eyes.

'You weren't praying for me, were you?' Anna asked.

'Yes,' said the nun. 'That your pain should be relieved.'

'Is it that obvious?'

'It is.'

'Well, thank you,' said Anna. 'You know I've never really had a proper chat with a nun. What do I call you?'

'You can call me sister.'

'That works for me, sister,' said Anna. 'That's what I've been calling my women friends since I was seventeen—that or comrade.'

'I prefer sister,' said the nun.

'Okay, so I've seen you pray to God. But I don't think you rely entirely on her protection,' said Anna, pointing to the sealed emergency handle above the door that was almost beside them.

The nun responded with a smile, her pretty, plump face framed by her white veil. 'Because I chose the exit row?' she asked.

'Yes,' said Anna and at that moment the plane hit a pocket of turbulence, as if to rebuke her insolence.

'We are all in her hands, my dear,' said the nun. 'But that doesn't mean we shouldn't take sensible precautions.'

•

After a bumpy ride, the plane hit the deck hard and rolled to a stop in front of the terminal. Through the window, Anna saw a hokey, old-fashioned sign, 'MOSTAR AIRPORT', screwed on to the front of a single-storey cement building. It reminded her of airports in regional Australia—simple, functional and low security.

She passed quickly through Immigration, her passport stamped by a woman who never looked up, then she went to wait at the sole baggage carousel. The pilgrims gathered in nationality groups to wait for their luggage, while the nuns joined up with others from their particular orders, and Anna heard a babble of French, Italian and Spanish as they hauled their bags off the carousel.

When she'd retrieved her Briggs & Riley, she waved goodbye to the exit row nun and made her way to the public section of the terminal.

At the front of a small crowd, Anna saw the veteran journalist Adin Genjac just as he shouted her name and started limping fast towards her on his stiff leg. She had spoken to him recently, but they hadn't seen each other for thirteen years.

He was still a bear of a man and the rolling gait seemed to emphasise his girth. His thin hair, now almost white, was pulled back from his brown face in a long ponytail. He wore a padded Israeli military jacket over a khaki T-shirt; a red pack of American cigarettes, most likely counterfeit, poked out from its top pocket.

He hugged her hard and kissed her forehead.

'Welcome back!' he cried as he pulled her away from a column of pilgrims lugging their chattels towards a waiting bus. 'You have to admire these Catholics. This is some money-spinner. Ninety per cent of the tourists flying in here head straight for "Apparition Hill", all because a few silly peasant girls got some bad LSD in 1981.'

'Maybe you should go see if the Blessed Virgin can fix your leg,' said Anna, and he let out a boisterous laugh.

'I'm too old for virgins, Anna,' he cried. 'But I do think my people should get in on this action. We should forge a document saying the prophet, peace be upon him, once came to Mostar for a sabbatical. Stand back and wait for the stampede.'

'Careful, brother,' she said. 'You'll end up with a *fatwa* on your head.'

Genjac's expressive face darkened, and she saw it was still a perfect barometer for his changing moods. 'Anna,' he said taking her arm and leaning in closer. 'We have bigger problems than an imaginary *fatwa*. Come, come, we must go. Ena is waiting outside.'

He led her to a boxy monster in the airport pick-up zone. Anna recognised it as a special Land Rover, one of those vehicles that rich media companies once used to transport their journalists and crews during the war, often with a security consultant sitting up front.

'You like it?' asked Genjac as he threw Anna's gear into the back. 'It's a Defender 110. I bought it from CBS when they packed up and left.' He bashed the machine's flank with his fist. 'Armoured chassis, bulletproof windows, 4.2 litre V8.'

'You think we're going to need all that?' said Anna.

'Ha ha ha, maybe,' he said. 'You sit up front with Ena. I stretch my leg in back.'

Anna climbed up into the passenger seat and found Genjac's daughter gamely gripping the monster's steering wheel. She guessed Ena must be about the same age as Rachel. Sometime during the last thirteen years, she had taken to wearing a hijab. Her face, framed by the silk garment, was still luminously beautiful. Anna had a fleeting thought about the nun and what it was about women's hair that required it to be hidden.

'It's good to see you again, Ena,' she said.

'Hi,' said Ena, giving her a tight smile.

Genjac leant over from the back seat. 'I don't get around too good anymore,' he said. 'In this past week, I sent Ena far and wide for you, searching for the men we talked about. I have not heard from any of them for years.'

During the long wait to get permission to see Marin Katich, Anna had trawled back through her files and found the list of names that Adin Genjac, from his hospital bed in 1992, had pressed into her hand. It was a list of the Muslim fighters under the command of General Cvrčak whom he trusted.

She had found the old Bosnian still working as a journalist in Mostar, and hired him to try to locate these men, whom she reasoned would be witnesses to the events set out in the indictment. Only yesterday Genjac had called her back with a simple message: *Come as soon as you can.* The expression on Genjac's face now told her she had been right to move quickly.

'Ena has found much information,' he said. 'These things I did not think it safe to talk about on phone. Tell her what you found, daughter.'

Ena nodded and turned to Anna, unsmiling, earnest.

'The list Adin gave you—the six men he knew and trusted in *Cvrčak*'s militia—here it is.' Ena handed Anna a sheet of paper. 'All of them survived the war, but five of them have died in the past six months. I have set it out in order.'

Anna looked at the list and read through it:

Haris Osmanovic: *Age 39—Killed in hit and run accident, driver not found, Mostar. 19 August 2005.*

Seid Silajdic: *Age 41—Found dead in Sarajevo apartment. Heroin overdose, not known user. 1 September 2005.*

Osman Dedic: *Age 43. Shot to death by unknown assailant in Tuzla. Police believe the shooting was gang related. 14 October 2005.*

Edin Zukic: *Age 38. Body found in the sea at Hvar. High blood-alcohol level, ruled death by accidental drowning.*

Barisa Halimovic: *Age 46. Found dead in bathtub with wrists slit in his farmhouse near Jajce. High blood-alcohol level, ruled suicide.*

Amir Ramic: *Age 42.*

Anna looked up at Ena. 'This reads like a hit list.'

'In each case, the investigating police were suspicious,' said Ena. 'But they found no evidence. In the case of Osmanovic, the first killing, there were no witnesses to the accident; it happened late at night. Silajdic was found by his girlfriend. I spoke to her and she swears that he never used heroin. Osman Dedic had a criminal record, so police easily concluded he was killed by a rival. Zukic was in Hvar with his wife and two children. He went out to meet someone for a drink one night and never returned. His wife does not know who he went to meet or why. Barisa Halimovic was found by his son; he had divorced five years earlier and was living alone, but his son had no idea that he was suicidal. He had seemed happy two days earlier.'

Genjac reached over from the back seat and took the list from Anna's hands. 'In each case, the police thought they were looking at a one-off incident,' he said. 'The detectives in Mostar had no reason to talk to detectives in Sarajevo—or Tusla or Hvar. They seem like isolated incidents unless you put the names together with the list that I gave you. That makes *me* a link between them, but I know I did not organise the deaths of these men. So who did? Someone who is trying to erase evidence from the past. This man, Marin Katich, who we once knew as *Cvrčak*, he might have a motive if these men could be witnesses against him, but he is in a prison where all communications are monitored. How could he orchestrate five killings in different places?'

'Impossible,' said Anna. 'But I think this does explain why the indictment against Katich, or *Cvrčak* rather, remained sealed. If the investigators knew that men from the possible witness list were dying mysteriously, they would have a real reason to suppress it until they knew what was going on.'

'It's unlikely, yes, but not impossible,' said Genjac. 'Can you be sure this Katich is not killing these men?'

Anna thought about it and shook her head. 'It wouldn't make sense, Adin. I was looking for these men to see if they might be witnesses *for* him. The person with the biggest motive is the man who took command in Ljubuski after Katich was shot,

General Jure Rebic. It was Rebic who told me that Katich was dead. I just learned in Zagreb that Rebic is now the head of a crime syndicate.'

'Yes, it does all point to Rebic,' said Genjac. 'And if that is right, this list could get us killed. I am worried for Ena.'

'Stop, Father,' said Ena sharply. 'I was careful only to speak to relatives of the men. I know the police are corrupt. I stayed away from them.'

Anna felt a shudder run through her body. 'Ena, I'm so sorry I got you into this.'

'You could not have known what I would find.'

'This started as your story, Anna,' said Genjac. 'But now it is ours. These were men that I knew in the war. Good men. This Rebic is an evil and dangerous creature. I have been making my own inquires about him, carefully, with trusted contacts. He has been almost invisible for years, gathering money and power. They tell me that in this past year—especially in Split, where he has two casinos, but also in Ljubuski, where he has a villa and a winery—he has come out more into the open. He is making himself a public figure, donating to charities, to churches, to schools and to local politicians. The rumour is that he will run for president in the next Croatian elections.'

Anna considered this information. Jasna Perak must have known that, but she hadn't mentioned it.

'The last man on the list, Amir Ramic,' she said. 'Have you found him?'

'We have,' said Genjac. 'He is in a safe place. You will meet him today, but we have to go somewhere before that. Ena, we should move.'

Ena started the powerful engine and it rumbled ominously. When she put it in gear and pushed into the street, its roar was deafening. It was obvious to Anna the muffler was shot.

'Sounds like a tank!' she shouted to Ena, whose face, framed by the elegant black hijab, was beaming.

'This is every girl's dream,' said Ena. 'To drive a tank.'

•

It was a cold day, darkened by clouds that flattened the impact of Mostar's sixteenth-century Turkish architecture. Ena drove them through the old town skirting the tourist zone along the Neretva River, and stopped near a small mosque. Genjac explained that its dome and the tall needle of a minaret had been destroyed during the war and rebuilt, just as the old bridge had been.

Genjac gestured to an entrance in the stone wall. 'Come,' he said. 'We are expected.'

They removed their shoes by the fountain in the courtyard.

'There's no need to cover your head,' said Ena. 'The imam is not conservative.'

Anna was puzzled as to why they were here, but asked no questions—her hosts clearly had a plan. She followed father and daughter into the mosque. The floor was covered in carpets and prayer rugs; a solitary worshipper was on his knees, bent forwards in prostration. The interior of the mosque was white and simple, lit by a great wheel-shaped chandelier beneath the high dome, and largely unadorned except for some finely painted trees and decorative work above the doors and windows.

They were met by an older man, a solemn fellow who led them out the back into another courtyard and across it to a separate stone building.

'This is the old madrassa,' said Genjac as they were ushered into a large room with cushions set around the edges.

A dozen men came into the room, each greeting Genjac but ignoring his daughter. Among them was an imam in black robes whom the others treated with great deference. His dome-shaped black turban was wrapped with cloth bands of the purest white. The face beneath it was grim and deeply lined. He had dark eyes and a short black beard.

The imam gave Anna a thin smile when Genjac introduced her, then gestured towards the cushions and said in English, 'Please sit.'

The men took their places around the room, leaving empty the three cushions facing the imam. As Anna sat in pride of place, flanked by Genjac and Ena, several men entered carrying copper trays on which sat white ceramic cups.

Anna smelled the rich Bosnian coffee before she saw it. A steaming cup was placed in front of each of them; beside each cup was a piece of Turkish delight, an ashtray, three cigarettes and a small box of matches. Most of the men lit up immediately and began sipping their coffee. Genjac followed suit, but Anna noticed Ena did not touch the cigarettes and so she left hers alone.

At some signal missed by Anna, the imam began to speak. He briefly addressed the room, then he turned to Anna and spoke to her directly:

'Adin came to me seeking help and I have agreed to take the man Amir Ramic under my protection. I know that his life is in danger because of what he knows and that five other men have already been killed. I have spoken to Ramic and I understand that he does have information that puts a very bad light on the Croat, Jure Rebic. This puts us in a difficult position. We do not wish to do anything which could again inflame the tensions between our people. Croats and Muslims now live peacefully in Mostar—not in harmony, not in happiness, but at least in peace. If handled badly, the information Ramic has could cause the old tensions to boil up again. For that reason, I considered keeping Ramic from you and allowing these terrible secrets to remain buried. I thought deeply about this, and I thought about those men already murdered because of what they knew. My conscience will not let me remain silent—the souls of those men, and many more, cry out for justice.'

Anna nodded, looking at him through the blue veil of smoke that now filled the room. She was about to respond when Ena put a hand lightly on her arm. She said nothing, and the imam began speaking again.

'From you I will require an undertaking. If Amir Ramic is ever to give evidence on these matters to the tribunal in The Hague, his life will be in serious danger. He will need the strictest conditions of anonymity, and he and his family will need to be relocated and put under protection. If you can guarantee that, I will release him to go there. If not, he will remain under my care and my protection. Do you agree?'

'Imam,' she began. 'Let me first say thank you for your deep thought on this matter. I can't speak for the Tribunal, but I can go and make your case to them and explain that these are the only circumstances under which Mr Ramic would agree to come and give evidence. But I will need more to make that case. If I can meet him and speak to him confidentially, to hear what his evidence is, then my argument will be immeasurably stronger. And if it is as persuasive as you seem to believe, then I can't imagine that the Tribunal would not grant him its protection.'

'Yes,' said the imam. 'I anticipated this would be your answer and we are prepared to take you to him, but you must submit to being blindfolded for the journey. I am sorry that this condition is necessary. It is not that we do not trust you. The precaution is for your own protection as much as his.'

'I understand,' said Anna. 'And agree.'

'Very well,' said the imam. 'Arrangements have been made. There is no more to say. This is a dangerous path that we have chosen. We hope that no more blood will be spilt, *inshallah*.'

With that, the imam rose to his feet and left the room. Most of the men followed him, but two remained, and after a brief consultation with them Genjac turned to Anna.

'There is a van waiting out back,' he said. 'Ena will go with you. I have more business with the imam, so I will wait here for you both to return.'

'Thank you, Adin,' she said.

'You handled that well, Anna,' he said. 'Now we must pray for the best.'

'You do that for me, will you?' she said.

•

Anna and Ena were put into the windowless cabin of a delivery van. One of the men wrapped dark cloths around each of their heads and sat with them in the back for the journey. Anna lost track of the time, but guessed they must have travelled for at least an hour before they reached their destination.

The van stopped; she heard the scrape and creak of heavy gates opening. She heard the driver climb back in and edge the vehicle forwards. He stopped again and she heard the gates close behind them. Only then did the silent man beside them remove the blindfolds. She climbed from the van and saw that they were in the interior courtyard of a walled Ottoman house.

The two guards left Anna and Ena in the courtyard and tramped up the wooden staircase to a room off the second-floor balcony. Anna looked back at the large wooden gate behind them: it could have withstood a besieging force, and perhaps it once had. There were tall arches around the interior of the courtyard. A group of women around a long table were making something, which they placed on steel trays and slid into a wood-fired oven.

'They are making *burek*,' said Ena. 'I hope perhaps for our lunch.'

Anna heard a noise and walked over to a straw-filled room under one of the arches. When her eyes adjusted, she saw that an old woman was rocking a baby in a painted wooden cradle. She rocked it in a fast motion, which produced an eerie creaking rhythm: *Cree-crak, cree-crak, cree-crak.* The old woman offered no greeting and stared implacably at Anna, her narrow face and mouth set in lines of disapproval. *Cree-crak, cree-crak.*

Eventually their two guards returned and took Anna and Ena upstairs to a dimly lit room set up like the one in the madrassa, with carpets on the floor and cushions around the edge. A middle-aged man wearing a cheap black suit was brought into the room by the guards. He sat on a cushion and Anna saw his fear-ravaged expression, his trembling hands. Ena said something to him, and he turned to Anna.

'I am Amir Ramic. I speak some good English.'

Anna carefully spelt out the deal she had made with the imam, Ena intervening from time to time to translate. Once she was sure Ramic had understood her, Anna said that she would need to take back to The Hague some evidence that he truly warranted being put into their witness-protection program. The man simply nodded and reached into the pocket of his coat. He produced a photograph and held it out to her with trembling fingers.

Anna rose and took the photograph. She carried it to a window to examine it in the light. The moment she realised what she was looking at, her own hand began to tremble.

Ena came close and they stared at it in silence. It was a full-length portrait of a man in camouflage uniform. Behind him were destroyed buildings. His face was fixed in a hideous grin and he was holding something up in his right hand. It was a severed head, unmistakably that of an Orthodox priest. The bearded face, its eyes screwed shut at the moment of death, was being raised in the air by a fistful of long black hair. The triumphant uniformed man, also unmistakably, was Jure Rebic.

31

SCHEVENINGEN PRISON HOSPITAL, THE HAGUE

24 DECEMBER 2005

MARIN PROPPED on his elbow to watch Rachel leave the ward, then collapsed back onto the pillow. She was his daughter. His daughter! The thought was overwhelming: the unheralded miracle of her existence, her hallucinatory presence, and now his breathlessness in her wake. When the pain flooded back, he hit the morphine button again and again, but he soon reached the self-dosing limit. He rang for a nurse and complained that his pain had become unbearable. She returned with a fentanyl lollipop, raspberry flavoured, and he sucked it like a child down to the stick.

Marin lay staring up at the demon's eye in the ceiling and, as the narcotic high came on him, he felt the flush rise from his neck to his scalp and render him weightless. The red light of the eye pulsed on and on and he was pinned down under its implacable gaze. As his eyelids fluttered and closed, he was imagining what Rachel would say to her mother, and then in this dream state his thoughts drifted naturally to his own mother, Samira.

•

Marin knocked on the door of his mother's old limestone house in Mostar. He had waited for the muezzin's call and watched her husband—a handsome, upright, elderly man—leave the house at midday for *salat al zuhr*.

The door opened and there was the woman he knew only from childhood memories and a single photograph. Samira had aged well, but her beautiful face was bemused.

'Hello, Mother,' he said. 'It's Marin.'

After a moment's hesitation, Samira pulled him inside, but before she could say anything he blurted out, 'I'm in bad trouble. I need your help.'

Marin was then twenty-one and a fugitive, on the run from Tito's security forces. Samira was silent, and one hand came up to cover her mouth as if she could not allow herself to utter a single word. Marin saw her wide, startled eyes and their familiar colour. He saw in them the moment of recognition, too, and the wash of calm that seemed to go through her body. Samira dropped her hand then and spoke to him for the first time:

'Come, I'll make tea and you can tell me what has happened.'

She took him to the kitchen and sat him down, staring at him from time to time as she performed the well-practised ritual of preparing mint tea.

'I knew you would come one day,' she said, pouring the sweet herbal infusion into his cup. 'I have much to tell you, Marin, but your story is more urgent.'

He explained in a rush that he had been sent to Bosnia by his father, one of twenty men, to start an insurgency against Yugoslavia's communist regime, an operation planned and financed in Australia. He and a companion had split off from the others and escaped a massive dragnet, but his friend had been killed by a farmer. He had no idea of the fate of the others, although he thought most of them must have been killed or captured.

He was sure that agents would be waiting for him at every border crossing.

'I will help you, of course,' said Samira. 'We will tell my husband, Ali, only that you came here looking for me. He is a good man. He will understand. Now, I'm sorry Marin, but I must tell you some things about your father. They will be hard for you to listen to and maybe hard for you to believe. Let me first ask: did you get any of my letters?'

'No,' said Marin. 'Not one.'

'I left a long letter for you and Petar when I ran away . . .'

'I never saw it.'

'This is what I feared,' said Samira, and Marin saw in her face what the years of guilt and shame had cost her. 'I can't imagine what you must think of me. For some time after I left, I wrote you both every week, and telephoned as often as I could. Your father became very angry with me when he picked up the phone. He said he would hurt me if I kept trying to contact you, but I didn't stop—until one day a man came to my house here in Mostar. He told me that Ivo had sent him. He forced his way inside. He had a gun. He warned me that if I continued to make trouble for Ivo by calling and writing to you boys then he would shoot me dead, but first he would kill Ali . . .'

Samira paused then, remembering something important.

'Marin, please wait here for a minute.'

While his mother was gone, he sat still in the old kitchen in which every object—the waxed wooden benches; the patterned tiles; the beaten copper pots and pans; the fine plates on the wall; the jars of spices and coffee and tea—seemed effortlessly placed to set one at ease . . . And yet his emotions were roiling as the missing pieces in his life began to fall into place. Samira soon returned with a large, beautifully carved wooden box. She put it down on the floor in front of him and knelt beside it.

'After that man came, I did not try to call you on the telephone, but I still wrote letters to you both. Since I was sure that Ivo was destroying them, I kept copies. They're here in this box.'

Samira took his hand, then, and looked up at his face, still on her knees as if begging his forgiveness.

'You can read them if you want. I have kept them all these years, hoping that one day you would come to find me.'

•

Over the next few days, when they were alone, Samira told Marin the story of her violent marriage to Ivo Katich. She had been just a teenager when she met Ivo, one of many thousands of refugees in the Bagnoli Displaced Persons camp on the outskirts of Naples. It was 1947 and her own father had been forced to flee from Tito's communists with his family, accused of collaboration with the wartime Ustasha regime and complicity in its crimes. There were many such men in the camp: collaborators, Ustashi officials, fighters, and they lived under the constant fear of deportation to face summary justice in Yugoslavia. The Allies ranked them black, grey or white, depending on the severity of the allegations made against them. Those designated 'black' were accused of war crimes.

Among that group were Samira's father and the young Ivo Katich. Unlike her father, Ivo seemed sublimely sure he would not be sent back. He was a top dog in the camp: handsome, self-assured and dapper in his fine Italian clothes, and when he turned his full attention on the young Samira he was a charming, thoughtful and apparently kind suitor. Months into their courtship, Samira discovered the source of his confidence. Ivo Katich had a protector, a man he referred to as 'my angel'. In human form, this angel was an American intelligence officer, Colonel Lewis Perry. It was Perry's job to recruit Nazis deemed capable of building anti-communist networks behind the Iron Curtain. Samira would learn that her itinerant boyfriend had multiple aliases and travelled freely under forged papers between Naples, Rome and Trieste. Only after they were married and he moved her to an apartment in Rome did she come to understand that Ivo was building for his angel a guerilla force of former Ustashi known as *Križari*—the Crusaders—and that he was undertaking missions to coordinate with *Križari* networks inside Yugoslavia.

Due to his clandestine work, Samira saw little of Ivo in the first years of their marriage. From time to time, she got word that he had been arrested by one of those branches of the Allied occupying force who still believed their job was to bring Nazi war criminals to justice. On each occasion, the angel Perry intervened to have him freed. By 1950, Belgrade had put a bounty on Ivo's head. He could no longer travel into Yugoslavia and UDBA assassins were after him in Italy. But his angel saved him again: the American spymaster saw to it that Ivo Katich's war crimes were 'cleansed' from his record and organised for Ivo and Samira to emigrate to Australia.

In the new country, Ivo Katich immediately set about building his own network of crusaders, a secretive organisation known as the Croatian Brotherhood. Samira bore him two sons and soon understood that, as far as her husband was concerned, her own mission in life was complete. They would never be *her* sons, only his. Ivo became totally dismissive of her and progressively more violent, worse when he drank—and he drank more and more. There were too many incidents for Samira to recount, but she told Marin one story that he would never forget.

One summer's night Ivo had been sitting in the backyard, engaged in a long drinking session with his mate Branko Kraljevic. The two men, old comrades in the wartime Ustasha and disciples of the great Poglavnik, were telling each other stories as they downed glass after glass of Ivo's hypnotically potent *rakija*. They were laughing uproariously in a way that Samira found sickening. At one point, she crept outside and stood concealed behind the edge of the house to listen. It was only by such subterfuge that Samira had learned many of her husband's secrets. In this way, she heard the two men recalling atrocities they had witnessed or perpetrated, as fondly as old friends might tell tales about a football final they had both played in as young men. They joked about the last moments of men, women and children, and the methods of their killing. Samira refused to describe the details except to say that, as with the slaughter of spring lambs, they favoured the knife.

When Branko finally stumbled off into the night, Ivo came to their bedroom, filling it with his huge and brutal presence. Her husband stank of his homemade *rakija*, the rancid, sweet sickness leaking from his pores. Samira knew she should stay quiet, pretend to be asleep, but she could not hold inside her what she had heard. She switched on the bedside lamp and saw her husband blink like a wild animal in a spotlight as she confronted him with his own drunken confessions of crimes beyond imagining.

Samira told her son that she wondered if, at some deep level, she had wanted to be punished for her own complicity in marrying a monster, but still she could not have imagined the consequences. Hearing this, Marin had instinctively known what was coming and he wanted to cry out: 'For God's sake, don't blame yourself! He is to blame. Only him.'

Ivo beat her savagely and as she lay there, battered and bleeding, he 'had his way with her'. Had his father been close by at that moment, Marin had felt he would have been capable of beating him to death.

Samira escaped the house the next day and borrowed money from friends who helped her evade Ivo's searchers and leave the country. She went back to Mostar, the city of her birth, and a place where many of her extended family still lived, and they embraced her and took her in as a prodigal daughter. In time, she met Ali, a gentle man who treated her with deference and great kindness. Ali was older than her, a widower, and he brought her to live in his elegant house with its Ottoman arches and ancient rugs, and the courtyard where she and Marin now sat with its flowering lemon tree and murmuring fountain, and this house became her sanctuary and place to heal.

When she finished her story, Marin came and took her in his arms for the first time.

'Mother,' he said, and she wept on his shoulder long and hard.

•

It was pain that woke Marin from the dream of his mother. His eyes opened to darkness. The red light in the ceiling winked compulsively, and he imagined he could still feel the weight of Samira's head on his shoulder. Despite the fluids still being pumped into his arm, his mouth was parched, and he took a long draught of water. The pain spread from the side of his chest up into his left arm and shoulder, thumping pain worse than the stabbing blows that had nearly taken his life. He hit the morphine button again and again until the regulator stopped him overdosing.

As he lay there waiting for the pain to subside, he remembered clambering, dusty and sweating with other rescuers, through the ruins of that once-gracious Ottoman house and digging out from the rubble the battered bodies of his mother and her gentle husband. He remembered the unbridled rage that overcame him as he led his men that night up the steep mountainside to attack the Serbian artillery position which had rained death onto the old town. He remembered the scattered bodies on the hillside of those Serbs who had tried to defend themselves and he remembered the faces of the men who had been dragged from their tents, still drunk on the *raki* they used to numb themselves. These were lined up, shaking in their boots, on the cliff edge. He remembered only one of them, a blue-eyed, redhead, a Montenegrin conscript, a boy from the Black Mountain.

Marin had paused in front of him, smoke drifting from the barrel of his gun, and asked him: 'Do you have anything to say?'

'Fuck you all,' said the boy.

32

LJUBLJANA, SLOVENIA

24 DECEMBER 2005

IT WAS DARK when they landed at Ljubljana Airport. This being the night before Christmas, there were so few travellers that the terminal was near empty. When Pierre went to get the keys for the hire car, Rachel realised it was already morning in Sydney. She slumped into a wave-shaped plastic chair and sent a text to Leah.

Happy Christmas x

Rachel imagined Leah, pious once more, in her parents' house. Rachel had only ever seen it from the outside. The house climbed up a steep hill to a veranda staring out over the harbour and the humpbacked bridge; a house within the eruv, marked out by walls, poles and wires; a house with no Christmas tree; a house in which no one talked about Rachel but everyone thought about her.

They drove through light snow beside the Ljubljanica. The city's black river was lined with Viennese-style buildings, many with green copper spires, and it was spanned at intervals by art nouveau bridges. One bridge was protected at either end by pairs of floodlit dragons—snarling, splay-winged, snake-tongued and ready, Rachel thought, to leap into the car and devour them both. She wondered if the few night walkers, wrapped in their long coats, would even be surprised to see people eaten alive by mythical reptiles in this town from a Grimm's fairytale.

The headlights picked up drifting snowflakes and she watched Pierre concentrate on staying in the black tracks through the slush made by the cars ahead of them. She was grateful that he'd insisted on coming with her, but it was strange to think of the journeys he'd shared with her mother in years gone by. Some thought she herself looked a lot like the young Anna and she wondered if it was equally strange for him. Pierre seemed to anticipate her thoughts.

'Anna hates being stuck in the passenger seat,' he said.

'Mum likes to be in control,' said Rachel, adding as an after-thought: 'In a nice way.'

Pierre laughed. 'Not always nice,' he said.

They found the hotel, a homely old place Pierre knew of, on an unfashionable stretch of the river. He parked the car under shelter, front out and ready for an early start, snow or no snow. The hotel had a little restaurant with an open fire and chequered tablecloths, and there were coloured lights around the frosted windows, whose handmade glass panes distorted the world outside. Pierre said he was hungry and ordered schnitzel and beer; Rachel made do with a chocolate *palacinke*.

'How do we get this priest to talk to us?' asked Rachel, picking listlessly at her pancake. 'What do we say to him?'

Pierre put down his knife and fork and took a sip of his beer, considering the question. 'What did you do in the war, Father?' he said at last with a smile, which Rachel returned only fleetingly.

'Seriously, Pierre, I'm not a journalist. We can't just pull him aside and say we think your life is in danger.'

'No,' said Pierre. 'We can't do that. We could say that an old friend of his asked us to come.'

'An old friend you used to know as Illija Lovric?'

'Yep,' said Pierre, resuming his meal. 'Or *Cvrčak*.'

'I need a drink,' said Rachel, signalling to the waiter. Pierre suggested they both try Slovenian *sadjevec*, a grape brandy with herbs.

Rachel threw hers back and, as she felt its warmth spread through her body, she ordered another one.

'This nightmare has really fucked up my life, Pierre,' she said. 'My girlfriend left me when I told her what was going on.'

Pierre removed his spectacles, and without the intervention of their thick lenses his eyes seemed sad.

'My first chance to act like a real godfather and I've got nothing,' he said. 'Look Rachel, I'm the last person in the world to give relationship advice. Except for this: if she was ever worth your love, she will understand that none of this has anything to do with you or who you are, and she'll come back.'

'She's a practising Orthodox Jew. She's gone back to her family.'

'Well,' said Pierre. 'She can't have been practising very hard if she was living with you. Have you thought of hiring one of those teams that extract people from cults?'

Rachel laughed in spite of herself. 'That's your godfatherly advice?'

'I warned you not to expect too much,' said Pierre. 'I'm sure I could get you a number.'

Pierre asked the waiter for another drink and told him to leave the bottle on the table. They sat for a while in silence, sipping at the brandy and enjoying the soporific warmth from the fire, until Rachel asked a question that had been on her mind: 'Why have you and Anna never got together?'

Pierre looked at her and she knew at that moment that she had found the source of his sadness—and that she must truly remind him of Anna.

'It's all about the iron-clad rules of attraction,' he said. 'If it all flows in one direction, you can never break them, no matter how much you might want to.'

Pierre downed his brandy and immediately topped up his glass.

'There's really nothing more to say,' he muttered.

Rachel saw that he meant it. She had touched on something deep and insoluble and Pierre clearly didn't want to elaborate.

They went up to their rooms soon afterwards, arranging to meet in the foyer at 5.30 am. Pierre said that, if the weather wasn't too bad, the drive to Motovun should take less than two hours.

•

The next morning the snow was no longer falling and, when Rachel stepped outside into the cold, she saw the sky was full of stars and the whimsical city wore a fine coat of virginal white. Leah had not replied overnight to her text message and the words *Happy Christmas* sat on the glowing screen of Rachel's phone like a rebuke.

Pierre was a few minutes late, but soon he came down the stairs tunelessly humming 'White Christmas'. His battered overnight bag was in one hand and in the other a wrapped present, which he held out to Rachel.

'Who says that old Trotskyite godfathers don't know how to celebrate Christmas?' he said.

Rachel took his gift and held it for a moment. 'Oh, Pierre,' she cried. 'I don't have anything for you.'

'You didn't have time,' he said. 'Go on, let's see what's inside.'

She unwrapped it and found a plain green, cloth-covered book: *Black Lamb & Grey Falcon*, Vol. 1, Rebecca West.

'When I lived in Zagreb I used to take this with me everywhere I travelled,' he said. 'Open it up!'

On an inside page she found Rebecca West's dedication:

To
MY FRIENDS IN YUGOSLAVIA
WHO ARE NOW ALL DEAD OR ENSLAVED

Beneath those words was a quote in Cyrillic and its translation: *Grant them the Fatherland of their desire and make them again citizens of Paradise.*

Pierre took the book from her hand, pulled out a fountain pen, wrote his own inscription and handed it back to her.

Rachel read: *To my Goddaughter, who I should have loved as if she were my own. Pierre Villiers, Christmas Day, 2005.*

Rachel tried and failed to blink away her tears, and hugged him instead. 'Thank you,' she whispered into his ear.

'We have to go,' he said.

•

Slovenia's wide southern motorway was clear of snow and virtually empty of traffic. It was still dark when they reached the border, where bleary looking guards waved them straight through into Croatia.

'That's a real bonus,' said Pierre. 'They've probably been drinking since midnight.'

They ran due south for an hour, shifting from freeway to highway to country road. As the sun began to rise, they saw ahead of them a pimple of a hill pushing up from a forested river valley. It was a cold day and the rising sun lit a triangular bank of clouds, which enveloped the hilltop like a multicoloured crown—yellow, red and purple. The stone fortifications reflected these colours and the terracotta-tiled roofs of the town glowed orange.

'It's like Tuscany,' said Rachel. 'I wasn't expecting that.'

'There's a reason for that,' said Pierre. 'The Venetians built most of it.'

'I thought they'd have stuck to the coast,' said Rachel.

'No, this is almost the dead centre of Istria. And this was a colonial stronghold protecting Venetian trade routes from the fourteenth to the seventeenth centuries.'

'Driver *and* tour guide.'

'I've been here a few times,' he said. 'The forest is full of truffles. They grow Teran and Malvazija grapes on the hillsides. It's been protected for as long as anyone can remember, but now—and this tells you something about modern Croatia—some fuckwitted billionaire developer is trying to build a massive resort and two golf courses right in the middle of it.'

They arrived at a mostly empty parking area at the base of the hill.

'Can't drive any further,' said Pierre. 'There's usually a bus to the top, but it won't be running today. We'll have to hike up.'

Rachel climbed from the car and slung her shoulder bag over her back, looking up at the steep climb. Part way up, she stripped off her coat and carried it over an arm.

'Thank God I kept up the yoga,' she said.

'Yoga, is it?' said Pierre, pausing to take a breath. 'Whatever happened to dropping acid and dancing all night, like a normal youngster? That's how we kept fit.'

Rachel picked up her pace, watching him struggle to stay beside her. 'I can smell an old fart from here,' she said. 'It's ecstasy these days, Pierre, and no one's called me a youngster for ten years.'

'It's all . . .' Pierre stopped again, clutching his side. 'Bit of a stitch, is all.'

'You okay?'

'. . . I was saying, age . . . it's all relative.' Pierre straightened up. 'One last push to the top.'

The church bells were ringing for the morning mass as they climbed a cobblestone laneway, passing the closed doors of stone houses and shops until they arrived at a level area with a chest-high stone wall, part of the outer fortifications. They paused to look down over the valley and the roofs of the lower buildings.

Only then did Rachel realise how far they'd climbed. The weak winter sun was still low and the light breeze chilled her again. As she pulled her jacket back on, the church bells stopped.

'The mass is starting,' said Pierre. 'It's up through here.'

They climbed a steeply canted cobblestone path up through a high arched tunnel built into the fortified walls of the keep. Inside was a wide, flat courtyard. To the right was the Hotel Kastel, its tables set out under eight old chestnut trees; to the left was the bright yellow Palladian structure of St Stephen's Church huddled next to a clock tower built from pale stone.

They went through the church's tall wooden doors. No more than two dozen parishioners were seated in the central rows of pews. Rachel peered into the stark white interior of the basilica and saw they were all old women dressed head to toe in black; they reminded her of a flock of crows. The church was of simple design with white columned arches on either side separating the nave from smaller altars to the left and right. Ahead of them, up four steps, was the main altar under a high dome. The priest was there, his back to the patient crows, producing puffs of smoke as he waved a brass incense burner over the altar, on which four tall candles were burning.

Only when he moved around to the back of the altar, waving the thurible all the while, did Rachel see him clearly. Father Ante Lovren's bare head was bald and shining under the low-hanging chandelier and his steel-rimmed glasses picked up reflections from the lights and candles. She read nothing in his impassive expression. He wore immaculate white vestments, with a crimson strip running from below his chin to where she assumed his knees would be; a large gold cross was embroidered at the top of the strip, and below it was a succession of golden emblems she did not recognise.

As he spoke to the crows, Pierre whispered a rough translation into her ear: '*Let us all confess our sins to the Almighty and admit to our brothers and sisters that we have gravely sinned in our thoughts and in our deeds. The blessed Mary ever-virgin and all the angels will pray for us. Lord have mercy. Lord have mercy . . .*

'The old woman are repeating that and on and on. Blah blah . . . The reading is from Isaiah. It's about living in the land of darkness but the people who walk in deep darkness have seen a great light . . . You can guess the rest . . .

'. . . Okay, his sermon is about baby Jesus in the manger, the shepherds are afraid because of the star that's moved above their heads, like some kind of UFO. No, he didn't say that . . . An angel comes down and tells them not to be afraid . . . This baby has been sent to bring us out of the darkness into the light . . . What could be less fearful, more lovable than a baby . . . I'm sure you know this story . . .

'Okay, he's blessing the wine and the wafers,' Pierre continued. 'This is the big moment, he's just transubstantiated them . . . Now he's cannibalising himself . . . drinking the blood, eating the flesh of Christ . . . Now, everyone else can go up and eat Jesus' flesh. Are you tempted? We haven't had breakfast. Well, you can thank the Almighty for one thing, it's almost over.'

When the last of the crows had left, Pierre approached Lovren. '*Oprosti otac,*' he said. '*Goverite li engleski?*'

'Yes,' said the priest. 'I speak English.'

Pierre turned and introduced Rachel. 'Father, this is Rachel. She is the daughter of an old friend of yours.'

'Oh,' said the priest, slightly alarmed. 'Who is that?'

'You knew him as Illija Lovric,' said Pierre. 'And by his *nom de guerre, Cvrčak.*'

Now Father Lovren looked genuinely alarmed. He glanced around to see if anyone was in earshot. 'Come with me,' he said.

Lovren took them behind the altar to the sacristy, where he shrugged out of his vestments and hung them carefully in an ornately carved cupboard. Stripped down to a plain shirt and trousers, he pulled a thick woollen jumper over his head and turned to Rachel.

'Well, Rachel,' he said, 'I have heard nothing from your father for more than ten years. I know from the news reports that his real name is Marin Katich, that was a surprise to me, and that he is in The Hague and they want to put him on trial. Again, this was a surprise—more than a surprise. Now I read that he has been attacked. How is he?'

'He's alive,' said Rachel. 'He survived. He says the attack was ordered by a man that both of you know. Jure Rebic.'

Ante Lovren drew a deep breath, looked at his watch and seemed to come to a decision.

'I have three hours before the next mass,' he said. 'My home is not far from here. I could offer you both some coffee and a modest breakfast. Would you join me?'

They followed Lovren to the end of the square and down a flight of stairs to the lower level of the ramparts. The priory was a short distance down a nearby narrow, cobbled lane.

Lovren produced a large key, unlocked an ancient-looking wooden door and ushered them into a comfortable, heated living room lined on two sides with books. He led them though the room to a small, warm kitchen and suggested they sit on wooden chairs at the table under an arched window. He busied himself making coffee.

'If Illija . . . I'm sorry, I should call him by his real name, *Marin*. If Marin has sent you to find me, he must be in need of help. He was not a man to expose his friends or to reveal their secrets.'

'Father, he sent me here because he thinks *you* might be in danger,' said Rachel. 'He sent me not to expose you, but to warn you.'

'I see,' said Lovren. 'That is something different.'

Rachel nodded. 'But I've also come for my own reasons,' she said. 'I've only just learned that Marin Katich is my father and I am trying to find out who he really is. I'm hoping you can help me understand that.'

Lovren screwed the lid onto the coffee maker, placed it on the stove and lit the burner beneath it.

'Perhaps I can help you understand him,' he said. 'As a personal matter. I don't want to be forced to give evidence at a trial. That would be like signing my own death warrant.'

'Just for me, then.'

'I will have to ask your friend to go and sit in the living room.'

Pierre agreed and left them alone.

'What is it you want to know?' asked Lovren.

'Is my father a war criminal?' said Rachel.

'No,' said Lovren. 'You father was, when I knew him, a hard man. You would not like him for an enemy. But he was a highly principled man, a moral man.'

'He told me you were with him when he executed a man who had raped and killed a young girl.'

'That is true,' said Lovren. 'The man he killed was a psychopath. He had raped many women and murdered many men. On that day, he ordered his men to massacre everyone in that village, and they did it. Your father was going to put all those men on trial. They are the war criminals, as are the men who gave them their orders. The worst of the worst was the man in command of them, Jure Rebic . . .'

At that moment the kitchen door crashed open. Two men pushed into the small kitchen; they carried handguns with silencers attached.

'Oh dear,' said the tallest of them, speaking in English. He was a silver-haired man with fearful, bulging eyes. 'Oh dear, oh dear. *Father* Lovren. You terrible sinner.'

The man called in Croatian to someone outside the door and a third man dragged Pierre into the kitchen, holding a gun to his head as he forced him to sit in the chair next to Rachel.

'So, let me introduce myself,' said the man with the protruding eyes. 'Father Lovren here knows very well who I am. That is why he's pissing his pants.'

Rachel looked at Lovren, standing quite still with a gun trained on his chest. The expression on his face did not suggest fear, but rather resignation. His eyes were closed, he had rosary beads in his hands and he appeared to be praying. Pierre straightened his glasses and Rachel saw that his hands were shaking as he did so.

'I think this man also knows who I am,' said the man with the protruding eyes, waving the silenced barrel of his weapon at Pierre. 'He was with the woman journalist, the Australian, who came to Ljubuski looking for General Cvrčak, as she called him. But I think we know now that she knew his real name was Katich. I was just myself, humble Jure Rebic, as I have always been. So.' He turned to Rachel. 'I heard you claim to be Marin Katich's daughter—is that really true? He told me many times that he had no children.'

Rachel said nothing.

'Well?' said Rebic. 'I'm waiting.'

When Rachel remained silent Rebic, in one fast movement, raised his arm and fired his weapon. A black hole appeared in the priest's forehead. The white wall behind him was spattered with blood and gore. Lovren slumped back against it and a trail of blood, like a haphazard swipe of paint, followed him down to the floor.

'Talk,' said Rebic. 'Or your friend will be next.'

Rachel's whole body seemed to have seized up. She tried to speak and nothing came out. She was aware of a terrible screaming sound and she thought it might be coming unbidden from her until she realised it was the coffee pot venting steam. Rebic turned the burner off and the wailing subsided. He poured a glass of water and gave it to Rachel.

'Drink,' he said. 'Then talk.'

Rachel gulped down some water.

'I am Marin Katich's daughter,' she said in a quavering voice. 'I was born in 1973. My mother kept it secret. Until yesterday, he didn't know of my existence. I only found out he was my father a few days ago.'

'I can see now that you have his eyes,' said Rebic. 'Truly, it would have been better for you if he had died the first time I killed him, or even the second. This Katich has many lives, but the people around him have only one. Now, listen to me, Rachel: I have learned that your mother is trying to find evidence to set him free. She is speaking to people she should not be. She has to stop that, Rachel. I'm going to take you with me to make sure that she does.' He reached a hand out to her. 'Give me your phone.'

Rachel fished the device from her pocket and Rebic threw it to one of his men with rapid-fire instructions she didn't understand. She saw the man scoop up her shoulder bag, put the phone in it and sling it over his shoulder.

Rachel reached across and took Pierre's hand. She was shivering as if someone had thrown open a door and an icy wind had come rushing in. Her whole body was shaking and, when her teeth began chattering, Pierre squeezed her hand firmly. That contact seemed to be the only source of warmth in the room; he was keeping her from tumbling into the abyss. She looked at him and he smiled gently.

'I'm here,' he said. 'You'll be okay.'

Rachel looked up at Rebic. 'What are you going to do with us?' she asked.

'Not *us*, Rachel,' said Rebic. 'Just you.'

She turned her stricken face back to Pierre, but there was no time. She heard the terrible muffled shot and the right lens of his spectacles was obliterated in a moment of shattering glass and blood. His hand gripped hers reflexively.

Rachel reached out to hold him, and fell with his body to the bloody floor. She clung onto him, screaming now, and resisted all attempts to drag her off him, until someone smashed the back of her head and she fell into the deep darkness.

•

It was dark and silent in Pierre's apartment when Anna let herself in late on Boxing Day. She found a note from Pierre on the refrigerator, telling her he expected to be back sometime that day. So where was he? She poured herself a glass of wine and went into the living room. Pierre had prepared kindling in the fireplace, and she lit it and sat down.

She opened her phone and scrolled through her messages. There was nothing from Rachel. She tried ringing; it went to message, where she heard her daughter's voice, coolly professional. She sent a text to Pierre: *I'm back at your place, where are you?*

She found some leftovers in the fridge, and brought a plate of food and the wine bottle into the living room. She pulled out her laptop and transferred onto it the interview she had recorded with the Bosnian, Amir Ramic. She had already made copies of her notes, and the documents and photographs that Ramic had given her; all these she had left in the care of Adin Genjac.

She would call van Brug in the morning and ask the lawyer to set up an urgent meeting with the Registrar. She had begun compiling a file of evidence on her journey back to The Hague and she was convinced Singarasa would have no choice but to free Marin Katich.

She was reviewing her next steps when the phone rang. The screen said *Rachel* and she snatched up the Blackberry, pressed the green phone icon and began speaking immediately.

'Rachel, at last, thank God, I've been worried sick . . .'

'And all the best for the holiday season to you, Anna . . .'

A man's voice! Heavily accented, American-inflected English.

'Who is this?' she shouted. 'What are you doing with my daughter's phone?'

'She is here with me,' said the man. 'I'll put her on . . .'

'*Mum! Don't . . .*'

'Rachel! Where are you?'

'She is safe.' It was the man again. 'Now listen carefully, Anna . . .'

'Who are you?'

'I think you know that already, Anna,' he said. 'We met when you came to Ljubuski. That was a long time ago, wasn't it?'

She knew, of course, and was filled with dread, awful in its intensity. A shiver ran through her body. She clamped her jaw shut to stop her teeth chattering.

'Did you hear me?'

She forced her mouth to work. 'Rebic?'

'You do remember.'

'Yes.'

'So you know what this means. If you want to see Rachel again, you must stop everything you've been doing. You will do nothing to help defend Marin Katich or Rachel will die. Marin Katich will say nothing. He can go to trial, plead guilty and accept his punishment. Or he can simply take his own life. That would be the best option to save his daughter. You will tell him this from me. He will understand that I mean it. If you contact the police, Rachel will die. Think about it. Gather together whatever evidence you have, the names of all witness you have spoken to, and wait. I call back soon.'

Rebic hung up. Anna called back immediately and Rachel's phone went to message. She sprang to her feet and began pacing the room. It was incomprehensible, crazy, but there was no doubting it was Rachel's phone. It had been her voice. Where was she? How had this happened? And where was Pierre? There were too many questions and no answers.

She tried Rachel's landline in Sydney, hoping Leah would be there. Again it went to the answering machine. She left a message asking Leah to contact her. She didn't have a mobile number for her daughter's girlfriend. What the hell was her surname? If she knew that she might be able to track down her family. Why the hell hadn't she paid more attention to Rachel's life?

She wracked her brains, going back over the strained conversation at the disastrous dinner party. She remembered Leah talking about her work at an art gallery in Paddington—that's right!

Anna ran upstairs and opened Pierre's computer. His account was locked, so she entered as a visitor with the password he had set up. She ran through the list of galleries in Paddington and found one that rang a bell: *Becker Contemporary Art.*

It was morning in Sydney, business hours, when she rang the number.

'Becker Gallery,' said a male voice.

'I'm trying to contact Leah.'

'Can I say who's calling?'

'Tell her it's about Rachel.'

A pause and then Leah's voice was on the line. 'Hello, who is it?'

'It's Anna Rosen, Leah,' she said. 'I'm sorry to call you at work, but it's urgent. Do you know where Rachel is?'

There was another long pause. Then: 'I thought she was with you.'

'Why would you think that?'

'Anna, I'm sorry, I don't want to talk about this.'

'Leah, it's very important. Something may have happened to Rachel. I'm trying to find her. Why would you think she was with me?'

'She told me about her father, Anna.'

'What did she tell you?'

'Everything,' said Leah. 'About his past. Who he is . . . I couldn't take it in, Anna. I needed a break. I left to stay with my parents. I went back to the apartment two days ago to pick up some things and she was gone. She had packed her bag, taken her passport. I thought she must have gone to see you.'

'Have you heard anything from her at all?'

'A Christmas message,' said Leah. 'Nothing else.'

'Leah, can you get into Rachel's computer? Do you know her password?'

'Yes.'

'Will you go to the apartment and check her computer for any emails, or anything that might tell us where she went?'

'I have clients here now,' she said. 'I can go at lunchtime.'

'Leah, I'm trying not to upset you, but Rachel has stumbled into something very bad. She's in terrible danger. I need your help.'

'What danger?' Leah demanded. 'What are you talking about?'

'If you have any love for Rachel, you will go now, straightaway. You have to trust me. We need some clue as to where she went.'

'I'll go now,' said Leah. 'But I want to know what's going on.'

Anna asked for Leah's mobile number and insisted that she write hers down, before hanging up. She thought carefully about her next step and decided that there was only one person capable of helping her—but could they be trusted? She decided she had no choice and, despite the late hour, she called Jasna Perak. They spoke for a long time.

•

At 2 am, Anna's phone rang. It was Leah.

'I got into Rachel's computer,' she said. 'There was an email booking flights to The Hague.'

Anna got Leah to read out the itinerary and was shocked to find Rachel had arrived in Amsterdam at 6 am on 24 December, over forty-eight hours ago.

'There's another email,' said Leah. 'To someone called Pierre Villiers saying that she's coming and when.'

'Oh!' cried Anna. Pierre! It felt like a physical blow.

'Are you okay?' asked Leah.

'Yes. Please go on, Leah, what else?'

'Rachel tells him that she has learned the truth about her father and says, "I assume you must have known." Then he replies that he has only recently discovered the news. He says that Rachel should come and stay in his apartment with you. Is that where she is? Where are you?'

'Is there anything else?' Anna asked urgently.

'Yes, this Pierre says: "You need to talk this through with your mother" and Rachel replies that she doesn't want to do that yet and begs him not to tell you that she's coming. He replies that he agrees reluctantly to do that and that he will meet her at the railway station in The Hague. That's all there is.'

'Thank you.'

'Now, what's going on?'

'I have to go,' said Anna. 'I'll call you as soon as I know.'

Anna hung up and sat there, numb. She rang Pierre's number, and again it went to voicemail.

LAST RITES

LAST RITES

33

SCHEVENINGEN PRISON, THE HAGUE

29 DECEMBER 2005

HELPED UP THE STAIRS by the ever-reliable Zwolsman, Marin Katich returned in the early morning to his cell in the detention centre. He had been deemed fit for release thanks to the wizardry of the Dutch surgeon. When the fellow came to see Marin in hospital, he explained that he had worked on many stab wounds to the heart during his time with Médecins Sans Frontières in Rwanda.

'Compared to what I saw there, yours was not so dramatic,' said the surgeon. 'And here we have echocardiogram and ultrasound, so I could be even more precise.'

'They like to keep their war criminals fit for trial,' said Marin.

'Accused *ja*, not convicted?'

'You're a good man, doctor,' said Marin. 'I didn't mean to sound ungrateful.'

'You'll be back on your feet soon.'

The surgeon was right. Marin had been up and walking around the ward for the past three days, as gingerly as an old man, but walking. And yet they still would have stopped him returning to his cell had it not been for the fact that his attempted assassin had been caught. He was a Croatian, as Marin had expected. His name

427

was Zoran Stolar and Marin smiled when he recalled that Stolar translates as 'carpenter'—it turned out the man had stabbed him with some kind of modified chisel.

More surprising was that, when they moved him into solitary, Stolar had swallowed a vial of cyanide he'd managed to smuggle in. He had ended up on the same hospital floor as Marin, although his attempt on his own life proved more successful. Marin wondered what hold Jure Rebic had over the man for Stolar to conclude he was better off dead. He assumed that the lives of family members must have been at stake.

It had been two days since Marin had last seen Anna Rosen. She had talked her way into the hospital to see him on the 27th, but she seemed so full of suppressed anger that he barely recognised her as the same person who had come to see him only days before that. She had certainly been agitated at their first meeting; but he believed there had still been a faint connection, like the sparking of exposed wires.

Worse than the anger had been her absolute refusal to discuss Rachel. Marin had tried to tell her that he understood why she had kept his existence a secret from their daughter. Yes, when he thought back on it, he had said 'their' daughter and perhaps that's what had upset her.

'I don't have time to discuss that now,' she said. 'I'm here to find out exactly what you told her.'

At Anna's urging, he repeated the long story he had told Rachel. He was conscious that, like an oft-repeated witness statement, it lost some of its impact in its retelling. Nevertheless, he recounted the details forensically: the massacre in the village; the rape and murder of the girl; his execution of the girl's killer in the village square; the insane behaviour of Rebic and his ultimate mutiny. Then he told Anna about his connection to Ante Lovren: how he had found him working as the parish priest at St Stephens church in Motovun; how the man had been his bodyguard on that terrible day; and how he had asked Rachel to pass Lovren's name on to her mother because he feared the priest's life could be in danger.

Anna listened intently to the story, then jumped to her feet.

'I have to go,' she said. 'I will be back to see you as soon as possible.'

In the two days since then, however, there had been no word from Anna, Rachel or the lawyer van Brug. Marin had gone from the absurd high of discovering that he had a child—an experience he likened to pressing the morphine button over and over again, with no regulator to stop him—to a strange kind of limbo. He told himself there was no reason for his disquiet, no reason for impatience, having waited so long. Indeed, there was a lightness to his mood such as he had not experienced since the day Moriarty had come to steal his life. Even the mocking ghosts had gone quiet.

Marin was dozing on his bunk in the afternoon when Zwolsman poked his head into the cell and woke him up. The guard, like a humble footman, was carrying a note from Slobodan Milosevic.

Marin read the simple message: *Chess 7 pm, after dinner?* He picked up a pen from his desk and scrawled beneath it: *Yes, if you don't mind being beaten again.*

He folded the note and handed it to Zwolsman. 'Can you take this to him?'

Zwolsman nodded and waddled back out of the room. His uniform seemed to be getting tighter, and Marin wondered if Milosevic was paying him in chocolate biscuits.

His floormates had left Marin alone since his return from hospital and he had assumed Milosevic would do the same—at best, avoid him; at worst, target him. Marin was sure the 'boss' would not have taken kindly to his subterfuge. He had been Tomislav Maric since he got here and now he was Marin Katich, with all that might imply to a student of history like Milosevic. And yet here was what appeared to be an olive branch.

At six o'clock, the cells were locked down and dinner was brought to each inmate on a plastic tray. From seven, they were reopened and the men on their individual floors were permitted to socialise in the common room until nine o'clock. So it was that when Marin passed through that room's wide doorway en route to Milosevic he saw the Gypsy and the Albanian engaged in a fierce table football contest, twirling knobs like mad things. They stopped when they saw him.

'Hey, Katich,' called Ademi. 'How does it feel, being skewered by one of your own?'

'I don't know, Ademi,' said Katich. 'How long would you survive on the streets of Pristina before some Kosovar hero put a bullet in your head?'

Hasimovic let go of the knobs that controlled his tiny footballers and came up close to Marin.

'Off to see The Boss?' he asked, then lowered his voice to a whisper. 'There'll be no protection for you here once he drops you.'

Marin knew he was in no fit state to tussle with these evil little weasels, but he couldn't stop himself. 'Stop puffing yourself up, Hasimovic,' he said. 'Maybe if you learned to play chess, rather than that stupid children's game, he'd have some respect for you.'

Marin straightened his shoulders against the pain in his chest and walked stiffly down the corridor to Milosevic's cell, from which he could hear the strains of a pop song. He pushed the door open wider and there was the old dictator slumped on his bunk, a glass of whisky on his belly, singing along to Celine Dion: 'Bewdy-fall, Bewdy-fall, Bewdy-fall, Bewdy-fall-boyeee . . .'

'I prefer the John Lennon version!' Marin said from the doorway.

Milosevic sat up from his repose, moist-eyed. He gulped down his whisky and pressed Stop on the CD player.

'Makes me remember Marko, when he's baby.'

'Cute,' said Marin, 'at least until he started running brothels and abortion clinics.'

The Serb's chin jutted belligerently, and Marin wondered how much of the whisky he'd already polished off.

'He's businessman,' said Milosevic.

'They call that horizontal integration, don't they?'

'What bullshit you're talking?'

'Brothels and . . .' Marin began, 'Oh, forget it. The important thing is that every day, in every way, he's getting better and better, right?'

'You don't look any better. You look sicker than me . . . Ha! I nearly said "Maric" and now you're Katich,' said Milosevic. 'First I'm in hospital, then you're in hospital. Did I miss much excitement?'

'Not much,' said Katich. 'Apart from the name change and the stabbing.'

Milosevic pushed a little bedside table between them. A chess board was already set up. Marin went to sit, but the old Serb gestured to him with the back of his hand, as if to a servant.

'Shut door, we need quiet.'

When he returned, Milosevic made another derisive hand movement. 'Better sit, Katich, before you collapse like overloaded donkey.'

As he gently eased himself into his seat, Marin saw that Milosevic had taken white without asking and already made his first move. He had pushed up his queen's pawn two spaces, so Marin met it with his pawn and in the next two swift moves they had their set-up.

'You play Slav Defence tonight,' said Milosevic. 'Ironic, yes?'

'Are you saying I'm not a Slav?'

'Slav or not,' said Milosevic, pulling the whisky bottle from a drawer, 'you Croats like most to cosy up to Germany. From Pavelic and Hitler to now. You want whisky?'

'I can't drink,' said Marin, trying not to slump. The deep ache in his chest was starting to grate. 'What I really need is painkillers.'

•

As the game played out, Marin, despite the pain, was starting to get on top. The old Serb kept drinking.

'So,' said Milosevic, 'why the alias? The shame of being a Katich?'

'I didn't want to be killed.'

'Because your father was big time Ustashi?'

'It was Croats who wanted me dead.'

Milosevic was ignoring the game now.

'I know your father, Katich,' he said. 'He was roving murderer in Bosnia, he kills hundreds of Serbs and communists, he's Ustasha hangman, he's bodyguard to Poglavnik. Then he escapes the noose himself, ends up in Australia, and from there he sends Ustashi killers back to Bosnia in the 1960s and '70s. I remember it. Were you one of them?'

'What is this?' asked Marin. 'Do I ask you about your father? Why he killed himself? And your mother—she couldn't live with herself, either. What were they ashamed of?'

'Don't you fucking talking about my mother! Your father sent terrorists to poison Belgrade water supply. That would be mass murder.'

'It didn't happen.'

'They had koala bears, toys filled with cyanide, you deny it?'

'It didn't happen.'

'Did you take Ustasha blood oath?'

'I was just a kid.'

'A blood oath is a blood oath. You really think I'm happy to play chess with Ustashi murderer?'

'I think you're drunk.'

'I think you're a fucking fascist!'

'You're the one they call the Butcher of Belgrade.'

'Fascist dog!'

'You call *me* a fascist? From the time you were a bawling infant, to a kid pissing in your pants, to a fucked-up teenager holding hands with Mira, you and all your fucking communist mates learned the history of the Ustasha like a fetish. Then you get power and you go ahead and repeat all their worst crimes: ethnic cleansing; religious massacres; rape camps to put Serbian seed in Muslim girls; death camps to slaughter their fathers and brothers. Now you sit there in court with your insane arrogance and you lie and you lie and lie and LIE!'

Milosevic rose to his feet, knocking over the chessboard, his face inflamed, the veins in his bulbous forehead throbbing, his mouth working hard, lips quivering. Marin was on his feet now, a tearing pain from the wounds in his chest, two men facing off over the fallen chess pieces.

'YOU'RE THE LIAR! FASCIST! NAZI!' screamed Milosevic.

Marin grabbed him by the collar and Milosevic thrust his hands around Marin's throat.

'GANGSTER! MURDERER!' screamed Marin.

They were intimately close, two invalids nose to nose, grappling with each other, each man's spittle spraying into the other's face.

Marin looked into the old Serb's eyes and he saw a moment of wild panic in them, and then their light suddenly dimmed. Milosevic made a spastic jerk and pitched backwards. Marin was still holding his collar; Milosevic was drooling.

Marin took his full weight and lowered him onto the bed. He felt for a pulse in the man's neck. Nothing. Milosevic's chest was not moving. His face was suffused with subcutaneous blood. He was dead.

Marin moved fast. He looked up into the ceiling, no cameras that he could see. He picked up the chess pieces and packed them away. He picked up the near-empty whisky bottle with the edge of a sheet and placed it on the bedside table with the empty glass. He stripped Milosevic down to his underwear and placed him in the bed, head on a pillow, facing the wall.

Then he pulled up the bedclothes and tucked them in so that, from the door, all you could see was the back of his head. He folded up the man's clothes and placed them on top of the dresser. He got painfully down onto his knees and looked around to make sure nothing was out of place. He found that the black king had rolled under the bed. He retrieved it, got back up and turned off the light, leaving only a small bedside lamp. He convinced himself that Milosevic appeared to be sleeping. He knew that there were surveillance cameras in the corridor.

He went to the door, pulled it open and stepped back into the corridor talking all the while to the body in the bed.

'Next time I'll play white. That was a tough loss. Yes . . . yes. No, I'm completely exhausted . . . A rematch tomorrow, then . . . Good night, Slobbo . . . Sure, I'll shut it.'

He pulled the door shut and limped slowly down the corridor. The cameras saw a man who'd had heart surgery just a week ago—knackered, harmless and exhausted. All of which was true. And yet he had just made another ghost.

34

BOSNIA

31 DECEMBER 2005

ANNA ROSEN crunched through the gears of the Land Rover Defender. It seemed she would never get the hang of driving this monster. It thundered through narrow passes, its startling, unmuffled roar echoing from the limestone walls. Genjac had offered to send his daughter as her driver, but Anna told him she had already put Ena in danger and she refused to make it worse. She had huddled in private conversation with him before she left, sipping his strong, sweet Turkish coffee.

'It is done,' said Genjac. 'The preparations have been made. You are sure you want to do this?'

'What would you be prepared to do for Ena?' she asked him quietly.

'Everything.'

'That's how it is.'

'God be with you, sister.'

'Thank you, brother, I might need her.'

Genjac laughed and slapped the armoured door. 'Go, go.'

•

Jasna Perak had acted quickly after Anna's panicked late-night call. She told Anna to book the first available flight to Zagreb and promised to dispatch a team to Motovun early the following morning to find Ante Lovren.

It was soon discovered that the priest was missing, having failed to appear for the midday Christmas mass. On that day, the church-warden and several parishioners had gone to his house, but found it locked up. They went around the back and broke in, worried that he might have been taken ill, but they found no sign of him inside. They told the investigators from Zagreb that they were mystified.

An old woman remembered him going off with two strangers after the morning mass. She described a pretty young woman and a middle-aged man with thick glasses. Several others remembered the same strangers had been sitting at the back of the church that morning.

Jasna's team went back to the priest's house and found traces of blood in the kitchen, two different types. Two days later a truffle dog had gone crazy, refusing to leave a patch of newly turned soil in the forest. The bodies of two men were found buried there. Both had been killed with single shots to the head. The corpse of Ante Lovren was identified by his housekeeper; that of Pierre Villiers by the passport in his pocket. A decision was taken in Zagreb to suppress the news.

When Jasna told her that Pierre's body had been found, Anna had gone back to her hotel room, locked the door and howled so loudly and for so long that the people in the next room started banging on the wall. Anna wanted to embrace the old Jewish traditions: to tear her clothes; fall to the floor; to lock herself away from the world; and to do nothing but grieve for him. But she didn't have time for that. The mortal danger to her daughter forced her to put Pierre's death to one side and just keep going.

She felt the adrenaline released into her body by primordial emotions. For the first time in her life she understood the impulse to violence, which had, for so long, consumed Marin Katich. She found herself in the bitter hours of that sleepless night calling on whatever spirits might intervene to alter her nature. She spoke aloud the remembered lines of Lady Macbeth, like an incantation: '*Unsex me here . . . Fill me from the crown to the toe topfull . . . Of direst cruelty.*'

•

Now she was on the road she had once before driven with Pierre. It took her in between two mountains, then back through the town of Medjugorje, on whose rocky paths millions of pilgrims had made the hard climb up to Apparition Hill, where the ever-virgin stood waiting for them to kneel before her. She remembered Pierre's gentle, mocking humour as he had described how pilgrims had blinded themselves by staring into the sun, looking for a vision and losing their own. The thought of him, alive and vital and funny, threatened again to undo her resolve.

It had been high summer back then, when she and Pierre had last broached these mountains in his dusty old Golf. Now it was winter and a layer of snow had crept down from the white peaks. When she reached the valley floor, the snow was patchier and strands of mist rose from the rocky karst and swirled about the dark-purple skeletons of bare trees and over rows of dormant grapevines. Ahead of her, the white ball of the sun shone through the clouds like a weak torchlight. It was setting over the saw-toothed mountain ranges and, as the distant peaks darkened into shadow, the closer layers of mountains were blue, then grey, then white.

Anna saw a bank of drifting fog on the road ahead. She slowed as she hit it, flicked on her headlights and was immediately over-whelmed with the sense that she had entered a netherworld.

•

From time to time, Anna glanced at the black shoulder bag, her only luggage, sitting benignly on the passenger seat. It was not the bagful of cash so typical of the kidnap stories she'd heard about all her life. Rebic had no need for cash. His ransom demands were more complex and she had done her best to fulfil them. The bag contained all the evidence she had gathered against him. Rebic had told her exactly what he wanted and she had told him it would take some days to comply with his demands.

After a period of negotiation, he gave Anna until New Year's Eve and ordered her to come alone to Ljubuski on that day. He warned her that if there were any signs of police activity around her arrival he would have absolutely no hesitation in killing Rachel.

It was dusk when she reached the outskirts of Ljubuski and the orange-tiled roofs she remembered from that long-ago summer were white with snow. The roads had been ploughed and dirty snow was heaped on either side of the streets. Anna followed the directions she'd been given, driving past the shopping mall and left onto the R424, on past the furniture store and the Restoran Avantgarde, then second right and first left to Hotel Trebizat, where she was told a room had been booked for her.

The hotel was a faux modernist monstrosity, comprising two cement boxes: a smaller white one superimposed onto a large pink one. Anna parked in front of the entrance, grabbed her shoulder bag and went in to the reception desk. She read nothing telling in the face of the young woman who checked her in and handed her a key.

Once inside her room, she threw back the curtains and found that it overlooked the car park. The last of the sunlight stained the low clouds red and purple. Beyond the car park, a row of leafless trees was silhouetted against the sky; the fine lacework of their branches reminded her of fish bones. Beneath one of those trees she saw the brake lights of a solitary car. It was a smart black German sedan and she made out the figures of two men in the front seat.

She had known they would be watching her, but it was still unnerving to see it.

She found a refrigerator stacked with miniature bottles of spirits. She cracked open the metal lid of a brandy bottle and took a long swig as a settler. On a tray above the fridge was a bottle of local red, two glasses and an old-style T-shaped corkscrew. She stared at the corkscrew for a moment and then slipped it into her coat pocket. As an afterthought, she put into the same pocket three miniature bottles of liquor, remembering as she did so the clinking pockets of Tom Moriarty.

She took off her coat, hung it carefully on a chair, closed the curtains, checked her phone and found no new messages. She lay on the royal-blue bedspread and stared at the ceiling. Soon her eyes were full of tears. She blinked them away and rehearsed the lines she had been working on for days.

After two hours, the room phone rang and she picked it up. 'Hello?'

'Go down to your car,' a man's voice ordered, then the line disconnected. She put her coat back on, picked up her bag and went out into the cold night. The German car she had seen earlier was parked alongside the Land Rover. As she approached, a big man got out of the car and waited. He had the mournful face of a practised killer, with a long scar that ran from below his right eye to the corner of his mouth.

'Get in,' he said. 'You will drive. Follow the car. Don't do anything stupid.'

'I just want to see my daughter,' Anna replied.

She started the roaring engine and Scarface looked momentarily startled. He rolled his eyes when she crunched through the gears to keep up with the German sedan.

They drove slowly through the centre of town, and she was surprised to see the bright lights of a winter market and hundreds of people thronging the streets. On both sides were glowing coal braziers; there were food tents with smoking BBQs and spitted meat, and crowded bars with gas heaters. In some of the tents, she glimpsed musicians and dancers, and a giant sign stretched high across the street from side to side: *NOVA GODINA NOVA HRVATSK*. She knew enough Croatian to translate it as *New Year New Croatia*, which sounded bizarrely like a political slogan.

Anna turned to Scarface. 'What is this?' she asked.

'The boss makes big New Year party for Ljubuski,' he said. 'People very happy tonight. Much drinking, food, dancing and later fireworks from old Ljubuski fortress on mountain.'

'Bread and circuses,' she said.

'No,' he replied emphatically. 'No circus.'

Anna followed the black sedan out of town and found they were driving alongside a fast-flowing river, foaming white over rocks. A chilling wind—she remembered that Pierre had told her this region was famous for what they called 'the breath of Bora'—had cleared the skies so that the countryside was visible in the moonlight. Up ahead, she saw some artificial light. Soon they came to a large floodlit stone structure spanning a narrow part of the river. It was an ancient stone mill with water rushing through three high archways at its base. Then they passed over a stone bridge and into a vast flat expanse of dormant vines—a large, well laid-out vineyard, framed by stands of old forest.

They came eventually to a set of electric gates, which Scarface opened by remote-control, and they entered a long drive lined with old chestnut trees. At the end of the drive Anna saw a walled compound and the upper floors of a French-style chateau. They reached the wall and a second set of electric gates, set in a high stone archway, swung open to reveal the chateau's courtyard. She drove in and the Land Rover's rumbling engine echoed off the walls in the enclosed space.

A number of guards with sub-machine guns slung on their chests stood waiting. She turned the engine off, left the keys in the ignition and climbed from the vehicle, pulling on her coat. As she looked around, she saw security cameras on the wall above the gates. She retrieved her shoulder bag from the back seat.

One of the guards produced a hand-held metal detector. As he passed it over her body, Anna was forced to produce her mobile phone and a metal pen, which Scarface took from her. When the wand beeped at her coat pocket, she gave an embarrassed smile and produced the three miniature bottles of spirits with the offending metal caps. The men laughed and made some sneering comments, she imagined, about the skinny Australian booze hound who'd had to get herself tanked-up to see the boss. Anna shrugged an apology and handed over the clinking bottles. The search was over and she made to move away from the car. But Scarface stopped her.

'Leave your coat,' he said, pointing back at the Land Rover. She was forced to shrug out of its warmth and regretfully threw it back onto the front seat.

Scarface took her roughly by the arm and led her through a pair of tall, carved doors into a wide entranceway with black-and-white chequered tiles. She was taken into a large, expensively furnished living room with high ornate ceilings and a fireplace big enough to walk into were it not blazing with huge logs. An old map above the fireplace, perhaps made in the eighteenth century, showed the layout of the house, the vineyards and the surrounding countryside. When she looked closer, she saw that the map was a counterfeit antique—a fake, no doubt masquerading as evidence of ancestral Rebic family holdings.

'Anna!' She turned to the familiar, oddly accented voice. 'Finally, you've come. I would say welcome, but . . .'

'Where's my daughter,' she said, trying to rein in the edge of hysteria she felt at seeing, in the flesh, this creature responsible for so much misery. She saw that Rebic had turned himself out like an imagined version of an English squire: brown brogues, a handmade tweed suit, a blue-striped Bond Street shirt, a Patek Philippe worn loose on his wrist like a fashionable gold bracelet.

'In due course,' he said, and the gibbous eyes narrowed. *I set the agenda here*, was the message. Scarface shifted his weight from foot to foot, as if awaiting the inevitable order to do violence.

'I want to see my daughter,' said Anna. 'I won't say a word to you until I know she is okay.'

'Very well,' said Rebic. 'I will take you to see her. Then there will be no more games.'

Scarface took her arm again, wilfully brutish now, hauling her almost off her feet. She was dragged down a corridor and into a doorway leading downstairs to a basement. To one side she saw the entrance to a wine cellar, on the other was a door to a locked room that must once have been servants' quarters. Rebic unlocked the door and let her in. There was Rachel, and Anna's legs buckled.

Her daughter was lying, frighteningly still, on a single bed, half-covered by a white sheet. Anna rushed in and shook her gently, but Rachel wouldn't wake. Anna looked around, her vision blurred by the rush of tears that came no matter how much she steeled herself. Beside the bed was a silver dish in which lay a syringe. She turned back to Rebic.

'You've drugged her,' she said.

'Naturally,' he said. 'Did you expect she'd be playing tennis and riding horses?'

'What is it?'

'Heroin, of course,' he said mildly. 'Very pure. I have to be careful with it. She'll come out of this as healthy as she ever was. Although she may have an expensive new habit.'

Anna checked Rachel's pulse. It was slow but steady.

'Wouldn't you rather just dream and dream through something like this?' said Rebic. 'I would say I have been quite humane.'

'You murdered my friend Pierre,' said Anna, choking back her revulsion. She stared at Rebic and thought of the photo of him holding up a man's head. 'Pierre was a gentle soul. He was Anna's godfather, my oldest friend, and he was just one in a long list of your victims . . . And you call yourself "humane"?'

'He was in the wrong place at the wrong time,' said Rebic coldly. 'But that is enough of this nonsense. Kiss your daughter goodnight. We are running out of time.'

'What do you mean?'

'I have a speech to make at midnight,' he said. 'Come.'

Scarface tore her away from Rachel and dragged her back up the stairs to the living room, where he thrust her into a tall wing-backed chair. Rebic sat opposite her, pop-eyed and expectant.

'First,' he said. 'The location where they are hiding Ramic.'

Scarface handed Anna her shoulder bag and she began rummaging through it.

'Don't fuck with me, Anna,' said Rebic. 'People are waiting.'

She produced a sheet of paper with a map and directions.

'This was hard for me to get hold of,' she said. 'When I went to see him, I was blindfolded.'

'Amazing what a mother's love can accomplish,' said Rebic staring hard at her. 'This better be true. Both Rachel's life and yours depend on it.'

'I know that,' said Anna. 'You needn't remind me. I am giving up a good man to be killed to save my daughter.'

'Oh,' said Rebic, standing to pluck the note from her fingers. 'He is not a good man. I think you are a poor judge of good men, Anna.'

Rebic walked across the room, carefully reading the note. Then he called to Scarface who brought him a satellite phone. Rebic pressed some buttons and was soon speaking rapidly into the receiver. Anna understood little of his monologue, but she was aware of him repeating directions from the note. Eventually, he disconnected and handed the phone back to Scarface. He looked at the gold watch.

'Now we will see,' he said. 'My team has been waiting in Mostar. They are about an hour away from the location. When they call back, you will know if you live or die. How interesting for your future to be so simply defined. And the future of Marin Katich—of his line, I mean. It could all come to an end before midnight. What drama!'

Anna found she could not remain silent. 'Is it a form of sickness,' she asked, 'that you take pleasure in threatening the lives of others, and in murder?'

'It's no pleasure for me,' he said. 'I just do what is necessary. The war taught me that, and it taught me how fleeting life is. How it turns on the merest chance. But you have more for me, no?'

Anna pulled the Rebic file from her bag and handed it to him, watching as he flicked through it.

'Ah!' he cried, holding up the photo of himself with the disembodied head of the Orthodox priest. 'The mythical photograph—so it does exist! I must say I doubted it.'

'You don't seem bothered,' said Anna.

'Oh,' said Rebic. 'That was a fun day. I must have been over-enthusiastic, shall we say. I don't remember posing for a photo.'

'It would make an interesting TV ad if you really do run for president,' she said, and Rebic laughed.

'Why?' he cried. 'It's such an obvious fake. Leftist propaganda, don't you see? A blatant imitation of an old Ustasha photo from 1943, and we know those images were all faked in Tito's propaganda labs. But here's the funny thing, Anna—if my opponents did ever dare to put this outrageous forgery out there, it would probably win me many more votes than it loses.'

'This is the world you're pleased to inhabit?'

'This is the world I'm pleased to *create*, Anna. Do you really not see that the time is right for men like me?'

'The world will always reject men like you,' she said. 'Like a bad virus.'

'Oh, yes. So speaks the great idealist,' said Rebic. 'Just like your precious hero, Marin Katich. Well, I should say that his father certainly was a hero. He kept the brotherhood of the Ustasha alive after the Bleiburg massacre; after the assassination of Poglavnik, he kept the light burning in exile. That *is* a hero. But his pathetic son? No! It's funny to me that you think this man is pure as fresh-fallen snow? I know him better than you. He's as much of a killer as anyone.

'I will tell you a story. You know, don't you, that his blood is not pure? He is half Muslim from his whore of a mother, Samira. Such a man could never have been trusted with the future of our people! There came a day, during the shelling of Mostar, when his mother was killed by a Serbian shell. What does he do? I admire him for it, actually. He leads an assault one night on the Serb artillery positions in the hills above Mostar. Crazy-brave action, even I admit it.

'His men reach the artillery position in the middle of the night. The Serbs, they are mostly drunk. Many of them are young conscripts. These were Serbian and Montenegrin kids, what do they know? They are snoring, drunk in their tents. Katich and his men begin killing them all. Those who are not dead in the first assault are rounded up. These are unarmed prisoners now by the Geneva laws, yes? And among them are these boys, not men at all. He takes his pistol and goes along the line executing them one after the other—just like he killed my poor brother-in-law.

'Now, I tell you the truth, Anna—I cheered when I heard this story. It became part of the legend of *Cvrčak*. But the murder of prisoners? This is a war crime, yes? In The Hague? Yes, it is. And he would be tried and convicted for it. Lucky for him I already silenced the witnesses. This is a real irony, no?'

Anna said nothing. It was too much for her to fully comprehend, and she knew this man was a liar by nature. And yet . . . There was something about the story that rang true to her. Look here, he seemed to be saying, I admit I'm a monster, but one thing I recognise is the true nature of men like me.

At 11.30 pm, Rebic took a call on his satellite phone.

'They are in place,' he told Anna.

•

Six men, with the alien profiles created by night-vision equipment, rose from their concealed positions and moved towards the walled Ottoman house. One remained in the vehicle with the satellite phone—an expert driver, ready to extract them once the job was done. The men moved through the darkness that was artificially bright for them. They moved expertly, silently, weapons at their shoulders.

They reached the gate and attached a small explosive to it, then crouched to one side as it detonated. They rushed in, the interior courtyard visible in their goggles, looking for stairs and doorways.

At that moment, bright spotlights came on from above them on each side of the courtyard. The men were suddenly blinded by the flaring in their own night vision. Then came the murderous rattle of automatic weapons from above. They were caught in crossfire from all directions—the perfect killing trap, fish in a barrel.

At the same moment their driver looked up, startled by the extent of the gunfire. A sniper's bullet pierced his window and entered his brain above his nose.

Every man in Rebic's assault team was dead in less than a minute.

•

Rebic waited five minutes before he started to worry. He called the satellite phone again and again. Then he looked up at Anna.

'You treacherous whore!' he shouted. 'What have you done?'

Anna had no time to respond. At that moment, the assault began on Rebic's compound. Black-clad soldiers, who had come across the back wall, were already in his house. Short bursts of gunfire marked their confrontations with each of Rebic's men. Then the front gate blew open and Anna saw through the front windows that more men were rushing in. Scarface cried out, his massive handgun pointed straight at her.

Anna was cringing away from Scarface when the back of his head exploded in a red spray. She saw Jasna Perak, in black from head to toe, standing in the braced position as a wisp of smoke curled from the barrel of her gun. Then Rebic was shooting at the black shadow and Jasna ducked back through the door.

Anna ran for the corridor, trying to get to Rachel in the basement, but Rebic was on her before she reached the door. His arm was around her neck, his gun to her head. He dragged her fast through the door, shot one of the black-clad soldiers and threatened another that he would kill Anna if he interfered with their escape. A fierce gun battle was going on in the courtyard as the remnant group of Rebic's men fought from behind cover.

In the confusion, Rebic managed to drag Anna to the Land Rover. He threw her into the passenger seat, fired up the engine and spun the big vehicle around to face the gateway. Two soldiers stood in front of the vehicle, their weapons trained on the windscreen. As Rebic powered towards them, they aimed bursts of fire at him. The bulletproof window shattered at multiple points, but it remained intact as he accelerated towards the men.

Anna tried to jump from the moving vehicle, but Rebic held her back with one arm, steering through the gate with the other and accelerating down the tree-lined entranceway, reaching high speed as rounds continued to ping off the armour plating.

'Where are you going?' cried Anna. 'There's no way out of this.'

'Shut your mouth, whore!' Rebic screamed as she looked into the barrel of the gun pointed at her head. 'I should blow your brains out *now*!'

Anna stayed silent as they tore down the road next to the river, past the floodlit mill. She felt her coat at her feet and slowly reached down for it. Pushing her hand into the pocket, she found the T-shaped corkscrew and drew it out slowly, gripping the wooden handle in her fist.

She thought Rebic must be headed back to the town, but he took a sharp left into a forested road and they began climbing swiftly and dangerously up a steep switchback road, ascending the mountain, which towered over the north end of the town. She knew where they were going.

The ruins of old Ljubuski, the ancient Croat fortress, were above the town at that point. As they pushed on fast, up and up, she wondered if Rebic had tipped over into madness; if he intended to make some kind of last stand in the ruined stronghold of his warrior ancestors. They climbed higher and there was mist on the road, but Rebic ignored it and the breakneck journey became even more perilous.

Finally, they rose above the mist and Anna saw the broken-backed ruins were lit up, jagged as a set of uneven teeth in a skull. The stone walls of the fortress seemed to grow organically from the limestone mountain. Parts of it were better preserved and, under the low spotlights, the high, crenulated battlements seemed to her eerily like a film set. Other parts of the wall had fallen as if in a slow-motion process of tumbling down the sheer cliff face.

Rebic stamped on the brakes and they skidded across a section of icy snow, thumping into a low wall. He leapt from the Land

Rover and dragged Anna out of the passenger door, hauling her into a snowy stone courtyard, where the foundations of the crumbling fortress were laid out like a floorplan.

She heard a *krump*, a sickening noise that reminded her of a mortar firing. Then came a secondary explosion and the sky above them lit up like a thousand white stars. Then another high explosion and another, and colour blossomed in the sky, each bloom of light growing from the core of the explosion and expanding out like burning, circular rainbows. The midnight fireworks, paid for by Rebic, now stopped his progress.

Explosion after explosion first blinded them then rained down burning embers. Lit by these flashes of colour—in reds and blues, in greens and oranges, and in silver light—Rebic's gaunt face and his ghastly protruding eyes seemed inhuman. Anna saw, in each flash-frame of his face, the panic of a trapped predator.

But still he dragged her up and up, until finally she saw his purpose. In the widest of the stone courtyards, high within the ruins, sat a small helicopter with drooping blades. She understood now that he had intended to descend into the town square of Ljubuski at the conclusion of the fireworks in his flying machine, like a God, and address the crowd he had fed and entertained. She imagined that he might have even timed this night, crowned by the triumphant murders of those who could give evidence against him, as the moment to announce his intention to run for president.

She had seen film crews in the night market and guessed now that the whole event was propaganda. She had no doubt at all that she and Rachel would have been his final victims that night. How could he have let them live with what they knew?

All these thoughts raced through her mind as he pulled her towards the machine. Another succession of explosions above them, bright starbursts, signalled the final flurry of light and noise. When they reached the machine, Anna cried out, 'No!'

Rebic turned on her, his face full of rage. She took the one chance he had offered and plunged the corkscrew into his bulging left eye. Rebic screamed and let her go. She scrambled away from him and, slipping on the icy snow, found cover behind a stone wall. Rebic fired at her wildly, screaming all the while in agony.

Then the fireworks ended and all was black and quiet. Drifting smoke and the stench of gunpowder filled the air. Anna's eyes were burning. She heard the whirring sound of a helicopter building up enough revolutions for flight and saw the lights of its instruments.

Then Jasna appeared out of the acrid smoke like an apparition. Anna saw her black form fleetingly—seen and then lost, then seen again—and raced after her. The chopper was above her, its spotlight raking the ground. Rebic was holding the controls with one hand, hovering precariously as he fired at the two of them through the open doorway, before commencing to rise high and fast.

Jasna propped herself against the outer walls of the fort, using the battlements to steady her weapon. She fired at the ascending machine in short bursts, and Anna saw a line of bullet holes punching into the fuselage until they hit the fuel tank and the machine exploded.

Anna's last sight of Rebic was as a blackened silhouette in the flames. Then the machine plummeted, tumbling down the cliff face, rolling and burning and disintegrating.

35

SCHEVENINGEN, THE HAGUE

3 JANUARY 2006

THE GUARD ZWOLSMAN had been given the job of escorting Marin Katich out of the prison. Marin sat on the bunk, his bag packed, waiting for the guard to unlock the cell and come bumbling in. Eventually he did, his simpleton's smile broader than ever.

'Come along, Mr K,' said Zwolsman. 'The sky is blue today. I will take you to the outside and you can look at it for as long as you like.'

'Thank you, Zwolsman,' said Marin, climbing to his feet and shaking the man's hand. 'I won't miss you.'

Zwolsman chuckled. 'That's all right, Mr K. Did you say that to Mr Milosevic when you said goodnight to him?'

'What are you getting at, Zwolsman?'

'Nothing, nothing.' The guard chuckled again. 'Time to go.'

Marin picked up his bag. As Zwolsman pointed out helpfully, it was small enough to fit in an overhead locker. Inside were his clothes, toiletries and a few books. He found a chess piece in his pocket, a black king. He looked at it for a moment then threw it into the bag.

He followed Zwolsman out of the cell for the last time. The guard unlocked the steel door at the end of the corridor and took him down the familiar stairs to the exercise yard. It was empty, but he had a moment of fight-or-flight panic and clutched his chest as he remembered the fast thumps and the blade plunging through his ribs.

Zwolsman seemed not to notice, but then he turned to Marin and said, 'No more basketball games for you.'

They went through another locked door into a corridor, and past the glassed-in meeting room where he had seen Anna Rosen for the first time in more than thirty years. The conjugal room was close by, a mocking reminder of what would never be. At a reception-type desk near the entrance, a uniformed man handed him a sealed package, which contained his wallet; a few hundred Croatian Kuna and a thin wad of Euros; his credit and debit cards, neither of which were out of date; and his waterproof watch, which hung loose on his wrist when he slipped it on.

Alberto Rossi had sent him a letter recently, assuring him his apartment in Rovinj, full of his belongings, was waiting for him and that the old man had been keeping up the maintenance on the antique Venetian boat while Marin was away. Rossi must have been the only person Marin knew who thought he would ever be free. The old man said that a table would be waiting for him at Giannino's with a carafe of malvasia and a chessboard.

So close now to walking free, Marin still refused to let himself think about it as something real. Zwolsman's joke about Milosevic had been like a trigger that set his nerves on edge. Would he be met at the entrance by Dutch detectives, handed an indictment for murder and marched straight back inside, this time to be remanded into the general prison?

But Rossi's letter and the promise it contained had produced the first taste of renewed life on his enervated palate. For a fleeting moment, he imagined his daughter sitting in the bright sun in the back of the old water taxi; he would take Rachel out of the boat harbour, past Katarina and out over the sapphire waters to the islands in Zlatni. He blinked and Anna was there too, sitting in the back with her arm around Rachel; she would have seen what he had named the boat and be happy for it.

'Mr K?' Zwolsman brought him back to reality. 'We must go. They are waiting for us.'

'Who's waiting?'

'The whole world is waiting,' said Zwolsman. 'Did no one tell you?'

The guard led him out of the war crimes unit, through the wire, past the prison hospital and through another locked door into the reception area of the general prison. There, beyond the security zone, he saw Anna Rosen and the lawyer van Brug. Zwolsman took him through the zone.

'I will leave you with your lawyer,' he said. 'Goodbye, Mr K.'

'Thank you,' said Marin and turned away, too distracted now to think of anything else but the fact that Anna was there. He had not seen or heard from her since news broke of the raid on Rebic's compound.

The lawyer came forward and shook his hand. 'I have your release papers,' said van Brug. 'You are free to leave. We have a car here. But I must warn you, there are very many cameras and journalists waiting for you outside.'

Anna continued to hang back and he saw the tension in her face. He ignored the lawyer and spoke directly to her. 'I'm really sorry about Pierre.'

She didn't answer, but instead turned to van Brug and gripped his elbow.

'Willem,' she said. 'Will you give us a minute alone?'

'Of course,' said van Brug.

Only when the lawyer had moved out of earshot did Anna look up at Marin.

'You should be sorry about Pierre,' she said. 'He died trying to help you.'

'I know that,' said Marin. 'I still can't believe it. I read that he was in Motovun with Rachel.'

Anna stared at him and he was surprised to see anger flaring in her eyes. When she spoke her tone was icy.

'Why did you send your own daughter into such danger?'

'I didn't!' He stepped back as if she had slapped him. 'I told her that Lovren's life could be in danger and that she should ask you to get him police protection.'

'She never called me,' said Anna. 'She was angry with me and wanted to find the truth about her father for herself. She decided to go to Motovun–and Pierre went along to look out for her. They walked straight into the hands of Rebic. You should have been much more careful about what you told her, Marin.'

'You think it's my fault? Rachel came to see me in hospital. Can you imagine what that was like? I didn't know she existed. You had lied to her and kept the truth from me. Look, I get it, I don't blame you for that. But I don't know Rachel. I had no idea she was so headstrong.'

He looked at Anna, beseeching her to understand, but her hard gaze was unchanged so he stumbled on.

'I was in bad way, Anna. Rebic had come after me and I knew he would go for Lovren. I just wanted you to warn him, to protect him. I never thought for a minute that she would race off to find him.'

'Pierre and Lovren were both killed in front of Rachel,' said Anna and now her eyes were glistening.

'Oh, dear God!' he cried. 'I didn't know that.'

Marin dropped his head to stare at his feet.

'I've only seen what's in the papers,' he said, looking back up. 'I tried calling you. I left messages for van Brug . . . Forget that. This is terrible, Anna, horrible. How is she?'

'She's still in hospital,' said Anna. 'Here in The Hague. She's recovering physically, but what she went through was unimaginable. Right now she's being interviewed by Croatian security people. She's expecting us to bring you to see her.'

'That's all I've been thinking of.'

'I don't think you should see her,' said Anna and he was struck again by the coldness in her voice.

'Why are you saying that?'

'There's a reason I haven't been to see you since she was rescued.'

'What do you mean?'

'Do you remember the letter you wrote me?'

'Of course.'

'You said you didn't recognise yourself in the picture I sent you. That you'd done too many bad things, things that still burn in your soul.'

'That's true,' he said. 'They turned me into a killer.'

'Yes,' said Anna. 'An assassin. A man who kills in cold blood.'

'The men I killed were killers themselves,' he said, aware that a babble of voices was welling up in his head. 'They had all done terrible things, but that doesn't mean their deaths don't torment me.'

The voices were roaring now in unison, indistinguishable cries of outrage, and in Anna's face he saw contempt.

'What about the boys?'

'What are you talking about?' he said, and now he could barely hear his own voice.

I told you.

His father cut through the cacophony, as he always could.

We are the same, you and I.

'NO!' said Marin. 'I'm not.'

'What?' said Anna, confused by his outburst. 'I'm talking about those you executed in revenge for your mother's death, the Serbs you executed on the side of the mountain before you destroyed their guns. Rebic told me about this. He said many of them were young conscripts, barely out of school. He told me how much he admired you for this action, how he cheered when he heard about it . . . Marin, did you hear what I said?'

The lawyer was now moving towards them, disturbed by the confrontation, but she waved him back.

'What do you have to say for yourself?'

'The ones I killed had murdered hundreds of innocent people, they were old enough to do that,' said Marin loudly. 'I thought I was delivering justice, but it's true that I wasn't in my right mind.'

Anna weighed up his words before speaking.

'No. I'm sure you weren't. But the element of the crime is that you murdered prisoners of war. I don't know how many you killed or all the details yet, but that is a war crime, no matter what your state of mind was. You understand that don't you, Marin? I told van Brug when I began working on your case that if I found evidence of war crimes I would be bound to report it.'

'You have evidence?'

'I expect you to confess.'

'All war is a crime,' said Marin. 'I'll confess to that. There are no rules but the ones you make up for yourself. I had one rule: protect the innocent.'

'I'll find the evidence, Marin. You know I will. I'm writing a book about you, and it will be the full story as I know it. Yesterday, I spoke on the phone to Amir Ramic. Do you remember him?'

'I thought he was dead.'

'He was in hiding because Rebic was trying to have him killed. Amir was in Bosnia under the protection of a powerful imam. As far as we know, he was the last man alive, apart from you, who knew the truth about Rebic. We found that Rebic had systematically murdered all the others. Now that the monster is dead, Ramic is safe and his testimony was necessary only to set you free.'

'I heard that Rebic had him killed back in 1992 when he purged our Muslim fighters, but Amir would certainly have seen the worst of Rebic's crimes before then.'

'And your own, Marin,' said Anna. 'He was with you on the mountain that night, wasn't he?'

'Yes,' he said. 'He was there.'

'I know Ramic,' she said. 'I sat with him in Bosnia. He's a decent man, an honest man. He wouldn't talk about it on the phone, but I'm sure I can convince him to tell me what he saw you do to those prisoners.'

'Have you told Rachel about this?'

'I want you to tell her,' said Anna. 'But if you don't, I won't protect her from the truth any longer. That was a terrible mistake. Pierre died trying to find the truth about you. Rachel was kidnapped and traumatised and nearly killed trying to prove her father was not a war criminal. But now I know for sure that you are . . .'

Marin's ghosts cried out at this. Their voices swelled up, hissing and shouting until the chorus of condemnation almost drowned out Anna's words. His hands flew up to his ears and he grimaced. Anna was alarmed.

'What is it?' she asked.

'Nothing,' he said and voices subsided. 'Nothing.'

Anna scrutinised him for a moment, then continued.

'I thought deeply about this in the past few days, Marin. You might think I'm completely heartless, but I intend to tell the world who you really were and who you are and what you have done, the good, the bad and the very bad, and if I find the evidence and witnesses you'll end up back in here facing a new war crimes trial. You'll walk free today, but every day you'll be looking over your shoulder.'

The voices died away. The ghosts were still and expectant, and he stared in silence at the woman he still loved who would now be his prosecutor.

•

Marin Katich walked through the prison's central gateway, which seemed, with its stone towers on either side, like the entrance to a castle. Leaving this fortress, he felt exposed, suddenly naked. He had been safe hidden away inside under another man's name—at least until they found out who he was and came to kill him. He remembered what Zwolsman had said and paused to look up at the clear, blue sky. He was alone beneath it. His foolish daydream of ferrying Anna and their daughter through the waters off Rovinj had evaporated like morning mist.

Anna Rosen and Willem van Brug followed him out, but stayed back as he made his way to the small podium. With the vast array of microphones clamped and taped in place, the podium looked like an electronic hedgehog. He gripped the edge of it as if this flimsy object would keep him upright and steady. In front of him were dozens of television cameras, photographers and sullen muttering journalists. It was a familiar scene from a lifetime of looking into television screens at thousands of press conferences, but it was completely different to be the one looking out at the ravening pack.

He glanced from face to face and saw not a single sympathetic expression. Hard professional cynicism was the main impression. A few clicks and flashes, then multiple flashes began across the pack. He expected a barrage of questions but, looking out again, he realised they were expecting him to say something first. He raised his head, picked a spot above the pack as his father had told him to do when he was fifteen years old and about to address a large crowd in Sydney Town Hall. He chose a stately old house on the other side of the raised roadway. He was about to speak when he saw a reflective object glinting in the attic window. He was instantly distracted. Then more blinding flashes came from the cameras nearest him. He blinked and looked above the cameras again.

Something glinting, attic window.

He looked back to where Anna was standing with the lawyer, ten paces behind and off to the side. Her face was grim, implacable. As much as he longed for it, there would be no redemption. Marin turned back to the cameras and gestured lamely over his shoulder.

'I want to begin by thanking my legal team,' he said. 'Without them, I would still be behind bars on false charges.'

He dropped his head, smiled, then looked back up.

'Above all Anna Rosen . . .'

Attic window, glinting.

'Anna Rosen,' he repeated as the nagging thought became an epiphany.

Sniper!

A flash.

The bullet hit him in the top right of his forehead. Everything blurred. Unbearable red-black, red-black pain. Burning scalp, bone, brain matter. Falling.

'Such a long . . .'

We're waiting.

'. . . time.'

Waiting for you.

Don't fight it.

Come join us.

You're here now . . .

He saw Anna above him. She was on her knees, sobbing as she cradled his head in her lap. She stroked his face with bloody hands as the light in his eyes went out. Then Marin was floating on his back in the Towamba River. It held him as gently as a mother. The shadows of iron bark and ghost gums reached out to him. He looked up and the blue sky went on forever.

36

SCHEVENINGEN, THE HAGUE

3 JANUARY 2006

THE MAN BENDING OVER the rifle stood up quickly. Pulling the weapon back through the window, he laid it on the floor. It was clean and untraceable; he left it where it sat. He pocketed the shell.

He left the attic, went quickly down two steep flights of stairs and out the back door. His car was a block away; he climbed in and drove fast to another neighbourhood. He peeled off the surgical gloves, pulled out his phone and sent a simple text.

•

Jasna Perak was sitting by Rachel Rosen's bed, listening as another officer questioned her about Jure Rebic. Then her phone pinged.

'Excuse me, honey,' she said. She left the room and walked down the corridor to an empty waiting room. She sat down and pulled out her phone. She opened her messages and read:

It is done.

Jasna sighed, thinking for a moment of the young woman down the corridor in the hospital bed. How sad that she would soon get the news that her father was dead. What a pity it could not have ended differently, but the half-blood had always been a threat to the homeland. Old Franjo knew that when he ordered his assassination the first time. Imagine a resurrected General Cvrčak returning to Bosnia now as a hero to remind the world of Croatia's crimes against Muslims. What damage could he have done to their European ambitions? History was a weapon. It needed to be managed with extreme care. She was proud that they trusted her to do that. So much needed to be forgotten for the country to move on.

Jasna went rummaging through her handbag. She pulled out a plastic bag of loose cigarettes and tipped a few onto the coffee table. She picked out the straightest one and lit it with a plastic lighter. She was exhaling a stream of blue smoke when a nurse walked into the room.

'No smoking,' said the nurse, pointing to a prominent sign. 'You must put that out.'

Jasna dropped the cigarette into a half-full plastic coffee cup. She looked up and saw the nurse was still watching.

'Fascist!' she said.

POSTSCRIPT

In the summer of 2006 there was an outdoor ceremony in a leafy, shaded courtyard of the Ministry of Defence in Zagreb. The Croatian president was there with a few of his officials. The ceremony was also attended by a handful of veterans of the War for Independence, a few journalists, intelligence officials and two women from Australia, a mother and daughter.

•

Earlier that day, Anna Rosen left Rachel with a list of things to see in the Croatian capital and went to meet the most senior of those intelligence officials, Jasna Perak.

'I brought you a copy of my book,' said Anna, after warm greetings.

Jasna paused to light a cigarette before responding. 'If I'm in it,' she said, 'I may have to detain you in basement cell.'

'Not by name, or even gender,' said Anna, handing her the book. 'I kept your secrets.'

'Funny title,' said Jasna, scrutinising the cover. '*In Darkness Visible*? I think it makes no sense.'

Anna smiled at that. She knew it was fanciful to think of Marin Katich as one of Milton's fallen angels, though he had certainly dwelt most of his life in darkness. Writing the book had been cathartic. Urged on by Leon, her editor—who was desperate to capitalise on the intense public interest in the drama which his writer was at the heart of—Anna had done it quickly over three months. She had flown back to Sydney with her daughter, nursing Rachel in the apartment as she mapped out a structure. She had gone to Canberra see the dying Tom Moriarty and taken down what was, in effect, his final confession. The corrupt old spy did not live to read her account of his own treachery and manipulation.

When Rachel was well enough, Anna had flown back to Croatia and travelled to Rovinj, the town where Marin had hidden himself away for so many years, living under the name Tomislav Maric. There, searching for people who knew him, she had met the old historian Alberto Rossi. She found that Rossi had not only been a good friend to Marin but also his landlord. At his suggestion she had rented the apartment, which was still full of Marin's belongings. It was in this apartment that she finished the book.

Anna spent many hours working at the long table in the front room, the shutters open to the view over the boat harbour and out to Katarina Island. As she wrote, she felt Marin's presence in that beautiful place and she imagined that this was *his* paradise lost. She had naturally searched the apartment but found remarkably few clues to his past. Those few she did would make their way into the book. The first was an old black and white picture, which she recalled he had shown her back in 1970: it was a faded picture of Samira with her two sons, the baby, Petar, and Marin, the resolute boy beside her. Then Anna found another picture of Samira standing arm-in-arm with an elegant, white-haired Bosnian man. They were next to a sparkling fountain in the courtyard of their

Ottoman-built house in Mostar, the house in which, Anna knew, they had died together.

The front room was lined with bookshelves, and among Marin's eclectic collection of classical literature and history she found her own book, *Australian Nazi,* about his father. When she opened it another photograph fell out. This one was of herself in 1970, before the year went bad. She was sitting in the revolving captain's chair at her desk in the Glebe house. The chair was tilted back on its springs and the young Anna was looking up at the photographer, Marin it was, with a loving smile. Anna barely recognised in herself the serenity she clearly felt at that moment. As she sat transfixed by the forgotten image her mind leapt forward to the terrible event outside Scheveningen Prison and she saw again Marin's bloodied head in her lap, his eyes losing focus, his essence draining away.

It was Alberto Rossi who helped her to reconnect with the absent man. He took her out in the beautiful old wooden boat named *Anna,* which was still tethered at the back of the fleet in the harbour. Like most of the town's inhabitants, Rossi was at ease on boats and patiently taught her how to drive the finely engineered machine and to harness its power. Later, he helped her with the paperwork to buy the boat, which had become by law an object in a deceased estate, and to take over the highly sought-after mooring. Rossi agreed to maintain the boat, as he had for Marin, for as long as he was physically able to.

So it was that when mother and daughter came back to Croatia in summer for the special ceremony, Anna first took Rachel down to the Adriatic coast to Rovinj. There she was able to astonish her daughter by taking her out in a boat to picnic and swim in the unpopulated islands south of the town. She imagined that Marin would have done this with his daughter had he survived his brief moment of freedom.

•

In Zagreb, the simple ceremony was coming to a close. At the appropriate time, Rachel was urged to come forwards to where the president was waiting with an open wooden box in his hands. As she got closer she saw, nestled in the velvet-lined interior, a golden medal. The president mumbled a few words, which she understood to mean that this was being given to her with the thanks of a grateful nation. The box he handed to her contained the posthumous award for her father, Marin Katich. It was the Order of Petar Zrinski and Fran Krsto Frankopan, the tenth most important medal given by the Republic of Croatia. The order, which was founded on 1 April 1995, has two levels. For reasons no one could explain, nor did anyone seek to discover, Marin was given the golden award for valour in combat.

Jasna Perak, watching the simple ceremony from one side, whispered to another senior intelligence officer. 'This is too good, honey. We love our martyrs, but we need for them to remain dead.'

ACKNOWLEDGEMENTS

Thanks and brotherly love to a pair of old friends, Mark Aarons and Pierre Vicary, for allowing me to borrow aspects of their lives to meld into the fictional lives of key characters in this book and for their enduring political passion, their Balkan expertise and their fine companionship over many years.

Many thanks again to my literary mentor Richard Walsh, without whom neither of my novels would have existed. And my immense gratitude to the wonderful team at Allen & Unwin—Annette Barlow, Angela Handley, Rebecca Starford, Aziza Kuypers and Luke Causby—for their perceptive comments, judgement, editing and artistic talent.

Above all, to Sarah—it is simply impossible to thank you sufficiently for the enduring love which makes life worthwhile.

ABOUT THE AUTHOR

After a cadetship with ABC Radio, Tony Jones joined *Four Corners* as a reporter in 1985, winning a Walkley award for his exposé of the Waterhouse racing dynasty. Soon after the fall of the Berlin Wall, he became an ABC Europe correspondent and covered the civil wars in Yugoslavia, the collapse of communism in Russia, the fall of Kabul to the Mujahideen, the end of the apartheid regime in South Africa and the first US-led invasion of Iraq. After a brief stint back in Australia, he went to Washington as a correspondent and finally returned to become presenter of *Lateline*, winning three Walkleys for broadcast interviewing. Today he hosts *Q&A* on Monday nights. He is married to fellow ABC journalist Sarah Ferguson. *The Twentieth Man*, his bestselling first thriller, was published in 2017 to acclaim. *In Darkness Visible* is his second novel.